J. R. Johnson was born
California. He is the
company specializing
based on his personal
a second novel.

J. R. JOHNSON

Takeover

GRAFTON BOOKS

A Division of the Collins Publishing Group

LONDON GLASGOW
TORONTO SYDNEY AUCKLAND

Grafton Books
A Division of the Collins Publishing Group
8 Grafton Street, London W1X 3LA

Published in paperback by Grafton Books 1989

First published in Great Britain by
Grafton Books 1988

Copyright © J. R. Johnson 1988

ISBN 0-586-20027-4

Printed and bound in Great Britain by
Collins, Glasgow

Set in Palatino

All rights reserved. No part of this publication may
be reproduced, stored in a retrieval system, or
transmitted, in any form, or by any means, electronic,
mechanical, photocopying, recording or otherwise,
without the prior permission of the publishers.

This book is sold subject to the condition that it
shall not, by way of trade or otherwise, be lent,
re-sold, hired out or otherwise circulated
without the publisher's prior consent in any
form of binding or cover other than that in
which it is published and without a similar
condition including this condition being imposed
on the subsequent purchaser.

Prologue

Kurt King studied his reflection in the bathroom mirror, ran his fingers over his cheeks and the planes of his jaws and decided he had better shave. In half an hour his senior executives and Minneapolis staff would gather in the Radisson South lobby to go to the dinner he had promised. He had time enough. Digging the shaver from his bag, he began to mow the dark stubble that had grown since he left Toronto for Minnesota that morning. In the glass, he noticed his eyes had lost that bloodshot look that came from long, strenuous evenings and lack of sleep. He thrust his strong chin upwards to shave its underside. Only one chin and no jowls, he thought with some pride. Finishing his shave, he slapped aftershave lotion on his face, wincing from the sting, then brushed his well-barbered dark hair, now shot through with grey at the sideburns. He straightened his tie and had a last look at himself. Thank God he appeared younger than his forty-six years. He felt fit, on top of the world and was looking forward to the dinner meeting.

As president of King Corp, he had for years kept up a hard-driving travel schedule, logging more miles than many airline captains. Simply because he lived and breathed business. No ivory-tower executive, King believed in going out to meet his company staff at every level from top management to the factory floor. His corporate faith began and ended with people, and he preached that commercial success could only come from the efforts of outstanding people, properly motivated. Factories, machines, tools, ideas, products and good fortune all counted in any enterprise – but only if they had the right people behind them. So, he journeyed regularly over his widely scattered companies to meet face to face with the individuals who made things happen.

In the last couple of weeks, he had clocked up more than 40,000 miles in his company jet, which he used as an office, to talk non-stop business with top executives in England, Italy, Canada and now in Minnesota.

Those who did not know him well thought the success of King Corp had inflated an already strong ego; those who knew him better realized it was natural self-assurance, justified by what he had achieved.

As King reached for the jacket of his suit, the phone rang. It was Kate Foy, his director of investor relations. 'Mr King? You have ten minutes before the others are to arrive. I have your messages, but there's nothing urgent, nothing that can't wait until tomorrow.'

'Okay, Kate, thanks. I'm just leaving. See you in the lobby.'

Slowly he replaced the phone, staring at the instrument as if it were a visual conduit to the black-haired, sloe-eyed embodiment of the voice that had been on the line; mentally tuning in her well-rounded attributes, mumbling to himself the admonition raised by her happily married status, then saying aloud to no one, 'It would be nice.'

On his trip to Toronto and Minnesota, King was accompanied by Chip Boyd, his chief financial officer, Dean Hubert, his operations wizard, and Mrs Foy. All aspects of the visit had worked out well. In both cases, the equipment and factories were in first-class shape and the review of current results was as satisfactory as the forecasts for the coming year. When the Minneapolis meeting had broken up at five, King had invited the senior executives to a six o'clock dinner.

Again, he adjusted his trademark, a Countess Mara knitted tie, slipped on and buttoned the coat of his Oxxford suit. He was reaching for the door knob when the phone rang once more. 'Damn phones,' he said under his breath and turned back into the suite to jerk the instrument from its cradle. 'Kurt King,' he said.

'One moment, Mr King. Would you hold for Kenneth Jackson, please?'

'Yes, yes.' He had heard and discounted every argument from those busy people who insisted on having the party they were calling on the line before they spoke themselves. In his book, it was another example of secretarial one-upmanship. Not only did he place most of his own calls, he answered his own phone. Kenneth Jackson was a senior partner in Jackson & Jackson. In addition to being corporate counsel for King Corp, he was a good friend, one who would track down a client only on an urgent matter. Puzzled, King waited.

Jackson came on the line. 'Kurt, are you sitting down?'

'No, Ken, as a matter of fact you caught me on my way out the door. Almost missed me. What can I do for you?'

'I was serious when I asked if you were sitting down, Kurt. I think you'd better. What I have to say is most unpleasant and makes me very uncomfortable. I'll keep it short. In fact, I really can't say much.'

King realized his knuckles were turning white on the receiver. He relaxed his suddenly moist palm.

'As of right now,' Jackson went on, 'I must disqualify

myself from representing King Corp, and I am hereby so doing. You probably know I also represent Zanadu Corporation. Their president, Norris Thomas, will call you in a few minutes to inform you he's making a takeover bid for your company. Frankly, I know nothing more than that. He tells me he's been unable to reach you and asked me to contact you. Now I've done that. Please wait there for Thomas's call.'

King had heard enough. His well-being of a few minutes earlier had given way to an incredulous, bitter anger and a rush of nausea. 'Thanks, Ken, that's wonderful news, just lovely. I've no intention of waiting for Thomas or anybody else to call me and tell me they want to take over my company. I'm leaving for dinner.'

'Why don't you wait, Kurt?' Jackson sounded a note of concern, and caution. 'Can Thomas reach you later? Remember, I'm only acting as an intermediary.'

'When's this going to start?' Agitation had lifted King's voice in pitch and volume.

'I understand they'll announce tomorrow.'

'Jesus Christ! Then why is Thomas calling me if it's all set. Is he trying to be nice?'

'I guess it is all set. But you can still be courteous.'

'Courteous!' King's wrath exploded. 'Thomas is not very damn courteous. Tell him to go straight to hell. I have no use for raiders, leeches who steal other people's companies under cover of bad law. You can also tell Mr Thomas to get ready for a fight and not to waste his money calling me. I'm simply not available now, and tomorrow I'll be in Kansas. If he wants to see me he can wait, like a gentleman, until I get back on Friday. I'll see him then. But if his mind is already made up, then screw him.'

Jackson obviously thought it best to move to another

point. 'You understand, Kurt, I cannot represent you in this matter. But I advise you to engage another firm. Now, today. Let me suggest Hart Eversole. They're a good outfit and they know you. If you intend to oppose Thomas, every minute counts.'

'Okay, Ken.' King had heard enough. 'Thanks again for the good news.'

He banged the phone back. A taste of bile rose in his throat and he felt he might be sick. But suddenly the feeling left, replaced by an unusual elation. That phone call was going to change his life drastically, and perhaps for the worse. Yet, he had an instinctive love of conflict and any new stimulus which gave him a lift. Even a fight for his survival would be emotionally satisfying.

For a full minute he glared at the phone, willing it to divulge the name he was seeking, the lawyer he wanted to call instead of Hart Eversole. He had never really liked that huge, prestigious firm. In a real knock-down street brawl you didn't want a pack of stodgy attorneys who fought by the Queensberry Rules. This was going to be in-fighting. So, he wanted the full attention of the senior partner; he needed bright counsel who would not quail at the sight of blood, or be afraid to play rough. He had the right man in mind, but the shock of that call had numbed his mind. 'Be calm, relax, think,' he told himself. A moment later the name leapt into his mind: Schutt.

Although Stephen Schutt's firm had never represented King Corp or its president personally, King had met the fortyish lawyer three or four times and had always been impressed by him. Once, over lunch and with no thought of a fee, Schutt had accurately and politely explained that a dividend plan King was keen to promote just would not work. King admired his mind and manner.

Although the lawyer was in conference, the secretary who took the call read the urgency in King's voice and put him through. 'Stephen Schutt? Kurt King. I'm calling from Minneapolis and I have a big problem. My company is about to be raided and I need a good lawyer. Two questions: are you and your staff any good, and two, do you work for Zanadu?'

'Well, it's self-serving, but I think we're good,' Schutt replied. 'No, we don't work for Zanadu.'

'Zanadu's my problem. They're making a takeover bid for King, which I understand they'll announce tomorrow. Will you represent us, and can I be assured of your personal involvement on a full-time basis? I'm sure your people are good, but I know you and I want you in the act.'

'Goddammit, what a lousy deal . . . dirty bastards. Yes, you'll have my personal attention. Now when can you be in LA? Time is extremely important in these matters.'

'Frankly, I haven't thought that far. Maybe it's best to cancel the rest of my trip and fly back tonight. Let me think and I'll call you back. In the meantime I'll have my secretary get some records over to your office. Oh! an idea – why don't you place an order for 5,000 shares of Zanadu stock? Buy it in the name of King Corp. Maybe we'll make a tender offer for them. At least it'll confuse the hell out of everybody. I want to make some other calls, so I'll talk to you later.'

Again, as he cradled the phone, he felt ill. In the bathroom, he slowly sipped half a tumbler of water and that helped. He recognized the need for something stronger. 'Twelve years,' he said to himself as the reality

10

of what was happening began to take hold. 'Twelve years spent getting this company shaped up and running like it should and some rotten bastard is going to steal it. Son of a bitch.'

No, it was more than twelve years. His whole life had revolved around this company ever since he could walk and talk. He had grown up in that oily, metallic smell of workshops making aeroplane and other components. This company was his birthright. His father had created it out of nothing, with Uncle Ray's help. It had been stolen from them and it had taken him half a lifetime to win it back. When it was teetering into bankruptcy, he had given it the kiss of life and rebuilt it into a thriving hi-tech firm with great prospects.

And look at the sacrifices he had made for King Corp! It had come between him and his wife and was destroying their marriage. If he didn't watch out, it would lose him the girl he now loved. His social life, his sex life, his friends – everything had run a poor second to the company. Father, mother, wife, mistress – that's what it had become. Almost everything he had done in life had its source in that company. And now somebody who understood no more about King Corp than its convertible assets, its profit-and-loss figures and its yearly sales of nearly a billion dollars was doing what amounted to a smash-and-grab raid on him. Yet to King the money was a secondary consideration. It was the company he cared about. Hell, this was like somebody running off with your wife or best girl. He felt queasy again. Curiously, the same sensation he had experienced when he had proof that his wife, Carolyn, had been sleeping with another man.

Suddenly, he recalled Chip Boyd's warning some months back that King Corp was doing so well it might

11

become a target for a takeover raid. For several reasons King had disagreed and now cursed himself. What they desperately needed was what Boyd had suggested as a defence – a 'friendly' or White Knight. Another company that could step in and outbid the raider by offering a higher price. He knew such a company, Astroteknik, and knew their president, Bill Damen. They might help. That gave him some comfort.

Boyd and the others were now waiting in the hotel lobby, undoubtedly wondering what was delaying him. They'd have to wait. He had things to do. Call the office, try to reach his friendly, call Schutt back.

His phone jangled. He stared at it. Norris Thomas of Zanadu? He let it ring. Ten rings, then silence. When it stopped, he called Marianne, his secretary, in Los Angeles and haltingly explained the problem. Though as shocked as himself, she took all his instructions without interruption. Within the hour, the company's by-laws, minute books and other relevant documents were on their way to Stephen Schutt's office. King then called their specialist on the New York Stock Exchange and advised him that, because of the problems created by the takeover offer, trading in King Corp stock would probably be suspended the next day. Getting back to Schutt, he described the action he had taken and said he was returning to Los Angeles in the morning and would be in the attorney's office before ten.

His watch told him he was an hour late for dinner. As he left the room, the phone began to ring again. He slammed the door, hard.

His three executives and other guests felt something had gone wrong. When had Kurt King ever turned up ten minutes late for anything, let alone an hour? When had someone normally so garrulous sat silently pulling on cigarettes which burned like quick fuses? In the car on their way to the restaurant, his three companions said nothing, wondering if it were a death in the family, a law-suit or a strike at one of their plants. King, too, kept quiet until all his guests were seated before rapping on the table. He leaned forward and said, quietly, 'Ladies and gentlemen, I hate to spoil the party, but I've just had a bearhug call.'

'A bearhug call?' somebody echoed, puzzled, and the whole assembly turned to stare at King.

'You know how a grizzly approaches with open arms,' he said. 'If you're crazy enough to step into them, it's the death hug. That's what somebody wants King Corp to do. We've had a takeover bid.'

A babble of voices greeted King's statement.

'A takeover – it can't be true.'

'Who'd do that – and how? It's a joke.'

'Whoever it is, they can't get away with it.'

Everybody was looking at King, scanning his face, hoping it was a joke. He knew they felt just like him. Thrown off-balance, bewildered. Most of them were friends who had prospered with the company, who looked on their jobs as a great experience. Now, they were realizing their lives might be altered by what he had said.

Calmly, he explained how he had heard the news, how they had sprung their takeover bid on him when he and his most important executives were away from their headquarters. How Zanadu, the raiding company, had even caused him to lose the services of their corporate counsel.

They all knew takeovers were in the air; yet the faces round the table looked incredulous, stunned. Bernard

13

Limburger, who handled public relations for the Minneapolis division, looked at King. 'It's like a car crash or a burglary or a mugging – you think it can only happen to somebody else.'

Chip Boyd broke in. 'What a lousy deal,' he said. 'We know Zanadu, it's in our backyard. But it's a second-rate bunch making, hmm, low-tech stuff like sanitation equipment.' Shaking his head, he turned to King. 'They're barely half our size. I just don't see how they can do it. What's the deal, Kurt? What price are they offering for our stock?'

He knew nothing of the pending offer from his conversation with Jackson except that it was imminent. He explained to the people at the table that all he could say was that the offer would be announced the next day. To Boyd, he added, 'We're quoted on Wall Street at 21½ now, so they'd have to top that by 10, 11 dollars per share, wouldn't they?'

'About that,' Boyd replied, then shrugged. 'But that's nowhere near what we know the company's worth – or will be worth.' He halted, catching several of the others staring at him and seeing King's facial twitch warning him not to elaborate.

However, his remark had set King thinking. Had Zanadu somehow got wind of their real prospects? Who knew about those, apart from Chip Boyd? Somebody on the inside track. His mind flashed over various meetings they had held with people who might know Zanadu officers, but no one sprang to mind. What about Kate Foy? She'd have an inkling about the financial projections. He glanced at her, wondering what was going on behind those oriental eyes. She was a latecomer to King Corp, but he knew her well enough to rule out any treachery there.

Dean Hubert? He, too, hadn't done much mileage with the company, and he knew the whole operation, especially their glassworks project. Could he have tipped off Zanadu? King's inner voice told him, No. Bud Gorman, his financial vice-president? No, Bud wouldn't blab. He had too much to lose.

King found himself lighting one Chesterfield off another and mentally polling all his home-based executives, questioning which one of them might be the Judas. A couple of names leapt to mind, a maverick director and a frustrated former executive.

Suddenly, he stopped himself. 'Hell,' he thought, 'if I go on suspecting everybody, I'll turn paranoiac and the fight will be over before it's begun.'

Calling for silence, he told them about some of the moves he had already made after he heard the news at the Radisson South. He revealed he had chosen Stephen Schutt's law firm.

'Why not Hart Eversole?' Boyd queried. 'I thought Steve Schutt was a divorce lawyer.'

'No,' said Kurt, impatiently. 'His firm is an extremely capable outfit. They do a lot of corporate work, litigation, underwriting, that sort of stuff. Ken Jackson suggested Hart, but for me they're dead on their ass. Excuse me, ladies. I feel we need an aggressive bunch like Schutt's people. Anyway, it's done, the decision's made and that's how we're doing it. If I've read Schutt right, he and his lawyers are already at work.'

In a restrained voice, but firm enough to carry over the clatter of dishes, cutlery and the conversational hum in the restaurant, King outlined what Schutt had warned him about takeovers. Time was the vital factor in a stock-exchange raid such as Zanadu was mounting against them. Everything could happen fast, too fast for

15

them to take the right avoiding action. Zanadu had caught them completely off guard. If they didn't move immediately, they might find King Corp had been devoured by Zanadu in a matter of weeks.

'How did they discover the president and three of his top executives were out of town and where we were?' Chip Boyd asked.

'Yeah, they must have somebody on the inside.' King heard the remark come from a Minneapolis executive down the table. He held up a hand for silence.

'That's something we'll figure out later. Let me finish telling you how they'll go about grabbing our company, and probably a few hundred of our jobs.' King showed how uptight he was by lighting another Chesterfield, oblivious of the one burning away in his ashtray. 'First, there's the legal announcement which isn't just a full-page newspaper ad. It's an official document that has to be served on myself in person. At the same time, or immediately afterwards, they put out a press release then bombard our shareholders with newspaper ads in everything from the *Wall Street Journal* to local rags announcing in detail the offer they're making. Three weeks after the announcement, they make the formal offer which is outstanding for another three weeks. In that period, those shareholders who wish can offer their stock. That would bring us up to 2 December, six weeks from now. On that date, Zanadu buys. If enough stock is offered to give Zanadu a controlling interest, then that's it – Zanadu will own King. Unless we can come up with a way to sidetrack or stop them, King will be a part of Zanadu on 2 December.'

'But that's a shotgun wedding,' Jack Stoneman, president of the Minneapolis Division, said in his strident baritone.

16

'It's more than that – it's downright highway robbery,' his vice-president put in.

'It's neither of those,' King said. 'It's worse, much worse. It's rape.' He noticed Kate Foy's dark eyes on him. Sometimes, she could read his emotions, and this was one of them.

'Kurt, we've got to move, we've got to beat the bastards,' Chip Boyd called above the hubbub of talk which followed King's exposition.

'We've already started doing something, and we're going to fight for this company all the way down the line, and beat them.' King had filled the back of his menu with pencilled arrangements for the next day's changed plans; he had detailed the staff who would stand in for them at their Kansas meeting. Dean Hubert would stay behind while he, Chip Boyd and Kate Foy would fly to Los Angeles to keep the ten o'clock rendezvous with Schutt in his office.

It was a dreary dinner when it should have been a celebration. What they lacked in appetite, they made up for in nerve-steadying drinks. Just as they ordered coffee, King was paged to the phone. He took Kate Foy with him and she answered the call. Holding a hand over the mouthpiece, she whispered, 'It's Norris Thomas of Zanadu. He says it's very important for him to talk to you. He says tomorrow will be too late.'

King shook his head. 'Tell him I've already left for Kansas.'

Back at the table, Kate described the call. Boyd piped up with the question in everybody's mind. 'Has Thomas put a tail on us? He knew about this trip, he knew where we were staying and he even knows where we're eating. How the hell did he know that, and even the restaurant number?'

17

Jack Stoneman spoke up, saying he had left the restaurant number with his son, who was home alone, in case the boy needed to reach him. 'Maybe I should have, but I didn't tell him specifically not to forward calls here. Should I go and check?'

'Yeah, Jack,' King said, as mystified as Boyd and the others. 'Call your boy and let's find out.'

Stoneman returned to tell them a man had called his son and asked for King. He was sorry, but the boy had given him the restaurant number.

'Forget it, Jack. Not your fault.' King scythed his apology away. 'What I can't figure out is how Thomas got your home phone number. Kate, go and call Manny Newell in Kansas. He knew where we were to be tonight, knew we'd be with Jack. I've a hunch he got a similar call.'

She came back, nodding. 'Yes, Manny got a call from Thomas's secretary asking where we were. Manny asked if they wanted Stoneman's number, but the girl said they already had it. What does it all mean?' She looked from King to Boyd.

'It means,' Chip Boyd said, 'they've got hold of one of our confidential phone books, the wallet size. It lists all the home numbers. Our friendly lawyer, Jackson, probably told them we'd be at Newell's plant in the morning, so they started with him and worked back.'

'That's what it sounds like, Chip. But who would hand them the phone list?'

Boyd's forehead creased with thought, then he snapped his fingers and grimaced. 'Tillman, that's who. I'll bet anything it has to be him. He's been doing some consulting work for Zanadu lately and he's the only man who could have given out that information.' He

18

paused, shrugged. 'I hate to admit it, but I gave him a phone book months ago when he was working for us.'

King did not know Matthew G. Tillman well. An investment consultant, he had worked on contract for King Corp, assessing various new projects which interested the company. He certainly had inside information about them, but King did not know he had also been working for Zanadu. Anger stripped away his inhibitions and he forgot the presence of ladies. He banged a fist on the table, rattling crockery and glasses. 'That son of a bitch! And we helped him when he needed help badly. You know, it's conceivable he triggered the whole fucking deal. Jesus, now I think about it, he was privy to all sorts of information, insider stuff. There was a time when he was almost a member of the family. He sure knew how well we were doing. Still, it's hard for me to believe he'd do such a rotten thing.'

'Well, Kurt, we haven't had much work for him since the first of the year,' Chip Boyd said. 'As a result, he's been practically full-time for Zanadu. And, if you remember, he was very unhappy when you gave a study job to the Boston people.'

'He couldn't handle it, Chip. But now you mention it, I'm reminded that Tillman saw the Boston report. I let him read it, but wouldn't let him take it out of the office. That told him plenty about the real strength of the company. It sounds to me like he's involved, we'll have to find out how deeply.' King smiled for the first time that evening. 'But it could be a key to fighting off Zanadu. Using confidential information is illegal and the Securities Exchange Commission leans heavily on those who break the rules. We'll let our lawyers nail them on that.'

'It could also have been Grant Sheridan, who helped

with the survey of the Tri Corp acquisition,' Kate Foy put in. 'He knew a lot of the answers.'

'True,' King agreed. 'We'll file that one away as well.' He called for the bill and signed it, the signal for the evening to break up. To his three Los Angeles executives, he said, 'Go over every meeting we've had in the past six months with outsiders from other firms, investment houses – anybody who might have run a study on us and gone to Zanadu with the information. I'll get our other people to do likewise when we get back.'

They said their farewells to the Minneapolis staff, King shaking hands with each one and assuring everybody they would fight off this underhand bid for the company.

Back in his hotel room, he packed his things quickly and efficiently, ready to book out next morning and fly to Los Angeles in the company jet.

He dialled Frankie Shore, the girl who meant most in his love life. She was not at home, but her service informed him she had finished her interior decorating job at the Johns-Manville headquarters in Colorado and was probably now in the air, heading for Los Angeles.

'Has she had any other calls?'

'Yes, three.'

'Any from a Mr Thomas?'

'One from him.' Did Mr King want the message?

No, he said. He already had it. Replacing the phone in its cradle, he stared hard at the lights of Minneapolis. How in hell's name did Thomas and the Zanadu Corporation know Frankie and he were in love? How did they find out about Frankie? How much did Frankie know about King Corp prospects from their table talk and pillow talk? She'd done Jackson's office, so the lawyer would have given Thomas her phone number.

20

But why ring her? Why not? In a deal like this where a company worth a billion dollars in sales was changing hands, whom could you trust? Nobody. But surely Frankie couldn't have had anything to do with the leak. That was paranoia about his company talking.

Yet, it left a disturbing echo in his head. This man Thomas and Zanadu had evidently done their homework on Kurt King and King Corp. It meant he would be fighting against a ruthless, no-holds-barred opponent.

That bathroom mirror had changed its mind about him in the last four hours. Now he did look forty-six, and maybe a year or two more. He brushed his teeth, climbed into his pyjamas and into bed.

But there he lay, his tired mind conjuring images out of the glowing city lights and moving shadows in his room. His father's face as he sat at the controls of his aircraft, circling his new plant and looking angry, dismayed. His father liked to take his problems, and his sorrows, aloft. A God-fearing man, he might have thought like those old cathedral builders, the higher he went the nearer to heaven. His father's cry, almost anguished, rang in his head. 'King Company has always been mine and mine alone to be passed on to my only son and heir. And now I can't do that because I needed money and the only way I could get it was to sell shares to the goddamn public.' It took him a long time to understand how his father felt that day.

Now, as he drifted into that state between waking and sleeping, his mind went back to another plane ride, one he could never forget. His first.

BOOK ONE
Birthright

Fall 1936

I

With his keen young ears, the boy caught the first faint drone of the unfamiliar engine and screwed up his eyes to look into the California sunset, then point. Beside him, the stocky man in working overalls also noted the strange sound and peered at the sky. After several minutes, the child's neck began to ache, but he did not complain or cease to stare at the western sky. 'There he is,' came his high-pitched cry. 'There he is. I see him, Uncle Ray, I see him.'

Taking his eyes off the small shape in the sky to gaze at the boy, the man grinned with affection. 'Yah, I now see him. Okay, time to go hide. I go out by the strip.' He had a strange, guttural voice. The boy turned immediately and ran to an old Ford pickup. Scrambling into the back, he pulled a dirty tarpaulin over him, as excited as if he were hiding for the very first time. Through a crack in the tarpaulin, he watched the plane float towards them, level then touch down in a clean, three-point landing. Its tail-skid drew a straight line in the landing-strip sand before the pilot turned the ship and taxied towards the man. As the engine died, the propeller gave the illusion of spinning backwards several times before it chunked to a halt.

'Well, well,' shouted Ray Nehring, the man on the ground. 'You go ahead and buy it. Just like that.' His voice had a reproachful hint.

The pilot who climbed down from the aeroplane, carefully stepping on the walkway then leaping nimbly from the lower wing, was unusually good-looking. Obviously in high spirits, he yanked off his leather helmet and goggles, tossing them playfully to the other man. His hair was black, his complexion olive, his features sharply chiselled and set off by dark, flashing eyes that seemed to be lit from within. No one would have taken him for a Swede, though he had been born in Stockholm almost half a century before. His father's ancestors had come from well east of the Ural Mountains, which accounted for the dark complexion and the slightly slant eyes.

'Yeah, just like that.' His voice was rich and fairly deep. 'What do you think of her? She's a Stearman, 4E to be precise.'

'This the one called Junior Speedmail?'

'That's right, this is the baby. She's the nicest plane I ever flew. Easy as pie. I was upstairs for the better part of two and a half hours, and nothing's sore. Not my legs or my arms.'

'How's about the seat of your pants.' In Ray's German accent that phrase sounded quaint.

'Not even that.' He laughed, and patted the other man on the shoulder. Under his tarpaulin, the boy watched them circle the plane, sizing it up. The pilot, talking quickly and gesturing, was showing the shorter man the refinements of the new aircraft. He pointed out a feature he especially liked, a full cowling enclosing the Pratt and Whitney engine to improve cooling and speed.

'Kurt, you must be dry,' Ray said, interrupting and handing the pilot a flask in grease-stained leather.

'And how, I can use it. You know, Ray, I always follow the motto, "Twelve hours from bottle to throttle," but there are times when it's powerful hard to

26

resist offers. And I must say there were some interesting offers of various kinds in San Francisco.' He took a quick pull, made a face, took a longer drink and gave back the flask, shaking his head.

'Ray, Prohibition is over, so please buy better booze. That stuff belongs in her fuel tank' – he nodded towards the plane – 'not mine.'

'How much horsepower that engine has?' Ray asked, lapsing into German syntax.

'I was hoping you'd ask. That engine's a 420 Wasp and they reckon to kick it up to 450. She goes.'

'You can carry all your machines in that monster. Beats hell out of the Jenny, but they were special. Like real aeroplanes they looked.'

'All right Ray, the Jennies were special and you held them together with baling wire and chewing gum and I loved 'em as much as you, but they were boxcars compared with this. She just flies so nice, and she'll take all my adding machines.' He took the flask back and had another swig, grimacing and wiping his mouth with the back of his hand. 'Anyway, I'm carrying fewer machines each trip and I've just about papered the state of California over with Burroughs machines, so I don't have to sell so hard now.' He kicked the tyre of a front wheel affectionately. 'No, this plane will hold me for a while, and you won't have as much to do to keep her in shape. She's only four years old, 1100 hours but well maintained. A clean record and no damage. She practically takes care of herself, this little sweetheart. Like a cat, don't you know?' He was handing the flask back when he had another thought and took another mouthful, still pulling a face.

Ray was about to have a drink when he stopped. 'Damn, you've got me paying so much attention to this

27

new ship, I almost total forgot. You got a little surprise in back of pickup.'

Kurt King, who had been looking at a suspicious oil drip under the engine, swung round, his eyes sparkling and a warm smile creasing his face. 'No kiddin'. That's about the best news a man could hear.'

He walked over to the beat-up Ford and began to talk in a loud, stagy voice. 'Let's see now, where should I put this big, old plane engine? I guess I'll put it way in the back so it won't roll around too much. Then, on top of that old tarp there, I'll shovel this load of fresh manure, this good, strong horse manure.'

Suddenly, the tarpaulin flew into the air, the boy scrambled out, his voice rising in fear and delight. 'Wait, Daddy, wait! It's me under here, Kurt King, Junior. Dad, wait, oh please.'

King grabbed the boy under his armpits. Laughing, he swung him high in the air and when the boy spread his arms he raised and lowered him while making loud aeroplane noises which the boy tried, vainly, to imitate. After several revolutions, he brought his son to his chest and hugged him hard. Holding him at arm's length, he searched his face as if he feared something precious might be missing then, reassured, he pulled him close and kissed him fondly on the cheek.

'Dad,' the boy said abruptly, 'don't do that. Men don't kiss.'

'My oh my, aren't we getting old in a hurry? What are you now, anyway, five years old?'

'Six,' the child corrected, sternly.

'Six, like in our middle name, Sixtus?'

'Yes.'

'Okay then, Mr six-year-old Kurt Sixtus King, Junior,

I hereby and forthwith promise never to kiss you again. All right with you?'

The boy hesitated, dubious, gazing at his father then looking away. 'Well, maybe sometimes it'd be okay. Maybe you could kiss me sometimes.'

King looked at his boy, a lump rising in his throat; for a moment, he felt he was seeing himself as a child. The same dark hair and eyes, the same intensity softened only by the less prominent lines of Kurt's face, and the colouring he'd got from his mother. The same self-assurance. He moved him from his knee to a sitting place next to him on the pickup running board. 'Would those sometimes include birthdays?' he asked, gently.

'Yes, and at night, too, when you're home. But not when other people can see.'

'What! I can never kiss you in front of people? What about your Uncle Ray standing over there with that long face down to his knees?'

Young Kurt's face lit up. 'Oh, it's okay in front of Uncle Ray.'

'But no strangers, eh?'

'That's right. Never in front of no strangers.'

'Any strangers, Juney,' King said, a bit more harshly than he intended.

The child, who hated to make a mistake, frowned. He corrected himself slowly. 'Never in front of any strangers.'

'Fine, I promise. Now, how would you like to take a plane ride?'

'Can we really, Dad?' He jumped up and ran towards the plane, but Ray headed him off and made him wait for his father.

'Kurt, you shouldn't again go up,' Ray advised. 'I

29

don't mean them swigs you had. They was nothing much. But daylight you don't have any left to speak of.'

'Well, friend, I don't plan to speak of it, just to fly in it. Don't worry, I just want to take the boy up for a short hop.'

Persisting, the other man said, 'I'd say nothing if this plane had them fancy new instruments for night flying, which it don't, or if you knew instrument flying, which you don't.'

King cut him short, laughing. 'Ray, you worry too much. We'll be right back. Now come on and prop me.'

Ray was on tenterhooks for twenty minutes until he heard the Stearman approach. Swinging the Ford round, he trained its dim headlights on the landing strip. That engine pitch and the whine told him King was going to land hot, to give the boy an extra kick, he supposed. He shook his head, reprovingly. A minute later, King was on the ground. When the engine noise trailed off, Ray could hear the boy's excited voice then both father and son laughing. Ray, too, smiled despite himself, as he drove to pick them up.

'Lord sakes, Ray, don't you have shocks on this thing?' King yelled above the clatter as the Ford bounced down the unpaved road connecting the landing-strip with the parking lot behind King Corporation's main building. At each tremor, young Kurt bounced on his lap.

'I figured you'd say that, so I had this afternoon your new Packard brought over by a boy. It's at the back of your office and here's the keys.'

'Thanks, Ray, that was thoughtful of you. Say, why not come in the office with me. We'll have one more decent drink and I can discuss a couple of ideas with you. I think I've figured a way to overcome the flutter problem on the trim-tab, and I looked at a plant in Bakersfield that could cut our costs still further in the Therm-a-Jug division. I'd like to kick these things around with you – won't keep you long.'

'I think maybe tonight wouldn't be best.' Ray's big hands splayed out on the steering wheel as he spoke, quietly. 'It's Friday and since Sunday afternoon you've been gone.'

'Sunday!' King whistled in genuine surprise. 'Kee . . . rist, and I'd have sworn I'd been away two days, three at the most. Oh, oh! Now I remember. It was a roadhouse just outside of Sacramento.' He glanced at his son who had his head out the window to catch the early evening breeze. He lowered his voice. 'There was this fraülein . . . versteh du? Und . . .'

'Hold it,' Ray said. 'I don't want to hear about it. Not even in your godawful German. Some things in this business ain't my business.'

King laughed. 'I see what you mean, but I have to say you miss some good yarns.'

Ray did not reply. He pulled up beside a sparkling tan-and-cream 1936 Packard four-door sedan with chrome-covered spare tyres in each of the front fender-wells. It looked twice the size of the Model A pickup. King took the large keyring, opened the front door and told his son to wait in the car while he talked to Uncle Ray for a minute.

Young Kurt clambered across the seat, rolled down the passenger window and waited happily. He was still exhilarated by the marvels of that flight. How the wind pounded against them and the earth wheeled beneath as they flew across the California horizon. Why, he had seen two setting suns, one from up there over the sea, after the first one down here over the hills.

Uncle Ray said something he couldn't make out to his father who thrust his head through the window. 'Juney, I just remembered something,' he said. 'You know I don't want you to lie, never in your life. You know that, don't you?' Young Kurt nodded. 'Tonight, when we get home, if your mother doesn't ask you about any plane rides, then I don't see why you should say anything. What I mean is, for some reason your mother thinks boys of your age shouldn't be flying in planes. So maybe we'd better keep it our little secret, what d'you say?'

'Yes, Dad. Okay.' He looked puzzled then said, 'Dad, what's a froyline in German – what does it mean?' His father's eyes widened and the boy caught him and Uncle Ray giving each other a strange glance.

'Uncle Ray's German is better than mine and he'll tell you, when he thinks you should know.' He put up an admonitory finger. 'But just don't ask your mother, that's all.' His voice had acquired a cutting edge, his son noticed.

Uncle Ray was trying not to grin as they walked to the pickup. Young Kurt knew his father and he had been like brothers since they met over ten years ago when Ray was new to California and his father a 'native' of five years' standing.

Always the story-teller, King was saying, 'Raymond, I've got to tell you just this one I heard in San José when I was gassing up. There was an old fly-boy in there, and I guess he does some barnstorming now and gives a few lessons. He was full of yarns and this one's a beaut. Seems there was this low-time pilot who was having a helluva job wrestling through turbulence, and he tries everything to keep his ship level. Finally, he doesn't know what more to do, so he takes his feet off

32

the rudder bar, throws his hands in the air and hollers, "Here God, you take it, I've done all I can do." Know what happened next? God cracked it up.'

They could still hear Ray's laughter as he took the Ford through its gears. King started the Packard, and it was with his usual feeling of pride that he eased the big car into motion. Funny, he thought, how he loved to push an aeroplane as hard as he dared, yet in a fine automobile he always started off slowly and smoothly and drove with care.

The gate guard nodded respectfully when he saw them, and King swung the car on to the empty highway. It was dark now, and King knew only the greatest effort was keeping his young son from falling asleep. Reaching over, he pulled the child to him and, steering left-handed, he cradled the boy's head on his lap.

Young Kurt took a deep, sighing breath and, just before he gave in completely, said, 'You know, Dad, it wasn't really God's fault.'

2

Kurt Sixtus King, Senior, was a devout man if an infrequent churchgoer, so in his book nothing was God's fault. With the exception of the weather and natural disasters, he blamed all accidents on mortal failing or neglect, and he had little time for those who made excuses for their mistakes, inefficiency or laziness. His own rise to relative affluence he attributed as much to hard, careful work as to his native intelligence. In Los Angeles in the mid-thirties he was a good man to know, a hard man to cross.

Born in Stockholm in 1890 to a fair Swedish mother and a dark Swedish father with an Asiatic look, King was brought to America as soon as he was old enough to travel. His family settled in a small Minnesota town and there, in a Swedish-American colony, the boy grew up. He married a fine-looking if not beautiful girl from his own background.

Unlike her husband, Martha Enstrom King would have been content to stay always in any one of a dozen small towns along the upper Mississippi, towns that enjoyed hot, bright summers and crisp, biting-cold winters. But everyone knew Kurt King was ambitious as well as mechanically minded. He could take anything apart, from steam engines to pocket watches, and put them back together again so they worked better than before. When the Burroughs Adding Machine company offered him a job selling their product from a Minneapolis office, he accepted immediately, without even consulting his bride.

Martha King never confessed to her husband how much she feared and disliked the city with its clanging horse-drawn street cars and its hundreds of automobiles, most of which always seemed to her to be blowing their horns at the same time. She might be dismayed they could not afford a house, she still kept their five-room flat in perfect order and spent hours preparing meals for her husband. She was an excellent cook, never happier than when in her kitchen.

Six months after their move to Minneapolis, she realized she had been sick for a week straight and knew she was pregnant. Came her time, everything went without a hitch, even when she surprised everybody by giving birth to twins. Kurt was delighted.

For the Kings, the future seemed to have limitless possibilities. Kurt had been promoted and was generally acknowledged one of Burroughs' best midwestern

34

salesmen. He and Martha talked about buying a house and spent several Sundays looking at pleasant neighbourhoods. And then their world fell apart. In the harsh winter of 1919, Spanish Flu reached America, killing thousands. Both King babies died of pneumonia.

A few days after the funeral, King walked into the president's office at Burroughs and asked to be transferred to anywhere, provided it was far away and warm. Startled, the president revealed that, coincidentally, King's name had been suggested for a new territory out West, but everyone thought he preferred Minnesota.

'I'll take it,' King said.

'Don't you want to know where it is?'

'Where is it and when do I leave?'

'California, as soon as you're packed.'

His new territory turned out to be twice the size of California, in fact the whole of the West Coast states. As he boasted to everybody, he was the Burroughs man for every place from San Diego to Seattle with all stops in between. From the very first day, King took to California. He simply loved it. If his wife felt otherwise she never once mentioned it to him.

Since the Burroughs machine was an excellent product, King had no difficulty selling them in hundreds. However, the pessimists, and even the so-called business experts, said it could not last. Once all the banks owned an adding machine, the market and his sales would dry up entirely. Kurt King refused to see it that way. Roaming up and down the state, travelling the oceanside roads just for the sight and smell of those towering redwood forests and the rugged coastline, he sold adding machines to anyone with a minimal need for one. When he had installed a machine in the last bank on his list, he did an about-turn and started interesting earlier buyers in the new models. He searched constantly for new customers, scouring every local paper in his huge territory, tracking companies that were springing up in California and convincing them they needed the speed and accuracy of mechanical computation.

After only two years in California, King had jumped into the top ten of the company's representatives throughout the nation. Though pleased, he nonetheless strove to better his record. Now, if it didn't take up most of his time covering his vast territory, he could outsell everybody. In 1923, he found the answer to his problem.

One of his customers was a man who had tried to make a quick fortune by selling war-surplus goods. For his first adding machine he paid cash; but when King called on him several months later, the business was in trouble. Because he needed money so badly, he was going to offer King two items for three hundred dollars that were worth at least five hundred. Intrigued, King followed him to the storage yard. There, parked amidst piles of truck tyres and cartons of trenching tools, he saw two huge double-winged aeroplanes. At once, King realized they were the famous Jennies, the Curtiss JN-4D which the United States army had used as a training plane during its last-minute entry into the World War.

They looked dilapidated with grease streaks and broken, disconnected bracewires everywhere. But with his mechanical flair, King rightly sensed the planes were structurally sound. Taking a chance on the condition of the engines, King closed the deal. Within weeks, he taught himself to fly and became known as the Burroughs Flying Salesman, unwittingly pioneering the executive plane. He flew from the rear cockpit, carefully tying down his adding machines in the other. Twelve months later, he was Burroughs' number one salesman in the country.

Soon, he was selling adding machines to men whose small shops and garages were the precursors of the vast aeroplane factories of the future. For hours, he swapped yarns with aviation pioneers like Don Douglas, Allan Loughhead (Lockheed), Bill Boeing and Claude Ryan. They were all looking for innovations to increase performance, reliability, safety. It was Ryan who spotted King's talent for invention and asked if he could design and build some parts for the control surfaces of a prototype plane.

King talked over the problem with Ray Nehring, a German immigrant who had recently moved to California. Quiet and shy, Nehring had a first-rate mind and was that rare thing, an expert aeroplane mechanic. Between them, they formed a company to develop and produce aeroplane parts. Since King supplied the seed capital, Ray insisted on calling the company The King Company, later to become King Corporation then King Corp.

As King worked for Burroughs full-time, Nehring hired and supervised the small work force; he took King's many ideas and sifted, polished and tested them before attempting to manufacture. In three years, they scored with three products: the control surface parts originally built for Ryan Aeronautical; the first oleo-shock strut, a landing-gear part; and King's pride and joy, the rudder trim-tab which saved pilots the aches and pains that came from hours of pushing a rudder bar with one foot.

By the late 1920s, everything was going King's way.

He was outselling every other Burroughs field representative, his own company was growing steadily, and he had finally convinced Martha they were in California to stay. They started house-hunting and found a good-sized property off Sunset Boulevard. 'Not far from Will Rogers' house,' King would tell people, proudly.

Typically Californian, it was a low, robust wooden structure with broad overhangs supported by heavy wooden beams; the rear grounds had access to the interior through an expanse of glass. Bougainvillaea flourished everywhere, and Martha set out to redeem the garden that had gone to seed since the previous owners had moved.

Still, King drove himself harder at his job. He also drank more than was good for him. On too many occasions he had to stay an extra day or two in strange towns because he did not feel sober enough to fly home. Or because, as wagging tongues said, he had a lady friend or two in various towns.

During the Wall Street Crash of 1929, King blessed his foresight for resisting advice from bankers to finance company expansion by selling shares. He rode out the storm. At Christmas that same year, Martha announced she was pregnant once again.

On the evening of 4 July 1930, King was sitting on the verandah of the exclusive Los Angeles Country Club, which he had recently joined, literally praying Martha would give birth before midnight. Always a flag-waving patriot, nothing would have pleased him more than a son born on America's birthday. His hope vanished with the last sky rockets.

On 6 July, in the spare bedroom of their new home, Martha King had a seven-pound, eight-ounce boy whom his father immediately named after himself.

From the time he could walk and talk, young Kurt was groomed as his father's heir to the company. King brushed aside Martha's protests that he was spoiling the boy by giving him the latest in bicycles and setting up a workshop for him in their basement. King was delighted to see his son had his same knack for working with his hands and inventing things. At six, he introduced him to the factory.

'Know something, Martha, when he saw those big presses in the south wing, he wanted me to start them up and roll out the parts just for him to see? He just plain loved the place. And now he's in the factory one or two afternoons a week whether I'm in town or not. He sticks his head in my door and says, "Hi, Dad, okay to look around?" And I say, "Sure, but be careful." Some of my high-paid executives don't know the plant like he does.'

3

Manuel, their Mexican servant, met him as he came home from school. 'Mr Kurt, Sir, you have a message from your father. He wants for you to come over to the factory right away.'

Kurt stared at him. 'But he knows I'm there almost every day after school. Did he say why?'

Manuel shook his head. 'You want I call Bruno and have him drive you over?'

'No, I'll go over to the garage and save time.' Kurt cut through the big dining room into the kitchen where the coloured cook was shelling peas. 'Mr Junior,' she exclaimed, fondly. 'You come in here for somethin' to eat? What you want an' I'll fix it?'

'No, Millie, but thanks anyway. I'm just passing

through as they say.' In the doorway, he stopped and, concealing his grin, said, 'Your beauty is food enough for me.'

'Oh, Lor' in heaven, listen to the sweet stuff. Go on outa here this minute afore you turn this ol' head.'

It was a warm February day and he rolled down the Cadillac window. Bruno, the Italian chauffeur, was proud, boastful and his least favourite servant, so Kurt teased him by using his first name and talking about the war. Bruno had relatives in Italy who backed Il Duce and the chauffeur called them idiots for choosing the wrong side.

'Arthur,' Kurt said, and saw the man flinch, 'I'm going to be thirteen in a year from this July and my father has promised to buy me a motorbike for my birthday. But they've stopped making them because of the war. Do you think the war will be over by then and they'll be making motorbikes again?'

'I wouldn't worry, Mr Junior, maybe your father will see to it the war's over for your birthday.'

Kurt did not think much of that joke and cut short their dialogue. Ten minutes later, he was bounding up the stairs to King Company's executive wing. Spotting him, the receptionist pressed a button to operate the door release. Another of his father's new gadgets, he thought, as he entered the outer office.

'Why the special call, Mrs Olson? I was coming in anyway.'

She hesitated, then shrugged. 'I really don't know, but he's been like a wounded bear since he came back from downtown.' She buzzed and his father's voice crackled over the wire. 'Go right in,' she said, smiling at him.

'Sit down, son, I'll be right with you.' His father

pointed to a chair. 'I have to make a few phone calls then we can get out of here. I want to run over to the airport, take the Beech up and shake the kinks out of her. Thought you'd like to come along and maybe you can take the controls for a little practice after take-off.' He punched the intercom button and gave Mrs Olson the names of the people he wanted to talk to.

Kurt was elated, for he shared his father's passion for automobiles and aircraft. When he made a call, his father's dark, handsome face registered every emotion and he behaved as though the person was in the room, nodding and shaking his head and waving his hand to emphasize a No or a Yes; he also bawled into the instrument as though he thought it would fail before he got his message across. As usual, he was dressed soberly in a grey suit, dark grey tie and black shoes, his only concession to high style being the large diamond stickpin in his tie. Young Kurt noticed the picture of himself and his mother on the bookcase behind his father and, for the first time, realized it was a new picture taken every year just for the office.

A loud clanging noise startled him. Turning, he searched the room for a moment before being aware what had happened. A month before, smitten with a device at the Emporium in San Francisco, his father had installed an elaborate network of pneumatic tubes to shoot messages through his factories. As the main terminus was King's office, every so often a whooshing sound would signal a cartridge ending its run. But characteristically, King had not been satisfied with the new system, despite its efficiency, and had tampered with it. However, he had not finished his modifications and, as a result, the capsules no longer finished in their slot but shot through the air and crashed loudly against the base of King's desk.

Looking up and covering the phone mouthpiece, King called to his son, 'I haven't quite worked that out yet, but I will. It's a great system, a time-saver, and we think we can come up with a better one.'

Kurt smiled to himself. Even for an able and famous inventor like his father, things didn't always work out as they should. At the risk of being accused of family treason, his mother had told him about what she called, 'Dad's legendary blunders'.

His favourite story concerned the refrigerator his father had built some years back, a forerunner of mass-produced machines. A modified ice-box, cumbersome but effective, it used chlorine gas as its expansion and cooling component. The huge box chilled food just fine – until the day something came unstuck and the house filled with clouds of green, choking poison gas. After a day's forced eviction, the family and servants were able to return.

Then there was the oil-burning furnace King had his factory build to his specifications, confident it would beat anything then available and create another new company product. His idea was practical but lacked safety devices. That furnace worked well, heating the house like nothing else – until it blew up and all but took the house with it.

Even though Kurt's faith in his father's ability as an inventor was absolute, he loved these stories of failure, feeling they were the exception that proved the rule, to use a phrase he had recently learned in class.

Leaving the plant, they took their usual route through the various departments that most interested King – Product Development, Chemical Processing, Press

Department and Assembly and finally the Employee Cafeteria where they often picked up a sandwich or some fresh fruit. Young Kurt watched to see if his favourite Mexican girl was working the counter and was disappointed when he didn't see her. She always stared at him so boldly that he had to look away or blush, but he cherished the feeling she invoked, a new and growing pleasure.

4

Time and the growth of King Company had transformed the dusty trail leading to the airstrip into a neatly-bordered, two-lane blacktop. King hustled them over it in one of the company panel trucks, bringing it to a halt near the handsome, bright-red Beechcraft.

King reached up and patted the glowing red fuselage. 'Now, remember what I told you this type of plane, with this design, is called?' He stepped back, waiting for the boy's answer. 'Come on, now, you should remember these things, son,' he said as Kurt hesitated.

'Wait father, I'll get it.' He clenched his fists to help him concentrate. 'Ah, I got it. Staggerwing, right? Or is it staggeredwing? No, staggerwing – that's it.'

'Right, son. I knew you'd remember it. Come on, get on up there.' Kurt was light for his age, not much over a hundred pounds, and his father's hand-up almost sent him headfirst into the upper wing. But he steadied himself, caught the door handle and cranked open the passenger door.

His father walked around the plane, doing the outside part of the checklist in his head, then he, too, got into the cockpit. Kurt watched him scanning the multitude of gauges, going over everything that should be checked before starting the engine. Apparently satisfied, his father leaned back in his seat and snapped his belt together.

'And why "staggerwing"?'

'Because, ahh, the upper wing is set back farther than the lower wing instead of the other way around. Most doublewings are the other way, the upper wing is farther forward.' He sat back, pleased with himself as the engine burst into life.

Unlike King's earlier planes, the Beechcraft was an enclosed model. It could carry five people comfortably. Comparatively speaking, its power was enormous and once having reached its cruise altitude it was as quiet as an automobile. First produced in the late thirties, its clean lines, power and retractable landing-gear gave it the edge over every competitor. King was delighted to find one available at the beginning of the war and constantly added modifications from the company workshops to increase speed and reliability.

Racking the plane round, he pointed its nose towards the runway. Just then, he spotted a man off in the distance, half-trotting, half-walking towards the plane. He cut the power back and waited. 'It's Ray, and he can't see far enough to know it's me. He's wondering what damn fool is trying to take the plane up when the damn gasoline is rationed. We'll wait for him.'

Kurt watched Ray Nehring, known to him always as Uncle Ray, although there was no blood kinship. He was hobbling badly. Kurt knew why his father was waiting, for Ray would be insulted if they taxied up to him. It still hurt to see him limp like that.

'Did you ever know how Ray was hurt, Juney?' asked his father, lapsing absent-mindedly into the old nickname. 'Did anyone ever tell you that?' He glanced at the boy, who shook his head.

'It was six years ago. I was still selling for Burroughs then and had to make a last-minute trip to Seattle. We loaded the plane and I was rushing Ray – you know how slow and deliberate he can be. Anyway, I was flying the Stearman, you remember her, one of her last trips. She was due to be replaced, overdue.' King sat staring straight ahead through the windscreen, looking at nothing, talking in a low voice the boy had to strain to hear.

'Ray was kinda mad at me for insisting on taking off in light rain. I signalled to him to spin the prop. It didn't catch. I signalled again, hurried like. That time it caught. Just as it turned Ray slipped on the wet tarmac. The prop missed his head but it hit him on the shoulder. Slammed him right to the ground. God, I about died before I could shut the engine down and get to him.' He swung his head round and watched Ray get closer, watched his slow, lop-sided gait.

'He lay in hospital for two months. I got him the best doctors money could buy, but the damage had been done. Ray's a strong man, and he's come back better than most anyone else could have. But he's a broken man, in body and I think in spirit. And I'm the one responsible.'

'No, Dad, it wasn't your fault,' Kurt cried.

'Well, anyway, one good thing came of it. I quit Burroughs there and then and nailed myself to the drawing-board while Ray was in hospital. When he came out I'd finished my inertial starter design. Now almost every plane you see has a self-starter, and that one invention accounts for at least a third of our present business. We make more starters than anybody.' He turned a wry smile on his son. 'But that doesn't do much for Ray, does it?'

Once Ray had spotted his father, he signalled them on without even noticing the boy in the right-hand seat. At the end of the runway, Kurt sensed his throat begin to tighten then his apprehension was swamped by the din of the Beechcraft's powerful engine revving up. His father gave a grin and the thumbs-up sign. Suddenly, all the boy could feel was the incredible thrust of the plane as it hurtled down the runway. Gravity banged him back in his seat as they left the earth and started climbing. He heard the gear motor whine then the thud and snap as the wheels folded into place. He watched carefully as his father smoothly reduced power and set the propeller pitch to take a bigger bite of the clean air.

A thousand feet up, Kurt could still pick out familiar landmarks. His father flew over their home, past the Will Rogers' estate and over that of the cranky and mysterious Howard Hughes, who had made millions out of everything from oil-drilling equipment through aircraft to film production. He heard the engine note change as they circled the small mountain range behind the canyon surrounding the newest neighbourhoods sprouting north of Los Angeles. Just when he thought his father would ask him to take the controls, he was surprised by a question.

'Have you any idea why I'm jumpy today, why I'm not myself?' his father shouted above the engine din. Kurt shook his head. 'No, of course you don't. Can't expect you to read my mind.'

At that moment, they hit turbulence and the plane dropped abruptly and Kurt felt his stomach tighten. As they wobbled through another updraught, he searched for something to grab. The right-seat control bobbed in front of him, but he knew better than to touch that without a nod from his father. He put both hands on

46

the glareshield to steady himself. His stomach was heaving.

'Well, I'll tell you,' his father shouted. Then his voice dropped as the plane emerged from the troubled air and levelled off. 'I had to go to Spring Street this morning.' Kurt knew his father was looking at him, but would not turn to meet the stare. 'You know what Spring Street is, don't you, son?'

'It's our Wall Street.'

His father grunted. 'Yeah, that's what I call it, Los Angeles' Wall Street. Well, I had to go down there this morning and I had to sell a good bit of the company. My company. Yours and mine. Goddamn it, excuse my French, King Company has always been mine, owned free and clear by me, your father, to be passed on to his only son and heir in that same unencumbered condition. And now I can't do that because I needed money. And the only way I could get it' – he was almost screaming the words – 'was to sell shares to the goddamn public. And it annoys the hell out of me, son!'

Another swirl of turbulent air took all King's attention. When he had wrestled them through it, his anger had gone and Kurt was relieved to see the smile creep across his father's face.

'Ah, maybe I'm all wet. Many successful businessmen in California have taken their companies public when they needed big dollars to make improvements, to expand. You either grow or die. The banks wouldn't lend any more money. Said the only way was to sell stock. Now, for the first time, I've partners, hundreds of them. Son, I hated to do it, but I'd no place to turn. Maybe I've got some kind of stupid pride or something.'

He fell silent for a minute, and Kurt did not know what to say, so he, too, kept silent.

47

His father leaned over and slapped him on the shoulder. 'Well, I still have control, Juney, I still own more of King Corp than anyone else. And now I have the money to retool and take advantage of the head start I have in the aviation business that this God-awful war has dumped on us. I'm doing what's right for the company, so I guess I should be happy. When you're grown and I'm ready to quit all this, the company I hand over to you will be worth much more than if I hadn't done what I did today. So, maybe it'll work out for the best.' His big hand squeezed his son's shoulder. 'But it still hurts,' he said in a choked voice.

He said no more, busying himself with the task of handling the Beechcraft. And Kurt, now with hands and feet on the controls, followed him through the touchdown and rollout. He was too busy to think about what his father had told him.

II

Somebody shook Kurt gently and he opened his eyes. A woman stood by his bed, her tall form silhouetted by the hall light spilling through the open bedroom door. 'What in the world is Mrs Norman doing here?' he wondered, drowsily, as he finally placed the woman. From the dimly-lit alarm clock, he saw it was twenty-nine minutes after three on a chilly December morning. Rubbing his eyes, not yet able to ask her the question, he blinked at her. She moved a step closer to the bed. Though her face was in shadow he could see she held a handkerchief which she was twisting fretfully. Somewhere in the quiet house a clock struck the half-hour.

'Kurt, I don't know how to tell you this, but I guess I should get it right out. It's your father. There was an accident, in the plane, a crash . . .'

Kurt sat up straight. Everything about him seemed to have stopped. He barely heard himself whisper, 'Is he dead? Is my father dead?'

'No, he's alive. But he is seriously hurt.'

'Where's my mother?'

'She's downstairs. She got the news an hour ago and called me and asked me to come and sit with her while she waits for the doctor to phone again. She sent me to wake you, thought you should be told right now instead of in the morning.' She blew her nose loudly in the wrinkled handkerchief, seemingly embarrassed by the way she had got the news out. 'Why don't you put a robe on and come down?'

49

He shook his head. 'No, I'll get dressed.' He was fully awake now. 'Tell Mother I'll be right down. And Mrs Norman, thank you.'

On her way out, the woman stopped, turned to look at him as though to add something, but thought better of it. Struggling slowly out of bed, Kurt put on the school clothes he had laid out on the chair the previous night. Without knowing why, he felt it important not to wait in a robe. Apprehensively, he came down and went into the kitchen where the two women sat.

'Oh, Kurt, you needn't have got dressed,' his mother said in a thin voice. 'The call could come any moment now telling us he's all right.' She tried to cover her worry with a smile. 'And then you'll be right back in bed.' She sniffed into a tissue, and tried a more forceful smile.

'What happened, Mother?'

'It was outside Sacramento. A little field like I've been seeing in my dreams for all the years he's been flying. He was taking off when the engine stopped. The plane hit the tops of some trees and went down into the river. It took the ambulance a long time to get to him, and they had to cut away his coat to get him out.' She closed her eyes, shielding them with her hand as though suppressing the image in her mind. 'They forgot to bring the coat along, so they didn't have his wallet and they didn't know who he was until an hour ago when he came to.' She reached over and took his hand, gripping his fingers with such strength that the boy was more frightened than he had been before. 'Then he lost consciousness again. The doctor's going to call me back just as soon as they know his condition. Oh, Lord, how I hate that expression.' To Kurt's amazement, her grip on his hand tightened.

'Mother, it'll be all right,' he said after she had remained silent for a long, awkward time. 'You know how strong he is.' His words sounded hollow. All he could think of was Uncle Ray's repeated warning that his father had to stop trying to beat the darkness and the weather with one engine; he should wait for daylight or good weather. His mother was speaking.

'Thank you, son. You know, maybe you have the right idea. I think I'll get dressed, too.'

When she returned, Kurt did not know whether to laugh or cry. She was wearing a pink dress, one his father had given her for Christmas. Kurt thought it much too young for her, that it made her look, well, foolish. But he understood why she wanted to wear it now.

Without preamble, his mother began to talk, to ramble on about her husband and the accident; she looked neither at him nor at Mrs Norman, but kept mumbling and looking hard at the phone on the kitchen counter. When she began to repeat herself, Mrs Norman gave her a sharp look, got up and walked to the pantry. She brought back a bottle of whisky and a glass. She poured a half glass and added some whisky to her own coffee cup.

'No,' she ordered when Martha King started to pour the whisky into her coffee. 'Drink it straight down.'

'Oh, Marion, I couldn't.'

'Come on. It's the best thing in the world for you right now.'

Swallowing the drink brought a grimace to his mother's face, and Kurt wondered why anyone drank whisky. Only when he noticed his mother seemed calmer after a few minutes did he realize the wisdom of

51

the neighbour's idea. Why hadn't he thought of it first? He desperately wanted to help.

At five o'clock the call came. His mother hurried across to the phone. 'Yes, this is Mrs King, I'll hold the line.' She turned so that she wouldn't be speaking with her back to him. Kurt noticed she was biting hard on her lower lip and her hair, which she had put up hastily, was slipping loose. One strand, which looked pure white, fell across her cheek and she pushed it back absently. 'Doctor? Yes, you did . . . what?'

He would always remember how she uttered that last word. It came out high and piercing, like the cry of a sea-bird, then died into a moan. He watched the phone slip from her hand and strike the counter with a bang before his mother fell heavily to the floor.

2

Among the papers of Kurt Sixtus King was a document spelling out in detail how his last rites were to be conducted.

His friends at the Sunset Boulevard Congregational Church, which he had begun to attend fairly regularly in his last few years, were disappointed that he was to be laid out in the parlour of his own home with no church service. A woman minister King had met in San Diego was to give the eulogy, then the body was to be cremated and the ashes strewn off the California coast-line from an aeroplane. One of King's business associates, a native Californian, who still resented the Easterner's invasion, remarked in private. 'Even in death he had to be different.' When he learned of the comment, Kurt took it as a compliment.

He could not look at the closed casket. Earlier, at his

mother's insistence, he had knelt before the silvery metal box that everyone but himself seemed to have no trouble believing held his father's remains. So great was his aversion to the idea the metal receptacle contained his father's body that he choked on the prayer he said, and couldn't remember what he had said. When he had done his duty, he got up quickly and left the room, moving as far from the catafalque and casket as he could.

All afternoon his father's friends came. Dutch Kindelberger, the Boeing family, Donald Douglas, and many others from the aviation community, filed by quickly, perhaps embarrassed that they were King's friends but had not met his family. The Mayor of Los Angeles stayed for almost an hour, and there was a large stand of flowers from Governor Warren. Kurt noticed how many of his father's business friends clustered around the trio of aeroplane pioneers. That didn't surprise him. He knew that, although the end of the war had brought the California aircraft industry to a halt, it was now experiencing a resurgence.

His mother stood straight-backed, imperiously unemotional, at the corner of the casket for the entire afternoon, greeting each of her husband's friends, thanking them for coming by. Kurt marvelled at her composure, for he alone had heard the sobs that had floated down the hallway each night since his father's death.

Most of the people who passed through the rooms knew Kurt and would stop to talk, offering their condolences in quiet tones. He realized they meant to be kind, but he wished to be left alone. As yet, he had not sorted out his own feelings. He felt terrible for his father, and his only solace was that he died in a hospital bed and not alone and struggling in some dark river. He also felt concern for himself. What is it going to be like, he asked himself over and over, to go on without my Dad? But most of all, Kurt tried to keep his muddled emotions under control.

Throughout the afternoon his classmates trailed in like so many wraiths in his vision. All looked uncomfortable in their suits and dresses. He watched carefully for only two friends. One was Beverly Anderson, who lived a couple of houses down, near the ravine. She was a junior at Palisades High School, one year ahead of him, but lately she had become very friendly despite the age gap. He was surprised how often he found her outside her house when he came by; it intrigued him that her long, blond hair was always neatly curled and combed, and that she always dressed with style.

His other friend had absolutely nothing in common with Beverly Anderson. Whereas, at 16, she already looked like a woman, thanks to the California climate and her genes, Ronald Poole, at fifteen, looked exactly what he was – a young, adolescent male. Painfully thin and unusually tall, his penchant for sarcasm laced with obscenity immediately attracted the polite, reserved King, who listened to Poole's foul mouth, looked at his rampant acne and dubbed him 'Cess Poole'. As King was still shy with girls and Poole markedly unsuccessful, the two spent most of their free time together. The rest of their crowd, noting the disparity in height between the shorter King and the six-foot-plus Poole, called them Mutt and Jeff. This kidding only buttressed their friendship.

On the day of Kurt's father's death, when the news of the event swept through the high school lunchroom, Ron Poole got up from his table, his tray untouched, and walked out without asking for permission. He caught the first bus to the King house where he spent the entire day, not leaving until assured that his scared and exhausted friend was finally asleep.

When Kurt had finished accepting the condolences of his school friends, he went searching for Ron and found him in a corner of a room, alone. 'How long have you been standing there?'

'Only a couple of days.'

'Come off it.'

'All right, about an hour. You had a bunch of old people round you and I didn't want to butt in. Helluva lot of people come to . . . ah, pay their respects. Was that the goddamn mayor I saw going out? Jeez. Oh, my mother says to tell you how sorry she is. So, I just told you.' He grinned tentatively, as if testing his friend's mood and whether he could stand humour. When he noticed Kurt smile slightly, he continued. 'Did you see Janice Arnold? You must've. She doesn't look so bad dressed up.'

Kurt smiled. Poole's crush on Janice was an open secret, but one that Kurt would never joke about. Looking closely at his friend, he noted Poole's dark tie was slightly off centre, and the shirt collar was unbuttoned. 'Your mother made you wear that tie, eh?'

'Yeah.'

'Couldn't get you to button your shirt, though, could she?'

'Stick it in your ear, Kurt, will ya?' Then, embarrassed by his comment, he added, 'Hey, excuse me.'

Kurt gave his friend a reassuring look. 'I've got to go up front with my mother while the minister speaks. You're going to stay, aren't you? Wait around, I'll be back.'

Poole watched his friend move to the front of several rows of chairs which had been set up in front of the casket. As usual Kurt's suit – dark blue – fitted him perfectly. Poole had often kidded Kurt for the excessive care he took with his clothes. No other classmate dressed as expensively or as neatly. Yet today, Poole decided, that trait had become an asset. Kurt looked older in Poole's eyes, more mature.

Kurt was impressed with the woman preacher, who was attractive and the opposite of so many mannish females he had seen in the various Californian professions and even in business. But feminine though she looked, she had a forceful, matter-of-fact way of putting her message across. His father, he thought, would have liked that. When she had ended her brief prayer, she answered a question in many people's minds.

'As you know, my church is not in Los Angeles but in San Diego, and our friend and his family attended a church near his home. But I came to know K. S. King some years back when I had a phone call fairly late one evening. The caller, who identified himself as a Mr King, apologized for disturbing me so late at night. He said he was a businessman staying overnight in San Diego and he had been reading the Bible in his hotel room.' The preacher looked round at the people in the room, a small smile playing on her handsome face. 'I remember it all so clearly. He said, "No please don't get the impression I read the Bible all the time, 'cause I don't. But tonight it was either read the Bible or have a drink, and knowing I can never have just one drink, and knowing I have a plane to fly back to Los Angeles in the morning, I chose the Bible."'

A murmur of understanding arose from the assembled group, and several people nodded their heads, meaning it was typical of Kurt King. The minister continued. 'He said he had come across a passage he didn't follow and it bothered him not to grasp the meaning. So, he had found my telephone number and rang me. He said he always preferred Congregationalists, though he didn't say why. Well, we talked about that passage for a long time. It was from Proverbs, and I knew it well. It gave me some insight about Mr King. I'll quote it for you –

There be three things which are too wonderful for me, yea, four which I know not:
The way of an eagle in the air; the way of a serpent upon a rock; the way of a ship in the midst of the sea; and the way of a man with a maid.

'Kurt King's interests were many and he pursued them with relish. I liked the cut of his mind, I guess you could say. He showed up one Sunday morning at my church, attended the service and stayed after to compliment me on my sermon. He did that four or five times in the last few years.' She paused, and without looking up, Kurt knew she was gazing at him and his mother. He brought his head up, slowly, and met her eyes. 'I did not know Mr King well, but I knew him well enough to know this – he will be sorely missed.' With that, she closed her prayer book and slowly moved past the makeshift pulpit to speak quietly to Martha King. Kurt stared straight ahead, not looking as the men from the funeral parlour put screens round the casket.

Later, when the food and drink had been put out on long tables, Kurt joined Ron Poole. He was pleased Beverly was with him.

A highly emotional girl, Beverly had truly liked Kurt's

father, and now she found it hard to express her feelings. While groping for words, she put her hand on Kurt's arm; she was holding back her tears and chewing away most of the lipstick from her full, lower lip. Kurt covered her hands with his. 'I know, Bev, I know,' he murmured. 'And thanks.'

'Kurt, why don't we go downstairs?' Poole suggested. 'Your mother won't mind. She's got a zillion people round her.'

Kurt nodded. He knew the doctor had just given his mother another one of the pills that had kept her going for the last two days. 'Yeah, that's a good idea. Come on, both of you.'

His father had added quite a few rooms to the large, sprawling house as well as a huge swimming pool, but Kurt preferred the small basement workshop. This room, his father's special Christmas present at the beginning of the war, was exclusively his, the only one nobody else ever entered. Both his mother and the maid, he had noticed with growing concern recently, often entered his bedroom, though warning him. This was his den, where he worked.

Kurt had turned out more methodical than his father, who tended to work in huge bursts of energy on several projects at a time then forget or forsake them after a couple of weeks. While possessing his father's intense energy, Kurt had developed more tenacity. Once he committed himself, he saw an idea or a project through to the end. He knew what Uncle Ray meant when he remarked one day about one of his ideas, 'Your father would have run out of patience before he got half as far, like the man who cashed in his chips when he was on a winning streak.'

He hated disorder, and at the end of each day put

58

everything in its place. In his basement den he did his school homework even if his mother objected that she had bought a new oak desk, a special chair and a gooseneck lamp so that he could study in his bedroom. When he had finished his homework, he would close his books, turn on an extra bank of overhead fluorescents and work on his latest project, usually a model plane. He could never express, even to his father who had created this special world for him, how completely happy he was at such times.

His model building had the approval and encouragement of both his parents. Obviously his father liked it, but he could never figure out his mother's attitude. He did not dare ask her for fear of ruining a good thing. All she ever said was that it seemed 'constructive'.

Like so many contemporaries, he built scale models of American fighter planes that had helped win the war – P-47 Thunderbolts, P-51 Mustangs, the Grumman planes, Wildcat and Hellcat the Navy had flown. But he had a special fondness for old planes. Whenever he or his father found one, they bought a kit that days or weeks later emerged from the work bench as an early Curtiss, a Handley Page, a Graham-White Charabanc (which as far back as 1913 could carry a pilot and ten passengers) or a Martin Great Lakes Tourer. All of these miniature creations now stood on shelves or hung suspended on thin wires from his workshop and bedroom ceilings.

'Hey Kurt, you got any butts hidden down here?' Ron asked, flopping down on the old sofa that took up an entire wall.

Kurt shook his head, but Beverly spoke up. 'I've got cigarettes.' Fishing in her purse, she produced a pack of Chesterfields and passed them round. Before Kurt could locate a book of matches she snapped open a slim, gold lighter. Both boys stared at the expensive lighter as she applied the flame to their cigarettes. 'From an admirer,' she murmured, coyly.

'Some admirer,' said Ron with a rare display of genuine praise.

Kurt smiled at the girl. 'Only one of hundreds, right Bev?' He gave her a sincere look of affection and she turned her face and looked at him with open fondness.

'Jesus,' said Ron to himself as he watched her soft expression, 'if Kurt turned the girls in our class on the way he does Beverly, he could have them all.'

They lounged and smoked, talking about everything except the event that had drawn them together. After half an hour, Ron went upstairs and brought down a plate of sandwiches. They were hardly touched. Kurt knew he should be upstairs with his mother but he stayed.

'Hey, what's this? You got a birthday, Kurt?' Ron had been looking at the model planes lined up on the shelves above Kurt's workbench and had come across a gift-wrapped package. He lifted the package and handed it to his friend.

'I didn't see that,' Kurt said, puzzled. 'I wonder . . . there's no card.' He rotated the oblong package, shoe-box size, noticing his name written in ink by a familiar hand. Suddenly, he handed it to Beverly, sitting beside him on the workbench. 'Please,' he said, quietly, 'will you open it for me?'

She looked up at Ron, standing on the other side of Kurt. When he nodded, she began to unwrap the box. 'It's a model. Uh, wait a minute, it's a Sopwith Bat Boat and it says it's the world's first true amphibian.' She paused. 'Oh, and there's a card taped to the box.'

Beverly looked at it and her smile froze. She turned it over once, then staring at Kurt with an anguished look, handed it to him.

Kurt read the card, then a strange sound came into his throat, like a stricken animal. He tried to stifle it, but couldn't. A spasm shook him and he began to sob, long moaning sobs. He bent forward to hide his head in his hands, but the girl took his shoulder and drew him to her, placing his shaking head in her lap. Soon, the sobs grew quieter, more muffled, but his small back continued to rise and fall as the tears and sorrow he had held in check for three days and nights erupted despite himself.

He had dropped the card on the floor. Ron bent to pick it up. It was one of Kurt's father's business cards. On the back was printed in King Senior's fine, precise hand a date and a message. The date was three days before he crashed.

Here's the one we've been looking for. To a wonderful son, from a proud and loving father.'

Ron had to swallow hard to keep back his own tears. He saw Beverly was sobbing, silently. He noticed her firm breasts rise and fall. One hand grasped Kurt's shoulder and she reached out the other, which Ron took gratefully. He stood there staring straight ahead, his Adam's apple wobbling in his long, thin neck. He could hear two things: his heart thumping in his temples, and the painful sound of his best friend crying.

3

Although close friends of the King family, Arthur and Etta Kimble waited a month before calling on Martha. It was a friendly visit, but as practising attorneys they also wanted to express concern at the confusion in which Kurt King had left his affairs and to ensure his widow knew her rights. Arthur Kimble explained the position as he saw it, then came to the point. 'Martha, we're not suggesting anyone at King Corp would purposely deceive you or mislead you about your rights and interest in the company now that Kurt is gone.'

He glanced at his wife, who nodded her agreement. They sat, the three of them, in the smaller parlour, drinking tea and talking in subdued voices. Arthur went on, 'In fact, as attorneys, we probably shouldn't be here saying what we're saying since it amounts to soliciting business, but we know you realize that's not the case. What we're doing is declaring that we're worried about a dear friend whose position in life has suddenly changed and who should look out for her own best interests or seek dependable counsel who has no self-interest.'

Etta Kimble took up the next point. 'It would be different if Junior were older and in a position to step in and take over as his father's successor.'

'Which is exactly what his father always intended he should do,' Martha King put in.

'If he took over, you'd be sure of your rights,' Etta went on. 'But you are, to a certain extent, at the mercy of the people now running the company, men who were your husband's subordinates. Now, there's no evidence these people have any but the highest intentions as far as you're concerned. But we don't think it's particularly wise for you to assume they will deal with you equitably.' Deciding she had said enough for the moment, Etta Kimble reached for her tea cup, then paused to add, 'For them, their interests come first and you come second, Martha.'

Martha King rose, smoothed the skirt of her black dress, and walked over to the window. School was out for the year and Kurt and several friends were using the pool which she could see from the parlour window. She thought one of the girls was Beverly Anderson, but the mature shape of the girl in her bathing suit as she posed, laughing, on the diving board suggested somebody older. Martha realized she had been staring out of the window for too long. Slightly embarrassed, she turned back to her guests. 'I don't know what to do,' she murmured. 'There have been so many surprises already. Kurt talked about business all the time, but I guess I never really listened.' She broke off and glanced back at the swimmers, distraught.

The Kimbles exchanged quick looks; they did not like what they were seeing. Martha, always so strong and positive in her quiet way, had changed since Kurt's death. She seemed hesitant, full of self-doubt and indecision.

'I never really listened,' Martha repeated. 'I didn't even know Kurt had bought out Ray Nehring's interest and that took place years ago. Ray needed money for something, I guess.'

Arthur Kimble could have told her Ray Nehring had tried to buy several relatives their freedom from Hitler's Germany; he knew, too, Kurt King had tried to arrange the money as a loan, but Ray wouldn't hear of it.

However, he had made certain Ray's pension package was the best in the company, for which Ray should have been grateful today. What Kimble did not know but guessed accurately was that Kurt King had never found time to set up a similar package for himself. Nor that a sizeable insurance programme had been on his desk for signature. It had remained unsigned.

His widow was still talking. 'I knew Kurt had to sell some of his interest in the company. I well remember how upset he was about that. But I didn't know until just recently he sold so much of it. Why, all he had left was a little over half – 51 per cent.'

'Yes, Martha,' said Etta, 'but believe me, there's a world of difference between 51 and 49.'

Martha looked at her friend, puzzled. 'I'm sure you're right, Etta. You know about such things and I don't. But it all seems so much to have to take in all at once.' She dabbed her mouth with a handkerchief.

Arthur Kimble made one last attempt to ram home their message. 'That's exactly why we're suggesting you have outside counsel, a lawyer of your own to make sure the company treats you and young Kurt fair and square.'

Manuel had appeared in the doorway, a question in the set of his head. 'Ah, Manuel, is it so late already? Arthur and Etta, would you care for a glass of wine? We have some excellent California Chablis. No? Oh well, fine.' She shook her head and Manuel disappeared. She turned to them. 'Friends, I appreciate what you're saying and even more the sentiment behind it. But if I told the company I'd hired a lawyer, why that would be like telling them I distrusted them. Until I have some reason to suspect unfairness I will let Bob Clayton advise me. But frankly, I don't think they will ever give me any reason. I certainly believe Kurt meant for me to trust Bob or he would never have made him his next-in-command. I'm sorry, but I simply cannot start out on this new life by distrusting people I've known for years and years. I'm positive Kurt wouldn't have wanted it that way.' She smiled at them and held out her hand to bid them goodbye. 'They're already working out a plan for my security, and the boy's.'

The Kimbles left shaking their heads sadly.

4

Just turning sixteen, Kurt King Junior had little interest in the succession of his father's company. They were rich, and he took it for granted his father would have made the right decisions for his mother and himself in the event of his death. Anyway, his mother had never wanted to discuss business, saying she had little head for it; moreover, she had faith in her husband's collaborators. Yet, Kurt could not keep away from the plant with its heady smell of grease and gasoline, that tang of ozone from the electrical gear, those lathes and presses. That summer after his father's death, he worked fulltime at King Corp doing menial jobs in various divisions of the plant until after his sixteenth birthday in the first week of July.

Then, he became eligible for a counsellor's job at Camp Arrowhead. Indeed, he spent most of his birthday on the train, for he had to start on the 8th. Watching the heat-hazed California landscape through the train window, he felt relieved to have skipped all the birthday fuss. His father would have thrown a party for him and Kurt disliked the thought of celebrating without him.

65

That morning at the station, Ron Poole had slipped him a cylindrical package wrapped in brown paper festooned with a red bow, and not to be opened until the train pulled out. When he finally opened it, Kurt was fascinated; it was the summer issue of the *California Nudist*. A buxom girl on the cover, shown from the waist up, was leaping high for a ball, and the camera had left nothing to the erotic imagination. Beneath her picture, Ron had scrawled, 'What every sixteen-year-old male needs for his birthday – the magazine, I mean.'

Just looking at the girl's bouncing breasts brought on an erection. Kurt realized he was seeing Beverly in this nude cover-girl. He thrust the paper into his suitcase as though it smelled of hellfire. But his erection remained.

Beverly, who was also working as a camp counsellor at a girls' camp east of Los Angeles in the Lake Elsinore area, had called him the night before to wish him a happy birthday. She whispered she had something very special, something she was saving only for him. She gave a burbling laugh after she said it, and Kurt wasn't sure whether she was kidding him, or what she meant. Ron Poole did. Next day, when he told Ron what Beverly had said, Ron gave an exaggerated groan, grabbed his crotch and staggered round the end of the boarding platform.

Kurt smiled at the reminiscence. Ron, the sex fiend, spurned by the pretty classmates he chased. Sex filled his waking mind, and from what he confessed to Kurt, his dreams as well. Beside him, Kurt was naïve, backward. But then, Ron could have given Freud points on sexual exegesis and the hidden obscenities in everyday behaviour and language. Kurt was fascinated and awed by what Ron read into what he considered simple and straightforward things – even though it shattered his illusions.

'Hey, Kurt, listen to this.' And Ron would begin to chant, tonelessly, the words of a song on everybody's innocent lips:

> Mama dear, come over here
> And see who's looking through my window.
> It's the butcher boy
> And oh! he's got a bundle in his hand.

'Yeah, what about it?'

'Aw, come on. Bundle, don't you see? It ain't butcher's meat. He's flashing his dick at her, and so's the baker boy and the paper boy.'

'They didn't mean that,' Kurt scoffed.

Ron guffawed. 'To the pure all is pure,' he said, grinning. 'That's what they did mean. And she's a teenage nympho who's sending her mother out like a pimp to grab hold of all three for her.'

Kurt stared at him, annoyed he could read that sexual connotation into the song. But Ron gave him his interpretation of half a dozen popular numbers that had never struck him as suggestive. He'd always thought 'Hold Tight' was a song about a hungry man coming home for his supper, late at night. For supper read sex, Ron said. In 'My Heart Belongs to Daddy', Kurt had never questioned who or what Daddy was until Ron explained. Even 'Carolina in the Morning'. For most people, Carolina was the state – for Ron a girl of that name.

And jelly-roll. He'd always thought that described a style of keyboard jazz, or something out of a baker's window. Ron had to enlighten him about its sexual overtones.

It needed somebody like Ron to pare away his social and sexual restraints, but he was not yet ready to apply his friend's teachings. At camp, he barely stopped working for the two months. No other counsellor worked harder or won as many medals and awards with his charges. His free time he spent swimming or riding along the beach while other counsellors were whooping it up in town or holding illicit beerfests in the woods. He felt he needed to tire himself out so that he could fall asleep without too many baleful images like his hero who was no longer there, or distracting thoughts like Beverly's promised gift.

In the fall, he began his junior year at Palisades High. Still at odds with himself and everything, he had trouble in school for the first time; he argued with his teachers, fell down on his homework and would have worked full-time at King Corp if they had let him. Even at the factory, things were not to his liking.

After a short waiting period, the King Corp board had formally elected Robert Clayton company president. A preferred stock deal was worked out with the founder's widow that was agreeable to all parties. That year's annual report noted, 'King Corp provided Mrs Martha King with counsel from the company's legal department to assist her in any and all matters attendant to the estate.'

At the beginning of school, Kurt had gone to see Clayton, who had assured him several times, 'The door of your father's old office will always be open to you, Kurt.' Clayton sent him to see Harry Stephens, a middle-aged man who had not been one of his father's favourites. Stephens headed the New Products Division in the aircraft section, run for years by one of the company's first engineers, Rudy Knopf. After King died, Knopf had stayed around for a few months to see how the new management operated then decided he preferred retirement. Stephens, who replaced him, had an unkind streak. Knowing how fond young Kurt had been of Knopf, he welcomed him with open arms – only to hand him the job of cleaning the division's toilets. This had one asset: it quelled Kurt's desire to work longer hours.

Week after week for two to three hours a day, Kurt followed the same routine. First, he filled a large tin bucket, which was on wheels, with steaming hot water, an industrial cleaner and disinfectant. This he pushed down the long hallway, passing offices filled with men working at draughting tables, and into the cavernous lavatory at the far end. There, after sweeping out the discarded newspaper sections and the cigar butts and the dropped toilet paper, he carefully swabbed each stall, the floor in front of the urinals, and the rest of the room. Then, he replaced all needed articles. On Saturday mornings, he got down on his hands and knees and, using a thick brush and a pail reeking of ammonia, he cleaned each toilet until it shone. He felt lucky Stephens had not asked him to clean the ladies' room as well.

One rainy night after four weeks of toilet detail, he was leaving the building when a car horn sounded. He recognized behind the wheel Howard Smith, an engineer who had worked closely with his father. 'Get in, Kurt, I'll give you a lift.' Kurt settled in the warm, dry car. Smith looked over at him. 'How the hell you been, boy? I knew you were working in the place, and I think that's just great. What are you doing? Who are you working for?'

Kurt hesitated for a moment. 'I work part-time for

Harry Stephens after school and on Saturdays. I clean the men's toilets.'

Smith turned and stared at Kurt. 'You're kidding me, aren't you?'

'No.'

'That son of a bitch.' He said it quietly then fell silent for several minutes. When he began to talk again, he changed the subject, asking Kurt about his mother. When they reached the intersection where Kurt would get out, Smith said, tersely, 'Kurt, come see me tomorrow evening when you get to the plant. There'll be a different job for you. I'll fix it. Come direct to my office. Don't talk to Stephens. I'll take care of him, that son of a bitch.'

Kurt became the odd-job man and jack-of-all-trades in the Engineering Department which Smith ran. He spent most of his hours in the Commercial Product Section where he was soon the official guinea pig, and happy to be so.

One warm Saturday afternoon, he and Beverly were walking along the beach and she asked what he did at the factory.

'If you promise not to tell anyone, I'll show you.' Checking to see there was nobody much in sight on the beach, Kurt slipped his sweatshirt over his head.

'My God!' Beverly cried. 'What are they doing to you?'

'Come on.' He laughed. 'It isn't that bad.' She put out her hand, tentatively, and touched a spot that looked like sunburn on his shoulder then one on his back and several on his chest.

'Well,' she said slowly, 'they don't feel funny.' She peered more closely at the spots. 'How'd you get all

70

those marks, Kurt? You aren't doing anything dangerous in that lab, are you?' She sounded worried.

'No, I told you I'm working where they develop and
test all sorts of new products and they need somebody
to test them on.'

'And that's you, obviously.' She said it with a
resigned shake of her blond head.

'Yeah, and these' – he thumbed at the spots – 'are
from a new type of sunlamp we're perfecting. They
stick bits of adhesive tape all over me in different places
and try different lamps for different lengths of time.'

'You mean, they pay you to lay around getting a
suntan?'

'Lie around.'

'Oh, lie or lay, I don't care, smartypants.' She glared
at him, then smiled. 'The way you talk they'd think you
were the Senior instead of me. That reminds me, Sharon
Culver asked me if you were going with anybody. I
think she wants to ask you to the Back-to-School Hop.
She's your year, you know.' She gave an impish smile.

'I know she's my year,' he said, pulling on his
sweatshirt. 'But don't you tell her anything. You know
I don't go with anyone. How could I when I spend all
my free time with you?'

They had reached a spot where a length of old
boardwalk supports projected from the sand. Beverly
walked over and sat down, patting the place close to
her. Kurt joined her, obediently. She watched him
intently then spoke. 'Kurt, I know such things are
hardly ever done, especially in our set, but what would
you do if I asked you to be my date for the Senior prom
this year?'

'The Senior prom? You aren't serious? You'd get
kidded a lot, Bev, with me being a Junior.'

'You're not answering my question.'

'Anyway, why ask me with all the other guys you have chasing you? And that reminds me, my mother said you've been going out with that jerk Clayton. Is that true?'

Beverly stared at him and thought carefully before she answered, knowing how he felt about Nat Clayton, son of the man who now directed King Corporation. She felt like telling him all the girls referred to him as Clayton the Cretin, but decided it was unfair. 'Nathaniel Clayton is a nice boy who takes me, and a lot of other girls, to nice places. Oh, maybe he is given to bragging and talking about USC all the time, and maybe he is all hands sometimes.' She paused, noting the angry look that flooded his dark features. 'But he's definitely not someone another boy should worry about, if you follow what I mean.'

Kurt stared at her, watching as she loosened the piece of yarn tying her hair and shaking it free before tying it again.

'I'm not, ah, very good with girls, Bev. But I know one thing, and that's when I'm with you, I'm happier than at any other time.' She started to say something but he stopped her by putting two fingers, very softly, on her lips. 'Beverly, if you really want to, I mean if, when the time for the prom comes, you still want me to go with you, to take you, well, I'd be honoured.'

5

A painful year and a half after his father's death, when his mother reserved a lunch table in the exclusive Los Angeles Country Club for both of them, Kurt knew she had something serious to discuss with him. They were both aware his father had always considered his membership in the club one of the greatest privileges his wealth had brought him. Kurt had never set foot in the imposing white, two-storey clubhouse building sitting amid a 36-hole golf course like a palace in its own grounds. His father had loved this green oasis bisected by Wilshire Boulevard and surrounded by luxury homes, mostly owned by millionaires, movie moguls and rich film stars.

In fact, the Los Angeles Country Club was then the most valuable property in the world devoted to golf. Yet, when Joseph Sartori, a founder member and early guiding light, decided to move the club to its present location in 1904, he personally paid one thousand dollars for the option to buy the land for the staggering price of forty-eight thousand dollars. In 1907, members were informed:

. . . The portion to be allotted to the Country Club consists of level and rolling lands, with natural hazards well adapted to a golf course, and includes a commanding site for a clubhouse. Since this land was purchased . . . it has greatly enhanced in value, being estimated at considerably over one hundred thousand dollars at the present time.

During the next two years, it is intended to create a bonded indebtedness of about one hundred thousand dollars which will furnish the money necessary to erect a clubhouse and improve the grounds, finish paying for the property and provide a substantial working balance. It is expected the Club will spend about seventy-five thousand dollars in improvements . . .

In another letter, Sartori explained, somewhat apologetically, that moving the club from its Pico-Western location meant a longer journey for members, but they had a faster streetcar system. For members reading a

73

copy of that letter in the ˉmen's locker room, it is ridiculous to think of anyone apologizing for moving their club to Beverly Hills. So choosy was the Los Angeles Country Club that movie stars, no matter how famous or financially successful, had never been members. Stars like Bob Hope and Bing Crosby played their golf at Lakeside or Bel-Air. Randolph Scott owned a home overlooking the fourth tee, was an excellent golfer popular with the members and played frequently as a guest. But he was never invited to become a member. Only when oil made him another and more respectable fortune was he asked to join.

Although members' wives were welcome, the club was a male bastion with a separate entrance for men, a men-only card room and dining-room. Women were received and brought their guests to the main dining-room and bar, decorated in the Colonial-Victorian style of the clubhouse. It was here on a typically cool June day in 1947 that Kurt King joined his mother for lunch.

As she ran her eye over the menu, her son studied her. How well she looked! Her tailored suit, a beautiful shade of light blue, wasn't new but fitted her perfectly now she had regained the weight lost after her husband's death. Putting down the menu, she removed her gloves, then looked up and noted his stare. She smiled fondly. With the weight, she had also recovered her composure, and in ageing had become somewhat regal, holding her head high.

The waiter fussed over her, remarking it had been too long since he had seen her. Before she could order, he remembered her preference for a particular California Chablis, and flattered, she flushed slightly. Kurt had never considered his mother beautiful but had always admired her class and style. Today, he thought she looked marvellous.

For a while they talked quietly, postponing their order. She told him how pleased she was he had finished school near the top of his class. He had actually been third in a graduating class of more than a hundred, but that kind of detail always eluded his mother. When people asked, she told them Kurt had done extremely well. Instead of bothering him, he found this trait oddly endearing.

'When does Beverly leave for Europe, Kurt?'

'Next week. It's going to seem funny not seeing her all summer.' He shook his head and smiled thinly. 'I'll even miss the fights.'

'I know what you mean. You two have certainly had an on-again, off-again romance.'

Romance! That word was so like her, and he doubted if the word 'affair' even figured in her vocabulary.

'Ron says Bev used to get mad at me on purpose, so I would have to buy her a present when we made up.'

'He may have something there. You certainly have spent a considerable amount on her.'

'She's worth it.' He kept his head down, avoiding her eyes.

'I don't doubt it for a moment, dear. Ah, here's the waiter. Kurt, do you want the fish, too? Good. And a small bottle of the Chablis with two glasses, Arthur. My son is growing up, you know.'

The ate slowly, talking now and then and when their coffee came, they both lit cigarettes. Ron kidded him about his mother's smoking, saying it was out of character, but she had been smoking for as long as he could remember, and it seemed a part of her. Now that he had the occasional cigarette, he liked it that she smoked.

'That was nice. The fish is always excellent here.' She paused to look at him with that direct gaze of hers. 'Well, son, in case you were wondering if this luncheon has a definite purpose, it does. I've come to a decision recently, one I have been putting off discussing with you for too long. Now my mind's made up.'

Kurt had been watching some golfers coming up the tough eighteenth hole, playing into the strong ocean breeze which lengthened the hole by a stroke. His mother's tone, as much as her words, brought his gaze back to her.

'Wait, Mother, let me guess.' She paused, surprised. 'It's the house, isn't it. You're going to sell it.'

She nodded, seriously. 'I simply hate to have to do it, Kurt, and your father, Lord rest him, would hate to see me do it. But I don't have any choice. There just isn't the money there was for taxes, maintenance, gardeners, help. I can't take care of it by myself. It's too big.'

Kurt stared across the room, noting how the chandelier light reflected in the mirrors above the handsome bar. How odd to be talking about lack of money in such an opulent setting. He considered how much his camel hair jacket had cost, his perfectly-cut, lightweight wool trousers, his cordovan loafers. His mother, who was signalling the waiter for more coffee, looked as if she belonged in places like this. His head spun with conflicting thoughts.

His mother seemed relieved at having broached the subject and talked more freely. 'The cost is the main thing, of course. You know I've had to sell stock, but don't get me started on that. When I sell the house it will make it so much easier to let the help go. Millie and Manuel are getting on and have been talking about working less, or stopping altogether, for some time.

76

The others will have no difficulty finding places, and poor Bruno won't have to look so embarrassed driving a Cadillac that isn't this year's model.'

Kurt had to stifle a laugh at that.

She continued, 'I'll miss Millie more than anyone, but she'll help out occasionally. Well, in any event, it has to be done. I'm sure we can live comfortably for quite some time on what the sale of the house will bring.'

'But you're going to buy another house, aren't you?' he asked, alarm in his tone.

She looked as if he had said something foolish. 'Of course. How would it look if I had to rent someplace? No, I will definitely buy, but it will be something small and nice, with room for you and me' – she smiled – 'and the dogs. There are some nice small places, brand new, over in the Palisades with an ocean view and pretty little gardens.' She stopped abruptly, reached across the table to put her hand on her son's. 'Kurt, we're not going to change our standard of living.' He saw her determination in the hard stare in her eyes. 'We're going to live just as well as we did when your father was alive. The only difference is that we aren't going to do it as often.'

'Mother, I'm not complaining. Just puzzled. Dad did so well I never thought about money, and I guess maybe you didn't either. But I thought we were rich.'

'Son, there's been a lot of problems. Your father thought he was indestructible and, frankly, had made no plans. You don't know this, but on the day of the accident . . .' She stopped, drew a handkerchief from her purse and held it to her eyes before going on. '. . . on that day an insurance policy was found on his desk. It was for a million dollars, dated some weeks before he died and needing only his signature. Had he signed it, things would be a lot different.'

'But what about the company – King Corp?'

'Well, though we owned more than half, your father left little cash. Everything he had was in the business except the house which, thank the Lord, was free and clear. The estate taxes were severe. To pay that, I had to sell stock. Bob Clayton put a group together and they purchased enough of my stock to allow me to pay the government. That, of course, eliminated my control of the company, so I've had little say in its affairs. Then, to assure income for me, the company exchanged my common stock for a preferred stock that guaranteed me a dividend. This was what's called a subordinated preferred. I really don't understand all of this.' She stopped, shaking her head.

Kurt, his face perplexed, asked, 'Subordinated, what does that mean? Preferred stock guarantees a dividend, I know that much.'

His mother, troubled by his questions and the necessity to reveal her poor judgement, turned to her handkerchief. 'You're right, son, it is a guarantee, but subordinated to other needs of the company, subordinated to certain loans they've had to make with the banks. That's what they told me. I guess Bob Clayton saw the need to expand and they borrowed a great deal of money. The expansion was not wise, according to Howard Smith, who still stops in to see me occasionally. They've been losing money. Bob Clayton hasn't spoken to me in about a year, but six months ago he sent the treasurer, a new fellow I couldn't place.'

'Prentice. He's a cold fish.'

'That's right, Prentice. He came to explain the problem. They had stopped paying a dividend. He told me they were having trouble paying the bank loan interest, they couldn't pay any principal, and the banks insisted the preferred dividend be stopped until the company got its affairs in order. Now they owe us the money and he says we'll get it eventually, and I'm sure we will. In the meantime, we have to live. So, I've decided to cut way back, get rid of the big house and still be comfortable.'

Kurt, his face now worried, queried, 'Mother, isn't there something that can be done, something you can do? How about Uncle Arthur, Mr Kimble? Attorneys can do things.'

'No, son, everything's been done.' Not wanting to explain her refusal of the Kimbles' help, she brought the conversation to an abrupt halt with her firm remark and steady gaze. He sensed his questions had been answered as much as they would ever be.

His mother signed the bill and he reached for her chair a step ahead of the waiter. They left the room, her hand on his arm, nodding and speaking to people they knew.

A well-dressed man who looked about Martha King's age turned to his wife and said, softly, 'Isn't that Kurt King's widow and son?'

'Yes, it is.'

'Look like a million dollars, don't they?'

'Hummph,' the woman replied. 'And why the hell shouldn't they?'

III

Kurt King did not do too well in his first year of college. At least, not academically. Relying on the unsolicited advice from several King Corp executives, including Robert Clayton himself, he had enrolled in the School of Business Administration at the University of Southern California. Left to himself, he would have chosen engineering, but the businessmen argued the technical background would impede his management promotion not only within the company but anywhere else.

Halfway through the semester, Kurt began to suspect his course selection was wrong, began to doubt the whole idea of college. Had it not been for his active social life on the campus, he might have talked his mother into letting him drop out before the end of the year. Ron Poole was also having trouble adjusting from high school life, and the year was unsettling and troubling for both of them. One thing kept them there: Kurt's way with girls. He had developed a new, outgoing attitude towards girls, and Poole remarked that Kurt suddenly knew more girls than one person could date in a year.

For some time, Kurt rarely saw Beverly Anderson since she was studying drawing and design at a San Francisco art school. But it was Beverly who was responsible for his changed attitude to girls and sex. Exasperated by his backwardness, she had finally taken it upon herself to start his sexual education.

Two days before his eighteenth birthday, on a Fourth

of July, they were both sitting among a cluster of young people on the hill below the sixteenth tee of the Los Angeles Country Club watching the fireworks display. When the last sparks of the final huge pinwheel dissolved into the darkness, the group drifted apart, their voices melting into the warm night. Beverly sat still, smoking and saying nothing. When Kurt made to rise, she reached out and gripped his arm, upsetting his balance. Laughing, he fell back, put his head in her lap and shared her cigarette.

Soon, they were kissing. Kurt sensed Beverly's excitement in the darting penetration of her tongue and the way she sought body contact with him. She breathed heavily and slowly slid her body down until she was lying alongside him. He wondered what she was doing, but had little time to reflect. Now beside him and pressing her breasts and thighs against him, Beverly placed her arms round him and whispered something in his ear. Not certain of what she had said, he murmured an incoherent, 'What?'

'Remember two years ago I told you I was saving something for you?'

'Uh, uh,' he said. His hand slipped down her back, its movement checked by her bra strap. Contact with this private garment stimulated him and he felt his penis stiffen. Beverly felt it, too.

'I'm still saving it, but I'd like you to have it.' She kissed his neck, slowly, running her open mouth over it. 'Tonight.'

'Jesus, Bev!'

They broke their embrace, suddenly, when they heard another couple approaching.

'Damn,' she said in his ear. 'There's got to be a better

place than this. Where can we go? I'm tired of waiting. I want us to prove we love each other.'

He gazed at her face, dim in the reflected glow of the city lights. 'What do you mean?'

She was kneeling, facing him. Taking his hands, she put them on her breasts for a moment then gently pushed him away. 'If we truly love each other, then we should do it. That would be proof.'

'Do what?' he said, half in earnest, but pressing for the answer.

When the other couple had passed out of earshot, Beverly leaned towards him again. She undid the top button of his shirt and slipped her hand on to his chest, trailing a fingernail across the nipple of his breast. A new sensation developed as the nipple swelled and hardened to match the swelling hardness of his penis. 'You know exactly what I mean, don't you, lover?'

He was breathing fast, his heart was racing. He swallowed and said, thickly, 'Yes, I guess I do . . . I do.'

'Where can we go?' She was getting to her feet now.

'Is there a blanket in your mother's car, a beach blanket?'

'Yes, I'm sure. At least there was.'

'I know a place.'

He had to take Beverly's car, for their Cadillac had recently been sold. Swinging the small convertible out of the parking lot, he gunned it towards Wilshire. After a hundred yards or so he turned sharp right, plunged through overhanging bushes on to a dirt road then right again on to a track.

'Where are you going, Kurt? Do you know what you're doing?'

'Shsh, this is the service road the greenskeeper uses

when he brings the mowers round to cut the fairways. It comes out just behind the fifteenth tee. Nobody but the maintenance people knows about it.'

'How do you know about it?' She sounded suspicious.

He shifted into second to give himself time to phrase the lie. 'I found it when I caddied,' he said, and might have laughed had he been less anxious. One early spring night he and Ron, ashamed to admit they were still virginal males, had brought two Mexican girls to the same spot. While Ron and his girl went for a walk, Kurt tried to perform the sexual act that he had been groping towards for at least thirty minutes in the back seat. Even though she was willing and laid herself open to him, he could not contain himself and came on her thigh. A string of high-pitched Spanish curses greeted this effort, overheard by Poole and his girl. Later, he and Ron figured out what the girl had screamed. 'Crazy fool, don't you know about rubbers?' If he had missed out on sex, at least he took the hint about contraception.

Now, when his headlights caught the reflectors on a large tractor, Kurt knew they had run out of road. 'Come with me,' he whispered, grabbing the blanket and pulling it over their heads. 'Careful, these bushes are full of thorns.' He felt feverish, his face flushing in the darkness as they moved through the bushes towards the grassy slope.

'Oh, Kurt, I've wanted you for so long.' Beverly stood in the small clearing and looked up through the ring of trees at the star-filled sky, as though praying.

He spread the blanket on the soft grass. Beverly straightened an edge, knelt and drew him down beside her. Locked tightly in each other's arms, they slowly twisted to a horizontal position.

83

Something was happening to time and space, he thought at one hazy moment. All he could sense was Beverly's warmth. First, her mouth against his, then her breasts as he snapped the halter of her bra free, then the rest of her as they stripped off their clothes. 'Have you got it on?' she whispered, and ran her pointed fingernails up and down his back while he turned to slip the rubber sheath on to his penis before moving into her.

His mouth was pleasantly sore from crushing hers. His excitement had mounted to a pitch he had never experienced. He kept thrusting his penis with obvious and painful unsuccess against her groin. Finally, Beverly helped. She took him in her hand. It was a touch unlike any he had ever known. Kurt prayed he would not discharge at that instant. But somehow she moved and he held on. She pulled him into her, raising her legs, and they were together. He was inside her and crying softly to himself with joy.

Later, as they broke apart, Kurt could not recall if they had been together for hours or minutes. He did know he had experienced a special feeling, something great, something truly unique. He couldn't decide if he wanted to do push-ups or fall asleep, yell out like an animal, or close his eyes and remember it all. He pulled the blanket edges around them. He heard Beverly sigh. Never had he heard her make a sound like that before.

'Bev.' His mouth was open against her neck. 'Bev, I must love you, it was wonderful.' He added in a whisper, 'Thank you for saving it for me.'

She stirred, hugged him and said, softly, 'I've wanted us to do it for so long.' She was bothered less by her own lie than his qualified declaration of love.

* * *

84

Kurt became a changed person, at least with young and attractive girls, after Beverly's initiation. While she was home he had no interest in anyone else; but with her in San Francisco in the fall and him at USC, he gave his new-found sexual enthusiasm full rein.

He had pledged and joined Phi Delta Theta, known on the campus as the poor little rich boys' fraternity. Pledge parties, given jointly with sororities, provided an opportunity to meet the best-looking girls in the freshman class. In two months, Kurt's address book was bulging. Ron Poole, who pledged the same fraternity, was the grateful beneficiary of dates with a series of attractive girls, friends of the girls Kurt took out, and thus he found little reason to complain of the social life.

Unlike his long up-and-down relationship with Beverly, campus affairs were short-lived. But they were torrid, even if he always respected the popular belief that nice girls seldom went all the way on a first date, no matter how hot-blooded. Poole marvelled at the ease with which Kurt was able to introduce them to the wonders of the golf club service road.

Amazed at the variety of willing females, Kurt once suggested to Poole that perhaps there was something in the California air or the drinking water that heightened sexual activity. What he confessed to no one, not even Ron, was what happened to him one weekend when all their other friends had gone out of town for a football game.

He was sitting in Julie's, a tavern near the campus on Figueroa favoured by the USC crowd, nursing a beer and feeling annoyed no one he knew had come in to give him a ride home when Gloria Fenster slid into the booth beside him. Short with curly, dark hair, Gloria had the body of a starlet, and Poole dubbed her 'Glorious' Fenster.

Kurt knew she was one of the campus prick-teasers. He had never seen it himself, but Ron had told him their classmates used to congregate across from her house, in the bushes, to watch her undressing act. It was a strip-tease which, with precise artistry, just stopped short of baring her breasts or her sex. Quite a performance, with Gloria only too aware she had a captive audience.

As the only girl in the crowd who openly boasted she planned to marry for money, Gloria bluntly refused to date boys whose family bank accounts did not measure up to her rigid economic standards. Had Kurt's father been alive, she would certainly have said Yes had Kurt asked; in fact, one of the boys she dated was Nat Clayton, son of the King Corp president. Kurt knew Gloria's outspoken ground rules too well to ask her for a date.

'Hi, Kurt.' She said it quietly, smiling.

'Hello, Gloria. Where's Clayton? Aren't you with him tonight?'

'No,' she replied, drawing out the word. 'I'm all alone. I mean I was, but I'm not now, am I?'

'Ah, that's right, no you're not. Like a beer? What can I do for you?'

She put an eye lock on him as if trying to determine whether or not he was kidding, then gave a throaty laugh. Easily the sexiest laugh he had ever heard. Gloria moved to the edge of the seat and her knees rubbed his under the table. 'I've been watching you, Kurt King,' she said in her low, musical voice. 'And I like what I see. I'm not going to play games or waste time beating around the bush. I want to do it. With you. Tonight. I have my car. Do you know a nice place?'

'Do you happen to have a blanket?'

'Why, I'm sure I do.' She grinned, lewdly, and got up, leaving him to follow her.

She drove, and when he asked her to stop at Thompson's filling station, she smiled and said, 'I appreciate someone who's thoughtful and well prepared.'

'Oh, Christ!'

'What's the matter? You losing your nerve?'

'No, not at all. It's just – well, this is embarrassing – I spent my last cent in Julie's.'

She gave that low, gurgling laugh. 'Now this is definitely a first for me.' She fished a dollar out of her purse and handed it to him. 'I take it the prices haven't gone up?'

When he had bought the contraceptives and got in beside her to direct her to the Country Club, he said, 'You're really something, Gloria.'

'All I can say to you, Kurt King, is you'd better be worth that dollar.'

He tried to repay his debt and her faith. And Gloria? She taught him the pleasures of sexual restraint. With Beverly and other girls, everything happened with a breathless rush. There was a blind fumbling and pawing before they almost ripped their undergarments off in their haste to fuse their bodies together. Gloria took it gently, exciting him with her handplay and her suggestive whispers as she guided his hands over her sensitive parts. And when their time came, she was as smooth as a mouse's ear. Beneath him, she moved everything in slow rhythm, her body, her buttocks, her thighs, the muscles of her sexual organ to bring him and herself to an explosive climax.

Later, when she dropped him in front of his house, she took his face in her hands and gave him a long, soft kiss. 'Good night, Kurt. And, by the way, you were worth it. You are something special.'

She drove off slowly. He looked at his watch and was surprised to realize less than an hour had gone by since they had left the tavern. He thought, 'Lucky man, Nat Clayton.'

They were never together again. But whenever Kurt saw Gloria Fenster after that night, she gave him her slow, special smile. What pleased Kurt as much as the sexual encounters was the fact he remained on friendly terms with girls after they stopped dating. Ron Poole once asked how he managed that trick and Kurt said the only thing he could think of was that he never lied to any of them. Then, warming to the idea of lecturing Ron about sexual conquests, 'Never tell 'em you love 'em.'

'I never do, never.' Ron was almost solemn.

'I said it once, and I think I meant it. Anyway, it was a long time ago.'

2

But if Kurt had made a breakthrough socially and sexually he had still made no great hit in his classes at the School of Business Administration. In fact, the end of that year saw him determined to drop out and start some other career. Ron Poole felt the same way. Neither of them had a true recollection of how and why they decided to enlist. Only that they were smashed when the idea came to Ron.

In the middle of the third week of May they had finished their exams and had a small celebration that night, keeping the real wingding for Friday when everybody would have the term behind them. It was a beer bust for men only, on the beach, and they didn't waste drinking time on irrelevant ritual.

'D'you think next year's going to be better'n this one?' Kurt was doing his best not to slur his words and wondering, at the same time, if he could make it to the tub for another beer without getting a faceful of sand.

Ron started to answer, but Cliff Evans cut him short. 'Something wrong with this one?'

'Ha! joker,' Ron said, guffawing. 'If you have to ask, you'll never get the message. Hey Kurt, old buddy, if there's any beer left get me one while you're up. How about you, Evans?'

'Nah, but thanks anyway. You know, Poole, I think you don't like school because your buddy, King, doesn't like it.'

With some effort, Ron pulled himself into a sitting position. Firelight flickered across his long face giving the illusion of movement. 'You know, Evans,' he mimicked, 'you might be one hundred per cent correct, but I still don't give a flying fuck what you think. Like them apples?'

Kurt had returned hugging three opened bottles. When Evans again declined, he made a small hole in the sand and inserted the chilled bottle. Evans got up. 'I gotta take a leak. See you later.'

'Nice of him not to do it right here, don't you think?' Ron said.

'Indu . . . indubit . . . you're right. Jesus, I think I'm half-smashed.'

'Half?' Ron's laugh carried down the beach. 'Hey, you're no worse than me, or maybe only a little worse. But to get back to what I said, if you can remember.'

89

'I remember everything. What was it?'

'School. Another year as shitty as this one Poole couldn't take. Know what I been thinking?' He waited for a prompt and getting none he continued, 'I think I'm going to join the Marines.'

'What! For real? The goddamn Marines.'

Ron got on to his knees as if pulled there by the thought that had just hit him. 'Yeah,' he said. 'Yeah, at least it would be a challenge. Know what I mean?'

Kurt said nothing for a long time. He stared at his friend. A stick hissed and crackled as it burst into flame. In its light each saw the other was smiling.

'Ron, I'll make you a deal. Tomorrow morning when we're both sober, if you still have the guts to join the Marines, I'm with you.'

That brought Poole to his feet, his six-foot-plus swaying in the firelight. 'You're not shitting me? You really mean it, you'd do it? Hell, you're drunk.'

Kurt levered himself up and stuck out a hand. 'Absolutely and positively I mean it and I'm drunk.' They shook hands vigorously, looking determined and proud.

'Oh, shit!' said Poole.

'What's the matter? Changed your mind already?'

'Something worse.'

'What's that?' Kurt was startled.

'You just knocked over the last beer.'

3

On the colonel's suggestion Lieutenant King eased himself on to the hard wooden chair alongside the desk, placing his cap correctly in his lap and folding his hands. He said nothing, waiting for his superior officer

90

to speak. Lt-Colonel Foreman, the battalion commander, studied the file on his desk. As he read, King's eye took in the silver oak leaf pinned to his uniform collar and the panorama of ribbons spread across his chest. Finally, when the older man spoke, his friendly tone surprised Kurt. 'Your company commander reports you make this request with reluctance.'

'Yessir, with extreme reluctance.'

Foreman gazed at him, not unkindly. 'We grant hardship discharges only in the most serious cases as I'm sure you know, Lieutenant, but it says here' – he tapped the file – 'your situation is well within the regs. How old is your mother?'

'Actually Sir, I'm not positive. But at least sixty. I'm told she was forty when I was born and I turned twenty last month.'

Foreman allowed himself a slight smile. 'Yes King, I know. Word of your birthday celebration reached as far as this office.'

King winced but said nothing as his mind played back that all-night party. His commanding officer was talking:

'The medical report says your mother's stroke is partially disabling and she will need frequent care. Your being home will help, I'm sure, but what about the financial picture? Isn't that the problem?' Foreman spoke more softly. 'Officially it isn't any of my business, but I often wonder in these cases if we couldn't keep some of you young officers if we were able to pay you more.'

'I don't think it would make too much difference in this case, Sir. It's more of a question of my being with her. Though I'm sure there'll not be a surplus of money.'

Glancing at the file, the commanding officer turned a page, scanned it then spoke. 'Your family fortunes, so to speak, have changed quite a bit in the short span of five years, haven't they?'

'Yessir.'

'Most unfortunate for you – and the Corps. You've only been with us thirteen months but your fitness reports are excellent. Second in your graduating class at Quantico . . . first-rate leadership reports . . . good rapport with your men.' He looked up from the file. 'Your men will miss you and I'm sure they realize it. Anything you'd care to say?'

'Just thank you for what you've said, Sir. But I feel as if I've grown up in the Marine Corps, become more mature, learned a lot.'

Foreman nodded agreement. 'This outfit does that to a person. Well, once I process these papers it will be only a matter of time and I'd imagine you could be on your way home in a week.' He stood up and King snapped to attention. 'At ease, you're dismissed.'

As King turned to leave, the colonel said, 'Wait a minute, Lieutenant. There was something I'd meant to ask you but it slipped my mind. That demonstration you arrange for the closing session of your demolition classes is rather spectacular. Care to tell me how you do it?'

King nodded. It seemed what had started as an impulsive prank was threatening to become Marine folklore.

After boot camp in San Diego, both King and Ron Poole were sent to Quantico, Virginia, to platoon leader's school, a tribute to the impression they had made on Colonel Lyle, an old-school Marine often compared to the legendary Chesty Puller. Following their commissioning as second lieutenants, they were separated for the first time, Poole having decided on flight school at Cherry Point.

With enough hours from weekend flying at a local civilian school to qualify for a pilot's licence, King would have joined his friend; but a slight colour-blindness disqualified him. Since he had done unusually well in the demolition courses at Quantico, the instructing officer recommended him for a post in the Demolitions School at Camp Le Jeune, North Carolina. He became an Engineering Instructor. Every phase of demolitions and high-explosive weaponry fascinated him. And he discovered, to his surprise, he was a natural teacher.

Word spread quickly that 'if you took demolitions from Lieutenant King you really learned your shit,' and his groups were lively, enjoying the instruction which included the use of flame-throwers and bazookas. Fellow-officers kidded him that they didn't know which would be gone first, the Marine Corps' supply of explosives or the countryside around Le Jeune.

To round off the ten-day course, King and his team reviewed their teachings and ended with a final wrap-up in a small, natural amphitheatre with a pond as the stage backdrop. King had, however, concocted an idea for making the instruction stick and gave his training crew a secret briefing the night before the final session.

'And now, gentlemen,' he said, gazing at the amphitheatre audience which included several full colonels, 'you are about to witness two examples of explosive force after which you will be dismissed as graduates of Demolitions 101.'

He placed a detonating device in a block of TNT which was transported to the demolitions area by his men who snaked wires back from it to where King stood. Connecting the wires to a hell box, he shoved the plunger down sharply to set off the TNT. As the sound faded, everyone nodded, suitably impressed.

King took another primer cap to which he attached the wires. 'Gentlemen, you have just witnessed the destructive force of TNT. I want you to be equally impressed by the force of this little cap itself, which you may be careless enough to disregard when it's not in the company of TNT.' He held the primer aloft. 'Treat this badly and you could lose a few fingers or worse.' He noted the disbelieving faces in his audience and raised his voice. 'Let me demonstrate,' he said, handing the cap to an assistant who carried it to the lake, wires trailing. There, another man waited astride the largest branch of a tall tree overhanging the water. Inching out, he hung the wires so that the cap was suspended a few feet above the still, dirty water.

His men back to safety, King slammed the plunger of the hell box down.

His audience sat, spectating with mild interest, expecting something akin to a large firecracker. In fact, the primer exploded with a loud crack. But at the same moment there was a mighty roar growing in volume and intensity. Like a gigantic geyser, the entire pond mushroomed into the air showering the graduating class with filthy rain while King and his team watched with smiles on their faces, well out of range.

'Jesus Christ, King's blown up the whole fucking lake,' somebody shouted. It still took several minutes for everybody to burst out laughing as they realized the trick he had played on them, and the fact that only their uniforms had suffered. Cheers and applause followed.

King's grand finale became a regular feature of the course.

'I'm listening, Lieutenant,' Colonel Foreman said, bringing King back to the present.

'Excuse me, Sir. What we did was mine the far side of the pond. It really helps the men remember the course.'

'So they tell me, Lieutenant, so they tell me. And what did you mine it with?'

'TNT, Sir.'

'And how much, may I ask?'

'About a thousand pounds, Sir.'

The colonel shook his head but could not conceal his slight smile. 'All in the interests of training, eh?'

'That's correct, Sir.'

'Sit down again, Lieutenant. I have an idea which might keep you in the Corps a little longer with benefit to both of us. Your records show you did your basic training under Colonel Bertie Lyle. We go way back together, about a century it seems. Anyway, Bertie is now commanding officer of the Marine detachment at the Long Beach Naval Station which is practically in your mother's backyard. Maybe we could arrange to have you transferred there, and when you have to apply for a hardship discharge you can do so. How does that sound to you.'

'Terrific, Sir!'

And terrific it was. Lyle allowed him to live off the base, which meant at home. He made him the Marine detachment riot officer which meant he called in each morning to see if they had a riot. If they didn't, he was free for the rest of the day.

Now eager to finish college as quickly as possible, he enrolled simultaneously at both UCLA and USC; but this time, following his own bent, he took an engineering programme, choosing courses at each school to fit his interests and time schedule. When he got his first semester's grades and knew he could handle the heavy classroom schedule, he looked for a part-time job. He tried King Corp, but they were not hiring for other than full-time jobs, so he ended up working as a filling-station mechanic near the UCLA campus. His job, his classroom schedule, his tour as Marine duty officer every third night meant that he got little sleep. But he was happy.

The Marine Corps had quashed any remnants of false pride, so when old high-school or college friends came by the station – usually in their new cars – and asked in astonished tones why he was working, he simply replied, 'I need the money.'

Anyway, his old crowd had scattered. Ron Poole was now a service pilot, flying jets and chasing girls. When he came home on leave, King was amazed by the changes for the better. There was no trace of his teenage skin problems and his growth had topped off at six foot four inches; he had put on muscle and King thought he looked, in a word, rugged. King, too, had grown to a shade under six feet and a solid 175 pounds.

Beverly Anderson had finished art school and disappeared, the last rumour being she was living in Spain. As she was as poor a letter-writer as King, he had heard from her only once while in boot camp. Then, a week before he was to graduate from Quantico, she phoned to say she would be in Washington the next weekend, staying at the Sheraton-Carlton on 16th Street. He borrowed a car and drove up after the Saturday morning ceremonies. Over lunch, they made elaborate sightseeing plans only to scuttle them an hour later and go to Beverly's room which they did not leave, even for meals, until an hour before her plane left Sunday evening. Somewhere in her travels, Beverly had discovered oral sex, and she lost no time tutoring the newly-commissioned officer in this variation on the old-fashioned way she had taught him earlier. After that, he had received a Christmas card postmarked Key West, Florida.

Others he had known in school and through family contacts were on various upper rungs of the academic or professional ladders, except for the girls who had married. True to herself, Gloria Fenster had married wealth, the only son of a successful Sacramento banker. Rumour had it the son wasn't the only family member smitten with Gloria's charms. That made King smile; but what astounded him was the fact that several of his old girlfriends were already mothers.

One afternoon, sitting on a crosstown bus, he looked up from his physics textbook to see a former Palisades High School classmate making her way across Olympic Boulevard. She was carrying not a baby but a good-sized child. Safely over, she lowered the child to the sidewalk and, hand-in-hand, they walked into an apartment building. It took King ten minutes to find his place in the textbook.

4

His fraternity house was filled to bursting with boys and girls he had known at USC. Pushing through to the bar, he shouted for a beer above the din. At the end of the bar he spotted Nat Clayton, the flabby son of the man who had taken over King Corp. Clayton waved at him, but he did not return the gesture. He could not trust himself to keep his temper even with the blameless slob of a son. He was gratified to notice that already Nat Clayton had a couple of chins and a bit of a belly before he turned away.

'Hey, Kurt, where've you bin hidin'?' It was Cliff Evans whom he hadn't seen since that night-time beach binge when they'd all tied one too many on and he and Ron had lit out for the Marines.

'The Marine Corps. But I had to resign my commission and take a special discharge on account of my mother's health.'

Evans got them two more beers and they elbowed through to the ornate fireplace for a chat. Someone carrying drinks bumped into King and he stepped back and trod on a foot. 'Sorry,' he muttered over his shoulder.

'Somebody said they saw you working as a pumphand in a filling station.'

'A mechanic.'

'What's it for, the laughs?' Evans asked, and King marked him down as one that had not changed or learned much sense.

'No, for the money.' Just then, another man barged into King and again he stepped back.

'Ouch!' A girl's voice echoed in his ears. 'Are you absolutely determined to cripple me?'

'Excuse me. I'm really sorry but this joker in front of me just can't stand still.' King stopped when he saw her face. Her skin was pale almost to the point of being pallid; her straight, black hair was cut sharply at the shoulder line, one side pulled back by a thin silver clip, her eyes were a startling blue and she had a thin, slightly tilted nose set above a thin yet sensuous mouth

She was strikingly pretty and so elegant she made the deep-tanned California girls around her look gauche.

She was aware of the deep impression she was making and turned a beaming smile on him. 'I'm Carolyn Crowley, and you?'

'King, Kurt King.'

'How droll! Where's your castle? And your queen – is she here?'

'I, ah, don't happen to have either one,' he said. His composure was beginning to return. 'But I do have a princess or two tied up in the tower for my pleasure.'

'Well now, that's something.' She handed him her empty glass. 'Say, King, do you think you could help this princess and get me a fresh drink – some of that obviously spiked punch over there.'

'No problem, I learned to follow superiors' orders in the Marines.'

Her blue eyes widened. 'You're joking. No? Well now, that's really droll.'

When he had fought his way to the bar and back across the crowded room with the punch, still trying to remember exactly what 'droll' meant, she had disappeared.

Two of his former fraternity brothers with long memories spotted him and waved. Working his way through the crowd, he joined them. 'Hi, nice to see you again. Maybe you can help me with a problem. I went to get a drink for that black-haired girl who was standing over there' – he motioned with his glass, spilling some of the punch – 'and now she's gone.' He felt stupid, putting it that way.

'What black-haired girl? There's only about twenty of them here tonight.'

'Damn, I don't know. She was kinda tall and thin

with good boobs and a classy-looking face, pale, pretty, no suntan.'

The two young men looked at one another and smiled. 'Must be the girl who's visiting Micky Herman, his date from somewhere back East. Massachusetts or New Hampshire or one of those freeze-your-ass states. Micky brought her, but I haven't seen them together all evening. Hey, there she is, over there by the door to the can.' They nodded at him and went back to debating Adlai Stevenson's chances in the presidential election.

King forced a passage through the crowd to her. 'Here's your drink, or what's left of it.'

She looked at him, momentarily confused, then took the glass from him. Her fingers brushed his hand and he was startled by their coolness. She took a third of the drink in one gulp.

'Hey, are you okay?' he asked.

She continued to look at him for a while before she spoke. 'The girl standing next to me barfed in her handbag. I thought I'd better get her to the powder room before it happened again. I must say you people throw the most active parties I've ever attended. At least our drunks back East wait until they get outside before they throw up.' She gave him a challenging glance which he took for the usual Eastern disdain for those west of the Hudson.

'Maybe your drunks have had a lot more practice,' he said.

Those blue eyes fastened on him for some time before she said, brightly, 'Touché. It's just possible you're the most attractive man here tonight, Mr King, and I should know because I've been looking around ever since Micky disappeared.'

East and West having called a truce, King relaxed and

100

they chatted. She told him she was a junior at Bennington which he pretended meant something to him. She was born in Boston, but her family now lived in Old Lyme, Connecticut. King listened, trying to take in what she said, but mostly staring at her vivid blue eyes and perfect teeth and stealing looks at her partially covered yet cleverly exposed bosom, unusually ample for such a tall, thin girl.

He liked her careful, controlled laugh and he was about to ask her if she would care for a tour of the house when Herman showed up to reclaim her. King wished he had found the nerve and the opportunity to take him aside and say, 'Micky, old buddy, we're old friends and I know you don't give a damn about this cold fish with the jet-black hair, what do you say?' No, he told himself, it was too late and he truly liked Micky, one of the fraternity brothers who had suggested he join the party. Bluntly, he told Micky how much he envied him, how lucky he was. Micky gave him an odd look. As he started to move towards the punch bowl, the girl stopped him by putting out a hand. 'Mr King, it was truly a pleasure to meet you. Should you ever find yourself in Connecticut . . .' Her voice and the cool touch of her hand trailed off at the same moment.

He stayed for another hour, drinking and listening to the pledges sing. Every once in a while he looked into the living room, hoping to see she was alone – or that his good friend, Micky, had passed out. But all he caught was a fast glimpse of the back of her head, and Micky still on his feet.

At home that night, he carefully wrote her name on a scrap of paper. 'Caroline Crowley, Old Lime, Connecticutt.' It would be a long time before he learned the only thing he had spelled correctly was her last name.

101

Kimble and Kimble had their law offices in a one-storey building on La Brea Avenue, a half-block north of Olympic Boulevard. For early June, the temperature was unusually high, and King fanned himself with an old issue of *Colliers Magazine* as he sat waiting. His cord suit had been neatly pressed when he left home an hour before, but he felt messy and a bit tired sitting in the waiting-room while phones rang around him and people moved in and out of unmarked doors.

'Kurt, how wonderful you look.' Etta Kimble took his hand and led him into her cluttered office. Legal files and documents were piled on top of each other and ashtrays overflowed with cigarette butts.

'Now you see why I had to become an attorney,' said Etta Kimble, pushing papers aside and dumping the contents of a large ashtray into the wastebasket. 'No man would have put up with me, otherwise.' When King said nothing, her face softened. 'My old lies don't work with you any more, Kurt, do they?'

'I never thought of them as lies, Mrs Kimble. How's Mr Kimble?'

'Terrible, actually, to be blunt. His stroke wasn't quite as bad as your mother's last one but I don't expect he'll ever be able to practise again. Not full-time, anyway. And the damnable thing was he was the one who kept things straight around here. God! you didn't come in to hear my troubles.'

King smiled. He wished he could tell Mrs Kimble how much he liked her.

'Kurt, the picture is this from what I've been able to find out by going over old records and talking to some of the people who were with King Corp at the time. The company didn't cheat your mother, but it made an agreement with her that was clearly to its advantage, an agreement no attorney looking out for your mother's interests would have let her sign. But she was determined to trust those people and went along with them, though we tried to dissuade her.' She paused to take up a file and glance through it. She lit a cigarette and smiled at King.

'I know you're a college graduate now, and a former Marine Corps officer, and a pretty bright guy despite all of that, but I'm going to simplify the details anyway. In a nutshell, Clayton and the other major stockholders offered your mother a plan designed to give her – and you – financial protection. Or so they thought. They converted her stock, which had been your father's, into a preferred stock with no voting rights and that meant she had no voice in management . . .'

'Which she wouldn't have wanted anyway,' King interrupted.

'You're quite right,' Mrs Kimble agreed. 'But you should realize that if she had wanted to and had insisted, she could have taken over as president. Legally she had that right. But the idea was to give her a guaranteed income in the form of a preferred dividend. That would have been fine had the company stayed as healthy as it was when your father was running it. Unfortunately, that is not the case and the company discontinued her dividends some years ago.' She stopped and her face went into a fierce clench as she looked at him. 'But you can bet the management people have done all right. Their salaries get paid whether there's a dividend or not.'

103

'I've seen some of them and they're doing fine,' King concurred.

Etta Kimble got up, stubbed out her cigarette and again flipped through the file. 'Your mother always kept up appearances as you well know. But the bills became too much for her the year she had her first stroke, the year you were with the Marines on the East Coast. She managed by selling the preferred stock. She sold some for as little as 10 at a time when it had a par value of 100. Damn, it still maddens me to think about it.'

She sat down, groping blindly for a handful of tissues in a desk drawer; she dabbed her eyes then blew her nose, loudly. Her composure restored, she looked at him and smiled. 'Look, Hon, she did a fine job of raising you after your father died, and you always lived first-class. But now it's clear she'll need constant nursing care, there aren't many options open to you. You can sell the house which will take care of expenses for a while, though not for very long because it's heavily mortgaged. After that, you'll have to pay for your mother's care out of your salary, so you'll need a job. You'll have no trouble, but the sooner the better. It's not a rosy picture, young man, but that's how it is. We'll help any way we can.'

King thanked her and kissed her on the cheek as he left. Walking up Olympic to the bus-stop, he replayed that session in his mind. 'Whatever happened to the spoon?' he asked himself. 'That gold one that was in my mouth when I was born? If somebody didn't steal it, then I sure as hell misplaced it.'

He saw just what Etta Kimble meant about the King Corp officers when a secretary finally approached him and ushered him, reverentially, into the office of Robert M. Clayton. A three-hundred-dollar suit from Huttons in Beverly Hills, a fifty-dollar tie with a diamond pin flashing in it. A fat cigar from the arabesque box on the expensive reproduction Sheraton desk. Modern art on the walls. Persian art on the floor rugs. When he thought of how his father lived who built up the firm, resentment flared for a moment or two in King's mind, but he quelled it.

Clayton did not even lever his overweight frame out of his swivel chair to come round and take his hand. An arm flapped at a chair in the full glare from the window. 'Sit down, Kurt, sit down.' He flashed a smile. 'Well, well, the time has finally arrived. You've got your degree and you're ready to go to work for the company. I think that's just great.' His voice rang with sincerity, reinforced by a warm, steady gaze at King. 'It would have made your father proud, real proud, like a dream come true. Every father likes to have his son follow in his own footsteps, and I'm no exception.' He chuckled then went on, 'I think we just want to convince ourselves our decisions have been right and having a son make the same decision confirms one's judgement.'

King nodded politely, though he felt impatient to end the small talk and get down to the real discussion. Clayton nicked the end of a cigar with a silver cutter, lit up and followed the expelled smoke as it lifted into the room. 'Kurt, I'm sorry but I have to be brief with you. I have a pile of paper to get through and I'm due at the

California Club for an important lunch, and I'm running late. But you push along and see Seth Ord in Personnel. I've told him you're coming and he'll work out a programme to get you on board. Seth knows my thinking.' He got up and extended his hand across the desk. 'And Kurt, I really hope you accept his offer. We'd like to have you with us, and I know your dad would have wanted that.'

On the way to Ord's office, he stopped at a fountain to give himself time to think. Pressing the valve, he stared at the bubbling water. 'Accept his offer!' Clayton had said. But it had always been understood he'd come to work for King Corp when he was ready. What did any offer, or his acceptance of an offer, have to do with it?

In Ord's outer office he smoked three cigarettes, his annoyance growing with each one. This is lousy, he thought. Just plain impolite. No one can be this busy. Finally, after a series of buzzers and whispered dialogue with her boss, the girl behind the Plexiglas partition told him in an offhand way Mr Ord would now see him.

The personnel manager was a bland, nondescript, middle-aged man who listened with neutral courtesy as King outlined his background. He then declared the openings in King Corp were restricted by the fact that King's degree was in Engineering. His condescension showing, he went on, 'I think the only job worth talking about is sales – a sales spot in the Aviation Products Division.'

'That's a travelling job, isn't it? Travel's fine with me, and I've a good feel for aircraft, I kind of grew up with planes. I'd like to get going with the company. What are they going to pay me?'

'A weekly salary to start and a draw against commission after the first six months.' Ord picked up a paper clip, straightened it out then bent it almost into a knot as though that reflected his mental embarrassment. 'In fairness I should warn you it could take quite a while to make headway in the aviation division which isn't moving like it did ten or even five years ago, and we've some very senior people. You could expect to be in that slot for some time.'

'I see,' said King, now beginning to feel the first signs of real anger though taking care to conceal them. 'Again, how much does the job pay?'

Ord hesitated. 'A hundred and twenty dollars a week to start.' He sensed the other man's animosity building and added, quickly, 'With a break or two, commissions will add to that in time.'

King let out his breath slowly, fighting down any show of disappointment. To disguise his wrath, he laughed openly at Ord. 'A hundred and twenty,' he said, incredulously. 'That's not much more than I made as a junior officer in the Marine Corps over two years ago. I can't live on a hundred and twenty a week and I don't understand how you can't pay more than that.'

Ord's voice had gone cold. 'I'm sorry, Mr King, but that's all we have right now. We're just not hiring. This is the best I can do, though maybe later . . .'

King did not let him finish. Rising, he said, 'I'd better have another talk with Mr Clayton.'

Something flickered in Ord's bland face and King felt sick as he realized what it was: Sympathy. 'Mr King, I really don't think that would make any difference.'

Inwardly, King raged at the injustice of the polite rejection. This is how they had treated his mother. He kept his voice level, normal. 'I understand,' he said.

'Please tell Mr Clayton I'm compelled by family financial problems to decline his offer. He'll know only too well what I mean. I'm sure I can do better.'

He banged Ord's door behind him. Moving like a bull, head down, he would have knocked down anyone who stepped in his path as he strode down the long corridor, wanting only to put this place and its people behind him. When he had once loved the place! . . .

Suddenly, he halted in his tracks. Why let that pansy-faced personnel manager tell the usurper, Clayton, second-hand the sort of home truths he should be told first-hand? King marched back down the corridor, flung Clayton's outer door wide, brushed aside the secretary and stormed in. Clayton looked up from tidying his desk. When he saw King, he glanced at his watch. 'Kurt, I said I didn't have time, I have a date.'

'Whether you've got time or not you're going to listen. First of all, I don't want your rotten little job at a hundred and twenty a week which won't even pay my mother's medical bills.' Despite himself, he was shouting. Behind him, he heard the secretary shut the door he had left open. Clayton put his hands up, palm foremost, to try to quiet him, but he went on shouting. 'My father brought you into this company and gave you your chance which is more than you've done for me. My mother trusted you and your kind and what did you do? You turned round and stole her heritage and mine.'

'You know that's not true, Kurt.' Clayton's voice was quavering.

'Shut up and listen. You sold her on stock that had no voting rights so that she couldn't interfere when she could have been president if she had insisted. Then when she had to sell, you and your pals bought her stock at a tenth of the price.' He stabbed a finger at Clayton's face which had turned as white as his shirt collar. 'You did all right out of us, Mr Robert Clayton, didn't you?'

Clayton found his voice. 'Your mother had the best advice and the best deal we could give her.' His tongue moistened his dry lips.

'The best deal for whom? For yourself, you mean.' King banged his right fist on the desk top setting everything jumping and scattering cigars out of the arabesque box. 'You didn't even see she had proper medical insurance and you never even called to see her when she was ill.'

'You didn't do much, either,' Clayton came back, and that really ignited King's anger.

With both fists bunched, he moved round the side of the desk with Clayton backing off. King wanted to wrap his hands round the man's throat and at least put the fear of death in him. He saw the flash of fear in Clayton's eyes, then remembered someone telling him the man had undergone surgery for a throat growth. He stopped himself, brought himself under control. He lowered his voice, but glared at Clayton. 'I know I didn't,' he said, 'and I curse myself for that and for doing nothing to stop you and your good-for-nothing bunch of accountants and amateurs from flying my father's company into the ground.'

'Kurt, I'm sorry you feel this way, but there's always a job for you here. I'll have a word with Ord.'

'Stick your job.'

He charged out of the office and through the outer office, closing both heavy oak doors with a bang that reverberated down the corridor. He was crossing the main office, head down, blindly, when somebody called

109

his name. 'Kurt, hey Kurt, where've you been?' King raised his face to look at the figure in his path.

It was Nat Clayton.

'Where've I been?' He heard himself almost snarl the words. 'Where've I been? I've been having a heart-to-heart talk with your father, the president.' He became aware that everybody in the big office had stopped working and more than fifty faces were watching him, wondering.

'With Dad?'

'Yes, Junior, with Dad. And I forgot to give him something – but you can have it for him.'

Bunching his fist, he put all his 175 pounds behind it. He did not aim the punch to finish in Clayton's soft belly, but beyond that, at his spine and even beyond that. His big fist travelled no more than a foot before burying itself in the solar plexus up to the wrist. Clayton's cry of pain echoed round the vast room. His mouth snapped open. The air in his lungs and stomach burst out of him. As he jack-knifed forward King hit him twice more. A left went into his open mouth knocking his head back and setting him up for another right hand which almost dislocated his jaw. Clayton started to go back on his heels, twisted then fell forward on his face, knocking over a couple of desks before hitting the ground. He lay there senseless, but his legs still twitched.

'Take him in to Papa with my compliments,' King called to the office staff, crowding round. He pushed through them and walked away.

Even leaving the elevator, he found both fists still clenched and his mind still spinning with rage and resentment. He went and drank from the fountain in the entrance hall to cool himself down. There, reproach

110

set in. All right, I couldn't get back at Clayton because of his position, and I couldn't hit him because of his age. So, I hit Nat instead because of what his father did to us. It was like the office-boy coming out of a stormy interview with the boss and kicking the office cat. Now that his rage had evaporated, he hated himself for what he had done to Nat. Revenge is a dish best eaten cold – isn't that what they said?

Since it would be his last look at the place where he had spent so many happy hours, he wandered round the plant, peeking into the factories where they still made the oleo-brake actuators his father and Ray designed. When his ire had cooled, he walked back towards the bus stop. Stepping across the parking lot, he heard a voice hail him. It was Howard Smith. 'Jump in, Kurt, and I'll give you a ride into town.'

King climbed into the new Chrysler, and Smith waited until they had cleared the plant area before turning with a grin. 'I heard about your run-in with Clayton and Junior.' He slapped King's shoulder. 'You certainly learned a thing or two in the Marines, eh!'

'I don't like what I did to Nat.'

'I wouldn't let it worry you.' Smith flipped a Chesterfield out of his pack and handed it to King. 'With a touch of sticking plaster and a bit of fancy bridge-work, he'll recover.' He lit their cigarettes. 'It was the best thing you could have done – turn your back on them. Kurt, they don't want you around here, they're scared you'll stop Junior from stepping into Papa's shoes, see? So screw the bastards – you can do better.'

Buoyed up by Smith's encouragement, he bought a *Los Angeles Times* from a downtown stand. After counting the money in his wallet, he walked to the Windsor, a softly-lit restaurant, New York type, below street

111

level. He took his dates there when he could afford it – which was seldom. An unusually heavy noon crowd pressed round the bar but he found an empty stool and ordered a double bourbon and water. He had drunk bourbon in the Marines and found it more bracing than gin. This was an occasion for it.

Sipping his drink, staring across the room at nothing in particular, he felt his resentment give place to self-pity. But he shook this off and called the bartender. 'One more and bring me something to write on, a piece of scratch paper if you have it.'

By the time he had finished his second drink, he had searched through the *Times* classified ads, circling the more attractive prospects, copying them on to the paper. With small change for a dollar, he began to job-hunt by phone in the men's room. It was a unique setting for starting a new career, but now his attitude had swung full circle and his confidence was soaring.

That day, he declined two good job offers. Before the week was out, he had accepted a post with a medium-sized electronics company as a sales-and-management trainee. It paid one hundred and ninety dollars a week plus commission.

Intermission

10 a.m. 21 October 1976

With Las Vegas dropping away behind them, they began the long letdown towards Los Angeles. King lifted his head from the yellow pad which he had covered with notes and figures to pick up the intercom microphone and speak to the pilot. 'Roger, bring us in gently over South Pasadena and the Zanadu plant, will you?'

Kate Foy looked over at him with a grin. 'What are we going to do, bomb the hell out of it?'

Kate had a wry, dry wit which normally appealed to King, and on another occasion her remark would have evoked a responsive quip. But from her boss's stony face, she realized that had there been bombs aboard, he might have taken out the Zanadu headquarters at that. She had seen him as grim as this once before, when King Corp stock plunged following a phony Wall Street rumour.

At 6.30 that morning they had taken off from Minneapolis in the company jet, and for the last three hours had hardly spoken more than a couple of dozen words. On the previous evening, they had exhausted all the arguments about the takeover, and none of them had slept well.

Chip Boyd, sitting across the passage from King, was also filling a notebook with figures, working out methods they might use to block the takeover bid. Already, he had an idea about making various stock issues to prevent Zanadu from gaining voting control. However,

115

he was still concerned about the choice of Stephen Schutt's firm to represent them and mentioned this to King, who cut him short. 'Put the cover on it, Chip. I've a gut feeling about this guy and he's going to do a helluva job for us.'

Kate and Boyd left him to his thoughts and the sums he was punching out on his pocket calculator as they climbed to their cruising height of 35,000 feet.

In fact, King was reckoning how much he was worth, something he rarely did. Most of his money he had tied up in King Corp stock. At market price that would yield just over 5 million dollars; but Zanadu's takeover bid would boost the stock quotation and his holding to between 7 and 8 millions. Enough to buy a company or retire and live the good life. Not that he had any intention of doing either. He would stake this and his other investments as well as his bank balance on fending off Zanadu; he would pawn his watch and other trinkets, sell his car and all that pricy furniture Frankie had bought to trick out his flat rather than see anybody take King Corp away from him.

And if he lost it all, well hell, he had started from zero before in New York, a tougher business world than California with only his talent to back him. Everybody knew he had given his old company, Maxim, the kiss of life and left it affluent. Maxim and a dozen other firms would hire him at double his present money if Zanadu pulled off this smash-and-grab raid.

Jesus, what was he thinking! Nobody was going to take them over. Not after he had exiled himself for more than ten years in the East to raise enough to buy into King Corp. Not when he had worked his tail off for another twelve years to transform it into one of the

116

leaders in its field with its stock esteemed by Wall Street.

Tomorrow, or the day after, this bid would make a lead story in every business section of the national and regional press. He supposed he'd find out how many real friends he had when the *Wall Street Journal* carried the story. His wife and twins would read about it in the *New York Times*. He could make a good guess at what she'd say: he deserved to drop right in it up to the neck. She'd give that scornful, coloratura laugh of hers and murmur something with fine New England contempt about Californian hicks going up so fast they met themselves on the way down. Anyway, he didn't give a damn about New York and the East, even if he had married and started a family there.

Jessica, the third woman in his life, would read about it in her favourite *Wall Street Journal*. He knew what she would do – sell her King Corp holdings while the price was high. But then, Jessica was a girl who got her priorities right, neither confusing sex with love, money with sentiment, business with pleasure. He couldn't blame her.

That bearhug call had done at least one thing – made him stop and take stock, and look back as well as forward. He had always kept his eye fixed on the road ahead, and if he used his rear-view mirror, it was only to watch how quickly he was drawing away from the rest of the field. Maybe he should have watched his back a little more.

King had spent a couple of flying hours trying to plan a strategy to thwart the takeover. Maybe he couldn't count on the loyalty of his stockholders who would probably unload their stock when the price went up.

But the King Corp executives and several of the directors would walk out with him if Zanadu did win.

Someone else might quit, and that one man could turn the scales against Zanadu. Admiral Hyman G. Rickover, father of the US nuclear navy, had placed vital and profitable defence contracts with King Corp and trusted King – as far as that cranky and temperamental old man trusted anybody. Rickover might well cancel those contracts and leave Zanadu with a plant which would take a crippling loss.

As they came in over Pasadena, King looked down and spotted familiar landmarks like the Santa Anita racetrack and the Huntington library. Slightly to his left, between the Pasadena Freeway and Monterey Avenue, he identified the sprawl of low buildings that made up Zanadu's main plant. He could have lost that lot in a corner of the modern factory and offices he had built for King Corp. An image flashed across his mind – of a snake swallowing a wild pig twenty times its girth. Zanadu swallowing King Corp! How the hell had Norris Thomas lighted on them? Who had tipped his hand on how big the King Corp jackpot was going to grow?

'Better buckle yourself in, Kurt,' Chip Boyd called from across the passage. King complied, wondering how he had missed the pilot's announcement.

Rain spattered on the window and streamed over the wings as they began their final run-in to Burbank. Through the rain haze, King saw the cluster of high-rise buildings in downtown Los Angeles fill his port window. Over the years, he had watched the business district grow, and its peculiar skyline always reminded him of a group of office buildings in Manhattan which he had passed every morning after starting to work for Maxim's New York office.

An odd thing, memory. First impressions especially. New York for him wasn't setting up his first home, or Andy Garrott, his old boss at Maxim, or the dozens of other important people he had met, or sexy Helen Bader, or Jessica. New York wasn't the swanky clubs, restaurants, theatres. No, those two words so often conjured up a knocked-about face clamped over a pulpy cigar and set on a stumpy body. Popeye Schwartz, who looked after the apartment block where he had rented his first room. Popeye Schwartz and his Murphy bed.

BOOK TWO
Growth Stock
Fall 1955

IV

He had to be at least sixty, but the little man took the apartment stairs at a pace which winded King. His sleeves, rolled up to the elbows, revealed arms that were impressive not just for the bulging muscles, but also for the garish tattoos covering the forearms. He wore an old waistcoat, an odd-looking black cap was falling off the back of his head and an unlit cigar stub jutted from a corner of his mouth. On the fourth floor, he selected a key from a huge ring and unlocked 401. Snapping on the hall light, he stepped back, motioning his prospective tenant to enter.

'Married?' His question seemed to emerge from the cigar stub.

'No, not me,' King said.

'Good.'

When King chuckled, the little man held up a hand. 'Listen, mister, don't get me wrong, I got nothing against marriage. Hell, I bin married thirty-seven years mysel'. I got to say twenty of 'em were spent at sea in the Merchant Marine. It's just if you take this apartment it's pretty small for two people. Fine for one, though.'

King looked at the high ceilings, noticing the embossed pattern covered by sparkling white paint and the fine moulding between the vertical and horizontal planes. He guessed twenty feet along the exterior wall. Off the hallway entrance was a sizeable closet, and the wall to his left had a massive fireplace in black marble. The wall opposite the corridor wall was dominated by a huge pair of floor-to-ceiling windows partly covered by louvred doors.

He swung these open to find a small, wrought-iron balcony. Too small for lounging, but it nonetheless expanded the room. From there, he could see West End Avenue and a slice of the tiny park running from 80th to 84th streets.

'Some of my tenants put flower boxes and plants out there,' the landlord volunteered. 'You get about three hours of sun every day – when it shines. That's a special feature.' His cigar migrated to the other corner of his mouth to stress the fact.

On the fourth wall there were several doors. One led to a tiny kitchen. Beyond making sure everything worked, King had no interest in that facility. He assumed one of the other doors entered the bedroom. 'I don't understand,' he said, 'why two people couldn't live here. I mean, if the bedroom is even half the size of this room, the place is big enough for two.'

An odd, grunting laugh came from the cigar. 'The bedroom is exactly the same size as this room, 'cause this room is also the bedroom. This here's what's known as a one-room apartment. You read the ad, didn't ya?'

'Yes, but I assumed that meant one bedroom.'

'Where the hell you from, mister?'

'California.'

'That figures. Weren't you ever nowhere else?'

'North Carolina and at Quantico, near Washington.'

'That's down South. That ain't NOO Yawk.' He chewed on his cigar. 'In fact, only NOO Yawk is NOO Yawk.'

'That had struck me, and I've only been here a month.'

124

'You said Quantico.' The little man gave him a knowing glance. 'What were you doing there?'

'I was in the Marines.'

'That so!' He chuckled. 'How come you ain't mean-looking then?'

King was enjoying the repartee. 'It must be this New York suit I bought last week.'

'I noticed it was Fi'th Avenue.' He chuckled again then walked over to a double door on the far wall, grasped the centred knobs and folded each section back to reveal what appeared to be the underside of a bed.

'What the hell is that?' King stood staring at the grid-iron frame in the wall alcove.

'That, young fella, is a Moyphy bed, after the guy who first thought it up. Got a lot of 'em in these older buildings. Want me to pull it down?'

King shook his head, his forehead knitting with thought. He grinned. 'Let me ask you something. What do I . . . what if you have a young lady guest and she's, uh, in the right mood, but you have to open the door and bring that contraption crashing down at the moment of truth? I mean, how d'you handle that?'

Sharp, wheezing sounds broke from the little man's mouth until King grew concerned about him. Finally, he removed his cigar and wiped his eyes with the back of his hand, still laughing. 'Had a tenant a year ago, young lawyer about your age, and I hear he did a lot of that kind of entertaining. He bought himself the biggest sofa, parked it in front of the Moyphy doors and that solved his problem, catch?'

'Thanks, I get the point.'

'Go ahead and run the water and flush the head and all that stuff if you like. Everything runs fine. The rent's 175 a month, due on the first. Sometimes we require a security deposit of one month's rent, depending on how good a job you got.' He winked.

King took out his wallet and extracted a business card, handing it to the man who read it aloud, 'Kurt S. King, Maxim Products, Inc., Assistant Vice-President Sales, Eastern Region.'

'Very impressive for a young guy. You must be sharp.'

'Don't let it fool you, they make everybody some kind of vice-president these days.'

'What d'ya say, then? You can move in whenever you want.'

'Well, the rent is a little steep . . .'

'Come on, Mr King, you're smarter than that. If this building had an elevator, this apartment would be 275. I bet you've looked around enough to learn that.'

King nodded. He had also admired the lobby with its spotless marble floors and columns, and the way the brass around the mailboxes shone. 'Okay, you got me.' Flipping a cheque book out of his pocket, he began to write the amount. He paused to look at the man. 'Say, you haven't told me your name.'

There was a second's hesitation. 'My name's Schwartz, but on account of my looks and me being in the Merchant Marine an' all, everybody calls me Popeye.'

King handed over the cheque. 'I'd prefer to call you Mr Schwartz.'

The man studied the cheque, folded it carefully and tapped it into his shirt pocket. He looked keenly at his new tenant then said, quietly, 'Mr King, I think you're going to get along just fine in NOO Yawk.'

He motioned the younger man ahead of him as they left the apartment, then said, 'There are a few things about living here I can tell you, so you don't get took if you see what I mean. For one, you didn't ask me for a receipt when you gave me that cheque. If you don't get a receipt, somebody will find a way to screw you.' He was still handing out advice when they reached the lobby.

2

Andrew Garrott, Maxim's head man in New York, stopped at his secretary's desk, turned his best smile on her, chucked her under the chin and said, 'Jenny, see if King's got here ahead of me and shoo him in to see me, will you?' Had he looked back before disappearing into his big office, he would have seen her answering smile change to a grimace.

A few minutes later, King sat facing Garrott, cradling a mug of black coffee in his hands, obviously relishing the steam that wreathed his face.

'Jesus, you still cold?' Garrott asked, incredulous.

'You're damn right I am.' King used the free-and-easy manner his superior encouraged from the few executives he liked. 'I don't think I've been warm since I got to this asphalt jungle.'

'Don't say we've been reading these modern novels, too?' Garrott went in for gentle irony.

'That's right.' King laughed. 'I take a night off from the social whirl once in a while.'

Garrott shook his head in mock despair. 'You bachelors break my heart with your sob stories. It must be tough to be young and single and overpaid in this Babylon. My mind boggles just thinking of all the fresh young things that get bedded down by you young studs.' He sighed, profoundly.

Everybody knew that Garrott – Handsome Andy or Randy Andy to the typing pool girls – had at least one and maybe two mistresses stashed in Manhattan apartments, so King deemed it prudent to drop this line of conversation, merely grinning at the last remark.

Garrott, a trim, energetic man of fifty, went on, 'Kurt, I wanted to talk to you about the progress report on your new capacitor project. It looks as if you're stalled for a couple of months until the lab finishes the tests on temperature drift and humidity. Your sales beat's covered for now, right?'

'Yeah, right. There's very little I can do until we get those results.'

King had been working hard in his own time to design and develop a new type of capacitor to improve the tuning system of TV sets. If he succeeded, Maxim would manufacture it as one of the many components it made for the radio and TV industry.

Garrott was playing with his silver paper-knife which he pointed at King. 'Good – I've a job for you, something out of your line but I think you can handle it. As you know, we're looking for companies to buy that will expand our line and simplify our operations by eliminating the need to go outside for certain goods and services. So, I've had my eye on a small New Haven outfit with a big name, New England Industries. It's an old family business that owns a grab-bag of smaller companies including a string of textile mills located up the coast from here to Maine. We like the mills but to get them we'd probably have to take the whole shebang. I'd like you to look at the whole package, study it and give me a detailed report – sales, profit and loss, balance sheet, people. Does that excite you?'

King reflected before answering. 'It does, very much.

I really enjoy seeing how other places are run, how they could be run more efficiently. Only . . .'

'Only what?'

'This may be going against my best interests, but aren't I a little young for this type of assignment? I mean, the present management, especially if they're older men, might take offence.'

Garrott's eyebrows lifted at the younger man's humility and good sense. 'Yes, they might, and that's why I'm sending Bill White along with you. Officially, he'll be in charge and you're his assistant, but it's your report I want to hear. Bill understands that, of course.'

Of course, King thought, Bill White would have to understand it. With a dicky heart and three years from retirement, with a son at Harvard and a daughter at Sarah Lawrence, White would make no waves. Fortunately for King, Bill was too decent or too pragmatic to take out his disappointment on others. 'Sounds like you've thought of everything, Mr G.'

'They don't call me the ageing boy wonder for nothing. Okay, you leave tomorrow. Jenny will have your tickets. I'm sending you up on the train so you can see the trees.' He flashed his smile at King then leaned back and lit a cigarette which signifed he had something else on his mind. King lit his own cigarette while his boss went on, 'You do this job right, Kurt, and I'll give you more of them – that is, if you don't mind being taken away from sales.'

King hesitated, wondering if this was another of Garrott's test questions, veiled by the smoke from his cigarette. What the hell! He enjoyed the verbal cut and thrust that terrified most of his peers but set Garrott's adrenalin pumping. He gave a straight answer.

'No, I don't mind. I like sales and my record's nothing

to be ashamed of.' Noting Garrott's affirmative nod, he added, 'In fact, I'm damn proud of it. But I like these other areas, too. Product development really interests me and if my idea on the new capacitor works out, well that would tend to open up another area. You see, my father invented a lot of things and I'd like to think I inherited the trait.'

'Very interesting,' Garrott said, but in an offhand tone. King hurried to finish. 'And this idea of looking at other companies and evaluating them for acquisition – that appeals to me.'

'Sales is a wonderful field, Kurt, and most of us at the top in Maxim started there, so don't get me wrong, there's nothing I appreciate more than the ability to sell. But' – he pretended to throw the paper-knife at King – 'it's only going to take you so far. You've got to learn other key aspects of the business world – design, management, marketing, I don't care what it is, but if you've something else to offer you'll go much further.' Garrott grinned and turned the paper-knife towards himself making a stabbing thrust at his chest. 'And you, boy, you may turn out to be my first triple-threat.' He had his arm around King as he walked him to the door.

Back in his own small office, King reflected on what Garrott had said. No doubt, advancement would come sooner to those with more than just sales expertise. But it didn't hurt, either, if you were like Garrott and drank your lunch twice a week at the Yale Club with the board chairman. Shrugging, he turned to the mail piled on his desk and had answered it all before Jenny brought the rail tickets.

Harold Crowley, president of New England Industries, was a handsome, silver-haired gentleman who immediately took to Bill White and was genuinely polite to

130

his assistant, King. He was not fond of the idea of selling a company which had been in his family for generations, but they needed capital which Maxim had. King thought it odd he did not raise the question of new management, but said nothing. On balance, Crowley said they would be happy continuing as they were. 'No one in the firm is exactly starving,' he said, then added with a smile, 'We've all managed to keep the wolves from our doors for quite some time, and if you know these New England winters you will admit that's no small achievement.'

They talked at length about the company structure, after which they were scheduled to tour the local plant then finish the day with the financial people. The following morning they would be left alone with the books and after lunching with Crowley, White would return to the city and King would begin his swing north-east to inspect the branch plants. As they left the president's office, King halted, his eyes rooted to a large photograph in a silver frame behind the desk.

Three attractive young people were seated on a low, stone wall with a small lake in the distance. A young man and a girl were fair with strong faces like Crowley's, but the second girl was slender with black hair and beautiful, delicate features in marked contrast to the others.

'Mr Crowley,' King ventured, 'I believe I met one of your daughters. I mean, those are your children in the picture behind you?'

'Yes.' Crowley seemed surprised. 'Was it Connie?' He pointed to the fair-haired girl.

'No, Carolyn.' Although King had not thought of the girl for a year, her name leapt into his mind. Starting to explain, he stammered and could only point at the picture.

'Anything the matter, young man?' asked Crowley, looking at King's embarrassed face.

'No, Sir, it's just such an incredible coincidence. I met her only once, a few years back, in Los Angeles.'

An understanding smile lit the older man's features. 'That's Carolyn. She's always been the different one, the impulsive one. I remember that trip to Los Angeles.' He made the name of the West Coast city sound as foreign as Algiers, which it probably was to him. 'I absolutely forbade her to go. Of course, she went anyway.' He glanced at Bill White and got the sympathetic look he expected.

'Is she still at school? She was going to Bennington, wasn't she?' Remembering that surprised him, too.

'No, she finished last June. She's in New York, but I couldn't tell you what she's doing. Some foundation thing. I see her when she's home on an occasional weekend. She's a pretty free spirit.'

'Makes for home when she gets hungry, I expect,' Bill White put in.

Crowley nodded. 'Or needs money.'

'Home would be in – I'll test my memory again – Old Lyme?' King was proud of his total recall.

'That's where we lived when she made that trip,' Crowley said. 'But since then we've moved to a smaller place in Darien. The older children fled the nest, too, and Darien's closer to New York. Well, gentlemen, I don't mean to hold you up. King, I'll be happy to remember you to my daughter.'

King was on the verge of asking for her telephone number but held his tongue thinking it was too soon in

132

their business relationship to be that personal. 'Please do that, Mr Crowley,' he said.

The next afternoon Crowley was called away on a sudden labour dispute, and the lunch was cancelled. King and White shared a cab to the station and ate a sandwich in the rundown coffee shop. As they parted, the older man took a business card from his coat pocket. On the back was written, '312 East 51st'. He handed it to King.

'What's this, Bill?'

'Her address.'

'Whose address?'

'Crowley's daughter – the one whose picture had you frothing at the mouth.'

'How the hell did you get it?'

'We had a chat about the high cost of raising daughters and the information sort of slipped out. I would have asked for the phone number, but figured you ought to be able to do something on your own. And, believe it or not, I was young once myself.'

King shook Bill White's hand harder than necessary. 'And I'd almost stopped believing in Santa!'

3

He found her number and rang. And, wonder of wonders, she remembered him, too. 'The King with the two princesses cooped up in the tower.' Of course, she'd love to see him. Yet, when they dated each other several times, they seemed to find it hard to relate to one another. She had a low ignition point. If only he could read deeply into her character he might come to grips with her cool perversity. Never had he met anybody so enigmatic, so difficult to figure.

133

One night, after a date during which they had argued about the foreign movie they had seen and almost everything else, he took her home early. Back in his apartment, he mixed himself his East Coast drink, a couple of fingers of Scotch and water. He sat, staring out dismally at a light snow that fell softly, drifting through the balcony doors which stood partially open. He was trying to decide whether to go to bed or to rekindle the fire and have another Scotch when someone rapped, quietly, on the door.

Carolyn murmured something light-hearted and squeezed inside. Before he had a chance to say anything, she had wrapped her arms round him and was kissing him. Not a hurried, brief kiss like the others, but long and passionate. Cold at first from the weather, her mouth quickly thawed and her smooth, full tongue searched for his. Her soft thigh pressed against his crotch, and she rubbed it against his groin in an almost excited way – the first time he had known her to lose her cool poise. But it was all the more effective in rousing him. Just as King was beginning to think of slowing her down she backed away and leaned against the door.

'Why don't you put another log on the fire while I get comfortable?'

He tended to the fire, oblivious of its heat. He could hear her toss the cushions from the sofa. Then the soft and unmistakable sound of clothing being removed. Finally, static electricity crackled as she dropped her slip.

'Kurt.' Emotion had furred her voice. 'You, too, take off your clothes before you turn round.' As he complied, the room lights went out, leaving them in the fire glow and the street light filtering through the curtains.

He stood facing the fire, conscious now of the heat on one side, and the chill air moving against his legs, buttocks and back. He heard her approach from behind and felt her body press against his back. Her hands drifted over his chest before slipping down his stomach to encircle his penis. She rubbed her body against his, her large breasts warm and soft on the muscles of his back. Under the expert touch of her fingers, he became more erect.

He turned, holding her away from him to gaze at her body, testing the reality of his imagination. Her eyes were closed as if she did not want to see him look at her; but her hands reached out and pulled his mouth to hers. They sank, slowly, to the floor, washed over alternately by the heat from the fire and the snow-cooled breeze. Kissing her breast, gently, his hand slipped between her legs and he caressed her. Under the touch of his finger, she quivered slightly. Now, she was breathing heavily. When he entered her, she gasped then moaned slightly. Suddenly, she stiffened. He feared in his excitement he would come. Then she relaxed and he eased himself deeper inside her.

At that, she gasped and seemed to lose control. Grabbing his back then his buttocks, she began to buck furiously beneath him. He tried for a moment to slow her movements, but soon he was overwhelmed by her apparent need and began to thrust himself, slowly and rhythmically. She gave a long gasp, like a soundless scream, as he shuddered through his climax. She hugged him fiercely for long seconds then went limp. Soon, he withdrew from the wet, tight and warm embrace.

He found a wool blanket and spread it over them.

She held him tight in her arms for a long time. At one

point, she drew back and looked at him, wordlessly. He freed one hand and started to draw a pattern with his finger on her breast which delighted him with its size and firmness. She pulled his hand away and put her head on his shoulder. She dozed off, and King happily replayed their love-making in his mind. Maybe a little too fast and furious, he thought, though thrilled by her passionate nature.

When she woke, they talked. She confessed her small crop of affairs – the married professor in her senior year, the shy campus poet. King did not swop confessions, but told her how lovely she was and the love-making had been, how he had longed for years to meet her again after California. He was amazed at her vulnerability, something he had never seen or even sensed before.

At dawn, he called her a cab. She would not stay the whole night, for that clashed with her ideas of propriety. At the door of his building, in the darkened lobby, he began to tell her how wonderful everything had been, but she silenced him with a quick kiss then ran to the cab.

Still, King never knew where he stood with her. At Christmas, she fell into one of her perverse, broody moods again. Or so Harold Crowley told him one night as they drank what he always called 'Highballs', waiting for Carolyn and her mother to join them for a restaurant dinner. By mid-January they were back on splendid terms, but she would not sleep with him. In fact, they had made love only once since that first time, and King felt she was holding back. She said she had things to work out, hang-ups to get over. He wished he had someone, like Ron Poole, he could discuss her with, someone to confide in. In February, they had a fight the weekend of her birthday. Her sudden bursts of sarcasm or contempt disturbed and perplexed him. Especially when she had lost an argument and shouted at him, 'Well, what the hell do you know about things, anyway?' That really riled him. Then, as had happened months before, she had an abrupt change of heart and phoned to apologize, saying he should pay no attention when she was bitchy. They made hurried but elaborate plans to spend the weekend in the Pennsylvania mountains. He hung up, happy and excited.

That night, King had a wire from Etta Kimble telling him his mother was gravely ill and advising him to take the next plane to California. Carolyn understood and sympathized, saying there would be other weekends and making him promise to call when he returned.

He was in the air over southern Minnesota when his mother died. Although he had expected her death and it came with none of the blunt shock of his father's death, he wept openly. His sense of loss was so great he finally chided himself for reacting excessively then sat down to rationalize his feelings. He tried to argue away her last disappointing years, particularly the series of strokes that had systematically destroyed her. Eventually, the reason for his grief dawned: he still harboured a deep resentment towards the people who had seized King Corp after his father's death, who had virtually stolen their heritage. Indeed, he was surprised at how deep his hatred went.

When Robert Clayton approached him at McKinley's funeral parlour, King stiffened involuntarily. Both men still recalled that shouting match in Clayton's office and the assault on Nat Clayton. He searched Clayton's face as he spoke of his sympathy and offered his condolences. His voice oozed sincerity, but the eyes belied it.

Clayton had lost weight and the whisper had it he was suffering from a cancer. Not long behind him, his son arrived. King had not seen Nat Clayton since he had knocked him over the typing-pool desks. Nat had evidently put that out of his mind. Taking King's arm, he said, 'I'm deeply sorry about your mother, Kurt. She was the kind of lady you don't meet much any more.' His sincerity touched King and he thanked both Claytons for their consideration. In the father's case it was difficult.

It seemed the flow of people to pay their respects would never end. He remembered most faces if not always the names; the Pooles explained that Ron, now studying law at Stanford, was camping in the mountains and out of reach; Beverly's mother said her daughter was due in any day from Paris and would call him immediately if he had not returned to New York. That name evoked a rush of vivid memories, not always in keeping with the funeral setting.

Etta Kimble approached and asked for a private word. 'Kurt, your Aunt Helen has made a practical suggestion which she felt I should talk to you about since you and she really don't know one another well. She wonders if you would object if your mother was buried in Minnesota in the family plot of the Enstroms, your maternal grandparents.'

He stared at her, taken aback and speechless for a moment.

Mrs Kimble went on, 'Your mother died without leaving any burial instructions, but we both remember her saying she never wanted to be cremated. There's nothing in writing, not even a will.' She paused and shrugged her shoulders. 'And no great fortune left for you.'

'That doesn't matter, Mrs Kimble.' He thought for a moment then nodded his head. 'About the grave, Aunt Helen's idea could just be the most sensible course. I'm not sure I'd have the stomach for visiting graves, but if she were back there with her folks, well, I know Aunt Helen and her people would take care of the grave and visit it and all the things one is supposed to do.'

'That's the right thought,' Etta Kimble said with an approving look. 'If your father had been buried here it would have been different.'

He thanked her. 'I'll go and talk to Aunt Helen,' he said and started to walk away then stopped in his tracks. He stared at the archway framing the foyer.

There, Etta Kimble saw a tall, striking woman dressed entirely in black except for a pearl-grey blouse that accented her mourning costume and her white face and neck. Her hair was as black as her small hat and veil through which her pale and elegant features shone. When she came up to King she did not kiss him, like most women sympathizers, but pressed both his hands in hers. 'Kurt, I'm so sorry about your mother. I've been thinking of you ever since your call and I simply had to come.'

He continued to stare at her as though his speech had gone, but his eyes took in all of her. Finally, he said, 'Oh, excuse me, Mrs Kimble, this is Carolyn Crowley. We are friends, I mean we've been dating in New York.'

'I can see that, dear.' Etta Kimble smiled. 'Nice to meet you, Miss Crowley.' She turned to King, 'Please excuse me, Kurt, I'll go and tell Aunt Helen your decision. I'm sure you two want to talk.'

'Kurt.' Carolyn fixed him with those kingfisher-blue eyes. 'Would you please take me up to the front? I want to see your mother.'

Two days later, on the aeroplane headed back to the East Coast, King and Carolyn were the only passengers in the late-flight first-class section. They were over Lake Michigan when he asked Carolyn to marry him. As they passed Detroit twenty minutes later, she accepted his proposal and they toasted each other in champagne.

4

With the possible exception of two women, Beverly Anderson and Mrs Harold Crowley, everyone was delighted at the news, discreetly deferred for three months out of respect for his mother's memory. Invitations for the late June wedding went out in early May. Beverly never responded to hers, which saddened him.

Anita Crowley had always wanted her daughter to marry a professional man, but she hid her disappointment and carried on bravely, determined to make the wedding a social event which would impress all her friends. Her eldest daughter had eloped and her son had married into a family that could not afford a big wedding. So, she staked everything on Carolyn. She had invitations embossed on thick cardboard then went too far, in King's view, by hiring a calligrapher to personalize each card in Olde English script.

Wedding gifts poured in, their quality and elegance suited to a couple whose engagement had been announced in the *New York Times* with a stunning picture of Carolyn. But West Coast gifts tended to be on the practical side. King roared with laughter when an astonished Carolyn told him the Kimbles had sent a vacuum cleaner, something she claimed she had never tangled with before. Gifts from the Crowley inner circle reflected a more graceful and aesthetic choice. Never had he clapped eyes on so many place settings of the expensive china Carolyn and her mother had selected after an extended tour of the New York shops, or so much silver, or so many pieces of beautiful crystal. Shortly before the wedding, he told Carolyn the huge, unused ground-floor study where the gifts were displayed looked like the Darien branch of Tiffany's. He meant it as a joke; she interpreted it as a great compliment.

Her mother might well have ordered the wedding day, it was so perfect. Bright sunshine and temperatures in the high seventies. The Gothic massiveness of the First Congregational Church of Darien passed muster with her as well as the cultured lawns and fairways surrounding Weeburn Country Club, scene of the wedding reception.

Only three of King's friends attended. Ron Poole, the best man, seemed in awe of all the Crowleys, Chip Boyd from King's office, who was a groomsman, and Andrew Garrott. All the others were Carolyn's friends and relatives. For King, the day swam by in a pleasant haze produced by excellent champagne. Shortly before the cake-cutting and bouquet-tossing, he noticed Ron Poole and Andrew Garrott had teamed up, and he shuddered at the prospect facing those nubile young women at the reception when those two Lotharios got to work on them.

He was pleasantly tired when the plane levelled out and headed south. His wife – the word startled him still – was dozing and had a slight champagne flush on her cheeks. He lit a cigarette and thought about the parting comments of three men – his best friend, his father-in-law and his boss.

Ron had gripped his hand hard enough to crush his

141

knuckles and slurred his words as he said, emotionally, 'I always knew you'd end up with someone special, and she is. Good luck and God bless you both.'

'My boy,' said Harold Crowley, affectionately, his normal Yankee reserve having dissolved in half a gallon of wine and several double Scotches, 'I'm mighty happy she chose you. I feared she would end up with one of those pale, proper types.' He waved his Scotch at the bar where look-alike young men in look-alike suits stood talking quietly. 'Not that you aren't proper, you understand, but you're what I call a real man. Well, I've said enough. I'm proud to have you for a son-in-law.' King felt a new warmth for the older man.

Just moments before King left to change his rented tails for travelling clothes, Andrew Garrott stood looking at him, a Cheshire grin on his incongruously youthful face. He had switched to real liquor quite a few drinks earlier, but unlike Ron or Harold Crowley, he seldom showed the effect until the party had run its course. His 'tilt' indicator lit up when he swallowed a double in two gulps.

'King, you're okay, and you've married splendidly as we say hereabouts. But more important, you're doing one hell of a job for me. When you get back to work, come in and see me first thing. I have a surprise for you.' He winked, and turned to join a young lady he had cornered earlier near the bar.

Their honeymoon on the Caribbean island of Antigua passed the way King had expected. Carolyn had been excited for weeks beforehand, and he was intelligent enough to realize she could not shake off her tension immediately. They partied every night, ate well, drank too much and slept late. Carolyn kept her fair skin out of the brutal Caribbean sun which tanned King handsomely. They did more sightseeing than he would have liked and their love-making lacked the total passionate release he had hoped for. But there, too, King was also patient. They had, he knew, an infinity of days and nights ahead of them.

He was astonished at the number of books, mostly novels, Carolyn devoured. He was also intrigued when, by the middle of the second week, he realized he was anxious to get back to work.

5

Garrott had to put off his surprise until late July. But it was worth the wait, for it turned out to be the official announcement that King's new capacitor design had passed all its tests with excellent results. In fact, the company viewed it as the most potentially profitable new product it had developed in years. For King, it brought a big increase in salary, but it also triggered his first serious disagreement with his boss.

He thanked Garrott for the praise and the larger paycheque but argued for his rights. 'Andy, don't think I'm being stubborn, but I can't buy the argument it's traditional for the company to hold the patent. This was an idea I had, all alone, years before I joined Maxim. I wasn't working to perfect someone else's concept. I think the patent should be in my name and consideration given me in some share of the profits.'

Garrott was equally blunt in rejecting that argument. Now look, Kurt, I hate to be difficult, but the patent must be assigned to the company. Your name will be on it, but that's the way it's done at Maxim and, for that

143

matter, anywhere else I know of. I think you're asking for too much.'

'Too much! Jesus, Andy.' King felt his blood rising and he cautioned himself not to lose his temper. 'That gadget is going to make millions for this company in the next few years.'

'That's overly optimistic, I think.'

'Don't kid me you haven't reviewed the projections.'

Garrott had the grace to smile. 'Well, as a matter of fact . . .' He broke off with a laugh. 'All right, it's a surefire winner, but even if I agreed with you, which I don't, I'd have to go to the board of directors with it. Look Kurt, you sleep on it and we'll talk again next week.'

Several nights later, King asked Chip Boyd, who was on the low end of Maxim's legal hierarchy, to have a drink with him after work. They walked to a Third Avenue bar, down the block from overcrowded Pat O'Brien's and King ordered a second drink before quizzing Chip.

'Yeah Kurt, I've checked it out, though a couple of honchos gave me funny looks, wondering what I was doing looking into patent procedures. Anyway, and stating upfront I'm no patent attorney and don't set company policy, I found the standard procedure is this – when they hire guys who're likely to be inventing things, you know, chemists, engineers and weirdos like that, they have them sign a release form. Maxim calls it an "Invention and Secrecy Agreement". You know what that is without me giving you legal gab.'

'Yes, go on.'

'Okay, so there's this document right out in the open, and the guys know they work on what they're told and try to invent stuff that will pull profits for the company.'

He paused and took a long swallow. 'Anyway, that's for those kinds of guys. But what happens when a guy like you, a management and sales type, comes along and invents something really worth dough – well, what's the form then? And remember you'd done work on this in school, before you ever came to Maxim.'

'Knock it off, Chip, the suspense is killing me with thirst.'

'The practice is there ain't any practice. Maxim has never been faced with this problem before. You're *sui generis* – it's Latin, go look it up. What's more, you're the only assistant vice-president – I know 'cause I did some checking – who's doing evaluation and acquisition work. Let me be serious for a minute, Kurt, you're not even twenty-six years old but you're already ahead of guys who've been here twice as long. On top of that, you're Andy Garrott's golden boy whether you like it or not. From where I sit, I'd say your future with Maxim is unlimited. I wouldn't push this too hard.'

'Jesus, Chip, don't get me wrong. I'm not that ambitious.'

'Save your false modesty for somebody else. I'm not telling you something you don't know.'

King smiled and nodded assent. 'Chip, I really appreciate your help. Still, on Monday I tell Garrott I insist on some financial recognition.' He drained his glass.

Boyd shook his head in sorrow. 'Is that the only way it is?'

'Well, sure, what else can I do?'

'Pray to the good Lord. Garrott can hang tough.' Boyd emptied his glass then looked at King. 'By the way, why're you so set on this?'

'Pride, Chip, pride. My father had thirty-one patents

145

granted him. I just want to think he'd be proud of me. Then, there's the money.'

'The money makes sense, but I don't know if Garrott will understand the parental patent thing, but I sure can.' Boyd signalled for another round. 'My father's a banker, an investment banker, but on a small level, back home. And like father like son I've always hankered for that kind of work.'

'Then why did you become a lawyer?'

'Oh shit, that's just one part of my Five Year Plan. I'm going to Columbia at night, getting a master's in Finance. Then it's back to work with Dad, back in beautiful Santa Barbara.'

'What! A Californian! I'm from LA.'

'That must be why I liked you right off. Jesus, why did you ever leave the sunshine for this shithole?'

'For the experience, and the kicks.'

'Yeah, I know what you mean. Well, Kurt, it's getting late, and you have that lovely girl waiting for you uptown. Just let me tell you what I think you ought to ask for from Garrott. But I warn you, wear your flak-jacket, for he's going to hit the goddamn roof.'

6

A week later, King threw open the apartment door and bawled, 'Carolyn, Carolyn, where the hell are you. I've got great news.'

'What do you mean, where the hell am I?' she called from the kitchen. 'I'm either in the room you're in or I'm in one of two others, if you can call this closet of a kitchen a room.'

King flung his raincoat on the couch and placed the flowers and wine on the coffee table. He could hear

146

Carolyn's voice reflect her growing exasperation with what she often called their 'crackerbox apartment'. He eared he might have made a mistake talking her into staying on the West Side, in his building, rather than the new high-rise she preferred, because of its East Side ddress. Not even the larger apartment Schwartz had aved for them on the second floor with its separate edroom and view of the park had changed her mind. Nonetheless, she had done a fine decorating job on ttle money, creating a charming and comfortable set-ing. He enjoyed entertaining, but his greatest pleasure vas returning from work to find candles lit and the drink fixings ready.

Carolyn stood in the kitchen doorway, her hair cov-red by a pale-blue scarf. Remembering how hot the mall kitchen could get, he felt a rush of sympathy. He icked up the wine and flowers and handed them to er.

'My, my,' she said, softly, her mood beginning to hange. 'What's the occasion? You hollered something bout good news. Don't tell me. Wait and save it till ve're comfortable.'

Deftly, one-handed, she flipped off the scarf then hook out her hair, lengthened considerably in the four nonths since their wedding. That movement, swirling he tousled hair perfectly into place, caught his atten-ion, impressing him anew with her dark, rich beauty. he asked him to be patient while she put the flowers 1 a vase. When she returned to the living room her rms cradled wine, glasses and a corkscrew and one and held the tastefully arranged flowers.

She smiled approvingly when he remembered to sniff he cork and sample the wine before filling her glass.

147

He thought all this a bit affected but he was learning to trade off minor concessions against bigger ones.

'Not so much, Kurt, never a full glass. Oh, and you bought California wine again. I swear you must be the only man in New York who does.' But her lilting tone told him her anger was past.

They sipped the wine and King said, 'The good news is that Garrott told me this afternoon the board approved my request. I get the patent in my name, assigned to the company of course, and I get the upfront payment I asked for.'

Carolyn forgot all her mother had taught her and almost spilled her wine. 'You get the money, you really do? Twenty-five thousand?'

'Every beautiful green bill. Twenty-five ain't-it-grand. All ours in one lump sum to be paid on the first of next month. And to think I wouldn't have had a penny of it if it weren't for Chip Boyd.'

'Chip Boyd? That funny little rumpled man in the W. C. Fields suits? You can't be serious.'

'It was Chip who came up with the idea of asking for a fixed figure rather than a percentage of the profits. He knew they'd never go for that because it would set a precedent they couldn't live with downstream. They'd have gone to court before letting go of a percentage and that would have been messy. When I proposed a lump sum it solved the problems both sides and they jumped at it. Chip directed the whole play from behind the scenes. He's a sharp guy.'

She sighed. 'If he's so sharp, why the circus outfits. He needs a keeper when he shops. He's either colour blind or colour-happy.'

King laughed. 'Yeah, he really isn't what you'd call a snappy dresser. Yesterday, he had on a suit with tripes, over a striped shirt and a striped tie. He looked ike a barber's pole on the move.'

Carolyn lowered her wine glass to the floor, stretched on the couch like a cat and kicked off her shoes. 'Why doesn't my big, money-making genius of a husband come over here and relax?' She unbuttoned the top three blouse buttons. 'But before you do, be a lamb and turn the oven down to low, very low. We can eat after a while.'

Much later, she lifted her head from his lap. She slipped into her blouse without her brassiere but put on her panties before stepping into her skirt. King was dozing. She leaned over and kissed him on the cheek. She had a big smile on her face.

'You leaving me?' he asked, stirred by her movement.

'I have to call mother. She was telling me about a perfect little house she saw for sale. She said it's made for us.'

'But I thought we'd agreed to postpone that for now, Carolyn – until we're ready to have a family.' His voice betrayed his concern.

'We did.' She gave a short, controlled laugh. 'But that was before we struck it rich.'

King sat up, suddenly, and looked at her across the dim room, intrigued by the implication in her reply. 'This isn't a subtle way of telling me you're pregnant.'

'Certainly not,' she said, leaning hard on the negative. 'As a matter of fact, if I am pregnant, the doctor who fitted this diaphragm is going to get hit with the biggest malpractice suit he ever saw.'

Laughing at her own humour, she stopped in the bedroom doorway and turned back towards him. 'It's funny, but I never thought about you making much money. I mean, I knew you had a good job or you

wouldn't have asked me to marry you. But making a lo
of money? – that was what people like my father did
not a young man like you. I never dreamed it. But wha
a pleasant surprise.'

He could hear the click and ratcheting sound of th
phone. Was that a compliment she had just paid him
He wasn't at all convinced it was.

V

As he turned on to East 54th Street, King braced himself against the thudding wind which bored through his dark-blue cashmere topcoat, chilling him. He welcomed the sight of '21's familiar iron railing, its black paint and brass gleaming in the afternoon sun. On his way down the stairs, he patted the colourful cast-iron jockey then went inside to leave his coat. He knew Andy Garrott would be waiting at his usual table in the crowded room. He favoured this particular spot rather than the quieter sections, and his choice had nothing to do with the ambience or the décor or the crazy-quilt of objects hanging from the ceiling. Garrott liked the waiter who knew his signal and could replace his empty glass so swiftly that nobody noticed. Another of his compulsive actions was leaving the office half an hour earlier than anyone else to make sure they wouldn't give away his table if he were late. Garrott had learned the small but sinister stratagems of the hardened lush.

'Well, well, if it isn't King Kong.' His shout carried to other customers, who stared at King.

'God,' King groaned to himself, 'It's going to be one of those lunches.'

That inept nickname and the shout indicated Garrott was at least two drinks ahead. King studied Andy closely as he lit a cigarette and was relieved his hands did not shake. And from a brief eye exchange, he noted Garrott did not have pupil flutter and was reassured.

'Kurt, let's get our business out of the way then get

151

down to some serious drinking.' He caught King's worried look. 'Hey, boy, relax, I'm only kidding. You know I save my real drinking for after work.' He shook his head reprovingly. 'Sometimes I think I created a monster when I talked the board into promoting you to senior vice-president. You're too goddamn serious. Now relax.'

'You do keep me on the go, Andy.'

'Sure, but you thrive on work. Don't kid me. Shit, I look at you and see myself all over again. And you sure as hell better take that as a compliment.'

King laughed and ordered a J and B and water. He saw Garrott brush his glass stem with a forefinger, his signal for another martini.

'I hope I'm not working you too hard, Kurt. Everything okay at home? How's that fancy dwelling?'

'The house couldn't be better. You know, I was scared when we bought it I was getting in a little deep, paying forty grand for a house at my age, but Carolyn says we had a call from a realtor last week when I was in Kansas City offering us sixty for it. Of course, we've no intention of selling, especially now Carolyn's pregnant.'

'She doing all right?'

'Fine, thanks. It was rough at first but now we're in the last six weeks it's pretty much routine. She isn't nuts about being pregnant, though, and she bitches a lot.' As soon as he said this, he felt guilty and sipped his whisky to keep himself from saying more.

'Shit, they all bitch. I remember when Marie was carrying Janet she gave me a ration of crap every time I walked in the door. But I put a stop to it.'

'How'd you do that?'

'I stopped walking in the door.' Garrott burst out laughing, so infectiously that several people at nearby

152

tables turned and smiled. 'I didn't come back for two weeks and it scared the hell out of her. When I came back she couldn't have been nicer.'

King wondered how much of the tale to swallow. But knowing this mercurial man, such a tactic was not out of character. Garrott had risen to the top of Maxim by a series of brilliant but unorthodox business coups. He was one of the few executives King had met in any firm whose personal and professional lives were equally flamboyant. In his year and a half as Garrott's right-hand man, King had come to admire the soundness of the man's instinctive business approach; but he was dismayed at the way he so often jeopardized it by his drinking and carousing.

'Why the hell did you buy a house in New Canaan?'

King had answered that question several times before, but politely repeated the explanation. 'Carolyn's parents live in Darien and she wanted to be near them. That first year we visited them so often my car drove the Merritt Parkway on its own. We couldn't afford Darien so Carolyn's mother house-hunted in the next town west, New Canaan. For her, it was tragic that we couldn't be in Darien, but she bore up and so did I. Though it was definitely a rung or two down the social ladder, don't you know, old chap?' King affected a British accent.

Garrott nodded, well aware of every degree of snobbish refinement in that society. He signalled for another drink and let King continue.

'I can't say I love the New York, New Haven and Hartford Railroad, though it seems I've been travelling it for thirty years instead of three. The town's kind of postcard pretty, but to tell the truth, I wish we were still living in Manhattan. I feel left out living in a place that closes up at nine every night. I bet we're the only couple in our neighbourhood under thirty. Aw hell, Andy, get me off this topic, I really have nothing to complain about.'

Garrott put his glass down. He looked, for the moment, absolutely sober and serious. 'Kurt,' he said in a lower, more confidential voice, 'be careful. Don't let things get messed up at home while you're young and busy climbing the ladder. I know whereof I speak. In fact, that's the only thing I'd do differently if I had it all to do over. That, and making sure I never got started with this stuff.' He raised his glass, then catching King's eyes, he looked away. His voice still quiet, he went on, 'You may think I enjoy all the catting around I do, but there are times when I wish I could have been the pipe-and-slippers type. Funnily enough, my reputation as a wildass has helped me. The board thinks of me as a highly successful maverick, which I am, goddamn it. But if I make one serious gaffe I'll be out on my can before I know it. It's anybody's guess how long I'll be running Maxim, Kurt, but when I stop it'll be because I chose to step aside. And as far as you and a few others are concerned, I want to leave with the feeling I've been an example and not an object lesson.'

As abruptly as he had turned serious, Garrott gave his boyish grin and said, 'Shit, this is getting downright morbid. Look, I wanted to talk to you about the shopping trip you're taking to Chicago next week. I said it would be for a week or maybe ten days, but I've had a couple of ideas that might keep you on the road longer. Do you mind?'

'No, of course not.'

'Okay. Now, as soon as you finish your reports on the two component manufacturers in Elgin I can decide which one I want you to evaluate further.' He paused to sip his fresh drink.

King lit a cigarette to give him time to consider his reply. The reports Garrott had mentioned went to him over a week ago. Finally, he said, 'Ah, Andy, maybe you'd better ask Jean if she mislaid those reports. I know I gave them to her.'

'You did? When?'

'Two, three days ago. She's probably filed them.' He felt no qualms about shuffling the guilt on to the secretary. Once he had pointed out one of Garrott's oversights to the man himself and would never forget the look that clouded his boss's face. A look of confusion tinged with panic.

'Yeah, that's probably it. Boy, I sure do miss Jenny. Every goddamn time you train a good secretary, they up and get married on you.'

King swallowed that one with another sip of whisky. How in hell could Andy say, straight-faced, Jenny had left to get married when the entire office knew he had promoted her to a small apartment on Houston Street in the Village where she tried her hand at water colours? Her only other task was to keep herself free on those evenings Andy decided to drop by.

Garrott switched back to business. 'Okay, so she must've missed something and Elgin's complete. You still have to hit Chicago. Take your nutmuffs. That wind off the lake makes this town feel like Miami Beach.'

2

When King opened the door of the hospital room, he had never seen Carolyn looking so mad. She was sitting, bolt upright, in bed. Normally, her eyes were blue, that soft, iridescent blue on a kingfisher's neck feathers. Angry, they turned another kind of blue. Gunmetal. Her voice, too, had a metallic ring as she shouted at him. 'Kurt King, I find it impossible to believe you wouldn't tell me before we were married.'

He wanted to laugh, but something warned him it was untimely. He had come directly from the airport after cutting short his Midwest trip on hearing Carolyn had been rushed to hospital in labour. When he became the father of twins, a boy and a girl, he was literally up in the air, 20,000 feet up.

'I'd forgotten it, I really had. I never thought to tell you.'

She sat up even straighter in bed. Although she looked the picture of health and beauty, her face was still twisted by the memory of the pain. As she did in crisis moments, she lost her breath momentarily. 'How . . . how could you possibly forget your own mother had once had twins?'

'Look honey, it was a long time before I was born. I know I'd been told as a kid, but those things don't stick.' He started to add the twins had died as infants but thought better of it. 'Gee Carolyn, I would think you'd be happy about having two babies instead of one.'

'Oh you do, do you? Do you have any idea how much that hurt, how much . . . Oh, what's the use of talking about it? You men think it's so easy to have a child. Hell, I just had children. If I hear one more man tell me about Indian women who have their babies in the field and go right on working, I'm going to scream.'

'They have different medicine men,' King said with a grin, trying to mollify her. But levity was out. Her tirade continued, if anything growing more bitter. 'If I'

156

known the history of twins in your family I'd have thought twice about having children.'

'You what?' said King. He had expected her to be happy, not outraged. His own anger started building. Maybe you wouldn't have married me,' he suggested.

She refused to give. 'That's entirely possible,' she said, and kept on complaining before he could respond. You know, the doctor said it was dangerous for someone with my narrow bone structure to have too many children. And he was talking about one at a time. For God's sake, Kurt, they almost had to do a Caesarean.'

She stopped and looked up at him. His hurt expression softened her anger and she spoke much more quietly. 'Oh, I'll be all right. I just need to get over the shock. But if you think I'm upset, wait until you talk to mother. She's convinced the only way you can conceive two babies at one time is to do something indecent. Now, get out of here and let me sleep before someone brings those little mouths back in here and they start to attack me again. Go to your club and hand out cigars. But be sure to get two boxes, one with a blue band and one with pink.'

He was halfway out the door, thinking Carolyn never forgot the proprieties, even in a crisis, when she called, All your business buddies will laugh and tell you what a great stud you are. But go ahead and have a wonderful time while I'm stuck here all stitched up like a Thanksgiving turkey.'

She began to cry.

King opened his front door and tested the night air. Relieved to find the temperature had not dropped, he decided against a heavy coat and pulled on his windcheater. At the corner of Lower Weed and Elm he bore right along his regular early-morning track to the commuter depot. Head down, hands in his pockets, he swung along ignoring the handsome dwellings. Ten o'clock and not a thing moving, not even a cat. Passing the deserted train station, he crossed the tiny business district then headed west up the hill. In the parking lot of the inn, a party of diners were regaling each other with a last story, or maybe one of the men was making a final pitch for one of the girls. That thought set King smiling.

Another ten minutes and he reached the duck pond next to Route 123 that led to Darien and the big, old brick Crowley home. The ducks glided away in line ahead at his approach. Hell, he wished he'd brought some fresh bread to feed them!

He cupped his lighter and hands round a cigarette and lit it, turning his back on the ducks. How had things got so mixed up? He put the question earnestly.

A week ago, at the farewell party for Chip Boyd who was leaving Maxim to return to California and his father's firm, King had overheard another Maxim executive say, 'I don't think I've ever been happier in my life. I'd like to move ahead faster like King, but other than that I haven't a complaint in the world. My wife, my son, the house in Mount Vernon – everything's just the way I want it. I pray Garrott doesn't get a brainstorm and transfer me out to the boondocks, because things are just fine with me.'

For days, that joyful speech kept echoing in King's head. He envied the man. But why in hell was he so goddamn content? King tossed his cigarette, almost resentfully, into the pond as he put the question.

Retracing his way, heading home he thought about his own situation, groping for how, why and when

158

hings had begun to change. Odd, and hard to pinpoint. Certainly, that very first year they had spent in the apartment had been the best. Those evenings he'd be excitedly bounding upstairs and catch Schwartz's popeye face grinning with understanding. Now, he no longer rushed home to Carolyn. What had changed?

Outside the train station, King noticed a couple sitting in a car. The Smithsons? He raised his arm then froze his greeting. Oops! One Smithson, maybe, but definitely not two. So, Smithson had his problems, too. Who was the woman?

His mind returned to grapple with his own problem. The first year in the new house was too hectic to bother about anything else with the place full of workmen, full of Mrs Harold Crowley and Carolyn combing town and country for nest-building materials. Again, she had done a spectacular job of decorating, though a bit too 'Eastern' for him. But what had happened to the two and a half years since then?

Of course, the twins – Randal and Alexandra – had changed things. For Carolyn, anyway. His routine was much the same. But what else? Two years seemed to have gone by in a blur of cocktail parties with friends and colleagues, an occasional theatre and celebration. Perhaps he was conveniently forgetting the travel. All those trips week in, week out when he carried the gospel of Maxim to the hinterland, as Carolyn had once phrased it. That had been an outsize bone of contention. He vividly recalled a fierce shouting-match when she had told him how much she hated his habitual absence. He had flung back at her that if she hated it so much she had a funny way of showing her pleasure when he got home, referring to the fact that she was invariably sleeping when the airport cab pulled up at the house on Lower Weed.

He heard sudden laughter and saw several people emerging from a doorway down the block. Someone on his train had talked about a new restaurant and bar in New Canaan. He waited for the customers to get into their cars and pull away before entering. Once inside and seated at the bar, he knew Carolyn would dislike the place, with its dark panelling, red-leather banquettes and muted lighting. He ordered a brandy and as he sipped it, he rationalized his work habits, defended his ambition and countered Carolyn's objections. Her father, as she so often reminded him, never left home before 8.30 and was home by six, whereas her husband, when not out of town, always caught the first train to the city and the last one back. Sometimes he missed the 'owl' and stayed over. When his commuting routine was new he had sat down and tried to explain to Carolyn how exhilarating he found his work. Her blank look convinced him communication had broken down. She did not understand. Or was she jealous of the hold his company and his work had over him?

He, too, felt mixed up. Garrott's warning about not letting work ruin his marriage echoed in his mind and he often fell to wondering if he would wind up like Andy, using the bottle as a crutch for his crippled personality and his broken marriage. As well as seeking solace with the clutch of mistresses he would have stashed in various suburbs.

If he could only figure out what she wanted then maybe he could straighten things out, get them back on track. Another brandy didn't help, so he paid the bill.

'Quite a walk you had.' Carolyn was waiting for him in the doorway.

'What are you doing up?'

She closed the door without bolting it. 'You had a phone call, the Westchester police. Your free spirit boss has been at it again. This time he wrapped himself and his car round a light pole.'

'Is he hurt?'

'Drunks don't get hurt – it's the others who do.'

Funny how he'd been thinking of Garrott. 'His car?' he said. 'But they took away his licence the last time.'

'That's only part of the problem. He happens to be stinking drunk and told the cops what he really thought of them.' She leaned towards him. 'You've been drinking, too, and you're stinking if not drunk. Can't you find a drink that doesn't smell so awful?'

He knew better than try to explain. 'What do the police want?'

'What do you think? For you to come, bail him out and get him home.'

'But you'll need the car tomorrow.'

'Of course. But I can work something out. I'll call Janice or mother or somebody. You might as well stay in Garrott's guest room again. You can go on to the office in the morning. I've packed a bag for you.'

Driving along the quiet parkway, King was still feeling good about her thoughtful gesture in having his bag ready. It wasn't until he crossed the line into New York he remembered it was Wednesday night. Now, because of the restraints placed on their sex life by Carolyn's gynaecologist, he would have to wait until Sunday before he could sleep with her. He wondered if she had even thought of it.

In May 1959, King spent three days fishing off Cabo San Lucas, the vacation trip justified by testing a new depth-finder developed by a Houston-based Maxim subsidiary. On the second morning, the captain neglected to switch on the ship-to-shore phone and it was the following day before King learned his father-in-law had died from a coronary twenty-four hours previously. Although he came straight from the airport, he was late for the funeral and joined the cortège at the cemetery. That did not please Carolyn.

Two weeks later, the family foregathered in the Crowley living room at Darien to watch the lawyer open and read the will. Surprised that such scenes were enacted outside of murder mysteries and movies, King suggested withdrawing since he was not a blood relative. His wife insisted it was his place to stay. From the proud note in her voice, she wanted him to witness at first hand the disposition of the fortune.

To King's surprise, after the short reading she quickly made excuses, saying they had to return on account of the twins. He knew the housekeeper could easily handle the children, but kept quiet. On the drive back, Carolyn sat mute. Once home, she instructed the housekeeper to feed the twins and put them to bed early. King heard ice clinking in the cocktail pitcher, the signal to join his wife in the new den off the living room.

Carolyn sat in a large chair, head back, shoes off, feet splayed on a hassock. She pressed the chilled martini glass against her forehead.

'Headache?'

She said nothing and was staring at nothing, so he ventured, 'Tough afternoon, but I thought your mother looked well, considering.'

Her silence set him shrugging and he reached across her outstretched legs to retrieve the dripping pitcher and fill his glass. Judging by the gin she had poured, he realized this was no two-martini cocktail hour. He gave her time to break her silence. The television was on, its sound muted, so he lipread Cronkite and sipped his drink.

Carolyn drained her glass and, after several minutes, started to speak then suddenly stopped on the first word as though she had a mental block. She looked at the muted newscast until it ended and the commercials came on. She spoke in a low, toneless voice. 'I never dreamed, I simply never dreamed this could happen. I didn't think he had left a fortune, like some DuPont or Rockefeller, but I never thought it would be nothing.'

King shook his head, incredulously. 'Carolyn,' he murmured, 'you can hardly call quarter of a million dollars nothing.'

She turned and shot him such a filthy look he was startled. 'Mother will live for at least ten years,' she said in that cold, even tone, 'and if you don't think she can spend twenty-five thousand dollars a year without half-trying you haven't been very observant. By the time she's gone there won't be a penny.'

He had expected some disappointment about the size of the estate, but those bitter words and their sound and the hostility in her attitude stunned him.

He tried reason. 'There's still the business, a fairly substantial asset, and the house.'

'No,' she said, positively. 'My brother will run the business into the ground. He hasn't a tenth of my

163

father's skill as a businessman. The house is mother's and it does nothing for me – at least, not now.' She poured herself another stiff martini, sat down and started again without looking at King. 'You don't understand, I wanted money. Money of my own. Now. If I couldn't have my father alive, at least I wanted money of my own.'

He had never suspected her of having such a hunger for money, but he had long ago given up trying to follow the convolutions of Carolyn's mind. What did that remark about her father really mean? Without thinking things through, he made a comment which led to an angry exchange which would haunt him for years. 'Maybe you ought to be thankful your father left as much as he did,' he said.

'What!' She barked the word then turned so quickly she spilled drink into her lap, upsetting her even more. 'What the hell do you mean by that?'

'What I mean is this' – he spoke slowly and evenly – 'if you want to talk about money and the worth of the company, your brother may well do better with the business than your father.'

'That's a crass thing to say.'

'No, Carolyn.' King felt his control going. 'I know what I'm talking about.'

'How could you?' she said, derisively, the gin slurring her voice.

'I know, because before I met you for the second time, I made a study of your father's company, and it was apparent it wasn't well run. Maxim was interested in acquiring New England Industries but backed off on my recommendation. Too many problems.' He swallowed the last of his martini before continuing. 'Your father was a wonderful man, Carolyn, and I'll always

164

remember how nice he was to me, but he was not a good businessman. My father once said . . .'

'Your father!' She was now yelling wildly, and loud enough for the housekeeper to hear. 'Your father! What in the world could that cowboy tinkerer know about the business world my father lived in?'

King felt his hand almost crushing the martini glass. Whatever reserve he had vanished. 'Your father lacked the necessary skills to operate successfully. He hired the wrong people and turnover was high, his inventories were out of control and overstated. When he got into trouble, he ran to the banks. He never cut loose a division in the red. If he hadn't inherited a good company he'd have been working for somebody else, and probably happier and still alive.' To his embarrassment, King realized he was brandishing his empty martini glass at his wife.

Carolyn had not moved an inch. She sat, frozen in the same position as though his shouting had not affected her. Then King noticed that gunmetal look in her eyes. Again, in that same low and awful tone, she said, 'Get out of here, you miserable prick. Get out, you asshole, son of a bitch.'

Knowing counter-attack was useless, he went into the kitchen and was relieved to see the housekeeper had gone. He hoped she had prevented the children from witnessing that awful row. From a cabinet under the sink, he took a radio that had stopped working six months before to his basement workshop. Two hours later, he plugged it in and it worked. That provoked a smile.

Upstairs, the TV was still flickering in the quiet den. Carolyn was asleep on the couch, her skirt drawn up to expose her thin but shapely legs. He took a light blanket from the corner closet and draped it over her, carefully. He snapped off the TV set and went up to sleep in the guest bedroom.

4

Maxim Industries Eastern Division took up the sixtieth floor of a huge skyscraper near Times Square in mid-town Manhattan. On 30 June, 1960, when King arrived at the late hour of ten – delayed by a dental appointment – he ran into something like an electric charge as he hurried through the glass-fronted lobby. Small knots of people had gathered at unlikely spots with heads together and voices lowered. Ten minutes later, his secretary buzzed to say Garrott wanted to see him. He stopped by her desk.

'Sue, I almost got electrocuted by all that static when I came in. Any idea what's going on?'

She grinned, pertly. 'It reminds me of the day Mr Oster forgot he'd sent his pants to the cleaners and walked into the typing pool. The place is buzzing.'

King laughed, already discounting what she was going to say. 'Remember what I told you about rumours, Sue?'

She flashed him her best Georgia smile. 'I certainly do, but this is big stuff.'

'Okay, give.' He moved closer, head lowered.

'Mr Garrott's gonna resign, or he's gonna get fired, one of the two.'

'Hold it a minute.' His voice had risen above the conspiratorial whisper. 'Rumours are one thing, but that's out of order. Sue, I can guarantee Andrew Garrott is not about to be fired, and I'd know if he were thinking

f resigning. Lord, he can't be resigning, he's only fifty-
ix.'

'He's that old!' she said in mock alarm. 'You'd sure
ever know it from the way he, ehh, looks, would you
ow?'

'You're terrible. If you weren't such a great secretary
ou'd be in danger of losing your job.' But he laughed
s he uttered the threat. 'Do you talk that way about
veryone, or just the boss?'

She straightened her glasses and smiled at him. 'Oh,
ositively everybody. You should hear what we say
bout you.'

With his hands over his ears, he headed for Garrott's
ffice. People were still huddling together; the rumour
ill still functioned.

'Kurt.' Garrott boomed the greeting, a hand over the
hone mouthpiece. He motioned King to a chair and
aised his coffee cup in an offering gesture, but King
hook his head. After a second or two, Garrott hung up
nd swivelled to look at the younger man. 'Well, how
oes the song, "The hills are alive with the sound of
umours"?'

'Andy, you've really got them going this morning.'
King decided to be blunt. 'What's all this shit about
etirement, or resignation, or whatever?'

'Ha! ha! is that the latest version? I'm surprised they
ren't saying I'm getting canned.'

King did not respond.

'Last night I called for an emergency board meeting,
nd once the telegrams had gone out the grape-vine
tarted transmitting. Look, I wanted to see you earlier,
ut you had that appointment. By the way, you've got
 smile like a goddamn model. What do you go to the
entist for, insurance?'

King laughed. 'Actually, he said my teeth are fine but my gums will have to come out.'

Now it was Garrott's turn to smile. '1940 Bob Hope. Old joke, but not bad. Okay, so the board members are due any minute now, but I wanted to talk to you first. Kurt, I'm going to have to ask you for your promise you'll never tell anyone – anyone – what I'm about to say.'

'You have it.'

'Thanks.' Garrott nodded his appreciation. 'I'm asking the board for a leave of absence . . . six months . . . medical reasons. You've met Bill Walsh, my doctor. He's prepared a medical report that's a perfect cover and the board will probably go along without question or suspicion. But you and I have been down too many roads together for me to try to con you.' He had been staring directly at King, but suddenly spun round to gaze out of the window. 'Funny, how tough it is to get it out,' he muttered. He swivelled back, jotted something on a piece of paper and handed it to King. 'That's where I'm going.'

King drew in his breath, involuntarily, at the two scrawled words, Silver Hill. It was the best private sanatorium on the East Coast and, among other things, specialized in drying out alcoholics. Ironically, it was in New Canaan.

'I'm going to take the cure, Kurt. If I go on boozing like this, my insides and my liver will give out. But, for obvious reasons I'm not telling the board. Once I've got it licked I'll be back and we'll give the competition hell as usual. But it's going to be rough going and, well, I was kind of hoping you might drop by once in a while when I get to the stage where they let people see me.'

King nodded, not ready to trust his voice. Garrott

ose, slowly, his shoulders sagging. For once he looked
his age. But he straightened up, flicked some unseen
dirt from his sleeve, and smiled. King was wondering
who the board would bring in to run the Eastern Group,
Maxim's largest, in the absence of Garrott's one-man
show. Garrott cut across his speculation.

'There's one more thing I'm putting to the board,
Kurt, something I'm equally confident they'll approve.'

'What's that, Andy?'

'I'm asking them to name you acting president of the
Eastern Group.'

5

His promotion brought the same reaction from Carolyn
as did all the other aspects of their marriage: polite
indifference. She was merely pleased. Not proud, not
happy for his sake. But she did sound genuinely understanding about his having to postpone his vacation. He
realized, of course, that she, the twins and her mother
would have to leave as planned, next day, for the Jersey
shore where King had rented a cottage for July and
August. He promised to join them for a weekend as
soon as possible. A hollow promise, since he and she
knew his weekends would be given over to work
throughout the summer.

To his vast surprise, he saw his twins, Randy and
Sandy, were actually disappointed that he was staying
behind. He felt guilty about spending so little time with
them. As the car pulled out of the driveway, he waved
and the two small faces pressed against the window as
they waved back. Alone, he mixed a weak drink and

took it into the den where he had a whole weekend's work spread over his desk.

The Fourth of July fell on a Thursday, and he was mildly angry at the interruption of his working week. On the following Saturday, he and his secretary were still in his old office at four o'clock when a call arrived on his private line. His secretary answered. Her voice became more and more friendly as she talked, then she said, astonished, 'It is! Why that sly old hound-dog never said a word to anyone. Imagine that, Mr King is thirty years old!' She beamed at her boss, holding the phone out to him. 'It's a friend of yours, a Mr Poole. He sounds real nice.' She drawled the last word to show how he had impressed her.

King laughed. 'Wait till you see him. He's a regular Paul Newman.'

Sue rolled her eyes then surprised King by licking her lips in feigned sexuality. How odd he had seen Sue Anne Marshall almost every day for more than two years and had not noticed she was as sexy as she was pretty.

'Ron! This is great. Where are you?' He noticed Sue was trying too hard to look as if she were oblivious of his conversation. As he replaced the instrument, he smiled at her. 'Ron Poole is quite a guy,' he said.

'Happy Birthday, Mr King,' she said with warmth. 'I wish you'd let us know and we'd have planned some kind of celebration.'

Hesitating for a moment, King said, 'I, ah, think we might have one after all. Ron's meeting me for a late birthday drink and dinner. And he insisted you come along, if you'd like to. You certainly don't have to if you don't want to, or if you have other plans.' He was

170

beginning to feel a little foolish. It took him a minute to decipher her questioning look. 'It's okay, Poole's single. He's one of the last great independents.'

She brightened. 'What does he do?'

'He's a financial consultant and analyst who specializes in corporate problems, deals, mergers and the like.' She had him elaborate. One reason he liked her work was that she asked questions and did not pretend to understand as other secretaries did. So, she made few errors.

'Some financial consultants help companies put deals together and find the money, much as investment bankers do, but Ron Poole can evaluate the entire deal rather than merely find the financial backing. Consequently, he puts his reputation on the line each time. His judgement's excellent and his batting average phenomenal.'

'Sounds like the kind of help we could have used on the Stokely antenna deal last year.'

'You're so right,' King said. 'I tried to get Andy to hire Ron on a couple of occasions, but he said he was too young. He's my age. Well, I guess I can hire him myself now.'

'That's right, you're calling the shots now.'

Forty-five minutes later they were in a booth at '21' whose *maître d'hôtel* had already heard of King's promotion and found them a privileged seat. Ron winked at Sue Anne, who sat between them, and before King could order he had sent the waiter for a bottle of champagne. 'I don't care how expensive it is as long as it's from California,' he told the puzzled man.

The first sip was faintly acrid, but King was pleased with the wine which went down easily and began to loosen him up. He looked at Ron, who was wearing a

171

neat, grey suit with a faint plaid design that set off the deep maroon of his knitted tie. His face still bore faint touches of his boyhood skin problems, but he looked rugged. King could see Sue Anne approved of him. They were talking easily, then she suddenly stopped and looked at them both.

'Oh, mercy Miss Mary, I forgot all about Helen.'

'Helen?' said the two men.

'Here am I drinking champagne and having the best time, and my friend, Helen, is sitting in her apartment waiting for me to call her. I'm supposed to have dinner with her tonight, and I forgot all about it. Excuse me, I'll be right back.' As she got up, King wondered if it was his imagination or if she had pulled in her back and pushed out her already ample chest for Ron's benefit.

'Hold it a second.' Ron reached for her hand and stopped her. 'Why not ask Helen to meet us here? There's plenty more champagne.' He cast a glance at King but gave him no time to intervene. 'Tell her she doesn't have a thing to worry about. Old King is totally harmless. Don't tell her he's actually over thirty – that might scare her off.'

Sue Anne hesitated, but when King did nothing more than look mildly embarrassed, she said, 'Great, I'll do that,' and went off to phone, smiling at the thought of inviting her friend. Sue did not care for Carolyn King, who treated her so condescendingly.

Helen Bader came from Minnesota which made small talk easy for King since his parents had been raised there. Attractive in a quiet way, she also had a rather subdued personality which made her the perfect foil for the outgoing Sue Anne. She had strong features and waveless, dark-blond hair that stopped at her shoulders. Her gaze was direct and her laugh solid and genuine and more frequent after the first glass of champagne. King noted, too, she was quietly self-possessed and neither flirtatious nor prying. She heard Sue Anne talk about Mrs King without surprise. While Helen and Ron had a brief but lively discussion about her job as a computer programmer, King caught Sue Anne smiling at him.

'Your friend's real nice, Mr King,' she whispered.

'Thanks, so's yours.'

Emboldened by the champagne, Sue Anne said, 'You don't step out on your wife, do you, Mr K?'

King had also drunk enough to take her question in his stride. 'No, I don't and never have.'

She fixed him with a long, frank look. 'It's nice to hear a man say that. But I can't help wondering, and forgive my cheek, if you have enough fun.'

He could see her big, dark eyes peering at him over her champagne glass. 'Fun? Jesus, I haven't really thought about it in such simple terms in a long time. I have fun doing what I do.' Unwittingly, he had raised his voice, drawing the attention of Ron and Helen. 'I'm serious, it gives me a lift to create a change – whether it's adding a new product or acquiring an entire company – and seeing it turn out the way I had envisioned a long time back.' Suddenly, he realized the other three were watching him intently. Although he felt a bit foolish, he was determined to make his point. 'We bought that New Hampshire can company two years ago when it was going to be shut down by the conglomerate owning it. I spent a week studying the deal and advised buying because we could manage it better than the seller. Last year it broke even and this year it turned a profit for the first time in a decade. But the real good part, the fun part, was that we saved over four hundred

173

jobs and the economy of a little town up there in the hills. When I went up there this spring, the union boss picked me up at the airport, and that doesn't happen often. And, damn it, that's fun.'

He stopped, aware he had been rhapsodizing about Maxim in the way he might have talked about a girl-friend. A change of some sort had come over Helen Bader's eyes as she looked at him, but he could not decode it.

'Hey Kurt, old buddy,' said Ron, fondly, 'that's real nice, but it's the last time I want to hear anything about business this evening. We have a nice fun-loving, hard-drinking group right here, and I don't want to spoil it. Now, Helen tells me that she and this little Georgia Peach were planning to go to some Dago restaurant in the Village for dinner.'

'Why don't we all stay here?' King suggested, sud-denly feeling expansive, 'and it'll be my treat.'

'No,' said Helen with surprising firmness. 'You can't treat, it's your birthday celebration.'

'What about this idea?' Sue Anne interrupted. 'Why don't we all go to the restaurant where Helen and I were going anyway? The food's terrific and it's a family place. They don't even have a booze licence.'

'Hold it, no booze, no dice.' Ron was laughing.

'You go around the corner and buy your booze and take it with you. Come on, let's go there. It's really fun.' She caressed the last word, looking at King and laughing.

As they rode to the restaurant, squeezed tightly together in the cab, King realized a line had been crossed and it was too late for him this evening to think about his formal relationship with Sue Anne. He was gratified to discover he did not give a damn.

174

Dinner was an athletic affair with much knocking of elbows around the small table and passing of plates so that they could all sample the four different dishes they had all carefully ordered. Learning it was King's birthday dinner, the proprietress dug through her stack of phonograph albums until she unearthed what Poole had secretly told her was his friend's favourite record – Mario Lanza's songs from *The Student Prince*. When the record came on, Poole was really worried that King was going to burst into tears.

When the wine in the gallon jug of Chianti had gone, they all felt mellow. They lit cigarettes and Helen mentioned she would like some coffee and asked if anyone else would, too.

'Coffee!' Ron repeated, incredulous.

'He's right,' said Sue Anne, who was holding hands with Ron under the table. 'If we have coffee, we'll lose our, our . . .' She searched for the word then said, 'I've got it, our buzz.' She leaned over towards Ron. 'That's the word, isn't it, sugar?' she said in her Georgia drawl.

'If you say so, honey.' Ron was grinning. King knew that grin well, having seen it so often on other occasions when they had both had one drink too many. He felt himself beginning to slip back into a tunnel of memories long suppressed. Ron's voice snapped him out of it.

'Hey, birthday boy, where's this place you said you'd take us after dinner?'

As the small nightclub was also in the Village, they walked. In the smoky atmosphere, they drank some more and watched the floor show. They saw everything and everyone through an alcoholic haze; the mediocre comedian was great, and their own repartee sounded brighter and funnier with each drink.

When the small dance band took over, Ron and Sue

175

Anne were the first couple on the floor. King hesitated, unsure of the propriety of dancing. Then his hand accidentally brushed Helen's. With an urgent movement, she grasped it and brought it under the table and against the inside of her soft thigh. Something like an electric shock went through King at the warmth of her.

Soon they, too, were on the dance floor. King knew it would only be a matter of seconds before Helen became aware of his erection. When it happened and when he felt his penis press against the yielding flesh of her thigh under the light clothing, Helen gave a shudder and pulled herself closer to him. When the music stopped they broke apart reluctantly, but another slow tune brought them together again. King gave in to the pleasure of the moment. It had been a terribly long time since he had felt this way.

There was a napkin over King's glass when they got back to their table. He recognized Ron's scrawled handwriting. 'Happy Birthday, Kurt. We've split. See you in church. Ron.'

King tried to pay the bill but found Ron had taken care of it and the tip. He and Helen walked a bit unsteadily out of the club arm in arm. An empty cab waited at the kerb. In the darkness of the back seat, he kissed Helen and she responded. When he tried again, she whispered, 'Wait, it won't be long.' He sat quietly, his arm cradling her, breathing heavily with pleasure at the sensations that ran up and down his leg as Helen softly stroked it. Each time she brought her warm fingers closer to the bulge in his crotch. And each time, as she stopped just short, she would laugh softly. When the driver pulled up at her building, he asked if he should wait. 'No,' Helen said, firmly.

He could hardly wait to get into her apartment. As

176

soon as she had shut the door, he wrapped his arms round her and crushed her to him. Her mouth felt full and warm and her tongue began to play with his, rousing them both. Still standing, they stripped one another gently in alternate moves. Helen could not wait, either. 'Leave my stockings,' she said, thickly, and peeled off her panties. 'Hurry,' she urged, her voice husky with desire.

Her breasts were firm and he bent his head to kiss them. But she was already wrapping her legs around his and grasping him by the shoulders. 'Hurry,' she breathed again. He wasted no more time but put both hands under her buttocks and raised her up towards him.

Helen opened her legs wide to let him enter her then tightened herself around him, using her legs as a vice and starting to rock back and forward on him. He knew, as soon as she began to thrust, he would come within seconds. He tried to tell her this, but she knew. Her face burned against his naked shoulder. She called out, 'No, don't stop, go ahead, we'll go slow the second time.' He started to move in time with her and they both groaned with the wondrous feeling as they reached their climax together.

When the dawn light woke him, it took a moment for things to fall into their place in his mind. He saw the sleeping form next to him. How peaceful and quiet she looks now, he thought, his mind lit by the sudden and vivid memory of their coupling. Helen had been right, they had taken each other more slowly the second time, in the middle of her living-room floor. Then, to her amazement, when they slipped into bed King had turned to her again, proving how hungry he was for love. And that third time they almost frightened each other with the animal passion that seized them both.

King left her a note telling her how much he had enjoyed himself, feeling rather foolish as he penned the words. He promised to call later in the day. She was still asleep when he let himself out.

He had a headache, a hangover. But oddly, he felt relaxed and at peace with himself. There were no cabs in sight so he took the subway to Penn Station. He leaned back, stretched his legs and closed his eyes. He knew he should feel guilty, but as he dozed off he could not stop smiling.

VI

he Silvermine Tavern on the Silvermine River is not
r from the famous Silvermine School of Art; the
estaurant is also near Silver Hill, where, on a sunny
fternoon in the fall of 1960, King picked up Andy
arrott for lunch. They sat on the deck overlooking the
ver and Andy ordered a ginger ale. When King placed
e same order, Garrott scowled and growled at him.

'Jesus Christ, Kurt, order a drink. At least, order a
eer. How the hell am I going to get used to seeing
ther people drinking if they all have soda pop like me,
st to spare my feelings?'

'Okay, okay, point taken.' King asked the waitress
or a Budweiser.

'Well, what's the picture? Has the place fallen asun-
er without the golden boy?'

It was Garrott's first question on every visit and it
aised King's smile. 'Yeah, I'm sorry. The stock's plung-
g and four directors quit last week and Miss Appleton
the library is pregnant. And that's just the good
ews. Seriously, Andy, tell me about yourself first. You
ok like a million dollars.'

King was not exaggerating. Garrott looked fit and
nprobably youthful for a man in his fifties. He had a
eep tan, heightened by his yellow blazer and white
aCoste shirt. His eyes were bright, alert. They were
eated at a large table and Garrott had his legs stretched
ut in front of him. King had never seen him looking
ealthier or more relaxed.

179

Garrott kept the soft drink cupped in both hands and took rare sips. He had never opened his mind about the drying-out process but King had the impression on previous visits it had been tough but Garrott had followed doctor's orders in the alcoholics' wing.

'I haven't felt this good in twenty-nine years, Kurt, maybe more. My only regret is I didn't sign in here sooner. Pardon my saying it, but you look as if you could use some sun. Haven't you been taking any time off?'

'Sure, but not until fairly recently, and then the family was back from the shore. I'm starting to play golf again on Sunday, but don't ask about my scores.'

'Well, how's Carolyn and, hmm, everything at home?'

'Maybe you'd better ask about my scores after all. Shit, it's okay at home, but nothing great. Do you know what I mean?'

Garrott shook his well-barbered head. 'Unfortunately, yes, if memory serves.'

'It's funny the little things that get all blown out of proportion. Carolyn and I were talking about the election next month, and I said that, even though I find Nixon pretty stiff, I'd probably vote for him anyway because I've always voted Republican. Then I said, half-kidding, "Besides, Nixon's from California." Well, she didn't like that and started touting Jack Kennedy whom she'd never mentioned before, and said she might just vote for him.' King paused to shake his head at the recollection of the scene. 'And then I said, still not really serious, "Don't let Maxim's board members hear about that." Well, that set her off, and we had a hell of an argument. The upshot was she went downtown the next morning and volunteered to work for the Kennedy

mpaign.' A small groan reached King from the other
de of the table. He went on, 'Fortunately, she only
sted a day and a half. Seems the Kennedy people
ere too down-to-earth for her, especially their lan-
uage. I don't know what she'll do when Nixon wins.'

'You mean, *if* he wins.'

'Come off it, Andy. Kennedy hasn't a hope. Who's
oing to put an Irish Catholic in the White House?'

'Kurt, the polls are showing him ahead.'

King shook his head and took a pull on his beer. He
oked and sounded tired. 'Andy, I have to confess I've
ead nothing outside the business pages since you came
ere.'

Garrott looked at his soft drink, grimaced and took a
p. 'Which brings us rather neatly back to the first
uestion. How're things at the office?'

King hesitated, groping for time to make his
esponse. At that moment, the waitress brought their
od and he quipped that this wasn't a working lunch,
ey'd wait until they had eaten. With coffee before
em he could no longer avoid the issue. 'Well, I found
ings were, eh, pretty messed up. And now I'm into
e figures, I can see we have serious problems! It's not
omething new, Andy, it's been in the picture for quite
ome time. But I'm sure that doesn't surprise you.'

Garrott had been lounging on his chair, but now he
at up straight. He gazed at King for a long moment
en sighed. 'I thought it would take you a little longer,'
e murmured. 'What are the problems as you see them?
Come on, let me have it straight.'

'Poor management, for one.'

'Ouch! You don't make it easy on a guy, do you?'

'Andy, I'm not saying it's all your fault. There are a
ot of Save-Your-Ass memos in the files from top guys.

181

Sometimes I think there's been more time spent writing memos back and forth than anything else these last couple of years.'

'Thanks for trying to protect me, Kurt, but I was the one who let things get out of hand. But go on, be more specific.'

'Well, not only is production down, but no one seems to have done anything to find out why. And the customers are getting nervous, especially the big ones. There hasn't been a decent idea out of product development in at least two years, and in my opinion, we ought to fire everyone responsible for quality control, and . . .'

Garrott waved him down. 'Okay, okay, that's enough. Jesus, you do go on. Shit, I was certain a couple of those things were about to turn around. But to level with you in confidence, Kurt, my judgement has been clouded for a long time. Now, being off the hard stuff, I can see I really let things slide.' He managed a weak grin. 'You can only dazzle them with fancy footwork for so long before they catch on. So, what are your suggestions?'

They emptied the coffee pot, talking over the problems and King's solutions. Garrott would nod or shake his head then make his own suggestions with which King filled the backs of two menus. When the clock struck four and they realized the Silvermine was empty, King looked at Garrott apprehensively. 'Hey, they'll have my hide for getting you back this late,' he said, making to rise. 'We can elaborate on some of these ideas next month, and then it'll only be another month before you're back.'

Garrott was an energetic man who did everything quickly; but King noticed his deliberate way of taking

ut a cigarette, tapping it against his lighter then light-
ng it, all in slow motion. He looked over the river,
lowing the smoke carefully away from them then
urned to King. 'The thing is, Kurt, I'm not coming
ack.'

King felt his stomach muscles knot. 'Andy, what are
ou saying?'

Garrott beamed at the effect of his statement on his
ompanion. 'I sent the chairman of the board a telegram
his morning. My resignation is effective from Monday
norning. I'm not pleased, Kurt, having to do it this way
ince I've left a mess for somebody else to clean up. But
ve learned something at Silver Hill and that's the
elationship between pressure of work and my need to
rink. If I try to turn Maxim round with all the pressure
hat involves I'm not sure I can fight off the booze. So,
or once I'm choosing the wise course and Marie is
ehind me one hundred per cent.' He sipped his coffee
regs and called for the bill. 'That is, she says, as long
s I take the pledge about all my previous vices, too.'
He gave a boyish grin.

King smiled, beginning to accept the startling news.
But what are you going to do? You're much too young
o retire.'

'I appreciate that, Kurt, even if it's true. We're plan-
ing to move out to the farm in Bucks County and live
ke rich people for a while. If it takes, we'll sell the
carsdale house. I've a bit of money, I'll do a little
onsulting work now and then and try my green finger
n the stock market which I've always wanted to do.
ife will be different, but better, I think.'

King could only shake his head which had a thousand
hings going through it, but nothing came out.

Almost as though it were an afterthought, Garrott

murmured, 'One more point, Kurt, I've recommended you get the job for real, no more "acting" crap.'

Tongue-tied for a moment, King finally got out, 'You're serious, aren't you?'

'Yup, and I already know off the record the board will agree. One or two members will bitch about your age, but they did the same when they hired me. There'll be no problem with the majority. So, let me be the first to congratulate you.'

King remained in a mild state of shock during the ride back to Silver Hill. Andy Garrott got out of the car, shook hands and walked away, whistling.

When King walked in the door, he heard the rattle of icetrays from the kitchen. Carolyn was standing there mixing gin and tonics in a pitcher. 'Hi. This's the last batch of the season. We'll have to switch back to martinis soon. How was Andy?' She smiled at him, a pleasant reception by recent standards.

'He looked and sounded just terrific. Know what he told me?'

'Oh, excuse me,' she butted in. 'You had several calls. I wrote them down. They're in the other room on your desk. All except for one who wouldn't leave her number.'

'Her?'

'A Miss Bader, or Baker, I'm not sure which. Who's she, Kurt?'

Was that question casual, or loaded? He played it back, trying to detect more than simple curiosity. Those blue eyes were scanning his face. Keeping his voice level, he said, 'That would be Helen Bader, a friend of my former secretary's. Maybe she wants a job.'

'Odd she should call you at home.' Carolyn went on

arranging the pitcher and glasses on a patterned plastic tray.

'Yes, it is a bit. But then it's been an odd day all round. Why don't you bring those drinks into the living room. It's chilly on the patio – and I've got something to tell you.'

2

Everything worked out as Andrew Garrott had predicted and Maxim's board voted unanimously to elect him president. Their confidence flattered him, but still left him shaken by the mammoth challenge of turning the company around. During the first months he had time for nothing but work, cutting everything out except social activities related to his business. Carolyn groused, though she seemed pleased when her friends called to say they had seen the notice of her husband's promotion in the *New York Times*. Fortunately, his work acted as a tonic and even his normal sixteen-hour day did not tire him unduly. During the week before Christmas, he did take time off to deal with a problem that had been bothering him for weeks.

At first, Helen Bader was cold, distant over the phone, but after some fencing she agreed to meet him on the library steps at 42nd and Fifth Avenue. Even though he made a stop on the way, she was late and he kicked his heels impatiently among the Christmas shoppers until he finally spotted her hurrying towards him. She wore a storm coat with a light fur collar and a bright red knitted cap with a matching scarf. He was relieved the sight of her did not knock him off his stride emotionally.

In a small, snug bar off Fifth Avenue, they laughed

as they peeled off gloves, scarves and hats. 'Well, well, Mr King, it's so nice to see you again,' she said, teasingly.

Since July, he had seen her only three times, the last over a month ago; yet, she had been on his mind more than he cared to admit. Each time had begun with a quiet dinner and drinks in an out-of-the-way restaurant downtown and ended with an ardent physical session in Helen's big bed. With his wife no longer on vacation, King could not spend the night, but his growing sexual urge, which plagued him for days after their love-making, told him he would not be satisfied for long with the present casual arrangement. He had thought the whole thing through and concluded he must break off the affair before it went beyond control.

During their first drink, he tried vainly to unload the speech he had rehearsed. It stuck in his throat. Helen looked vibrant, and he found himself thinking of her musky warmth, the aura of spent passion that gripped him as they stayed in each other's arms afterwards. Be careful, he warned himself.

'Kurt,' she said, none too gently, after refusing a second drink, 'why don't you come out with it? It's written all over your face. You want to stop seeing me, don't you?' Embarrassed that he had let her make the running, he nodded but said nothing. 'Oh, don't look so crestfallen. It's not as if you're saying goodbye to your mistress, now, is it?' Her voice had developed a new edge.

'Please don't use that word.'

Tilting her head back, she smiled at him. 'It would have come to that, and at least that would have been my preference. The only problem is you're so straight, which is really too bad, because you're great when you finally decide to let go.'

Ill-equipped to handle this line of conversation, King reached into a pocket and produced a long, thin package, gift-wrapped in tinselled silver. He set it in front of her. Helen's expression did not change. She removed the wrapping without a word, but when she saw the name of the jewellery store she stopped. With her fingers poised to open the box, she said in a softer tone, 'Whatever this is, you didn't have to do it, you know.'

'I know.'

She took out the gift, wide-eyed. 'Christ, darling, it's beautiful. I've never ever seen one of these outside a *New Yorker* ad. It's a Patek Philippe isn't it. Oh, Kurt, I'm stunned.' She looked at him, her eyes scanning his face. 'I should say, "How can I ever thank you for this?" but that sounds like a cheap movie.' She leaned forward and took his hand and began to caress the palm in a way she knew excited him. He drew back.

'Helen, I'm sorry but it won't work.'

Her expression changed to bittersweet. 'Oh, Kurt, I almost wish you were more like the others, and yet I don't.' Abruptly, she smiled, slipped on the watch and held it closer to the dim booth lamp, admiring its slim elegance. She nodded when the waiter appeared. 'One for old times' sake or for the road. But just one.'

King smiled too. That ordeal behind him, he relaxed and lit a cigarette. Helen swallowed some of her bourbon and ginger and said, 'Are you ever going to leave her?'

King was taken aback by the question. 'Jesus, Helen, I guess I don't know.' Then, as if he could not stop himself, the words tumbled out. 'It's not as though mine's the worst marriage in the world. I see guys

187

who're having it a helluva lot tougher and I can't think my picture is hopeless. Anyway, how many couples do you know who're as happy as when they first got married?'

Helen smiled thinly. 'The old give-it-one-more-chance, uh? Well, I don't know whether to wish you luck or not. The married men I've known have always said they hated their wives and, to your credit, you never said that. Maybe there's a chance for your marriage, but really' – her look hardened – 'this is not my favourite topic.' She lit a cigarette, held up her arm again to gaze at the watch and sighed happily.

Later, King despaired of getting a cab and walked back to his office, cursing the wind. 'The married men I've known' – that flat-toned phrase of Helen's had stuck in one of his mental grooves. He pulled up his coat collar and pulled down the brim of his stylish hat. He had never felt colder.

3

King's first move as president was to put through a call to Chip Boyd in California. Without bandying words, he said, 'Chip, how would you like to come back to work for Maxim as vice-president reporting directly to me and at twice your old salary?'

'You're not kidding me, Kurt.'

'Like hell I'm not. I've got one bitch of a job here and I need you and that financial brain of yours. I'm in Chicago the day after tomorrow. Meet me for dinner at the Drake and I'll give you a better idea of the whole thing and pick up the tab for your fare and expenses. Don't say No until you hear me out in person, Chip.'

When Chip Boyd said Yes, King's next move was to

postpone the monthly board meeting for two weeks to get a better idea of how to put Maxim back on the track.

When the meeting took place, King was ready. Normally, these gatherings followed a relaxed parliamentary agenda, and it took only a few minutes to approve the minutes and dispose of old business. That routine settled, King addressed the board. He noticed several poised pencils and guessed why. Alvin Schuster, Maxim's venerable chairman, was in hospital recovering from an operation and his closest associates were taking notes to report the meeting to him. What the hell! King thought. They can tape me if they like.

'Gentlemen, my voice is a bit quavery, for two reasons: I don't have much experience of addressing you; and two, I'm sure you're going to hate what I have to say.'

That straightened the heads and created a small epidemic of coughing. Several coffee cups were tabled with a clatter. And William Graham Jevons, a senior director, began to beat a tattoo with his fingernails on the table.

'No amount of sugar-coating is going to hide for long the plain fact Maxim is in trouble, deep trouble. I have spent every waking minute of the last two weeks checking if my negative evaluation of our present situation is accurate. It is, and I wish it were otherwise.'

He noted the distressed expression in the eyes of Fred Bradley, a banker who also happened to be a close friend of Andy Garrott.

'Gentlemen, in case you think I'm slurring my predecessor, when I have finished I shall hand out a letter from Andy explaining why, as one of his last official acts as president, he instructed me to open this meeting with the statement I have just made. That on the record,

189

I'll proceed. You have every right to demand that I back up what I'll say, and in spades.

'As you will know, our most important products are those used in TV set manufacture and the "flagship of the fleet" is our TV tuner. I'm sure, like me, whenever you see a TV set, you look closely to check it's the kind using our tuner.'

That raised a few chuckles and nods around the table.

'When we first brought out our tuner it was so good that in a relatively short time we led the league. Well, we let our early success lapse into complacency. For years we have literally coasted on our lead to the point where we have become fat, dumb and happy.' He wondered if these hard colloquialisms were bothering anyone, but no, he had everybody's attention.

'Now happiness doesn't worry me, but being fat and dumb does. Let me sketch the picture with more specificity.' He rolled out all five syllables of the word, slowly. 'Because of the huge sales volume generated mainly by our tuner in the early TV years, we added personnel at a startling rate and expanded. That was fine – if we had enough new business to keep the plants loaded. Well, we passed that point a couple of years ago.'

'We're still making a profit,' Jevons called from the end of the long table.

'We were, until this year,' King corrected, welcoming the challenge, then tapping the pile of folders in front of him. 'These reports will show we'll have to pass our dividend at year's end if we don't put things right. We'll just about break even.'

At this, everybody sat up and directors looked at each other, incredulous. King drove home his message. 'Gentlemen, we've become top-heavy with admin ypes, people who push paper around most of their ay. Our files are massive monuments to the memo nventor, and most of these memos are self-justifying. he truth is we have lost our competitive edge, but we aven't yet admitted it or tried to do something about ..'

He took a mouthful of coffee to ease his throat and ive time for remarks or comments. His hand shook on he cup, but he noticed his audience was equally nerous from the sound of shuffling papers.

'Because of this complacency and lethargy, we are ot serving our customers as we used to. Delivery romises are broken, product development is almost ead and product quality has slipped badly. Not surrisingly, customers are unhappy. I'm reliably informed wo of our biggest customers are seriously considering oing elsewhere because there are now two pretty good uners that are ten per cent cheaper, are of good quality nd are being delivered on time. That, gentlemen, is ot just a deplorable situation, but one that could break ur company if allowed to continue.'

C. H. Lavin, the chairman's closest crony, was sitting ack in his chair, stroking his chin. From his expression, e agreed with King's analysis. And he knew from arrott's frequent comments that, as Lavin went, so did he board. Yet, in spite of that flicker of support, King xperienced a flash of panic. 'What if they decided to huck me out along with all the others and come up vith a whole new team?' he thought. Too bad if they o, he told himself. He had to give them the truth as he aw it.

'Some of our line accounts are sticking with us ecause of our former reputation, but I can't say how ong they'll continue. And, I need not remind anyone that, once a tuner is out of a set, it's mighty tough to get it back in. TV manufacturers can't afford the retooling costs, catalogues, service manuals – well, you know all the problems.

'I'd like to say the bad news stops there, but you'll have already made all the right deductions. Because of the problems I've mentioned we have also suffered through our sales attitudes. We have been relying too much on social selling, wining and dining and, ah-eh, things of that sort.' King decided not to get too specific. No board member, liberal or otherwise, wanted him to place on record mention of the young women 'companions' hired to loosen up prospective buyers on their visits to the big city. Nor did he want to mention Maxim had acquired a reputation, not unfairly, of being a hard-drinking bunch. Some of them knew that already.

He poured himself a glass of water and took a sip. As he put down the glass, he looked round the faces and was encouraged by the way they looked at him and the interest they showed. He went on:

'The full extent of the picture is contained in the report that will now be given to you. I shouldn't have to add it's highly confidential, but will for safety's sake. There is also the letter from Andrew Garrott. I'd like to take the last few minutes to ask you – not for a vote of confidence, because it would be too soon for that – for permission to make some wholesale changes.'

To emphasize his words, he leaned forward with both hands on the table. 'I intend to can anyone who is not pulling his weight. I'm going to shake up every department until each one is doing what it should or we know the reason why. I almost hate to tell you this, but as businessmen I'm sure you've already figured out I'm asking for approval to spend some money. Not to throw

192

ood money after bad, but to save what has been a fine, profitable company from going under. And believe me, I wouldn't recommend the action outlined in my report unless I were convinced it can and will work. I guess what I am telling you is this – I am ready, willing and able to take some drastic measures and I want you to wish me and all of us luck. Gentlemen, in blunt terms, I am going to kick some ass.'

King sat down amid complete silence. Then someone tapped the table with the flat of his hand and several others took up the applause. At the end of a minute the whole board was standing and clapping mightily.

He felt his face grow red, and loved it.

4

A few weeks later, King was stopped at the front door of Maxim's complex by a sign, reading: AUGEAN STABLES, INC. DO NOT ENTER WITHOUT A SHOVEL. He did not have to guess twice about the author. Chip Boyd had asked a Third Avenue hobby shop to run up the sign. King laughed but took the sign down and put it on a shelf behind his desk.

However, the description was apt, for he and Boyd were doing something every hour of every day to sort out Maxim's problems. One of their first moves was to visit every major customer personally.

King knew what the customers were up against. He could count on some loyalty, but knew that no rational businessman could stay with Maxim unless it improved. Hat in hand he went to them to spell out his difficulties as the new president and assure them he would put things right. 'However,' he cautioned them, 'the improvement at first will be two steps forward and one back. But slowly and surely, Maxim will produce a better product and deliver on time.' By showing customers that someone at the very top of the company cared, he bought Maxim a great deal of much-needed time.

Bringing production back on schedule and getting orders out on time would have been relatively easy had they been the only problems King faced. But there was a serious breakdown in quality control which Chip Boyd brought to his attention in a dramatic way. He burst into King's office one afternoon with his tie askew, and dirt and grease all over his striped suit and unmatching pants.

'Chip, knowing you, I'd say your car had broken down and you tried to fix it, but you don't have a car out here. What happened?'

'I just came back from the Jersey plant and it's a goddamn pigpen. No wonder we're shipping shit. This you've got to see for yourself.'

After noting Maxim goods with obvious defects at a customer's factory, King had instructed Boyd to drop in at the Jersey plant unannounced and look round to see why his own people could not spot the faults before shipping.

'Anybody give you trouble about walking out on the line?' he asked.

Boyd shook his head. 'I flashed my business card but the supervisor didn't even read it. It's a good thing our winding equipment isn't exactly secret any more, for anyone could walk right in and copy those machines. The whole place is sloppy, Kurt.'

'Did you identify yourself before you left?'

'No, I figured why tip them off.'

'Come on, Chip, we're going over there. I want to see

his for myself. And don't look so glum, this time we'll
ake a cab.'

The ride to Hoboken across the Hudson from the
Manhattan offices took an hour. When they entered the
plant, the oldest of Maxim's three production facilities
n New Jersey, several workers watched them but said
nothing. In fact, as they hurried through the plant to
he production line, no one took any interest, no one
questioned their presence. At the end of the line, Chip
showed King tuners with bent shafts, loose tubes,
missing covers, most of them improperly jammed into
shipping cartons. Those defects were obvious. Many
more were hidden.

'Jesus Christ, this is terrible,' King said, tossing a
uner on to the packing bench in disgust.

'Hey!' boomed a voice from a doorway halfway across
he cluttered room. 'What the fuck are you doing, Mac?'
A chunky middle-aged man leaned against the door
amb of the production area office. King guessed he was
he line supervisor. Behind him, on a desk sat a pint of
whisky. 'Hey, who the fuck are you?' he shouted.

King turned and began walking rapidly towards the
man.

'Oh, oh,' Boyd murmured to himself.

'My name is . . .' King started to say, but the stocky
man interrupted him.

'I don't give a shit who you are, you got no business
ouching anything around here unless you got my
permission. I know you ain't from the main office 'cause
ain't seen one of them bigshot pricks around here in
ears. Now get the hell outa here. I'm not gonna warn
ou again.'

'Look, I'm trying to tell you . . .'

'Goddamn it, I said fuck off!' With that, the man

moved forward. He shoved quickly with both hands, catching King full in the chest and sending him sprawling backwards.

Boyd, seeing the oil patch a few feet behind his stumbling boss, closed his eyes.

At the last moment, before his foot touched the oil, King reached out and grabbed the side of a huge metal press. He regained his balance, steadied himself then moved towards the man. When he was less than a couple of feet away, the man swung, but King easily ducked the blow. Before the man could recover his balance, King pivoted quickly and drove a fist into the man's ample belly, putting all his weight behind it. A grunt came from the man and he jack-knifed forward, his mouth open, arms dropping. King hit him once more in the stomach, sinking his fist deep, and the fight was officially over. Clutching his belly, the man staggered back against the office wall, knocking over a clock which fell with a jangling crash. He leaned against the wall, his eyes half-shut.

King stepped into the doorway of the small office; he stared at the two secretaries, the whisky bottle and plastic cups, the deck of cards on the desk. Finally, he looked at the other man in the office. 'I'm Kurt King and I run this company. When your loud-mouth friend feels like talking again, have him call me at my office. I'd like to tell him personally about the changes I'm going to make around here.' He smiled. 'I'd like to have his help.'

'You mean, you're not goin' to fire him?' He sounded amazed.

'Fire him? Of course not, it wouldn't be worth the trouble. Besides, I've a hunch he's going to see things my way from now on.'

Boyd waited until they left the plant before he burst
ut laughing. 'There's a bar across the street,' he said.
'll buy you a drink, champ.'

ews of King's run-in with the supervisor spread
uickly through the other plants and established him as
 tough but regular guy. But no amount of image-
uilding or personal popularity could eliminate the
ompany's problems. And then King did something
at threatened to bring the entire firm down about
imself.

Twenty-four hours after visiting the Hoboken plant,
e conferred with the chief engineer and established an
ite corps of Production-line Cops. These workers,
ationed at the end of each assembly-line and answer-
le only to the president, rejected every part failing to
eet rigid quality standards.

The immediate result was chaos. Boxes of unshippa-
le goods piled up at the end of the line and, as
ipments slowed, customers began to scream they
eren't getting merchandise, good or bad. Maxim's
roduction people began to complain King was ruining
e company. He was spending hour after hour person-
ly rejecting various parts and products and showing
roduction heads the junk they were making. He made
ersonal phone calls to customers, explaining the
nprovements he was making and begging for a little
ore patience.

When his new inspectors had rejected no less than a
uarter of an entire run, he took the production man-
ger aside. 'I hate to tell you this, but you're going to
ave to go all the way down the line and retrain
veryone who's retrainable. Those who aren't will go.
nd if you don't do it, I'll find someone who will. Our

union agreements aren't so iron-clad we can't fire incompetent people. They'll see either we clean up this mess or no one will have a job.'

If the production crew had fallen down, part of the fault lay with the engineers. Some products were actually too difficult to manufacture and had to be redesigned. This eliminated another bottleneck and sorted out those who could or would not do their jobs. King gave these people the opportunity to resign, as he put it to the board when he outlined his latest actions.

In the midst of these early changes, King spent an afternoon with an engineer he had known for years and had recruited from the West Coast. Bob Eland knocked at his door.

'Can I have a word, Mr King?'

'Come on, Bob, we've known each other too long for that.'

That pleased Eland, but he still said, 'Excuse me, but when a man is president, he deserves respect.'

'Okay, respect the hell out of me, but call me Kurt.'

Eland wanted to talk to him about the new design of a single-triode TV tuner on which he had been working for years. 'I think it's time to start field-testing,' he said.

'Hmm, it's come at a bad moment, Bob.' King caught a lock of his hair at the back of his head and pulled as he reflected. 'We've got so damn many other problems. What do the others say?'

'Other engineers? Well, I've only told them so much since you said to keep it quiet. Most of them say the thing will never work and we've got to stick with the dual-triode tube we've been using since . . . since . .' He searched for a phrase to convey his contempt. 'Since Ed Sullivan was a kid.'

'So, what would it cost if I isolate you and maybe one

chnician and you work on nothing but this until it
mes out one way or the other? How much and how
on?'

'Fifty thousand and three to six months. I'll need a lot
outside model work and at least ten prototypes.'

'As much as that?' King's eyes followed the smoke
om his smouldering cigarette. He snapped his fingers.
Okay Bob, go ahead. But not a cheep because I'm not
oing to the board for approval. I'll fudge it, steal it out
some other budget. I don't have to tell you to do a
ood job. Go!'

King's innovations slowly but surely took hold and
ventually chaos gave way to bedlam which became
igraine and finally only a simple headache. In three
onths, Maxim was shipping quality merchandise and
six months it was arriving on time and the customers
ere happy. Those emergency actions had sent costs
y-high, but they came into line as the larger problems
ere resolved. At the end of King's first year as presi-
ent, Maxim was solidly back in business, though the
ompany still had problems. If it had a superior product
its TV tuner, it still cost a tenth more than those
fered by the company's two major competitors. Costs
ad to be cut, though not at the expense of performance
quality. King's working days grew longer and longer;
ut if he felt the stress, it did not show.

He had a new mistress, a new tuner design.

5

contrast to his first directors' meeting, King's seventh
egan as a back-slapping occasion. He felt so good he
id not want to spoil it by having to tell them about his
test idea. Once the various reports were out of the

way and the board was convinced Maxim was back in the black, the mood was downright jovial. At that moment, King rose to put his new project before the board.

'Gentlemen, I want to tell you how proud I am of the way the company has come around, proud of the people here who've made it happen, and to tell you how much I appreciate your support over the last months. It was a rough time, but we are out of it and the future looks better.'

'Hear, hear,' said Jevons, who was not normally so effusive, and everyone laughed.

'Thanks, Bill.' King joined in the laughter. 'However, I don't happen to think it's anywhere near as bright as it can be. And because I feel that way, I want to offer a presentation today, a new tuner design that has the potential of making this company again first in its field. But I must emphasize this is going to cost money, and there's risk, considerable risk.'

There were stirrings and murmurings around the table and one or two directors looked as if they had questions. King ploughed ahead. 'Let me tell you what we have on the drawing board, although it's actually a bit further along than that.' An aide set up an easel and the first of a series of large cards, a black-and-white drawing of a vacuum tube and, below it, a drawing of the Maxim tuner.

'As you see, the bottom drawing is our tuner and the part pictured above the tube we use as the primary amplifier in that tuner.' He substituted a second card for the first. 'Now, this drawing shows a different kind of tube. It's a single triode but it performs exactly the same function, if Bob Eland, our design engineer, is right. He has developed a new circuit to use the single

riode and the result is excellent performance, maybe
etter, and at less cost.'

King was reaching the tricky part of his speech,
onfessing he had spent considerable money without
he board's say-so. 'I have to admit I secretly encour-
ged Bob to perfect this new circuit because everybody
xcept himself said it was impossible, and that's a
ghting word. I had to juggle with the budget a bit to
und the project and it ran to seventy-five thousand
ollars in the last five months.'

'That isn't peanuts,' Jevons put in, and several other
oices murmured in agreement.

'I know, gentlemen, I know. But time was important
nd I didn't want a lot of discussion until we were sure
f the project. And I can't say I'm sorry, because it looks
s though it will pay off.' At that, several directors
elaxed and some sighed their relief. King went on, 'But
we're to capitalize on this new and brilliant design,
he next step will be expensive.'

He indicated another drawing. 'This is the new tuner
hich incorporates the single triode. Now, compare it
ith the old one.' He stuck up the previous drawing
nd gasps of surprise came from the board members
ho saw the new tuner was half the size of the old one.

'Gentlemen,' King continued, 'it is a fact TV sets are
oing to get smaller with the trend towards bigger tubes
nd smaller cabinets. If we go with the trend and help
ioneer the changes, we'll lead the parade again, if we
on't we'll wind up with egg on our faces. So, I'm
roposing to commit ourselves to making the single-
iode circuit and scaling down our present tuner.'

He stood quietly, listening to the whisperings round
he table as various directors huddled together in dis-
ussion. A familiar voice rose above the murmurings.

'Tell me, King, aren't you talking about a major retooling?' It was old Schuster, who had rejoined the board recently after his operation. Trust him to see the main point before the others.

'Yes, A.J., that's exactly what I'm talking about.'

'Then, young man, just what would that cost in real money and without hiding expenses or stealing from other budgets? You know I don't like that.'

King swallowed quickly, hoping no one noticed. 'I would say slightly in excess of 500,000 dollars.'

That rocked them back and set them arguing for two solid hours about the new project. Half the board sided with King, but the other half urged caution. Hadn't they just levered themselves out of the red? Didn't they need a breathing space before embarking on risky, new ventures? The sort of money the new president was committing might bankrupt the company.

On a show of hands, the board was split down the middle. It looked as if King would have to shelve his proposal. Schuster saved him. 'We've heard what Mr King has told us about this new equipment with honesty,' said the old chairman. 'We put our faith in him as president and he has so far justified that faith. I vote we hold a ballot on his project.'

When he counted the voting cards, Schuster turned to King. 'Young man, you're home – but only by two votes. So, your hunch had better be good.'

'Thanks, A.J.' It was all King could get out before he felt his legs give way and he slumped into his seat.

That night, he told Carolyn, who was surprisingly interested. 'I've just put my whole career on the line. In about nine months Maxim will either be Number One again – or yours truly will be the biggest bum in the whole television industry.'

o one in the TV manufacturing industry saw things
ng's way. For months, he and Eland made the rounds
all their old customers and several prospective new
es with the prototypes of the new components.
eryone listened to their spiel about the Eland circuit
d the new mini-tuner which were a breakthrough in
technique. One by one, they shook their heads like
e diehard members of the Maxim board.

Not one expert said it would work and several execu-
es laughed in King's face when he begged them to
e the risk. One big firm called the project crazy and
olhardy and challenged all their results. 'A single-
ode tube just won't do the job,' they said.

They were the worst months in King's career. With
erwhelming technical opinion against him, it looked
though he had made a blunder that would cost him
job and send Maxim stock diving. In a last, desper-
move he approached the Turret Company, known
a progressive outfit which was beginning to lead
makers in new developments. Since Maxim had
ver done a pennyworth of business with Turret, he
d Eland went with little hope to meet Carl Green,
rret's vice-president for engineering. He listened to
eir story then called in his right-hand man.

'Nate,' he said, 'I think Maxim has something inter-
ing. Put a couple of guys with Bob Eland and test the
w tuner in the lab. If the tests are good, equip a
uple of sets with it and put them out in the field in
ugh areas. I'll give you a week to test and get back to
e.' With that, the meeting ended.

When Green called a week later, King walked into his

office with his heart in his mouth. 'Sit down, Kurt, an[d] relax,' Green said, reading his expression. 'Your tune[r] looks good. Now, let's talk some business. Before yo[u] and Eland showed up, we were about to build a ne[w] tuner ourselves. We were even talking about getting ri[d] of the dual triode. I have to ask a very direct question have you applied for a patent on your new circuit?'

'Yes.' King grinned with relief.

'Dammit, I should have filed something myself, but [I] wasted time dreaming while you guys went ahea[d.] Okay, enough hindsight. Turret needs 2,500 tuners [a] day. How soon can you produce enough to serve ou[r] needs?'

That order fuelled the turnaround. Nine months late[r] Maxim was supplying Turret with one hundred p[er] cent of its requirements and they established a lead ov[er] the industry in the number of sets sold. But so far a[s] King was concerned, the key point was that the Numb[er] One set in the country used the Maxim tuner. He ha[d] to try hard not to say we-told-you-so when calls arrive[d] from firms he and Eland had talked to, vainly, t[he] previous year. Commodore, for instance. King ha[d] lunch with their president in their posh dining room. [']hear Turret's doing very well with the new Maxi[m] tuner,' the president said. 'We're old friends, our tw[o] companies – why didn't you come to us instead [of] them?'

'But we showed it to your people first,' King sai[d,] hiding his smile. 'They said it wouldn't work and did[n't] want to test it. One of your engineers who knew Maxi[m] was in trouble accused us of grasping at straws.'

'No tests?'

'Not one.'

'I'll be a son of a bitch. Okay, the way Turret

ling, the damn thing has to be good. What's the
ice?'

'Ten per cent less than you're paying for your present
ner, and we make a decent profit.'

In just over a year, Maxim was leader in its field and
rt King was the boy wonder. For the first time in a
cade, Maxim declared a healthy dividend, and each
arter showed a bigger profit. In a unanimous vote,
e board raised King's salary and sweetened the details
his stock option.

7

on, other manufacturers jumped on the Maxim band-
agon. King felt proud of his accomplishment, his
ture with Maxim was bright and he had other projects
keep ahead of the opposition. To his surprise, how-
er, his board did not jump to support him, but urged
ution. Perhaps having been burned once by a presi-
nt who kept the true status of the company secret,
ey had decided to play it safe. Their decision to back
m on the retooling had been their one big gesture and
w they were saying, 'That's enough.' They were like
e roulette player who saw the first ball drop for him,
shed in his chips and went home.

In the fall of 1964, he went to the board with a
tailed proposal to acquire several companies which
uld level out Maxim's overall sales and earnings
rve which was heavily dependent on seasonal sales
e most electronic component manufacturers. They
rned down his whole programme, saying profit at
ar's end was increasing nicely and they were reluctant
change things. King left the meeting with a growing
astration.

One night, shortly before bed, he stopped in th doorway of Carolyn's room and released some of hi frustration. 'They've turned into a bunch of ol women,' he groaned.

She put down her brandy glass and stared at him amazed. 'Kurt, aren't you ever going to be satisfied You have a wonderful position with a fine company Why, every other man your age we know is jealous o you and would be happy to trade places. Sometimes think you ought to go with me and see Dr Sanderson.'

He sighed, loudly. Carolyn had a newfound passio for psychotherapy which he didn't share.

'All right, what in the world would you do if yo didn't run Maxim?'

'There are any number of other companies that nee help and would provide me with a challenge. Unfortu nately, I can't afford to buy one on my own, thoug I've been sorely tempted lately. I was offered the chanc to buy a string plant in Atlanta just last week. It wa cheap, no directors, just me and the banks.'

Carolyn laughed as she turned out the light. 'Kur that's simply ridiculous.'

Later, lying in his own bed, hands behind his hea he gazed at the moonlight seeping through the shad and thin curtains. Why had it never bothered him whi he was so deeply involved in getting Maxim back on i feet that his marriage was only a marriage in nam Carolyn often twitted him that Maxim was his true lov and he injected all his energy, sexual and physical, in his work. His children, Randal and Alexandra, were boarding school or camp, or at their grandmother' more than at home. As for himself, he released h sexual frustration with call girls. There was on especially who had a keen financial and business sens

d even with her he found himself talking shop more
an doing anything else!

He comforted himself by thinking most businessmen
his age had seriously troubled family lives as well.
t what truly bothered him was the lack of fizz in his
ily work. Maxim's board had dropped the boom on
n. But worse, he suddenly realized the fierce drive
at had burned up his energy while he was turning the
mpany around – that had gone. The moon had set
fore he got to sleep that night.

Had King not been so repressed, so open to the idea
personal and professional change, he might have
rned down an offer that came out of the blue in early
54. But even had he been happy, he might have said,
s. It was a very special offer.

On a West Coast jaunt to inspect the California
search lab, he ran into Gene Morton, an older man,
ho had been a successful Los Angeles businessman
as long as King could remember. Over lunch at the
untry Club, he was startled to be served by the
iter who had attended to his mother and him years
o. The man did not remember him.

Gene Morton had hundreds of business stories, and
ey fascinated King. Known as the dean of business
ctors, he was used by banks and investment houses
en a company was headed for the rocks. Morton
rformed the needed surgery to give the patient every
ance to recover; he wielded a sharp, quick scalpel and
mpanies and their boards looked nothing like their
evious selves when he had done. But he was a saver,
xer. Never a builder. He sought someone else to play
at role.

King asked about companies available to buy or run.
orton had a mental file crammed with them, though

none of them appealed to the younger man. Their lunch was almost over when Morton stopped his fork in midair and gave King a sly look.

'Frankly, Kurt, I've been holding back, testing you. There's a company that's perfect for your situation and I know it backwards and forwards. The banks have had me on it from time to time over the past two years. It's sick, but with enough sales to afford a young hotshot like you. You couldn't buy it, but you could sure run it with a free hand. They'd pay you more than you're making, all the extras and even throw in a good chunk of stock at bargain price, plus options. In fact, you could pretty well write your own ticket. If you're serious about leaving Maxim, this is your deal and I can call the tune.'

'What's the name of this dream opportunity?'

'King Corp.'

VII

When his plane made a scheduled stop at Chicago, ing sat staring through the window at the piles of irty snow they had bulldozed off the runway. That ymbolized something, he wondered what. Although is flight would be on the ground for forty-five minutes, e felt no urge to get out and stretch his legs. He was omfortable in first-class and had no desire to join the aos and confusion at O'Hare airport. A work-filled riefcase sat unopened on his lap, but he had no energy • start reading. Instead, he kept thinking of two very ifferent situations: the challenge that awaited him in alifornia, and the mess he had left behind in Connect-ut. Now he knew what that slush signified: his once-hite marriage.

After dinner the previous evening, Carolyn had half-eartedly offered to help him pack. Unlike their normal istom, both of them had imbibed too freely. At first, iey swapped meaningless chat. Then, with all the idden drama of an electrical storm, an argument broke ut. Carolyn rounded on him abruptly, catching him ff-balance.

'No, goddamn it. No, no, no. Is that too difficult for our male ego to accept, or should I simplify it? I am ot, the children are not, moving to California. We elong here and we are going to stay here. And so ould you if you had the sense to see the mistake ou're making.'

'Now wait a minute, Carolyn . . .'

'No, you wait a minute for a change. I like it here. It' my home, and the children love it here.'

King had a different opinion on that point but decide against voicing it at the moment.

'And where's your one good reason why we shoul tear up our roots and follow you out there like som . . . like some Scandinavian immigrant family!' Thos furious, gunmetal eyes were riveted on his and he kne she had chosen the analogy carefully, wanting it t wound. Her sudden rage confused him, caught him off balance.

'What the hell has gotten into you?' He could thin of nothing better to say.

'Nothing's gotten into me. It's what's gotten into you You had a fine position here, one that made us all ver comfortable. We had a damn good life. Oh, maybe the weren't going to give us an award for marriage of th year, but we had adjusted intelligently and maturely, i my opinion. Then you go off by yourself and decid we're moving to sunshine land like religious pilgrim and you didn't think to ask me about it.' She had a pi of shirts in her hand which she threw into the half-fille suitcase with such force two of them bounced on to th floor.

King picked up the shirts, placing them carefully i the suitcase, knowing his neatness would annoy her. I a voice he could barely keep at normal volume, he sai 'I always thought a wife was supposed to go where h husband went.' He wasn't certain he believed this, b it was what he felt like saying.

It had the intended effect. Carolyn sputtered, s angry she became speechless. She stopped and walke over to the dresser to pick up her drink. She took a lo pull and put the glass down. 'You may still be living i the Middle Ages, but modern families talk things out. And when they find they're having trouble communicating, they're intelligent enough to seek professional help. But you don't approve of that, do you?'

Stung, he lashed back. 'Carolyn, the only real problem we have in this marriage is that we aren't sleeping together. And that was your idea, not mine. Yours and your beloved shrink who sold you on the idea that nice couples only screw twice a week, and with the lights out.'

'You animal! Don't you dare talk to me like that.' She had stiffened totally as if his taunt had paralysed her. Her mouth opened and shut, yet no words emerged. She seemed to be fighting for breath or enough air to scream. Finally, she managed to speak.

'Your trouble is that you don't love me or the children, or you wouldn't do what you've done.' She drew in a deep breath. 'You love only one thing – your beloved business.'

Recently, Carolyn had dressed to downplay her prominent bosom, hiding it under blouses and baggy sweaters. Tonight, she had changed to a tight-fitting cashmere sweater. King could see her breasts move as she breathed faster. Though furiously angry, he found himself almost wanting to rape her. Her flushed face and those heaving breasts had set his groin tingling. What would happen if he suddenly threw her on the bed or the floor and took her like an animal? Would that bend her will to his and miraculously transform their troubled marriage? Some men bragged about the effectiveness of that approach and the appreciative response of their partners. King knew he could never attempt such a thing.

Though she had found her voice again, Carolyn still

had not moved. 'I should think,' she said in quavering tones, 'you've been enjoying more than enough of that sort of thing with that blonde slut you keep in the city.'

'What are you talking about?'

'Oh, don't deny it, I know all about your Miss Bader.' She gave that look of the hurt and wronged wife. 'In fact, we've even had some nice chats on the phone.'

'I still don't know what you're talking about.' He prayed he sounded firm yet bewildered.

'Stop it, Kurt. Don't insult my intelligence by trying to deny it. You were seen by friends of ours who were only too happy to report back to me.' She had herself under control now and was determined to go on. 'I don't know how they got her name but they did. Then she called one day and I answered the phone and we had the most civil conversation.' She spat out the last two words. 'Oh, you'd be surprised what I know about that conniving bitch.'

King's mind was whirling and he felt suddenly defenceless, bewildered. 'I swear Carolyn, it was the only time.' He hardly recognized that weak voice as his own. 'She was the only one and it's been over for a long time.'

At that, Carolyn moved for the first time in minutes. Her hand went to her mouth and she muffled a small cry. King saw the shock spread across her face and he knew instantly he had made a fatal mistake. Despite those positive remarks she had not known the truth but now she did.

With little idea of what he was doing, King reached for his drink, clumsily. He touched the glass which teetered, fell and shattered on the polished floor.

Carolyn looked at him and, mistaking the gesture

212

e shrieked, 'Are you crazy? Have you gone crazy and
rted to destroy things?'

She ran from the room, a frightened, hysterical look
her eyes. King turned back to his packing to keep his
nd occupied. He heard Carolyn enter the bedroom
d when he looked, saw she had a tiny bottle of
rfume in her hand.

'Here,' she shouted, 'this is almost as flashy and
eap as the stuff your whore probably splashes on
rself. It came in the mail, a free sample.' She pulled
t the stopper and shook the bottle over the open
itcase, leaving the cloying scent everywhere. She
ssed the half-empty bottle among the clothes. 'That'll
nind you of her.' She gave a terrible grimace.
emind you of your pig.'

King took his briefcase and suitbag and left immedi-
ly. He walked to the cab stand in the middle of town
d the night air washed the smell from his clothes but
t his mind. He paid the ludicrous forty-dollar fare to
anhattan without a thought. He'd finished with argu-
ents for one night. Next morning after breakfast, he
lked from his club to Fifth Avenue and bought a
all bag and half a dozen white shirts.

Flying west, he replayed their scene, trying to reduce
to reality and rationalize away his guilt. By the time
ey were descending towards O'Hare he felt better,
ving convinced himself that a few months of separa-
n would probably be good for both of them, and
fore long the whole family would be reunited in Los
geles.

Sipping a Scotch and soda, he thought about King
rp. Curious, how therapeutic work was for him.
nce his father's death, the company had grown sub-
ntially, though in fits and starts. A piecemeal expan-
n with not much pattern to it. Although it had

213

divisions outside southern California, the main plant
and head offices were still in the same Los Angeles
location, on Slauson near Sepulveda. His father's old
airstrip had given way to needed plant expansion.

King Corp was not doing well under Clayton. Before
King and the directors agreed on terms, he had been
shown a first-half statement indicating 150 million dollars in sales for a profit of 50,000 dollars. Nothing to
cheer about, but he was relieved the company was at
least in the black. King wondered if Gene Morton had
been overly pessimistic about King Corp's plight, but
Morton seldom made diagnostic errors about companies. Anyway, he told himself as he put down his drink
and reached for his briefcase, it was good to be going
home with a real job to do.

2

As his cab eased round the curves on Stone Canyon
Road, he was gratified to see no obvious changes in the
beautiful Bel-Air neighbourhood. Through the fading
light, he admired the broad sweep of the perfectly-kept
lawns and the huge homes set back from the road.
Gazing through the open window, he was reassured at
choosing the right place to stay. He felt as though he
had come back home.

His taxi turned into the small parking lot of the Bel-
Air Hotel. 'Damn,' King said, involuntarily, 'the place
still looks terrific.'

'Yeah,' the young driver concurred. 'I don't much
like driving all them curves, but it's sure a swell sight
when you get here.'

Though not many miles from the film industry capital, the Bel-Air Hotel was the antithesis of Hollywood

It would fit better in some other world, King thought, eyeing the place as the cabby unloaded. Rather than a single large building, the Bel-Air was a series of small, dissimilar structures, mostly cottages set in irregular patterns with connecting walkways. That and the canyon walls framing the site gave it a rustic aspect.

King handed a bellman his luggage and briefcase and crossed the stone bridge to go inside and register. Nothing had changed in the charming lobby area. He went to his cottage – a bedroom and small living room with a fine old fireplace – and took a fast shower. Then he walked quickly to the bar, marvelling at the freshness of the night air and trying to separate out and identify the fragrant smells he had missed in New York City. The bar lay in dimmed lighting, its mahogany panelling glowing. King took a stool. 'A Beefeater martini with a twist. Dry and cold, please.'

It was perfect. When the barman began a polite conversation, King said he had just returned to California, where he had been born and raised, to take on a new job.

'Welcome back.'

'I'll have another one and drink to that.'

After a dinner of steak and salad, he strolled slowly up the path towards his cottage, smoking a cigarette to prolong the feeling of well-fed contentment. He was anxious and excited about the job that would begin in the morning, but he wanted to savour the moment. A distinctive aroma hung in the still night, reminding him of gardenia.

Outside the cottage, he stood for a moment looking up at the stars, so bright they seemed to hover above the canyon ridge. With a start, he remembered it was not ten after one in the morning as his watch said, but

215

ten after ten at night, California time. Or was it? Slipping off his coat, unbuttoning his shirtsleeve, he removed his watch and set it on California time. He did so in the certainty he would never change it again.

3

His first day as president of King Corp would have sent a lesser man back to wherever he had come from, though it began quietly enough. He arrived early and fixed himself a pot of coffee and started reducing the stack of accumulated mail by 7.30. By eight he was sipping his third cup of sour coffee when a secretary entered, wide-eyed at seeing him this early. They talked briefly about office routine, and King made a point of telling her he liked his door to remain open. He explained that many businessmen he knew worked behind closed doors as if too important or too busy to be interrupted. Secrecy was not his style, he said.

'Actually,' he went on, testing her sense of humour, 'most of them are sleeping off lunch, or practising their putting, or maybe playing with themselves.' When her face reddened slightly, King made a mental note to monitor his bawdiness level in her presence.

She had a message for him. 'Mr Adamly left word with me last night he wanted to see you this morning – as early as possible.'

Brian Adamly arrived a few minutes later. King tried to relax the atmosphere by chatting to King Corp's chief financial officer by the window, from where they saw the traffic-clogged San Diego Freeway. Adamly was a bookkeeper's bookkeeper, but King found him bright and pleasant. He sat down, pressing his fingers together, tense. As King lit a cigarette, Adamly began

'First of all, welcome back and I hope everything turns out as you want it. But, ehh, I really hate to do this on your first day, but I had to tell you first thing, I'm resigning.'

'What!'

'Yessir, I know it's sudden and unexpected and of course I'll stay for a few weeks to help you get established. But after that, I simply have to leave.'

'Why?' King could not hide his total surprise.

Adamly kept his eyes on King's ashtray. 'Well, Mr King, it's like this, I'm a professional man with a good name and I cannot be forced into a position of signing my name to a financial statement I believe to be false. If you recall, the six-month statement you received from Mr Clayton was not signed by me.'

'I'm afraid I missed that.'

'That statement showed a profit of 50,000 dollars, but it's my belief that amount is based on overstated inventory figures in most if not all of our operations.'

'Oh, oh.' King's stomach tightened and it wasn't the foul coffee.

'When I questioned the figures and other items, Mr Clayton told me to accept them as reported.' Adamly threw his hands open in a resigned gesture. 'If I'd had the staff I'd have done some sort of internal audit, but I had no other choice than to consolidate the information furnished by the divisions. I can't work that way. At year end, the auditors will discover the truth. As I said, I'll stick around to help you get acquainted, but as of now I'm washing my hands of the whole mess.'

After he left, King sat deep in thought. He considered persuading Adamly to change his mind, to throw in his lot with the new management. But no, the man was gunshy now where King Corp was concerned. Even his coffee had gone cold on King and he set down the cup and dialled the old Maxim number, leaving word for Chip Boyd to ring him.

As he expected, Boyd was only too eager to return West. A week later, King met him at the airport, mismatched clothes and all. He had been telling his secretary about the financial wizard due in from the East Coast. When she first clapped eyes on Boyd wearing what he thought an appropriate California outfit consisting of checked pants, a Madras jacket and a plaid wool tie, she whispered to King, 'Is that really our Mr Boyd?'

However, the new Finance and Planning vice-president immediately proved his worth. Instead of waiting for the annual audit, he called in Price Water-house and that prestigious accounting firm confirmed Adamly's suspicions: instead of the projected annual earnings of 100,000 dollars, there would be an operating loss of 1,800,000 dollars. The only plus was the sale of some unneeded property reducing that figure by 600,000 dollars.

King's first reaction was to curse Clayton and his whole brood. Then, he cursed himself for walking into this mess open-eyed. Through deceit Clayton had stolen his birthright. Now, Clayton had hung what amounted to a company teetering into bankruptcy round his neck and was probably smiling at his smart-ness. Yet, there was something bracing about the challenge.

Over the first weeks, he began to see the complete picture. It was frightening. At times, he felt like the little Dutch boy with his finger in the dyke. To his relief, a careful study showed the situation was not completely hopeless, though he did not relish telling the board what Clayton had concealed from them.

Ironically, it was Clayton's incompetence which gave him hope. He reasoned thus: if the company was well managed and still losing nearly two million dollars, he might as well lock the doors and chuck the keys into the Pacific. But, since the company had been mismanaged, then the right changes might save it. His analysis proved accurate.

His first commonsense move concerned the corporation's insurance. A routine check revealed the insurance was handled by twenty-five different brokers and agents: old friends, relatives and cronies of Clayton and his management team, an expensive alliance. King called in two major firms, listened carefully, then chose one as the company's sole insurance broker. It saved costs, time and produced better coverage. Another problem involved the basic corporate structure which had five major divisions. Yet only two had a common fiscal year. One of them was on a cash-accounting basis like a mom-and-pop grocery which Clayton thought avoided tax problems. All five operations were put on the same fiscal year and one more headache was cured. But it was like a Chinese box, every problem giving way to another deeper one.

On the day Adamly quit, King took a call from an Air Force officer who shook him by claiming King Corp owed the government over three million dollars in rent for machine tools, owned by the government but used by the company in a defence-oriented facility. He explained that under an old lease programme dating back to World War II, King Corp had a number of machine tools belonging to Uncle Sam. The rent was due on those. King checked and learned the equipment

219

was rent-free only when used on approved government work. So, the Air Force was right. And since King Corp could not meet the bill, the company was technically bankrupt. Fortunately, the government was understanding and after a series of meetings with King and Boyd, agreed to a long-term payment schedule and a reduced rental charge. That put another problem behind them.

One afternoon, in King's third month as president, the switchboard girl buzzed. 'There's a Miss Rockefeller on the line, a Miss Jessica Rockefeller. Will you speak with her?' She literally cooed the magic name Rockefeller.

Had she known something of Jessica Rockefeller's background, her tone would have changed. She was King's favourite callgirl, and Rockefeller was no more than one of the *noms de guerre* she used in her profession. When things broke up with Helen Bader, King had looked for somebody who had a purely professional and mercenary outlook on sex, nothing that would tie or involve him emotionally. He had found Jessica Rogers, who not only had a flair for sex but also for playing the stock market. They had coined the name Rockefeller for her. She had cushioned his fall after Helen, in every way.

'Jessica!' King whispered into the phone as soon as the operator was off the line. 'How the hell are you, where the hell are you, how did you find me? You know, I didn't realize until I heard your voice how horny I am.'

She laughed, a soft musical sound. King had never been able to get used to her contradictions. She had the most pleasant voice he had ever heard, but a vocabulary

go with it that made his old Marine top-sergeant
und like a Sunday-school teacher.

'Where am I – in fucking LA. A friend was flying his
cking Lear Jet out and offered me a free ride. Free
de, my ass in a cactus bush. First time I ever performed
the goddamn clouds. Scared the shit out of me.'

'You scared? I don't buy that one.' King was
uckling.

'Aw, shit, I thought God was gonna stick his head
rough the window and say, "Naughty, naughty".
hich brings me to the point – you been getting any
ely?'

'No,' King admitted, sadly. 'Not a thing since I got
re. I've been a real boy scout.'

'Hey, how come you talk so clean?' she asked,
ruptly switching topics which was another of her
bits. 'You're a boy scout all right, a goddamn boy
out.'

Again, he laughed. 'Maybe it's because you're foul-
outhed enough for both of us, Jessica.'

'Fuckin' right.' She giggled, then her tone changed
d no actress could have done it better. 'Wait a minute,
u always used to say you liked my mouth.'

'Ahh.' He could feel his penis beginning to stir as if it
ere emerging from hibernation. 'Look, tell me where
u're staying and I'll pick you up, say around seven.'

'No,' she said, again in her seductive voice. 'Come on
er to the Beverly Wilshire. You'll probably be pretty
t and sticky after a day's work. You can take a shower
th me for company like we used to do in New York.
st you and me and the hot water, loverman.'

He swallowed and said, 'See you at seven.'

'Hey, if you decide to stay all night I'll give you
ecial West Coast rates.'

221

As he put the room number in his pocket, King was smiling and his startled secretary heard him begin to whistle the overture from *Camelot*. With his problems, she wondered what made him whistle.

At 8.30 that evening, King sat on the bed in Jessica's room staring mindlessly at the TV set. She had already performed twice. Using the mouth he remembered so fondly, she had brought him to climax in the shower then again on the bed. Now, he sat there with a slap-happy grin on his face while she ordered dinner. After a torrid sex session with Jessica, he felt as though somebody had opened a major artery and his life was ebbing away.

He shifted his gaze as he heard her ordering. 'For two, please, the abalone, but only if it arrived fresh today. Don't give me something you've stashed away in the freezer. And, let's see, maybe for a vegetable celery hearts. No, skip that. Artichokes with plenty of butter and mayonnaise. And a huge salad, one of those special ones you make that's almost but not quite a Caesar, and make sure it's served on very cold plates. Fruit and cheese for dessert. And two bottles of what ever California white wine your sommelier recommends, but be sure it's properly chilled. That's to be here at 9.15 sharp. Okay fine, but send up two very dry Beefeater martinis, doubles, right away please. Room 314, thank you.'

King shook his head, unbelievingly. Her voice, her diction, the way she handled that order was pure class. What a changeling, he thought, as she replaced the phone and walked to the mirror and began to brush her long, ash-blond hair. As she raised her arm with each stroke, her silk bed-jacket lifted to reveal the twin globes of her bottom.

'Fuckers,' she said. 'Joe Braun is out sick and I had to talk to some asshole. I bet the wine won't be chilled enough and the abalone stale. You'd think at these prices that wouldn't happen. Hey, you haven't given me any stock tips yet.'

King smiled. Jessica's interest in money and finance took up half their talk, and he wondered if, like a genuine Rockefeller, she wasn't making several times as much in the market as he was. And, in that case, why was he paying her and not on the receiving end. It always cost him an effort to remember Jessica had taken business classes at New York University and City College for several years, dressed way down and so low-profile she never asked a single question, but filled notebooks with her excellent shorthand. She saved her questions for him, and other businessmen clients.

King reeled off three or four names that would probably make her some money in the next six months; he jotted them on the hotel pad. She sniffed and smiled wanly at him. 'Jesus, I wish now I'd listened when you talked about Syntex. But tell me about this company you're running. Was it really your old man's? That's a pisser.'

'Yeah, he founded it, built it up then when he died the bastards who took over squeezed my mother out of the picture and had it all to themselves. It grew, Christ, couldn't help growing with all the aircraft business it had in California twenty years ago. But it started to putter a few years ago, and go downhill. In fact, they sold me a bill of goods to get me to come and run it, but I don't really care. It's so great to be running King Corp I'd almost do it for nothing.'

'Loverboy, you've been playing with yourself too much and it's gone to your brain.' Jessica smiled at him. 'But tell me more.'

A knock came at the door and Jessica, essentially unclothed, took the drinks from a young bellboy. He stood there so stunned he almost forgot to have her sign the tab. The first ice-cold martini made King shiver with approval. He lit a cigarette and motioned Jessica to a chair where he could look at her while he talked.

'The main thing that brought me back was I found I had a rare disease, incurable in my case.'

'Hughh!' She looked at him, alarmed.

'It's a disease called Californication.' She smiled and he went on, 'I only like to make love in the sun.'

'You big prick, you scared the shits out of me. Now, back to business.'

'Well, a few years after the bandits grabbed the company, its president, a man named Clayton, decided they'd diversify to reduce their dependence on the aircraft business and the Defence budget. But he bought badly, companies that had no common ground with King, and landed the company in serious trouble.

'At the same time, Clayton and his directors knew a group of investors who had bought a firm which did work for computer outfits and tried to build it up. But they brought in the wrong man to run it.'

'And he ran the fucking thing into the ground, that it?'

King nodded. 'These two companies, King and the computer supplier, thought by getting together the might solve their mutual problems. But instead of sorting out the problems, the merger compounde them. It was a classic example of negative synergism.'

'Synergism,' Jessica said, running a tongue round her full lips. 'I like that, it sounds porno.'

'Nothing so exciting, Jessica. It's a medical term to describe the heightened effect of taking two or three or more drugs together when, if you took them separately, they'd have a lesser reaction. See?' She nodded. 'It's becoming one of the "in" business words these days, meaning 2 plus 2 equals 5.'

'Well, go on.' Jessica had her chin in her hand, drinking in each word. 'Jeez, I really dig this kind of hi-tech shit.'

'Jessica, you've such an eloquent way with words you'd make a fortune at public speaking.'

For that, she gave him the one-finger treatment.

'What the Harvard Business School types mean is they can take one business – a 2 – and another – also a 2 – put them together, mutter the magic word Synergism and get a 5. Frankly, I think it's crap, but Wall Street analysts like the word and the notion. So, we have a lot of synergistic business marriages . . .'

'Which land on the rocks like King did.'

'Exactly. In their case, 2 and 2 came out to 1½ or less. Clayton had done it again. He bought badly, he managed the old and new businesses badly, with chaos as a result. Then it got worse.'

'Worse, how in the name of fuck could it?'

'Clayton developed a serious throat illness, though people close to him said it was psychosomatic and he had simply given up. They brought in Gene Morton, the company doctor who put me on to the company some months back. But even he couldn't do much but cut away deadwood.'

Their dinner arrived, and King and Jessica ate in silence, speaking only to praise the food and wine. But

Jessica could hardly wait to hear the rest of the story. 'Who controls the company then – the investors who made the merger, those guys?'

'Most of the stock is owned by people all over, though Californians have the lion's share. I have some with an option to buy a bundle later on. Anyway, it's a bad buy, having dropped from the low 20s when Clayton started expanding to about 3.'

'Jeez, some people must've got hurt. Say, should I buy some now you're the top boy?'

'Jessica,' he said, frowning. 'If I told you to buy or sell, it would be tantamount to giving insider information which is a violation of federal law. You wouldn't want me to do that, would you?'

'I sure 'n hell would if I can make a few dimes on it. Look, lover, if the whole thing's such a crock of shit, why did you agree to run it? I've never known you to be stupid – except where women are concerned.'

'Thanks for the backhanded compliment. I agreed because I felt the problems were basically those of management and I think I can turn it around. The fact it was my father's old firm swayed me a bit, but there were also some pluses.'

Jessica was digging her perfect teeth into a peach 'Such as?' she asked.

'King has a small contract to make nuclear power control components for Admiral Rickover.'

'The guy behind all those nuclear submarines, right He's a hot shit from what I read.'

'That's him. He's a technical and perhaps even political genius and I want a chance to do more busines with him. If you can satisfy Rickover, you can satisf anybody. Hell, he pushed the navy's nuclear deterrer force almost single-handed. Some guy!'

'But he's a crusty old fart.'

'I don't give a damn. The Rickover association is a good one, I'm going to work hard on it and develop it into big business.'

She poured coffee and they lit cigarettes. 'I forgot,' she said, suddenly. 'I was down in Jamaica last month and got some really great grass. We'll smoke some later on, if you're not still scared it's going to make your pecker fall off. It really adds something to my performance, maybe yours, too. Now, finish what you were saying about the job. It wasn't only the Rickover thing.'

'No, things were so bad that there were a lot of opportunities for fixes and many of the fixes were straightforward. Clayton had neglected nearly everything which proper attention and tender loving care could turn around quickly.'

'Where was Clayton?'

'Enforced retirement. He had a son that everybody thought would take over, but he went, too.' King held his tongue about the fight with Nat Clayton. 'Anyway, the day I went around the plant I was shocked. The place was dirty and rundown, a real mess.'

'Like how?'

'Oh, light fixtures without bulbs, peeling paint, and a bulletin on the board announcing a company picnic for two years previously. It rocked me, but it also indicated things were far from hopeless. I read up on the situation, I liked the Rickover contract and the equipment was up to date. I also met a couple of keen young engineers rarin' to work on the nuclear programme and other projects. After chewing it over for a week, I said yes.' He refilled their glasses with wine. 'One other thing, Jessica. I slipped and fell on the ice and snow going into Idlewild, but stepped off the plane at LAX into a 70 degree sunset.'

'I know.' She giggled. 'Only thing I'm sorry about is you don't live in New York anymore, so I'll have to get out here from time to time so we don't become strangers.'

She doused her cigarette and slid down slightly in her chair. Her bare foot began to inch up his leg, pushing aside the bathrobe she had provided him with when they had finished their shower. He smiled and closed his eyes.

Her voice had turned dreamy, slow. 'You know, lover, I think after we finish this first bottle of wine, I'd like you to carry me over to the bed and do me the good old-fashioned Mrs America way with you on top doing most of the work this time. Later on, we can smoke some grass, and when you're up to it – ha, how about that? – I'll show you a few tricks I learned in the Caribbean.'

4

Jessica Rockefeller's visit had been timely and it sent him back to his business problems with an energy that surprised even himself. He had needed that ego boost Jessica had given him, for King Corp was still in deep trouble.

In the fourth month of his presidency, King learned from Boyd that only one of the company's operations was showing a profit. Next week, a stunned King got a call that it had burned to the ground. He rushed in to inform Boyd who could only grin. 'What the hell are you grinning about, Chip?'

'Just I got an insurance binder on that plant three days ago.'

'You mean, it wasn't covered?'

'Nope. The previous owner objected to paying fire insurance, saying the building was brick and couldn't burn. Clayton missed that one, but I got our new broker to blanket-cover everything we own, so we're covered. You know it's almost humorous.'

'Sick humour, maybe. Somehow, I don't think the insurance company's going to laugh. Jesus, Chip, with our problems it'll probably look like arson.'

'Who'd burn down their only profit-making division? No, it's a lucky break. We deserve at least one.'

Boyd worked as hard as the president. He had made certain nothing was left to chance. In addition to negotiating a solution to the Air Force problem and straightening out the accounting department, he had quieted the bankers and helped King explain the current status to the major investors on the board. He had also convinced them to jettison an electronics operation which was not worth keeping. In one case when he could not find a buyer, he had simply closed down a small plant rather than let it continue in the red. Boyd was becoming a brilliant businessman.

One night, relaxing with a drink after work in King's office, he said, 'Kurt, the main lesson I've learned since I came here is to make decisions. And I've developed that because of you.' King started to protest, but Boyd stopped him with a hand. 'No, Kurt, don't deny it. If I've heard you say it once I've heard it a hundred times. "A bad decision is . . ." ' King laughed and finished the phrase with him " . . . better than no decision at all." '

His self-confidence boosted by King, Boyd handled the financial side, leaving the president to work on the operating problems. Under Clayton, a fundamental staffing flaw had occurred, something that would never have happened had his father lived. Although King Corp's product line was mechanically oriented, the engineering staff, located in the corporate headquarters, were headed by a Ph.D. with an electronics background; also, the man was a Clayton loyalist who, like almost all the personnel, had not been around in the founder's day. King discharged the man and deployed the engineering staff in divisions where their talents could be best used. Each division was given its own engineering section.

Having straightened out that mess, King hired a Cal Tech graduate, Willis Naughton, as his technical adviser and ordered him to assemble the engineers and support people that would develop the nuclear control system he hoped to sell to the Navy. He reasoned if the company had a strong engineering team, then no matter what it worked on primarily, there would be beneficial fallout for the company in other areas. A few short years later, Admiral Rickover himself complimented King on that wisdom.

King did himself and the company much good when he hired Marianne Connors as his personal secretary. A graduate of Los Angeles' best secretarial school, in her late twenties, she was married to a Santa Monica lawyer. She told King a teenage operation precluded child-bearing, adding, 'I mention it only because I missed out on one good job because they assumed I wouldn't work for more than a year or two before starting a family.' King was impressed, especially with her explanation that she had left her last job because she was bored with a boss who worked part-time. He hired her on the spot.

Marianne had been working for less than a month when she pointed to the pile of papers on her desk. 'Why do we have so many different logos, letterheads and forms? You'd think this was five different companies.'

She was right, and King let her find a consultant to advise on a new format for all company forms, stationery and business cards. He came up with a handsome, triangular outline of interlocking Ks. King, who viewed the company's paper image as something marginal, was surprised at its impact. Among the employees, it created *esprit de corps* which reminded him of his Marine Corps days; and when the customers reacted favourably, he realized the importance of the changeover. For them, it signified a new management solidarity in the company.

When Marianne expressed grateful surprise at the generous raise King gave her, he carefully explained he had authorized it to make sure she spoke up loud and clear the next time she noticed need for change.

King was spending long hours with division managers and other key people, striving to bring their operations out of the red. In some cases, it meant changing managers, in others the machinery. Sometimes, all that was needed was encouragement. Under Clayton there had been one major taboo – taking risks. Fearful of seeing earnings plummet even further, the previous management discouraged innovation and change. King had quite a job convincing people the management philosophy had altered. He had to push and prod and pep-talk his 'troops' into taking personal initiative in everything from design work to sales.

'Miracles don't happen,' he told them. 'There's no single panacea for any business illness and I don't look

231

for one. There's no single all-purpose answer to any design or production problem, and I have watched company presidents take an operation down the tubes because they wasted time searching for the miracle answer. That isn't going to happen to King Corp.'

When he had purged the unproductive people, the 'survivors' who remained gained confidence and became a closely-knit team.

On a February weekend, Carolyn and the twins flew out to escape a lingering, cold, eastern winter. She pronounced his Bel-Air cottage 'quaint' and they spent a civil if not greatly pleasant time. On Wednesday, he drove them to the airport then went straight to the office.

The end of King's first full year as president of King Corp had just been celebrated. Slowly, through his efforts, the company had been transformed from a bunch of hand-wringing alarmists who faced inevitable failure to a hard-working group who were convinced they could win.

Before the assembled board of directors, Kurt King could announce proudly that, at the end of his first year, the company showed a small but honest profit.

VIII

Flying head-on into the late afternoon sun, King was temporarily blinded as he glanced up from the instrument panel. Sunlight reflecting off the ocean surface combined with the atmospheric glare had dropped forward visibility to near zero. But by banking steeply left, he could pick out the coastline, and looking straight down could make out scrub-covered hills, a highway snaking seawards and a cluster of farm buildings to the north. His eye and watch told him he was still a good fifteen minutes from Los Angeles. He scanned the instruments and smiled to himself, remembering Ray's jibe about his father's seat-of-the-pants flying. King was no hot-shot pilot but had worked hard to learn instrument flying. Now, he postponed his radio call asking air traffic control to clear his approach. Like his father, he felt too good up here.

Recently, Chip had suggested replacing the two-engine Cessna with a small jet, but he had not pushed the idea. For him, this plane had something special, something more than the deep engine throb, its unique smell of fuel, oil, plastic and leather. It had personality - like his father's old Jennies.

Left, he picked up the sprawling shape of Santa Barbara and watched the breakers crawling up the beach. This was the place to be. He wished he could stay up all day, but a *Times* reporter was due in his office at five. He started his descent into the Los Angeles basin and his high-altitude euphoria began to evaporate, though his short time aloft had done him good.

'Mr King,' said the young reporter after a bit of small-talk, 'my editor feels there's quite a story in the way you've turned King Corp around, and we appreciate your willingness to be interviewed.'

'Why shouldn't I be willing? Hell, it's good publicity.'

'You'd be surprised how many company presidents feel any publicity is bad.'

'Well, maybe they have something to hide. All right, fire away.' As he lit a cigarette, someone rapped lightly on the door. 'Ah, Dean, come on in. This is Mr Bowen of the LA *Times*. They plan to run an article on us in their Sunday business section and I thought it might be helpful for you to listen to what I have to say about the early days.' He explained to Bowen that Dean Hubert, operations vice-president, had joined less than a year ago; he wished, privately, he could convey the contribution Hubert had made, to the company and to him personally.

After riffling through his notes and the King Corp annual report, the reporter began, 'How long have you headed up the company? A lot of this is in the reports, but I'd like it from you.'

'Five years. I guess you know my father founded the company, but he died when I was a kid – 1945. When left S.C. I lived and worked in the East before coming back in '64 to this job. So, I'm a recycled Californian and since I worked here, off and on during high school and college, I'm a recycled employee.'

'When you arrived things were in pretty bad shape weren't they?'

'That's putting it mildly. You can't print this, but gave me a bad bout of rectaloculitis.'

234

'What was that again?'

'Rectaloculitis. It's a well-known business syndrome that develops when a company goes from bad to worse; it tightens your sphincter muscles to the point where your eyeballs are pulled down to your rectum and you begin to have a very shitty outlook on life.'

They all three laughed before King sketched the early problems and the moves that had turned the company around.

'Okay, Mr King, now the company's out of the red and making a modest profit. But how did you get from there to reported earnings of 18 million dollars last year.'

'Some good acquisitions, good management and a hell of a lot of luck.'

'Luck? Can you elaborate?'

'Sure. This, for instance. I'd been president for just over a year when a broker friend called me. He understood I was looking to acquire companies related to our own business. Would we be interested in buying a concrete pump firm?' King gave a grin. 'Stupidly, I asked, "But who makes pumps out of concrete?" and he had to explain the pumps weren't made out of concrete but pumped the stuff. I said, Yes we're interested and made a date to see him over breakfast early the next morning.'

Head down, the reporter was filling his notepad, so King continued:

'That night, a problem cropped up at the guidance control plant and I didn't get home until two in the morning. At five o'clock my alarm went off, I dragged myself out of bed and started shaving. It occurred to me was crazy to drive forty miles to have breakfast and a business discussion on only three hours' sleep. I would have called and cancelled had I not felt it was unfair to wake the poor broker, who lived nearby the scheduled breakfast rendezvous.

'Our meeting went fine even though I was bushed. He gave me the right figures and told me the owner had just married a lovely young wife, wanted to retire and would sell for 800,000 dollars. It was a small but growing company which had earned 150,000 dollars in the past twelve months. I felt the price was reasonable, so we drove out to the pump factory after breakfast and the owner gave us a first-class tour. The plant was brand-new and he also had a lot of property adjoining it. He planned to keep the land and buildings and lease them to the buyer. I was impressed with everything, but the balance sheet was lousy and this created a substantial goodwill problem.'

Bowen looked up from his notepad, apologetically. 'I'm sorry, I should know what that means, but would you fill me in?'

'Goodwill, in business accounting in a cash purchase, is the excess one pays over what the books say the purchase is worth. The difference between what you pay and the company's net worth is goodwill.'

'I don't see the problem – I mean, if the price is fair.'

'The problem is that, in time, goodwill has to be written off the books and this has a depressing effect on earnings. Put another way, it means for every dollar of goodwill you have to make two dollars before taxes.'

'Aha! now I see the problem.'

'So, in this case, we'd have had to make a pretax profit of 800,000 dollars to satisfy the goodwill. Despite that, I felt this was a good deal. I did some quick mental arithmetic and made him an offer on the spot – hi asking price of 800,000 dollars, plus his actual cost on the land and buildings.'

'Wasn't that a bit of a gamble?' King could see that even Hubert was asking the same question as Bowen.

'Sure it was. And I made it at 10.30 in the morning on three hours' sleep. But I trusted the seller.'

'And?' The reporter looked up from his notes.

'He thought for a moment then shook on the deal, and King Corp was in the concrete pump business. The old gentleman was honest. His land and buildings had cost him 240,000 which meant we paid just over a million for the whole package. But when the property was appraised it had a value of 650,000, so the goodwill problem disappeared.'

'That's fascinating,' Bowen put in. 'But did it turn out to be a good deal?'

'A great deal. The first year, the concrete pump division made 300,000 dollars and the second year a little over a million. In less than three years we had our investment back. And that pump company gave the whole of King Corp an earnings base to build on – that acquisition got this company going again.'

'Lucky you didn't call the broker and cancel the meeting,' Bowen said with a grin.

King was lighting a cigarette. For a moment, he stared out at the late afternoon traffic before turning back to the journalist. 'It sure was, because later that day another company topped my offer. But the seller was a man of integrity and stood by his handshake.'

Two weeks later, King was going through the Sunday financial pages when his eye halted suddenly as it was caught by a familiar name in a headline: COMMERCIAL

TRANSITION ACCOMPLISHED BY KING CORP, by Alexander T. Bowen, *Times* Staff Writer.

Bowen had done them proud, and his article, which stretched over most of a page, had nothing but praise. Reading it carefully, King felt gratified the factual errors were minor. He made a note to send the reporter a card or even a gift if that could be arranged tactfully. On his way to the shower, his phone rang. It was Chip Boyd.

'Hey Kurt, did you see our ad in the *Times*?'

2

As a rule, King avoided the social whirl. His work schedule left him little energy for the cocktail circuit. He preferred a few drinks after work with Chip or another executive or a visit to some quiet bar in the sinful depths of Los Angeles with Dean Hubert, who seemed to know all the tiny, dark bars that attracted the fast, hard crowd. Those women he met in such places didn't seem to mind if he called them again or not. They appeared to enjoy one-night stands as much as he did, perhaps even more. And Jessica still swung West every now and again, so he had his share of sex and expert female companionship.

One beautiful fall afternoon, he made an exception to his non-partying rule. King Corp was represented by the law firm of Jackson & Jackson, and King felt their counsel was worth every dollar it cost, and they certainly knew how to charge. So, he went to a five o'clock opening of the firm's new offices. Once there, however, he regretted his decision. Small talk just washed over him and he considered it a meaningless art. Now Carolyn – she was superb in such settings, listening without hearing, smiling without amusement and nodding sideways. Why think of her? He hadn't seen her in over a year, and then she had cut short her visit because her mother became ill. Two days she and the twins had stayed, but then she was out of his thoughts as soon as she left.

King took a second glass of champagne from a waiter. The offices were tastefully done if a little stiff. But what law offices weren't? He zig zagged through the crowd to look at the Hogarth prints on a wall when he stopped halfway, distracted by the sight of a striking-looking girl. Tall, about five-foot ten, she had long, straight brown hair she kept sweeping out of her face with one hand while the other held a champagne glass and a long, brown cigarette tipped upward from the rim. Her face was full but not round, with features larger than normal. Eyes, nose, lips – they all exceeded the ideal standard, yet the combination was startlingly beautiful. She wore a tan shirt with half-sleeves over a dark-brown jersey top and a matching tan skirt, short enough to reveal half an inch of tanned skin above her knees. She had no ring, but thin gold jewellery flashed from her throat and one wrist.

Cynthia Jackson, the senior partner's wife, was standing talking to her. Although close to fifty, Cynthia was still an exceptionally attractive woman who took great care of her looks. Yet, beside this marvellous young creature she resembled Eleanor Roosevelt.

Noticing King's stare, the girl smiled. Not a come-on or the professional grin of the savvy secretary for the more important guests. A friendly smile. King started to move towards her.

'Kurt King. Just the man to set Mr Arandi straight about LBJ's new investment incentives.' Frank Pine, one of the firm's partners, pushed through to introduce him to a dark-skinned man in a Nehru jacket. He turned out to be a Pakistani on his first business trip to the United States. After twenty minutes, when he was able to break away, he scanned the crowded room for the girl. She was gone. Ten minutes later, he also left.

At the door, he complimented Pine on the new décor. 'Thanks, we're pleased with the way it turned out, but we'd seen other offices Frankie Shore did, and . . .' At that moment, his office manager called him away, and Kurt escaped.

He had taken a cab to the party, but the early night air was so refreshing he began to walk, wondering whether to return to the office, have dinner in town or head home to the Bel-Air. He bought a paper, glanced at the headlines then looked up at a crescendo of horn-blowing. A sports car at the light had apparently stalled and drivers behind it were honking their impatience. As he walked abreast of the small foreign car, he realized the driver was the tall brunette from the Jackson party. She was obviously embarrassed and angry. Impulsively, he walked over and looked through the passenger's window, noting her shapely leg as she pumped the accelerator and turned the key, trying to start the car.

'Excuse me, let me make a suggestion, okay?'

She stared at him before recognition and relief flooded her large, attractive features. 'Oh, please, before these idiots behind me blow my brains out.'

'There's no smell of gas, so I guess you haven't flooded the carburettor yet. Don't pump the gas pedal, floor it – put it against the floorboard and keep it there. Now, try starting it again, but in short bursts.'

On the second attempt, the engine caught, sputtered

once and roared into action, a fast and powerful sound. Keeping the engine revving quickly, she leaned over and tugged on the small leather strap and opened the door. 'Get in,' she said. 'The least I can do is give you a lift.'

King slipped into the passenger's seat without hesitation. 'Thanks. My name's Kurt King, by the way.'

She gave him a lovely, wide smile. As they passed beneath a street light, he saw her face was still flushed with excitement. She looked exceptionally appealing. She told him her name, but the engine noise drowned her voice. 'Actually, I'm the one who should be saying thanks,' she said. 'I just got this car and love it, but sometimes it stalls and I have trouble getting it going again. I suppose I should take it back to the dealer and have them check it over.'

'Well, maybe they've just set the idle too low. Why don't you pull into that shopping centre – the one with the lights – and I'll have a look?'

She flashed him that marvellous smile. 'Okay, but if you break it, you have to pay for it.'

That set him laughing, too. When she stopped, he checked the tachometer and found the car was idling at 750 rpm. With a pocket knife, he adjusted both the Stromberg carburettors. For good measure, he changed the fuel and air mixture to a richer setting, figuring she would prefer to waste a little gas to keep the engine running. When he had finished, the engine idled smoothly and the tach needle steadied at 900. 'Try it,' he suggested. After the fourth stoplight, she pronounced it 'perfect'.

'But why was it set so low?'

'Oh, a lot of mechanics do that because you get a slightly better mileage that way. But they sometimes go a bit too far, as in your case. They had your best interests in mind but were a little optimistic. It'll run better now and you won't have to worry about it. There's nothing worse than a new car that acts up.'

'Amen,' she said. 'I've wanted an MG for so long, and when I finished the Jackson job, I bought this one. British racing green and a tan leather interior with a tan top. Nice, huh?'

'I've always liked MGs . . .' He stopped and looked at her. 'Did you say the Jackson job? Then you must work for this guy, what did Pine say his name was? – Shore, Frankie Shore. You work for him?'

She looked at King for a moment, bewildered, then said with a chuckle in her voice. 'I guess you didn't hear me when I introduced myself. I am Frankie Shore. If you expected a man, you're out of luck.' She smiled at his obvious embarrassment.

That, and the dinner that followed at Perino's, was their first date. Before the evening was over and she dropped him at his office to pick up his car, King learned Frances Elizabeth Shore, twenty-five years old, almost fourteen years his junior, was a most unusual young lady. A graduate of neither college nor design school, she had gone to work for a top interior designer right after high school; she had worked there until she was twenty-one at which time she saw she would almost certainly remain a 'gofor' and the opportunity to design on her own might never come. She quit and became a Pan Am stewardess.

By the time the airline found out her French was not as fluent as she had claimed, they had relaxed their standards and she could have stayed. But she'd had enough of being 'pinched and propositioned' as she put it. She went to work at a small salary for a large decorator who promised her solo assignments, and surprisingly lived up to his word.

Several of her jobs were praised in newspaper and magazine features and spread her reputation. Her big drawback was that, although she could design well, she had expensive tastes. Her boss, scared his clients might look for someone cheaper, suggested she strike out on her own – which was what she wanted to do and didn't have the heart to tell him. When she and King met in 1968, she had been on her own for almost a year and already had all the work she could handle.

'I spend three or four days of the week making money,' she recited, happily. 'The rest of the time I do whatever I want. I rent a nice place on Malibu beach where nobody bothers me or my friends. I have a big, old station-wagon for hauling stuff and people around, and I have the MG. I'm doing what I want.'

They were having an after-dinner drink that first night when she reviewed her career. He expressed admiration for her success, then asked, casually, 'And what about your social life. Is there someone special?'

She looked at him directly with no coyness or guile. 'Sometimes there is, though at the present time there isn't. My choice, by the way. One of the things I like best about my life is' – she smiled with candid seductiveness – 'I seldom know how a given day, or night, is going to turn out.'

'That,' he said to himself, 'is a come-on if I've ever heard one.' Yet he hesitated, and their first night ended on a polite and almost formal note. He had the feeling she wanted to see him again, and their age difference meant nothing to her. Her attitude made him realize he was more out of touch with California life than he imagined, even if he had been back for five years.

* * *

243

Several months later, King woke one morning with an unsettled mind. It had taken time, but he now realized his fellow-guests at the Bel-Air were much older than himself, or looked much older. Before he had finished shaving, he had made up his mind to move. An apartment he could find for himself, but when it came to decorating, well he would need professional help.

'What a nice surprise,' Frankie said when he identified himself over the phone, and it was clear she meant it. They arranged to get together within the week he had given himself to find a suitable apartment. She recommended several places.

When he checked out the first, he was pleased it was not a haven for swinging singles. That sort of life did not interest him and he appreciated Frankie's comprehension of this. That apartment was too big and too far from his office; but the second, overlooking the Pacific Coast Highway at the end of Sunset, was exactly right. Coincidentally, it was near his childhood home. After half an hour touring the grounds and the penthouse apartment he signed a year's lease and a cheque for two months' rent.

Frankie met him there on a Sunday afternoon and he could tell by her face she was more than impressed with his choice. 'I should have known,' she laughed, 'you'd take the penthouse, even though the two-bedroom layouts below are more than large enough.' Suddenly she turned and stared at him. 'Or, are you planning to bring your family out here?'

'No, no, I'm not.' He was taken aback, but recovered. 'What made you ask that?'

'Well, it occurred to me if you were, I'd do the place quite differently than if you plan to live here alone.' She smiled and gazed at him steadily as though expecting

244

him to elaborate. He went on, 'I have two children, twins, a boy and a girl eleven years old. I see them every six months or so, briefly, in Connecticut where they live with my wife. We are separated, but not legally.' He looked at her swiftly to see if she would let him off this hook, but her eyes still interrogated him. 'We might as well be divorced,' he said. 'In fact, I recently wrote her offering a generous settlement so that we could both get on with our lives. I haven't received an answer yet.'

He turned to look at her, not quite certain what to say next. She spoke before he could decide.

'I'm sorry, I didn't mean to pry. In fact, I already knew you were separated, but I guess I wanted to make sure things hadn't changed recently.'

'You knew? How?'

'Oh.' She gave that beaming smile. 'I checked around. Now, let's see what we have here.' As he followed her, he could not help but notice and admire the way her hips moved inside her tight, tailored white slacks.

The apartment had two bedrooms and a den. Each room was larger than those on the lower floors, and the penthouse had a structural overhang. Frankie said little, but uttered low, approving murmurs as she moved from room to room making notes on a small, leather-covered pad then sticking her gold pen behind her ear in a swell of dark hair maintained by a leather slipknot.

King tried to study the rooms to see if he could visualize them with her professional eye. He found himself looking at her instead. She wore sandals and a knitted red top, and he noted that, though relatively small, her breasts were high and firm. 'Jesus,' he said to himself after a long, furtive glance. 'No bra.'

With an effort, he brought his mind back to the

apartment and listened to Frankie's suggestions. Finally, her careful inspection and measuring done, she slid open the balcony doors and they went out on to an enormous balcony. 'My God,' she said, 'you could grow oranges up here, or have your own little vineyard. Seriously, we could put in deep tubs of good soil and you could grow anything that doesn't require a lot of shade. Home-grown vegetables, for instance.'

King laughed. 'They'd wither on the vine, Frankie. But some little trees might be interesting and give it a private garden effect.'

'No problem. But don't let's plan too much for out here until we decide how to furnish the inside. Is any of that stuff at the Bel-Air yours?' He shook his head. 'Good, we can start with a clean slate.'

He liked the 'we' and conjured up a quick fantasy of what it might imply, then something occurred to him. 'Frankie, I just remembered, I have a whole houseful of good, old solid California furniture and even some antiques in storage downtown. They've been there ever since I sold my mother's house after she died.'

'You mean that heavy, Spanish effect, like in those Dolores del Rio movies you see on the Late Show?'

'You have the picture.' He grinned.

'Forget it.' She made a face. 'That would be fine if you were sixty years old and widowed and planning a once-yearly dinner for your board of directors.'

He was flattered she did not see him as a stuffy type. Knowing his artistic limitations and the demands on his time, he told her to go ahead and do the entire apartment as she thought best.

'Wonderful, I was hoping you'd say that. I'm sure you won't be disappointed.' She leaned against him and pressed his arm with delight. After she left, turning

246

down his dinner invitation because of another engagement, he wandered about the empty rooms. Several times he caught himself rubbing the spot on his arm where she had touched him.

3

Two months to the day she was finished. King slotted his pearl-grey Coupe DeVille into his assigned parking space. He had taken Frankie Shore to dinner the previous Friday night and imagined he could still catch her perfume in the rich car upholstery. She had admired the car, but stated she would still like to see him in a sports car. He remembered her gentle laughter when he explained the King Corp car arrangement.

First, all company cars had to be American because, like his father, he was patriotic. Then he had laid down a rigid classification: salesmen could drive a Chevrolet or its equivalent; division presidents could have large Buicks or Oldsmobiles; Chip Boyd and Dean Hubert could drive a Chrysler, Lincoln or Thunderbird; and only the top man, King, could drive a Cadillac. Any company officer could upgrade his car, provided he paid the cost difference. Anybody foolish enough to insist on a foreign car paid the lot himself. Frankie had called him a dictator, but kissed him goodnight anyway.

King fished in his jacket pocket for the key, slid it into the lock and then hesitated. This would be his first sight of the apartment since he had seen it completely empty. Frankie had insisted on working entirely alone, ruling out any suggestions from him. And no previews. His apartment was off-limits until everything was finished.

When he opened the door, the first thing to fill his eyes was himself. Mirrors lined the upper half of the

247

foyer wall opposite the door. Below was a long, low table holding several potted plants. An expensive chain lamp hung in the corner and cast a muted light. Altogether, a rich effect.

He turned into the living room and was surprised by the feeling of space, despite all the furniture. Everything was modern in what he judged Danish or Swedish style. Frankie must have been thinking of his ancestry. He moved slowly from room to room, impressed with what she had done, though not entirely sure if everything suited his taste even if the overall effect was handsome. The couches and chairs were all low and functional, in deep earth-toned colours. Modern abstract paintings and prints hung on the walls. A teakwood bar stood in a living room corner and he saw it was already stocked. Under the bar was a small refrigerator with an icemaker next to it. King built himself a good-sized Beefeater martini and wedged a lemon slice on the rim of the striking Dansk tumbler engraved with a fitting K. He carried the drink with him as he continued his inspection.

A long, low cabinet on the inner wall turned out to be a high-fidelity system. He pushed a button and the FM came on. Segovia filtered into the room from hidden speakers. Plants were strategically placed in several corners, mostly miniature palms, which seemed to stretch the height of the room. Almost every light had a dimmer switch.

Heavy tan curtains of burlap material, lined so that the brilliant afternoon sun did not seep through, covered the balcony wall. King drew one aside and looked out to admire what Frankie had begun to create on the balcony. A line of small, leafy trees in large wooden tubs stood along the railings. In the middle of the patio was a table and chairs finished in bright yellow plastic beneath a huge green-canvas umbrella. Two well-pillowed *chaiseslongues* sat on the other side and a garden hose was coiled on a wall-holder. Frankie had been thorough. The whole feeling was of something open yet private, and he loved it already. She had turned the balcony into a secluded outdoor room.

He checked the kitchen and the guest bedroom in the same methodical fashion. He found the simplicity of the den particularly satisfying and saw she had lined an entire wall with bookshelves, had selected a mixture of current best-sellers and classics to give the place a lived-in look.

He went into the master bedroom and halted in his tracks at the immensity of the bed. 'Jesus,' he said aloud, 'it's the Hollywood Bowl!' There was a long bookcase headboard filled with Harvard Classics with several pieces of abstract sculpture serving as bookends. A three-globe light fixture, reminding him of a pawnbroker's sign, hung from the ceiling.

His eye went to the ceiling and again he said, 'Jesus.' Mirrors ran from one end to the other, reflecting the whole room and, impressively, the mammoth bed. What had Dean Hubert once told him? – the only thing he still wanted out of life was bedroom mirrors. It almost made King laugh. He was still standing there, gazing upwards, when he heard a quiet knocking on the apartment door.

'Hi.' Frankie glanced, quizzically, at him as she thrust a package into his hand.

King looked at the large straw basket which contained two chilled bottles of Tattinger's, and a large, lumpy-looking package wrapped in butcher paper. Frankie smiled at him. 'It's champagne and lobster tails for the new tenant and, I hope, satisfied customer. Well, aren't you going to let me in?'

Two hours later, the remains of their meal on the terrace table, they sipped coffee and held hands as they watched the sun slide into the ocean. Without looking at him, Frankie said, tentatively, 'You do like it, don't you, Kurt? I mean, is the apartment as they say in my business, YOU?'

He stubbed out his cigarette before answering. 'To the first question, a definite Yes. I wouldn't know whether to say it's ME, that's for others to decide. But at the moment, I'm so over the moon I don't care if it's me or you or Sam Yorty.'

He got up and crossed to where she was sitting, her long superb legs stretched out on the *chaise-longue*, and knelt next to her. She turned her head to be kissed, and he marvelled anew at the size of her lips. Then he was kissing her, lost in the softness and warmth of her lips and tongue. She let out an unexpected moan then slipped off the *chaise-longue* to kneel next to him and put her arms around him.

Swiftly, he dragged several cushions on to the terrace floor and built an impromptu bed. Above them, the evening sky had gone almost dark. They could hear the hi-fi music from the living room as they lay there kissing. He unbuttoned her thin, shirtwaist dress. Soon he had forgotten the music, the night and everything else as he explored her body, soft and firm and young. He was too excited for preliminary sex play, and so was she. When she drew him into her and he entered her gently, the constriction of her sexual organ round him sent an electric flare of youthful memories through him. It had been a long time since he felt so sexually fulfilled.

When they had pried themselves apart, she still l

250

with her left leg over his right, nipping him with small kisses from time to time. 'What a wonderful idea, to make love under the stars,' she said. 'But I didn't design things for that reason.'

King reflected for a moment then decided against telling her the real reason he had chosen the outdoor setting was he did not feel ready to face the ceiling mirrors.

4

In July 1975 when he turned forty-five, Kurt King was surprised that the milestone seemed to bother others more than it did him. What did age mean if he felt as youthful as he did? But he conceded his youthful state of mind had a lot to do with the good influence of Frankie Shore. Like his relationship long ago with Beverly Anderson, this one had its up-and-down and on-off periods. It progressed of its own momentum, as Frankie once commented – though after too many drinks. Without agreeing with her evaluation, King had to admit he did not have anything like the same control over his personal life that he exercised in business dealings.

One reason was Carolyn, who insisted she saw no point in changing what she called a very convenient arrangement. If he truly wanted a divorce, he had better be prepared to bring the action himself. As he explained to Dean Hubert one night, Carolyn knew he would never do that unless greatly provoked.

Hubert, who had become as close to King as Ron Poole in his boyhood, screwed up his face. 'Aw shit, Kurt, you're just being too goddamn nice. Either that or you're the only man I ever met who was too busy to get divorced. 'Course boss, I must admit you do seem to have the best of both worlds, if you know what I mean.'

'I believe I do,' King replied with a harshness he did not intend.

In August, Hubert, Frankie Shore and Ron Poole, having finished a consulting job in Los Angeles, arranged a belated birthday celebration for him. A long weekend stretching into five glorious days aboard a sixty-foot motorized sailer. Frankie had decorated the staterooms and the owner chartered the boat as a favour to her.

For three days they sailed and fished and on the fourth day they headed, slowly, for Los Angeles, tying up at Catalina late in the day. On the last night, moored in Avalon Bay thirty miles from Los Angeles, there was a vicious gin rummy game. Both Frankie and Poole tapped out early and went on deck for air.

Ron flopped back on a hatch cover and stared up at the brilliant stars which seemed just overhead. Frankie pulled her sweater round her shoulders and searched for a crumpled pack of cigarettes and a lighter. Ron waved away her offer, saying, 'It was so smoky below I want to clear my lungs for a while.'

After several minutes' silence, he said, quietly, 'I'm glad about you and Kurt. You seem real good together.'

'Thanks, I think we are, too. I really miss him when I'm on out-of-town jobs. But I suppose absence makes the heart grow fonder and all that jazz.'

Ron sat up, suddenly. She could feel him looking keenly at her, as though thinking. 'Would you marry him if he were free? I mean, you two might as well be married, you spend so much time together.'

His earnest attitude brought a smile to her face, then

she said, 'Did you know Kurt hired a private detective to find out if he might actually have grounds for divorce?'

'Are you kidding? No, you wouldn't, not about that.'

'No, I'm dead serious. And if she hasn't been Miss Iron Maiden as she claims, things could take an interesting turn.'

'Jesus.' For a moment Ron ran out of thoughts. He leaned over and hoisted two ice-cold cans of beer from the styrofoam tub. Pulling the tabs, he handed one to Frankie. 'I'll trade this for a cigarette,' he said.

They smoked and drank, hearing only the laughter from below and the slap of the waves against the hull.

Ron broke their silence. 'Well, Frankie my friend, I've known Kurt S. King ever since I can remember and I've never seen him happier than he has been over the last several years. My consulting practice takes me all over the world and I deal with company presidents every day. But I don't think I could name one as capable, as honest and, dammit, as decent as Kurt King. If there were more executives like Kurt, American business wouldn't get the bad rap it does.'

'Well, well, how's that for a commercial!'

Ron laughed. 'Excuse me, I was getting carried away. I'm bushed. This has been a great cruise and I'm about to hit the sack, but I wanted to tell you I think Kurt's life is really in the groove right now. I think he can handle his marriage mess. He's made his company stronger than ever and he's come to terms with himself, thanks to you. And that's what I wanted to say.'

Frankie felt her eyes grow moist. She grabbed Ron by the arm and gave him a fast kiss on the cheek.

He clattered down the hatch, his lanky form blotting

out the light from below deck. She could hear his strong voice.

'Hey, Kurt, get your ass up on deck. There's a hell of a woman up there waiting for you.'

BOOK THREE
The Raid
21 October 1976

IX

On the eighth floor of the Ticor building, King scanned the lobby walls for a sign to Stephen Schutt's office. Elegant, bleached-oak panelling enclosed the area and a massive double door filled most of one wall. But no sign. King grasped the huge brass knob, swung the doors open and led them into a large reception area furnished in identical panelling with opulent oriental rugs on a black and white parquet floor. On the walls hung paintings that would have graced an art gallery. Frankie would appreciate this, King thought. His more sober afterthought was: Schutt must be good, but hellish expensive.

Stephen Schutt came to greet King warmly and was introduced to Kate Foy and Boyd. Tall, dark-complexioned, Schutt had strong, pleasant features and a full head of hair tinged with grey at the sides. His clothes were stylish. King knew Schutt's father had been a Federal Court judge in California and had done much philanthropic work. Someone had mentioned the son collected German expressionist art.

Schutt introduced his partners, Paul Towers and Harry Mandel, and they briefly discussed the problem. King saw these men were bright, thrusting and appeared to grasp the situation called for fast action. He followed Schutt down a corridor covered with pictures and prints to his private office. He had one question in mind. 'Have you spoken with them?'

'Yes, Mr King . . .'

257

'Steve, let us deal in first names and save words, okay?'

Schutt nodded. 'Mr Norris Thomas, his attorney and shock troops will be here at two. Thomas has a speaking engagement at the Beverly-Wilshire and will walk over after that.'

'Frankly, Steve, I don't want to see the bastard. Since they're going to do it, why not just let them? Why put me in a spot where I might punch him right on the nose?'

'Kurt, relax. I know it's hard to keep your temper in these circumstances, but you don't have to be polite, only civil. Believe me, we'll spend enough time in court before this is over without having to appear because you flattened Norris Thomas.' He grinned suddenly, unexpectedly. 'Anyway, I don't handle assault cases. Nor divorce, for that matter. I've gone through three of them personally and my firm hasn't handled one.'

A quip flashed through King's mind. He'd have to tell Chip how wrong he was, Schutt wasn't a divorce lawyer but a divorced lawyer. 'Okay, I'll keep my hands in my pockets. But you haven't answered my question – why the meeting?'

Schutt motioned him to a chair and sat down himsel in a leather swivel chair behind his desk. 'It's all part o the ceremony, like an Indian ritual. This charade of a face-to-face meeting allows them to claim they acted like ethical businessmen from the outset, and theirs wa a friendly offer.'

'Bullshit. If that's the case, I refuse to see them. The can go straight to hell. It's . . . it's . . .' Anger blockin his thought, King finally said, 'I'm leaving, it's as simpl as that.'

Schutt's expression did not change. He slowly rolle

a pen between the fingers of both hands as he looked at King's grim face. 'Again, relax and listen. If you insist on walking out, I won't try to stop you, but just hear me out first. You're bright, successful, strong-willed – but also impetuous. Now, you've retained me to counsel you, though of course you make the final decision. However, if you won't listen to my counsel, I'll have to withdraw and you'll have to get another lawyer.'

King held up his hands. 'Excuse me, I accept what you say – only I can see no reason for meeting that bandit.'

'I know how you feel, but if you refuse to see them you'll be labelled a discourteous, unbusinesslike executive who puts his personal interest ahead of his shareholders' interests. And that initial black mark against you they'll play up to the hilt.' Schutt replaced his pen in a carved, wooden tray. He was no longer smiling. 'It's your duty as King Corp's chief executive officer to listen to any reasonable offer and to see it's passed on to your shareholders along with a recommendation. Now that recommendation does not come from you but from your board. It's a recommendation to accept or reject, but based on proper deliberation and with the benefit of outside counsel – not legal counsel but investment banking counsel.'

King started to interrupt, but Schutt stopped him with an upraised hand.

'I must also tell you there is a practical reason for not standing up the Zanadu people. They'd love to see that happen, because they could then attack you, personally, as a stubborn, intransigent individual. My advice is to keep the appointment, but the decision is yours.'

King rose and walked to the window and stared out at the congested traffic on Wilshire Boulevard. He

looked blankly at the Brown Derby entrance, the affluent shops on Rodeo Drive, the hub of one of the world's
richest communities. Yet he saw none of this; the shock
of the proposed takeover had numbed his mind. It
overflowed with obsessive questions. Why him and his
firm? Oh, he knew others had suffered the same blow.
But why pick on him? And why now? Why not later
when he might not have cared so much? He felt he was
being drawn into a street brawl, but on ground of his
opponent's choosing. Before the battle had started, they
had fouled him, and it seemed he would have to stand
there and take it. He replayed Schutt's remarks in his
mind and had to agree with his reasoning. Anyway, he,
Kurt King, had no background, no experience, no
insight into this sort of fix. Very few chief executives
did. Except for law firms which made their living as
mercenaries in the corporate wars, it was a once-in-a-
lifetime ordeal for a company chief. He glanced round
at Schutt, still sitting calmly behind his desk.

'Okay, you're right. I'll stay and be civil.' His voice
was quieter than usual. 'Now, how about some lunch?
We left Minneapolis in such a hurry we had no time for
breakfast. And you can imagine how much dinner I ate
last night after I got the news. It was kind of strange
I'd take a bite and it would seem to lodge right there.'
He tapped his breastbone.

2

Lunch was served in the firm's dining room, its wall
lined with a fortune in expressionist art. At one point
King overheard Schutt, deep in conversation with Kat
Foy, say, 'Generally, the German expressionists de
with stark reality, not beauty.'

260

'Stark reality,' thought King as he picked at his delicious lobster salad. 'He could have been talking about a takeover.'

Earlier that day, he had chosen an investment banking house as the qualified outside source to guide the directors on whether to accept or reject the Zanadu offer. After grumbling about investment bankers, whom he viewed as a necessary evil, he accepted Schutt's suggestion of Newcombe & Styles. Schutt thought Bob McGill of that firm was smart and strong enough if the fight dragged on.

McGill arrived shortly before two. They small-talked for a few minutes before he, King and Boyd went into Schutt's office to wait for their visitors. Since Thomas was late, McGill began to talk about the takeover. In King's opinion, the man smelled a fat fee and was trying to impress with his knowledge and insight about the situation. However, he had done his homework.

'Kurt,' he began with too much familiarity for King, 'this is a raw deal. Everybody knows Zanadu has gone nowhere. This morning, I ran some quick comparisons. King and Zanadu were about the same size five years ago with the edge maybe going to them. Since that time, Zanadu has been essentially flat while your company has grown almost fourfold. And importantly, most of your growth has been internal and it's my guess there's more to come. Am I right?'

'You've seen only the beginning,' King confirmed.

McGill picked up speed and assurance. 'In two areas, Canada and Indiana, where you both had holdings, you've expanded dramatically while Zanadu has closed down operations. Now, besides size and growth there another factor which a lot of people ignore – what I call the "social responsibility of job creation". Your good

261

management, hard work and creativity have resulted in many new jobs. According to that important yardstick, Zanadu has failed miserably.'

Noting King's smile of approbation, McGill ploughed on. 'Their annual reports show a continued layoff of people as sales have dropped off. They've closed plants, but managed to sell off the assets of those plants at inflated prices. That means they have cash and probably sizeable borrowing power. Put those two things together and they can buy you and thus achieve what they failed to do on their own – grow.'

King was flattered by these remarks about job creation, which had always been one of his aims; but he did not entirely agree with McGill's notion you could purchase growth. 'Sure, Bob,' he said, 'you can buy companies to achieve growth and we made quite a few such deals, some good, some bad. But I still can't see the point of trying to take a company like ours by force like this.'

'I'm sure you can't, because you don't work that way. I don't know Zanadu's problems in detail, but I know they haven't been able to make a significant deal in years. I'd guess no one wants to talk with them. Anyone who sells a business he has built up, whether he owns it or shareholders own it, wants two things – the best price, and the feeling he's putting his baby into good hands.' McGill paused to sip some water and clear his throat. 'But look at Thomas,' he went on. 'He has a need to grow, to justify his existence so that his board doesn't begin to wonder if he's earning his three hundred grand plus a year. He hasn't made Zanadu grow from the inside, like you, nor has he made any friendly acquisitions. He's sitting on a pile of unemployed cash, so he really has only one option.'

Boyd, who was getting tired of the banker's voice, cut in. 'To go out and steal a going concern like King Corp.'

'But why steal it?' King queried. 'Why didn't he just come to me and make an offer?'

McGill gave him an almost pitying look. 'Because he knew you'd laugh in his face, right?'

'Dead right.' King thought for a moment, then added, 'I guess I wouldn't have laughed in his face, Bob. I'd have listened, though I doubt if a deal could have been worked out. However, my duty to my shareholders compels me to listen to any reasonable deal. Had Thomas made a friendly approach with a decent offer, I'd have been forced to consider it. But an unannounced raid – never.'

'Okay, so what does Thomas do? He studies the hell out of your company, gets all your annual reports, press releases, write-ups, everything, including possibly some illegal inside information. He stalks you like a lion a gazelle, and when he's ready he goes in for the kill.'

McGill had worked himself up. King gave a quick glance round the room and noted the looks of admiration. Quite a speech, he admitted, and could find fault with none of it. If only he could have had this kind of warning counsel earlier when it would have alerted him about takeovers at far less cost!

But McGill had a lot more to tell them. He seemed to have struck a pose, with one hand on the back of a chair as he continued. 'But Mr Thomas's next move in the takeover game is a beaut. There are two New York law firms that specialize in operating for the raider or the victim, whichever one retains them first. Thomas hires both of them, Karl Gearhart and Larry Moss, who are usually at each other's throats in these cases. Clever Thomas!'

'Hold it a second, Bob.' King cut across McGill's monologue. 'Both Moss and Gearhart – how the hell do you know?'

'How did I know? Well, nothing improper, but Steve called me last night, said you'd be making the choice but our firm might be engaged to advise you. Knowing how urgent these things are, I did a bit of snooping with a New York contact . . . he called back this morning and confirmed the word was out Zanadu had grabbed both Gearhart and Moss.'

'So, how in hell does the word get out?'

Schutt, who had sat silent up to now, broke in. 'We stopped trading your stock on the opening, Kurt.'

'Yeah, I guess I knew that. Things do move fast, huh?'

'Too fast,' McGill said, shaking his head grimly as he looked at King. 'Consider yourself the chief executive of a sizeable public company about to be raped and plundered by another company whose president couldn't carry your briefcase. Be prepared for the fight of your life – and be prepared to lose that fight. I hate to say this, but I've been involved in a couple of these takeover bids and the odds are all in his favour.' In the months to come, King would remember McGill's words as he went on, 'Be prepared for an unbelievable series of events in which you will find a whole phalanx of people and organizations lined up against you – your banks, the Securities Exchange Commission, some shareholders, the courts and even some employees. I can see you can't and don't believe that now, Kurt, but I have seen it happen and it will happen to you.'

'It isn't going to happen to us,' King came back. 'We're going to fight this all the way.'

McGill gave a resigned shrug and nodded towards

Schutt. 'You have retained damned good and capable talent in Steve and his people – but these guys Gearhart and Moss are real barracudas. And this whole thing is a nasty, mean and dirty business, despite the ridiculous term "tender offer" which covers it.'

McGill sat down and there was silence, broken only by the tapping of Steve Schutt's pencil, then his voice. 'An excellent summation, Bob, and I'm sorry to have to say I agree with all the warnings, though I take issue with your prediction Kurt is going to lose. I admit the odds are strongly against him.'

'How strongly?' King put in.

'I'd say ten to one.'

'As much as that.' King's face had gone white.

'Let's not count ourselves out yet.' Schutt turned to McGill. 'One thing puzzles me. You said, and Kurt agreed, there is going to be a lot more internal growth. And Kurt replied, "It's only a beginning" or words to that effect. What did you mean, Kurt?'

King took out a Chesterfield and lit it with deliberate gestures. He stared at Schutt, a quick look of special pleading in his eyes. The others missed it, though not Schutt.

'Oh, Lord, I almost forgot a legal requirement,' he said. 'Kurt, you'll have to come with me to Paul Towers' office and sign one more paper before Thomas arrives. Sorry, but let's hurry.'

Schutt led him into a big, sparsely-furnished office. 'We're making this room available to you and your people as a kind of home-away-from-home. Believe me, you'll need it with all the time you'll be spending here. Now, that worried look. Was there something you didn't want to say in front of McGill?'

'You're very good, Steve.' King found an ashtray and

stubbed out his cigarette. 'I know I'll have to trust McGill to keep everything confidential, but not on the first day. He was right about King looking better and better. But only a few people know just how good we look. McGill may be long-winded, but he helped me piece a few things together. I'll try to make it as fast as I can.'

Schutt did not look at his watch. 'Relax,' he said. 'When Thomas shows up, he can cool his heels for a while.'

King was pacing the room while he spoke. 'You reminded me earlier today I work for the stockholders. Let's get one thing straight – I always have and always will work for them. Now, I say any price under 40 dollars a share is a sell-out. I guarantee we can liquidate the company for that, minimum.'

'Are you serious?'

'Absolutely. Chip worked out the figures six months ago, and he's conservative.'

Schutt shook his head and scratched his temple with the butt of his pen. 'If that's the case, then Zanadu must have inside information. I say that because our analysis indicates 29 to 33 dollars a share with 33 the maximum. Your balance sheet isn't strong enough, it shows too much debt.'

'Anything under 40 and my shareholders get a screwing. With what we have going for us, King will be a 50-dollar stock in mid-'78, eighteen to twenty months away. You and the public don't know what we do.'

'Maybe you should tell them.'

'I can't, not until it's certain. I don't like tempting Providence. But my top executives know, and Zanadu must know, and the only way they could know is by having inside dope, and I think I know where they got that. Let's get back and face the bastards.'

When Norris Thomas entered Schutt's office, King was struck by his resemblance to John Mitchell, the former United States Attorney General who had sunk in the mire of Watergate. He had the same bearish physique, the same look of bland insouciance. King thought, 'With this man we'd better be loaded for rhino.' Thomas was accompanied by a short, stocky man who turned out to be a junior partner in Karl Gearhart's law firm.

'Mr King,' Thomas began, 'I tried to reach you in Minneapolis last night to arrange this meeting and discuss our proposed adverse acquisition of your company, but you weren't available.'

'"Adverse acquisition". That's a damn clever way to put it,' King blurted out. He was already finding it hard to keep his promise to Schutt to be civil.

'Please, Mr King, we're here to make a proposal that will be good for you and your shareholders. I greatly admire the fine job you and Mr Boyd have done in building your company. We've followed you closely. We want this to be a friendly transaction.'

'Friendly! You could have called me a month ago. Why didn't you try to see me earlier?'

'I was advised not to by counsel.'

King started to tell Thomas what he thought of this way of doing business but checked himself. He looked hard at Thomas. 'What's your proposition? Let's get on with it, I'm very busy.'

At that, the Gearhart man extracted a sheaf of papers

well over an inch thick from his briefcase and, without comment, handed them to Schutt.

'This is your 13-D?' Schutt queried, and the attorney nodded. Schutt brandished the papers. 'I know I'll read it in here, but to save time why don't you outline your deal?'

'Read it,' replied the attorney, curtly. 'It's all there and in proper form.'

'Let's not play games,' Schutt came back. 'You prepared the documents and your client expects an answer. We are trying, in difficult circumstances, to act as gentlemen. A brief synopsis would help both sides.'

'Read it.'

Schutt's eyes narrowed. 'In that case, if we have nothing to talk about there seems little point in continuing this meeting – unless you want to wait several hours while we peruse these documents.' When neither Thomas nor his attorney said anything, Schutt added, 'You might as well go.'

Hardly able to credit this brusque legal exchange or the attorney's uncivil conduct, King turned to the Zanadu president. 'Mr Thomas, there are a few things you should know about King Corp, things that might have given you second thoughts about your "adverse acquisition" had you been courteous enough to speak to me. It's too late to discuss these matters, so I'll just tell you and you can listen – carefully. First off, I consider your action completely unfriendly. If my directors agree with me and you happen to acquire – through buying King Corp stock – more than 25 per cent of the outstanding shares, you will automatically trigger the payment of about 30 million dollars in accrued bonuses and pensions to about one hundred key employees of this company.'

'Just a minute.' Thomas had a startled look on his face. 'That's not in anything we saw.'

'This isn't a discussion,' King replied, firmly. 'Just listen. This company has an investment of close to 200 million dollars in special equipment producing control systems for the Navy's nuclear propulsion programme headed up by Admiral Hyman G. Rickover. I can tell you any takeover of this company will be looked on unfavourably by Rickover. He doesn't like raiders. He likes me and this company because we've done one helluva job for him. We are now negotiating contracts worth 350 million with him, but your action will delay if not jeopardize those contracts. Some years back, our directors considered selling the Control Systems division. The Admiral got wind of it and raised hell – held up all procurement to us for almost a year. It cost us a fortune. He hates change. You might like to think about that.'

That had Thomas wondering and glancing uncertainly at his attorney.

Watching him, King was reflecting: 'Rickover would swallow this man whole and spit out the bones.' He was remembering his own experience with the Admiral, probably the most eccentric character the modern American Navy has produced. Who didn't know of him and his legend? Hardened naval men quailed when summoned for interviews in the spartan, book-cluttered Washington office where he ran the Naval Reactors branch. His interview chair had a slippery seat and front legs a couple of inches shorter than the back ones so that the Admiral's victim skidded and slithered around like fat on a hot pan. At the same time, he was puzzled and bewildered by Rickover's trick of opening and shutting the Venetian blind like a semaphore. And the questions! 'You're in a plane out of control. Can you convince the other three men to let you have the only parachute?' When the victim said Yes, he found himself arguing for his life with three staff officers summoned by Rickover.

When King had been working a short time for Rick-over, the Admiral phoned him at home one Sunday. 'I'll be at your factory at nine tomorrow to look round,' he snapped. King turned out his staff to tidy up the place that evening and early next morning. Rickover, a wiry, white-haired little man close on seventy, ran them round the factory quizzing men, barking orders and probing with a finger for dust. Suddenly he rounded on King, 'Dammit, King, not a speck of dirt.' It sounded like a reprimand. 'You've cleaned this place up for my benefit, haven't you?'

'That's right, Admiral, we did,' King answered, honestly.

Rickover looked at King quizzically. 'Well I'll be damned. Every other vendor I visit tells me that their factories are always spotless. I know it's bullshit. Cleaned it up for my visit . . . ? Maybe you're honest!'

Thomas cut across his recollections by saying, 'I think we can handle the Admiral.'

'But can you handle the company?' King came back. 'My company's success is built on people who, I believe, are loyal to me, and the day you walk in I walk out and take my key people with me. That's all I have to say, so as far as I'm concerned this meeting is over.'

Thomas got up, walked towards King and put a hand on his shoulder. 'Let's take some time and talk this out. We can work everything out to your satisfaction.'

King kept his voice level. 'I simply refuse to discuss anything with you in these circumstances.'

270

Thomas and his lawyer left without a handshake or a goodbye. King, with his strong feelings of like and dislike, knew he had just met two men he would never be able to like.

When the door slammed, Schutt looked at King. 'You were almost civil.' He added with a shrug, 'Not that they deserved even that.'

4

Schutt hastily reviewed the papers given him by the attorney, riffling through them and muttering from time to time. After ten minutes, he looked up. 'Okay, I'll go over the basic offer. Zanadu offer 31 dollars per share and have arranged to borrow 100 million from banks to finance the purchase; they have already bought 40,000 King shares on the open market; they will pay 40 cents a share to brokers for handling; these papers have been filed today with the Securities and Exchange Commission, so Zanadu can purchase no more stock until the period of the tender offer expires. That's 2 December. At that time, they would buy all that was tendered up to 51 per cent of the outstanding shares. If more is tendered they would still buy no more than 51 per cent.'

Schutt stopped to look around in case anyone had a question before he continued:

'It's interesting, but the papers are silent on what happens to those shareholders who hold the remaining 9 per cent.'

'That's not interesting,' King growled. 'That's ominous.'

Schutt caught his meaning. It was a bad deal at 31 dollars a share because the stock was certainly worth more. For those who could not sell, the remaining 49 per cent, it was a much worse deal for they would see their stock slump.

Schutt led them back into the conference room to explain the offer to the others. 'There's something we all have to understand and reckon with – Zanadu will easily get 51 per cent of the stock unless we do something to stop them.' He turned to King. 'Kurt, you said earlier you control 16 per cent of the stock. If you recommend not to tender, probably another 16 per cent will go along with you. That's only 32 per cent. Enough of the rest to give Zanadu their 51 per cent will be motivated by fear and greed.'

'We'll find a way to stop the bastards.' King looked round the room. 'Damn, what was that great Churchill quote about never giving in, "in nothing great or small"?' He gazed at the other faces for help, expecting none.

But somebody spoke up. Paul Towers, one of Schutt's partners. He was in his late thirties, tall and thin with huge glasses and a modish hair style. He had a surprisingly deep voice. '"Never give in! Never give in! Never never, never, never – in nothing great or small, large or petty . . ." Ah, wait, I know it: ". . . except to convictions of honour and good sense." Right.'

'Another Churchill nut, like me.' King nodded his gratitude to Towers. 'Well, to my way of thinking that's our attitude. And when our board meets tomorrow, hell, I know they'll agree.' He turned to McGill. 'Bob, you'd best get to work on your opinion which we need to guide the directors. I don't want my views quoted until they've had your opinion and studied the offer. Steve, let's assume they oppose Zanadu, what legal steps can we take?'

'You'll have to get out a mailing, a letter to all your

shareholders, plus a printing of that letter in the *Wall Street Journal*, the LA, San Francisco and San Diego papers, and probably in the *New York Times* and *Chicago Tribune*. Will that cover it, Mrs Foy?'

'Yes, but that would be terribly expensive. Wouldn't one paper be enough?'

'Kate, if we're going to fight we can't worry about nickels and dimes.' King's voice, unusually harsh, brought heads up round the table.

'Mr K, we're not talking about nickels and dimes. That much space in those papers will cost a fortune, and we've never spent that sort of money on shareholder communication.'

'My dear, this is a different ball game,' King snapped. 'Just book the space for early next week or as soon as you figure you and the legals can have it ready. Get a draft finished pronto so we can check it out. Get it done!'

'Yessir.' She had hurt in her tone.

Kate Foy, the newest recruit to the company brains trust, handled the Investor Relations department. Although close to forty-five, she looked years younger. She had an Asian background though no more than a hint of this showed in her features and jet-black hair. Seeing her on the day she was hired, Chip Boyd had a double-take thinking she looked like King's sister, then remembered his boss was an only child. Married to a psychiatrist with an international practice, Kate had quit her last job when her last boss tried to palm off a Securities Exchange Commission charge on her for omitting vital facts from an investment brochure. She had walked out immediately she learned he had altered her copy without reference to her.

273

Schutt's secretary opened the conference room door. 'Mr King, a Miss Shore on extension 37.'

'Tell her I'll call back.'

Their discussion focused on the possibility of blocking Zanadu through anti-trust legislation. Paul Towers was scanning a pile of law books and notes. When Schutt called on him to explain how Federal anti-trust laws might stop the raider, he said, 'Does King Corp compete with Zanadu in any way?' When King shook his head, Towers gave him a sly smile. 'No, they wouldn't have started . . . Ah, but you could buy a competitor then call on the feds, the anti-trust guys, to stop the whole deal. It's one way, if you're gutty enough.'

'I'm gutty enough for anything, but we've got to establish one ground rule right now – whatever we do to stop Zanadu has to make good business sense. Break that rule and even if we beat off Zanadu, we could spend the rest of our lives defending shareholders suits.' He sighed as he put out his cigarette in the heaped-up ashtray in front of him. 'Don't forget, a lot of people will jump at the 31-dollar offer. They'll be wrong, but, as you all know, fear and greed are powerful incentives.'

'You're right, Kurt,' Schutt said. 'And when the market reopens on King stock you'll see heavy trading. At any price close to 31, a lot of people will drop their holdings at the first chance.'

'How can they, Mr Schutt?' asked Kate, confused. 'You said the tender doesn't start officially until 1 November, and Zanadu can't buy until 2 December.'

'You're forgetting about arbitrage, Kate,' King put in. 'The arbitrageurs will jump on this immediately.'

She nodded, knowing that these investment experts made their money out of short-term ups-and-downs

274

the market. Schutt was talking. 'And the arbitrageurs will take King stock to 31 or even a bit higher.'

'How can it go higher?' King looked at the lawyer, quizzically. 'The Zanadu offer is only for 31. At that price, the arbitrageurs would lose, or just break even.'

'But there's the broker's fee,' Schutt came back. 'Because they're in the investment business they get the broker's fee of 40 cents a share which means they could pay 31.35 a share and still make a nickel. With the kind of numbers they deal in, they could still make a hefty profit.'

Chip Boyd cut in. 'Let's get back to defensive tactics,' he said. 'What about buying something and issuing preferred shares? A few weeks ago, I played golf with the executive vice-president of Astroteknik, the White Knight firm I have in mind. They wanted to sell a couple of operations that might fit us. We could give them a preferred with voting rights and this would cut Zanadu's voting stock even if they bought 51 per cent of us.'

That brought King to life. 'A great idea, Chip. Give them a call and set up a meeting for tonight or tomorrow. Also, tell them I want to meet with their president, Bill Damen, as soon as he's available. He could be our White Knight if we need one.'

Chip went to a phone and the others split into various working groups. Kate Foy was already drafting the shareholders' letter while Schutt and his partner, Harry Mandel, were paging through a stack of law books. 'Hey, maybe we have something here.' Schutt had a grin on his long, handsome face. 'Under Delaware law which governs this tender offer, it is required that the offeror serve the 13-D on an officer of the company they're after at the company's principal place of business.'

'13-D?' Kate queried.

'That's the formal announcement of their intent to offer. Technically, Gearhart's man should have handed the papers to you, Kurt, at your own office. It's a technicality, but perhaps a major one. The law is written in a certain way for a certain purpose, and God knows, I didn't write it. But Zanadu hasn't complied with the letter of the law. Stupid on their part, but maybe helpful to us.'

'How does it help?' King asked.

'If their act of serving the paper on your company is improper they may be forced to do it again and that buys us what we most need – time. I'll call Tom Baker, an expert on Delaware law, and ask our best approach.'

Boyd returned to say he would meet with the Astro-teknik people later that evening. They thought his idea looked good, but the president, Bill Damen, was out of town until Saturday and they would have to wait for his say-so before making any commitment.

Schutt talked to Baker then hung up. 'He thinks it's got a shot,' he told King. To Towers, he said, 'He wants a copy of the documents to be sent to him tonight, so get the girls busy on the copiers and call Bor-Air and schedule a nine o'clock pick-up to get them to him tomorrow morning.' He sat back and allowed himself a long, slow smile. 'I think we've done everything we can today. I suggest everyone head home and we'll meet back here tomorrow morning.'

Driving home, King started to listen to the radio news then shut it off abruptly. He'd had enough news for one day. All in all, he did not feel low. In fact, he fe rather good. Schutt's people impressed him as competent and bright. Already, they had launched an attack and he had a deep-down feeling he was going to win.

Home again, he checked with his answering service. Steve Schutt had called asking him to bring certain company files with him in the morning. King shook his head, admiringly.

He thought about food, but decided instead on a cold glass of milk, then early bed. He fell asleep easily, but at 3.30 something woke him and he lay for a moment confused before remembering what it was. Damn, damn, he had not called Frankie. He punched up his pillow, pushed his head back into it and was asleep again within minutes.

X

On Friday 22 October, the news made the first page of
the *Los Angeles Times* financial section, in a mid-page
box set off by dark borders. It read:

ZANADU WILL MAKE OFFER FOR KING CORP

Zanadu Industries, Inc., of New York announced it is seeking
up to six million shares, about 51% of King Corp of Los
Angeles, at a net price of 31 dollars per share, cash. Zanadu
said the tender offer will be made on 11 November and will
expire 2 December. The New York company said it is attempting to meet with King management to discuss the offer. A
spokesman for King Corp said the bid is currently being
examined.

King tossed the paper on the yellow side table. He
slipped off his robe and, clad in nothing but boxer
shorts, he dropped lightly to the deck and began a
series of slow, boot-camp push-ups. Puffing, he
stopped after twenty-five to rest. Damn cigarettes, he
cursed, then did twenty-five more though with less
rhythm. He did another quarter of an hour and finished
drenched with sweat but feeling good. He showered
then breakfasted on orange juice, black coffee and a
single piece of toast.

'How do you feel?' Schutt asked when he dumped
the office files in front of him.

'Almost human.'

'Given the circumstances that's pretty damn good,
Schutt laughed.

278

A stack of messages awaited King and he began to return some of the calls. Many had come from brokers wishing to help King Corp fight off the tender offer. Hearing that he had already retained Newcombe & Styles, almost all the brokers wished him good luck. Except one, who seemed excessively disappointed and implied that King and his company owed him the job. Then Edward Foxe tried, unsubtly, to blacken the name of Newcombe & Styles. Foxe was no stranger to King; in fact, the young investment banker, a vice-president of F. G. Irving, had handled a few of his personal investments; their relations ended there, although Foxe had attempted to extend his role to handling King Corp's banking needs. McGill might be loquacious, but King preferred him to this hard-selling character.

Paul Towers walked in on him, complete with his outsize, yellow notepad. Towers was likeable, even if he had an unnerving habit of turning mental cartwheels during group discussions. 'We're going to need specialized outside help,' he said. 'A guy who can furnish expert opinions for affidavits and the like. As your counsel, it's off-limits for us. We need somebody who's been under fire both on the raiders' and the victims' side. There are three, four outstanding guys, all in the Big Apple and they don't come cheap.' He tapped his list.

'Is Ronald Foster Poole on that list?'

'Yeah! How come you know about him? He's one of the newer ones in the field . . . helluva reputation.'

'He's one of my oldest friends. We grew up together.'

'Hey, that might work real well. But wait a minute – his friendship won't cloud his judgement, and your own judgement?'

King thought for a minute then shook his head. 'In

fact, Ron knows me so well, if he sees me heading off in the wrong direction he can turn me around a lot faster than you fellows.'

Towers smiled. 'I'll give him a call right now and see if he's available.'

King halted him at the door. 'Paul, it's my guess he'll make himself available, even if it costs him something. So, make sure he doesn't shave his price. You know what's in line and what isn't.' He ran a nervous hand over his hair. 'Jesus, I get the feeling I'm going to be buying a lot of new cars for a lot of lawyers before this thing is over.'

Towers had the decency to look embarrassed. 'Oh, Steve wants to see you when you're free,' he said.

Schutt was on the phone but ended his conversation quickly and with such smoothness the person on the other end could never have guessed he was getting the fast shuffle. Schutt advised King to retain his Delaware colleague, Tom Baker, who thought they could delay Zanadu on a technicality. King gave him the go-ahead, pleased to have even a small reed to clutch at.

'Your directors will be here at 3.30 and I think we should run through the agenda now,' the lawyer said. 'I know this is normally your baby, but here some legal advice is called for. The first rule is – nothing but the facts, absolutely no opinions. I'll help with the presentation of the tender offer and its terms, then Bob McGill will give the board a professional opinion. Kurt, you may furnish the board with your earnings estimates for 1976 and the coming year, but keep it as factual as possible. No excessive predictions that might influence them.'

'Goddamn it, Steve, I've never distorted a presentation to influence the board in my life.'

'Sorry, but that warning's one of the things you're paying me for. I have the overall forecast for the rest of '76 and the next two years made by Bud Gorman, your financial vice-president. It's quite impressive. He says you can show earnings for the year of 4 dollars a share at least. From your look that doesn't surprise you, even though you haven't yet seen Gorman's projections.'

King smiled, though a bit wearily. 'Earlier this year, I told the Wall Street people we'd make at least 2.50. I knew we had some hay in the barn, thanks to Dean Hubert, who watches over our glass products divisions. It's safe to project 5 dollars per share for '77.'

'What are you going to tell the board about Tri Corp?' Schutt asked.

King and his top executives had kept the Tri Corp project under their hats, but they were certain it would reap big rewards for the company in a few years. Indeed, it was the sort of deal that might have triggered the interest of Thomas and Zanadu – if they had already got wind of it. Only days before the raid began, King and Hubert had returned from a short trip to Italy and England where they studied the feasibility of building their own float plant for large-scale glass manufacturing.

As head of the company's expanding glass operations, Hubert had learned of the chance to buy Tri Corp, a glass manufacturer close to bankruptcy. Hubert's division needed raw glass and Tri Corp had a float plant which had just gone on line. The purchase meant closing outmoded and unprofitable sheet glass plants and streamlining the management and workforce; it meant, too, taking on extra debt. But the float plant would make them profits in a year or two.

Their English trip was to visit the Pilkington Glass

281

Works whose founder had developed the float-glass process, and who controlled strong international patents, and licensed manufacture throughout the world. Using the Pilkington process, it would take three years and 40 million dollars to build their own float plant. They also rejected the Italian alternative, which was still in the construction stage, and returned with their minds made up to buy Tri Corp.

That was the week before they flew to Canada and made the midwestern trip to Minneapolis where he learned Norris Thomas was launching his raid.

'So, what do you say about Tri Corp?' Schutt asked again.

'The deal was good before and it's just as good now, Steve. I'm going to recommend purchase just as I would have if Zanadu hadn't entered the picture.'

'Okay, and I admire your point of view, Kurt. Some chief executives in your position would say "screw you" to everything.'

'That's as may be. But that's not the way I've ever thought about any company – and certainly not about King Corp.'

2

King met all his directors individually, asking how much they had heard while studying their faces. Did any one of them show signs of knowing about the offe before he did, forty-four hours earlier? If they did, non of them betrayed it. Not Sam Martenson, who knew everything. Nor Quentin Groves, who had friends an contacts everywhere in the California business world Nor Cass Byrd, the venerable, who had pull in all thre of Washington's power houses – the Congress, th

Senate and the White House. King knew them all personally, and with their business and family background, he doubted if any of them had turned Judas. But who could tell when so much money lay on the table?

At 3.30, he called the meeting to order, apologizing for having to convene the entire board outside its normal routine, but pleading the gravity of the situation. First, he reported on the excellent current operations of the company. Any other time, that news would have brought a handclap or even a backslapping joke or two, but now everybody was too preoccupied with the takeover bid.

King told the board about the Tri Corp project, hinting at another special meeting to review the final terms Hubert had negotiated. After that, he took a deep breath and plunged in, describing the tender offer with no flourishes and no personal coloration.

Clearly, everyone had been waiting for this and listened in total silence as King spelled out the facts. He had always had complete loyalty from his board, but paradoxically their strong support of him created a difficulty now. If the Zanadu offer was a boon for King stockholders, the board had to support it or violate their trust with the shareholders; but to accept the offer would mean Kurt S. King, Jr would almost certainly leave. They knew he would never work for Thomas and his departure would trigger a whole series of resignations.

King kept his presentation factual and unemotional. Nonetheless, when he handed over to Steve Schutt, the tension subsided. Schutt passed round a digest of the terms included in the 13-D Zanadu had filed. When the directors had finished studying the summary, questions began and Schutt handled most of them. Next, Bob McGill took the floor.

'Gentlemen,' said McGill, 'Newcombe & Styles has made a thorough review of all the factors in this offer. As a result, we report that 31 dollars per share for all the King Corp shares would be inadequate. Therefore, 31 dollars per share for 51 per cent is totally inadequate. Are there any questions?'

Hands went up, but went down again when McGill explained his firm's opinion would be presented in written form. King stood up. 'Now that you know as much as we do and have the professional opinion of Newcombe & Styles, may I have a motion?'

A motion from the floor rejecting the Zanadu offer was promptly seconded and carried unanimously. King felt elated and buoyed up physically by this support.

From halfway down the table came a mellow but no-nonsense voice. 'Kurt, get your PR people started immediately. It is essential the shareholders and the public know our side of this story. This is absolutely vital in fighting these people off.' The speaker was Cassius H. Byrd. An attorney, he had played a major role in the 1968 Republican victory and had served in Washington for two years in several key posts. He left in 1970 to become National Chairman of the Republican Party and thus escaped the stigma of Watergate. He still had contacts at the highest government levels. Although King had never exploited Cass Byrd's considerable influence, he wondered if this might not be the time.

'A good point, Cass, and we have already started work in that direction.'

He officially adjourned the meeting, but no one left and the room resonated with heated discussion. Sever more people arrived, from the public relations firm, from McGill's office. Phones kept ringing and half a dozen conversations were going on at once. The huge conference table disappeared beneath a chaos of coffee cups, coke cans, glasses and ashtrays as well as the tidal wave of papers and notepads.

Someone handed King a sheaf of papers containing phone messages. One was from Ron Poole, who had been contacted in Chicago and would arrive at LAX at 7.10 that evening. Just the thought of seeing him made King feel better. Another was from Frankie Shore and read, 'Don't worry about not calling. I understand perfectly. Call when convenient.' He was glad to hear from her and relieved she was not upset at his failure to call the previous night.

In the office Schutt had set up for him, King noticed someone had already· transformed things. Two small prints he had admired hung on the wall over the largest desk and plants had sprouted in several corners. He had his own bathroom, complete with small refrigerator. He peeked inside. The ice trays were full and the shelves contained bottles, both soft drinks and liquor. And his favourite brands of gin and vermouth, Beefeater and LeJon. How typical of Schutt! he thought.

He called in the lawyer then sent for Boyd. 'Chip, tell Steve about our two suspects.'

Boyd briefly described Matthew G. Tillman and the consultant jobs he had done for the company, and the fact that he had a lot of confidential information, including their phone list. He was their prime suspect, since he had done a great deal of work for Zanadu and could have fed them vital information about the King Corp prospects.

Another man, William Grant Sheridan, had also done

work for both companies, and he, too, knew a lot of inside information about their prospects, and their weaknesses. He might have triggered the raid.

Schutt noted all this in his precise hand and when Chip had finished, he turned to King. 'We'll get two subpoenas out and serve them on both men then take their depositions. If either or both has divulged confidential data to Zanadu, they could be prosecuted under the Securities and Exchange Act.' He drummed his gold pencil on the desk then looked at them. 'Anybody else who might have tipped your hand?' Both shook their heads. 'I'll get on to it,' Schutt said.

Left alone, King rang Frankie. She told him how sorry she was about the raid, but she was sure the war hadn't been lost. He appreciated that. 'Look, Hon, I don't think I'll be tied up here too late tonight. Would you be up to fixing dinner at my place? I'm in no mood to eat out. Oh, there would be three of us. Ron Poole's coming in at about seven, and I'll pick him up.'

'Of course I wouldn't mind. How hungry will you be?'

'Probably not very, if the last couple of days are any indication, but I should eat something. I think I forgot lunch.'

'I'll get some steaks and a big salad along with potatoes and a vegetable. How does that sound?'

'Beautiful. I'd better get back to the group. See you around quarter to eight.'

He hung up, blocking the sound of her kiss.

3

Despite having met on only three previous occasions, Ron Poole and Frankie Shore considered themselves fast friends. Their friendship was genuine, as is often the case when two people have deep feelings of love and affection for the same third party.

Frankie opened the door to him. 'Ron! you look great . . . good enough to eat.'

'Jesus, when Kurt invited me for dinner, I didn't realize . . .' His sentence tailed off and Frankie threw back her head and laughed.

'And I thought I was setting you up to say something feelthy. Welcome back to California.'

'Hey, Kurt,' he said, looking at King, 'how about leaving me alone with this gorgeous creature? We want to – how do you say it? – we want to get it on.' He slipped an arm around Frankie's waist and leered at her.

King laughed. Ron never changed. 'As a matter of fact I have to go into the den and return some calls. Bring me a drink in there will you, old buddy?'

Frankie looked at Ron. 'Which one of us does he mean? It better not be me.'

Ron walked over to the bar and fixed two drinks. 'What's yours, Frankie?'

'Nothing, thanks. I've been sampling wine in the kitchen for the last hour. Take Kurt his drink and come outside with me while I put these steaks on the coals.'

It was clear and pleasant on the terrace with only a mild breeze. The last streamers of sunset lit the darkening sky. Abruptly, Frankie turned and said, 'Ron, please fill me in on the seriousness of this whole tender offer

287

thing before Kurt gets off the phone. But make it simple if you can.'

For the next ten minutes, Poole briefed her about the crisis King and his company were facing. Only once did she interrupt him for clarification. Her concern showed in the way she listened to every word. 'But how do you fit in, Ron? When did you start to specialize in these takeovers?'

'About three years ago, shortly after I met you with Kurt in New York. I'd been working for Freeman, an investment brokerage house, and got involved in a takeover bid on the side of the victim, a guy who'd run his company for more than ten years, then boom, he was out on his ass. I felt for him. But it seemed people and companies could really get screwed, yet the whole thing was perfectly legal. I shot my mouth off when our guy lost, and one of the senior partners told me to cool it.'

'But why?'

'Because the firm was getting more and more involved in takeover bids, and usually on the raider's side. Then I learned how much Freeman was making through its arbitrage department.'

'Excuse me, but arbitrage . . . I'm floundering again.'

'Arbitrage is Wall Street's fast-buck game. The "arbs" – short for arbitrageurs – deal in the day-to-day stock market fluctuations. Generally, they deal in large volume and small margins, pennies, they get in and out quick, betting on a sudden upturn or downturn of the market. They love takeover bids.'

'It sounds more like Las Vegas than Wall Street.'

'You've hit it on the button. The "arbs" are betting Zanadu will win. Or better yet, somebody will come along and top their offer. They've only one worry –

288

somehow Kurt will figure a way to beat Thomas. The "arbs" will be calling Kurt hourly to see how the battle's going. If he's winning, down goes the stock, if he's losing up it goes.'

'They're like sharks going in for the kill.' Frankie had awe in her voice.

'For them, money's the name of the game. When they get in early on a sure thing, they stand to make a fortune. On a half billion dollar raid, they'll make 60 to 80 million, and if they're brokering the deal another 20 million. If someone has insider information before the action starts they can rake in a helluva lot more. That's illegal, but it surely happens.' He paused, reflecting on his suspicions, adding, 'and all that in a few days . . . real leeches!'

'But who pays for all this money they make out of nothing?' she butted in.

'Way downstream, the stockholders.' Poole ground out his cigarette on the terrace and sipped his drink. 'Anyway, I made it known how I felt about Freeman's involvement in raids and we had a civil parting of the ways and I set up my own shop, specializing in takeover bids. I prefer working for the victims, though sometimes I work for the raider.'

'Did Kurt know you did this as a speciality? I don't remember him telling me.'

'Kurt probably never thought twice about it because he never expected to be raided – even though it goes on all the time.'

'It's that common, then?'

'It's getting that way. This year there'll probably be twenty, thirty that make headlines, like Zanadu raiding King. Sometimes a raider will hire me to find him a likely victim because I've learned to spot them and size them up. I've been asked several times to look at half a dozen potential victims without even knowing who the raider is.'

'Wait – how can you be hired by somebody you don't know?'

'I'm hired by the attorneys, the real raid specialists. There are two New York lawyers who are the top experts – Karl Gearhart and Larry Moss. When either of those men comes after a company, it's in deadly trouble.'

'And one of them is after Kurt's company?'

'I wish to God it was only one. Zanadu's got both of them.'

'Oh, Jesus, what are his chances, Ron?'

'I just stepped in, so this is a guesstimate. I'd say twenty to one against him.'

Frankie suddenly became aware of that Pacific breeze and shivered violently. She made to say something but stopped when King appeared on the terrace, a third drink in his hand. Frankie looked at it and almost cautioned him that another drink might spoil his appetite, then thought better of it. The way things were going Kurt was entitled to it, and he was seldom affected by three drinks. As there was damp sea air wafting along the terrace, she served them a candlelight dinner indoors. The fine California Pinot Noir went perfectly with the steak, baked potatoes, roasted corn and spinach salad. They talked little. Both men had dined in their shirtsleeves, but when Frankie began to clear the table, she noticed King had put on the jacket of his suit.

'Cold?'

'No, I thought we'd sit outside for a while. Do you mind, honey?'

'Of course not, but don't you want dessert?'

They both refused, and when she was stacking the plates on the kitchen counter, she saw King had eaten no more than half his meal. He was taking this raid too much to heart. She joined them on the terrace where King was leaning forward, dragging on a cigarette and listening intently to Poole.

'To a limited extent there are laws against raids. At federal level there's the Williams Act requiring raiders to make certain disclosures about their companies and their intentions. And the SEC demands public information about the financing of the deal. That slows the raiders down a bit.' Poole stubbed out his cigarette and took the cup of coffee Frankie proffered. He went on talking since King had neither moved nor spoken. 'At state level Ohio, Delaware and New York have passed laws giving victims incorporated in those states forty days' grace, which does help a little. In other states, hell, it can be over in ten days, maybe less. Takeovers are a runaway express train – there's no way to stop them.'

'We've got to find a way, Ron,' King said through clenched teeth.

'Well, there's usually some device to slow things down and give a victim time to try to find a better offer from a White Knight – like the Astroteknik outfit you mentioned, Kurt. But even if the White Knight comes in it's still a lousy deal. You may not get raped, but you sure as hell lose your virginity.'

King reached over and laced Poole's coffee with cognac.

He nodded his appreciation and kept talking. 'The sad thing is the courts, banks and government agencies are pretty much on the raider's side. They take the view

291

if the stockholders get better than the market price for their shares, good luck to them and that's all that counts.'

'Maybe I shouldn't say this,' Frankie interrupted in a tentative voice, 'but isn't it a good thing? I mean, what's wrong with a stockholder getting more for his holding?'

'In a sense you're right, Frankie, but there's a lot more involved than money. People's lives are knocked off their stride by these things.' Poole glanced at King, whose features looked set hard even in the dim light. 'Excuse me, Kurt, but in these affairs good management usually ends up on the outside. It's the money men and the wheeler-dealers who win.'

King had noticed Frankie was trying, vainly, to disguise the fact she was beginning to shiver; he took off his jacket and draped it over her shoulders.

'But won't you be cold?' she queried.

'No, the coffee and brandy has warmed me up. That, and listening to Ron's spiel.' He walked over to the railing to peer down then came back and stood for a moment, saying nothing. But they noted his agitation in the way he drummed his fingers against the door jamb. Frankie reached up and put her hand on his and he stopped, looking at her as if surprised to learn what he had been doing. He broke his silence.

'This will probably sound as self-serving as hell, but you're the only two people I can unload myself on. Building a going company takes more than money. It takes brains, guts, hard work and the uncommon talent of developing other people's talents. That's something the raiders don't know and never will. And you can throw Wall Street and the banks in with that lot. It has given me a helluva kick to see the Wall Street geniuses fall flat on their ass. This week they're telling me how to run my company, next week their own company goes bust. In my opinion, Wall Street and the banks have become leeches living off the brains and guts of American entrepreneurs.'

King sloshed some coffee into his cup then spiked it with cognac. He lit a cigarette, setting its end glowing brightly as he sucked in smoke. 'Let me give you an example. Joe Doakes in West Cupcake, Idaho, invents a framistaris to grow Idaho potatoes – like we had tonight – bigger, better and cheaper. He has a little money, borrows a bit more and starts a factory which will benefit every spud-eater in the world and shorten the dole queues in West Cupcake. Things prosper, but eventually he needs money to expand and meet increased demand. His friendly banker can't increase his loans but recommends he talk with the local representatives of Bing, Bang, Bong in Pocatello. Within no time, Joe is sitting in Bing's panelled palace in New York City. Financing is arranged, stock is sold to the public, Joe gets his money and the framis factory goes forward. But good old Joe now owns only 20 per cent of the company he started, with the rest of the shares scattered throughout the country. Of course, everyone likes Joe who stays on as president of Framis Inc. Up to this point, the system works well.'

King paused, lit another cigarette, took a sizeable swig of his coffee and looked to see if he had the ear of Poole and Frankie. They were hanging on his words.

'But it's now the Wall Street boys begin to have fun. By story and by rumour, the Framis stock is promoted. What came on the market at 10 shoots right up to 30. The stockbrokers and the wise-boy investors get their cut, but the poor public is now paying 30 for stock that is worth only 10. Then the first shoe falls – some smart-ass analyst who doesn't know a framis from his navel writes up the company and says the business is in decline because potatoes are not only going out of style, they cause athlete's foot and alopecia totalis prematura.'

'Hey, what's that,' Poole put in. 'And is it true?'

'It's premature total baldness, and no, it's out of my head.' King was not smiling. He continued. 'OK, the stock hits 5 from 30, but it's still worth 10, and even more. Because something the analyst doesn't know and Honest Joe daren't tell him is that he and his engineers have developed a widget to hit the market next year and make a ton of money.'

Normally meticulous, King flicked his dying cigarette out over the terrace railing. They could see he was worked up, getting high on his anger. 'Then the next shoe falls. Word on the widget leaks out and both Gearhart and Moss hear about it and pour it into the ear of that well-known raider, Shitke of Vulture & Vulture. In a takeover bid, Shitke is prepared to pay 8 for the stock still sitting at 5. The scared and uninformed shareholders grab at the chance and Shitke gobbles up the company in two weeks. The shareholders holler "Wonderful!"'

King flopped down on the empty *chaise-longue* and sucked in a deep breath. 'Wonderful bullshit! The shareholders got a real screwing. Shitke doesn't know framis or a widget from a potato crisp and screws up the whole company. Employment in West Cupcake drops by 50 per cent. Joe and his key people have taken off, unable to live with Shitke.

'Ah, but people say, "Don't feel sorry for Joe". He got his money out at 8 and he's now worth a couple million. He can buy a condo in Hawaii, take up golf and sailing and live a little for a change. Only, Joe didn't want to do that, he wanted to keep on running his company. So, the country has lost an inventor, a leader, a fine manager, a builder, a man who created jobs.'

Without realizing it, King was standing waving his arms, splashing coffee over the *chaise-longue* and himself. 'Incidentally,' he went on, 'while the raid was in progress, Joe fought like hell to fend off Shitke, and he took stick from all the powers that be. Shitke, Wall Street, the courts, the SEC, the banks, the investment wizards – they all said he was just trying to hold on to his job. What's their beautiful phrase for it, Ron?'

'Yeah, I know – entrenched management.'

'But it couldn't be further from the truth. Joe had the widget up his sleeve, he knew his company was under-valued but was working too hard to tout his stock up and down Wall Street.' King lowered his voice when he realized he had been ranting a bit. 'American business has been slipping in public esteem, but not because of the Joes. It's the people who finance business, the banks and investment bankers who parasite off the Joes of West Cupcake – they have lost the public trust.'

He sat down hard, as though all the steam had gone out of him. His two friends were staring at him, in no doubt that his impassioned allegory had himself as its real martyr. For Joe Doakes read Kurt S. King. When no one had spoken for several minutes, Frankie broke the silence. 'A great story, Hon, but is that always the case?' It wasn't quite the question she had wanted to ask, but the silence had embarrassed her.

'Ron, you take that one,' King said in a whisper. 'I'm all talked out.' He got up and went inside, heading for the bar.

Frankie waited until they heard him mixing a drink,

then whispered. 'Kurt's taking this takeover bid so hard I'm scared he'll crack up. He was talking about himself in that story, wasn't he?'

'Yeah, 'fraid so.' Poole shrugged. 'But what do you expect? – King Corp's more than a company to him, it's his father, mother and everything else. His whole life.'

Poole left shortly after midnight, explaining he was still on Eastern time. Out of long habit, Frankie began to take her clothes off in the darkened living room. She stopped when she realized King was not watching her. He was standing at the terrace door, one hand on the latch, staring out at the few lights in the distance.

'Coming to bed soon?'

'Ah, yeah, honey. Look, don't worry, if you fall asleep I'll wake you.'

Frankie went to bed. She was aware of nothing more until a hand on her thigh woke her sometime in the night. She turned and took his hand, bringing it up to her bed-warm breast. She waited a moment or two for him to move then stared at him. He was fast asleep.

'Poor baby,' she sighed.

XI

King's makeshift office in the Ticor building was beginning to look like the command post of a warship at battle stations. Or a big news agency coping with a major catastrophe. Half a dozen phones never stopped ringing and lawyers, public relations men, bankers and King Corp staff were all holding forth to each other or to outside callers while secretaries criss-crossed with reports and messages. King, who was losing track of time, had to look twice at the calendar to check it really was a Saturday.

Paul Towers summoned them to a special meeting. An attorney friend had rung to say his client, Cross Industries, was having a legal hassle with Zanadu, who was resorting to every trick to monopolize the market and squeeze them out. Cross was accusing Zanadu of patent fraud, price rigging, below-cost selling, all of which prevented Cross from raising capital.

'How do we come into this, Paul?' King asked.

'Maybe it's a crazy notion, but one of the best ways to stop a raid is by showing the takeover would produce a monopoly or stifle competition to the point where the Federal Trade Commission would say No to the deal. Cross would like to be acquired. Perhaps King could buy them.'

'What do they make that competes with Zanadu?'

'Toilets.' Towers said the word so loudly several people chuckled. 'Chemical toilets, and Zanadu is a major operator in that field. So, acquire Cross and you could get a built-in anti-trust suit.'

King reflected for a moment before answering. 'Paul, it may not be so crazy. We've been looking to get into that business for some time, but evidently our people have never heard of Cross.'

'My lawyer friend says they have excellent products but haven't been able to get off the ground because of Zanadu. He claims he has a great law-suit but Cross probably won't live long enough for him to win it.'

King thought the deal sounded like a fit. King Corp made and distributed all sorts of equipment used a construction sites, such as barricades, signs and warn ing lights, a growing area. Months earlier, the man whe ran that operation had approached Chip Boyd with th idea of acquiring a chemical toilet company as it woul dovetail neatly with their other products.

'Chip, take a hard look at this outfit right away. Bu give it serious consideration only if it actually fits ou business needs and a fair deal can be worked out. S up a meeting with the Cross people and your evaluatio team for tomorrow.'

If anyone recalled the next day was Sunday, no or bothered to mention it.

Schutt buzzed King and asked him to come into h private office. 'I've got news about your two maveric who might have leaked your prospects to Zanadu,' said before King had sat down.

'The bad news first, Steve.'

'It's bad both ways, Kurt – but with a chink of hop With the point of his gold pencil, Schutt flipped throu several pages of his desk pad. 'We ran William Gr Sheridan to earth last night and Harry Mandel w over to Pasadena to take his deposition. I only have bones of it, but we think he's clean. He did some consulting work for Zanadu and knew they were interested in taking over King Corp. He affirms they didn't even ask his opinion about you.'

'They probably didn't have to since they got it all from the other rat, Tillman. Where are we with him?'

'In a word, nowhere. I can tell you he's left town for some assignment in Colorado.'

'Sure it's not across the Mexican border?' King stabbed his cigarette at the lawyer's notepad. 'Anyway, how do we know that much?'

'He phoned his lawyer who's a friend of ours. Tillman was scared by the news of the takeover bid.'

'He damn well ought to be.'

'Okay, Kurt, but he denied setting things up for Zanadu.' Schutt scratched his grizzling hair with his pencil point and pouted his lips. 'On the other hand he did let slip giving them a list of names.'

'Yeah, we know that – our confidential phone list. And a lot else, I'm certain.'

'Well, we'll see. Anyway, we'll keep chasing him and stick him with a subpoena, then he'll have to talk.'

'He's the bastard who triggered this raid,' King said.

He and the lawyer spent half an hour going over their strategy before King had to excuse himself. He had a meeting with William Damen of Astroteknik. At the door, Schutt stopped him, placed a hand on his shoulder and fixed him with those dark, intelligent eyes. 'Kurt, a piece of non-legal advice – don't get too emotionally involved in this takeover business. I know your father created the company, you were gypped out of it, you gave it the kiss of life and put everything you had into it. But don't start hating people like Tillman or even Thomas. In other words, don't let your heart

299

dictate to your head. We'll have more chance of beating the bastards if we keep our personal feelings out of it.'

King looked at him, hesitated for a moment then slapped him on the shoulder, aware Schutt had paid him a compliment by putting those thoughts on the line. Between him and this cultured and intellectual lawyer, a deep sense of trust and friendship had developed. 'I'll behave. Now, I've got to get with Bill Damen.'

Schutt looked at King quizzically, 'Damen? That's Astroteknik. From what you and Boyd had said I assume he's your number one candidate for White Knight. How well do you know him? Can you trust him?'

'Known him for ten years or so, not well. He was the top financial officer under Fulton Summers . . .'

'Oh, yes, Summers – died suddenly a few years back.'

'That's right. Great guy. We were very close. He was on my board. We used to hold an annual business and social outing in Palm Springs together – Astroteknik and King Corp. Damen became CEO after Summers' death. How well do I know him? It's one of those funny things. I know him because of the association with the company and Fulton Summers, but I really don't know him. Trust him? Well, Summers was one I could trust and Astroteknik has always been a friendly company. So, sure, he's OK.'

Schutt stared upward, looked back at King and said, 'Be careful.'

However, that meeting with William Viscott Damen put his pledge under stress. King took Chip Boyd, Ron Poole and Harry Mandel with him to the meeting at Astroteknik. King and Damen knew each other and shared some business interests, though they had never had any direct dealings. Damen was about ten years

300

older, short, stocky and on the portly side. He wore his hair old-style, short-back-and-sides, and this reflected his approach to things. Bad sight obliged him to wear tinted glasses, so nobody could tell what his eyes were hinting. King respected Damen as a businessman, though their approach differed. Damen, an accountant by training, did not look much beyond the dollar signs. He had a forthright style which strangers mistook for rudeness. King Corp and Astroteknik had shared some directors.

They quickly got down to discussing the takeover bid. Chip Boyd outlined his scheme for buying a couple of Astroteknik operations by issuing Astroteknik's preferred stock with voting rights to cut Zanadu's voting strength. King was watching Damen closely, aware he had already been briefed about the idea. To his astonishment, he realized the man was not even listening. When Boyd had finished his exposition, Damen quickly said, 'No, that doesn't appeal to me. I'm sorry about the situation that's developed with Zanadu, and I'll help where I can, but Astroteknik's my only consideration. Any action I take must be good for my company and I can't get involved in some Mickey Mouse scheme to save King Corp.' Damen ignored the shock and disappointment his blunt statement had caused and went on, 'We've played the White Knight role in a couple of tender offers and it didn't work out. But we could be interested. Tell me more about your company, Kurt.'

'I think, Bill, we'll prevail over Zanadu, but in the unlikely event we can't stop them, we would have to run to friends. If Astroteknik is interested, I would consider your company an excellent marriage partner.'

Damen had a sour expression on his heavy features.

He fixed King with a stare behind those useful glasses, but did not comment on the statement. Again, he asked about the company's business and prospects. At considerable length, King gave him a rundown on the entire company, its products, plans, growth record, present earnings and future projections. Damen was now sitting up and taking note.

'If what you say is true, Kurt,' he interrupted, 'I get a lot different impression of your company than I had developed independently. Frankly, I thought most of your growth had come about through acquisitions. This is a different story.'

That lifted King's mood, and he continued, 'Bill, what I've said is on the safe side. As for internal growth, listen to these figures – our sales were 250 million dollars in 1970, this year, six years later, they'll hit close to a billion which is a growth of 650 million. Of that, 500 million is internal and only 150 million through acquisitions. Incidentally, that's a net figure because we've sold off five or six small operations.'

Damen was nodding his appreciation and even threatened to smile at one point. 'Okay, what now?' he said.

'I suggest you send some of your experts to look at our figures in depth. We'll show you everything, no holds barred. As this will take time and money on your part, if we beat Zanadu we'll pay your costs. If we lose and have to send you an SOS, you'll have the information necessary to step in at the right time.'

'We'll worry about costs later. When can your people be ready to work with mine?'

'Hell, tomorrow, Sunday, if you like.'

'No, Monday's fine.' Damen hefted himself out of his chair. 'It goes without saying I wish you luck.'

Boyd and Mandel had another stop to make, leaving Ron Poole and King alone in his Seville to drive back to Schutt's offices.

'Kurt, how do you figure this man, Damen?'

'He's okay. Why do you ask?'

'I just reckoned he wasn't as nice a guy as you are.' Poole looked across at King. 'He reminded me of that old Greek story of the Trojan Horse.'

King took his eye momentarily off the road to grin at Poole. 'You're getting paranoid, too. Damen's fine . . . his tongue's a bit rougher than he is, deep down. He's all right.'

Poole fell silent for a good ten minutes, a long pause for him. Suddenly, he blurted out, 'Kurt, there's something I've got to tell you, something about professional ethics. My own. Now, there's no conflict of interest in my working for you, but something happened last summer I must explain because you might take it the wrong way if you heard it first from another source.'

'Ron, what the hell are you driving at?'

'I looked your company over as a candidate for a takeover bid.'

'You what!' In his agitation, King turned and stared at Poole, slithered out of his traffic lane without warning and a fanfare of blaring horns punished him. 'You what!' he repeated.

'Keep your cool, Kurt, and keep your eye on the road and I'll explain. First of all, in this takeover battle I'm completely on your side.'

'I'd hope so.'

'What I'm getting at is I've known Karl Gearhart for some time, and last summer he hired me to do a study of likely takeover candidates. If it was for Zanadu, he

303

didn't let on to me. Anyway, I did the job and collected my fee.'

'I don't get all this,' King interjected. 'Where do we figure?'

'Now, don't get het up,' Poole cautioned. 'The study criteria Gearhart gave me was a glove fit for your company. So, I took a hard look at King Corp, through your annual reports, 10-Ks, all the public information available . . .'

'So, you set me up for the kill.' King glared at Poole, his jaws clenched. 'My best friend, and you set me up!'

'Listen, Kurt. Just simmer down and listen.' Poole slid out the ashtray and ground his spent cigarette into it. 'About twenty-five companies including yours fell into the study group. King ranked way down, maybe as low as 23rd. What I'm saying is this – as a qualified appraiser of potential victims I didn't even consider your outfit as a candidate.'

'Oh! thanks a lot, pal.' King injected heavy irony into the remark, but he could not keep the relief out of his voice that Poole had not betrayed him.

'You know what I mean. But I didn't know then what you've just disclosed to Damen – the inside track on your prospects. Had I known that, you'd have moved up near the top of my list. Let me put this to you – now that I know the real dope about your company I'd say Zanadu had to have an inside steer because I looked at every public document available.'

'So, you think there must've been a leak?'

'Sure of it. Could someone on your staff have made few bucks by feeding information to Zanadu?'

King banged both hands on the wheel of the Seville in his anger. 'That annoys the hell out of me, Ron, slur like that. I know my people and I trust them completely.'

'Look buddy, take it easy. From handling these take-overs, I've learned you can't trust your bosom pals let alone the Damens.'

'Well, that may be your way, it's not mine. Oh, I get burned once in a while but my staff's clean.'

'There must be somebody.'

'All right, there is. A guy named Tillman who did some consulting work for us. I'm confident he tipped our hand to Zanadu, in fact he gave them a confidential company phone book. That's how Thomas was able to chase me round the Midwest by phone.'

'How do you know that?' Poole queried.

'Tillman told his lawyer who contacted Schutt. And he's hopped out of town until the battle's over.'

'Then get after the son of a bitch. The disclosure of inside information violates Regulation 10-b-5 of the Securities Act. Have you ever heard of Theophilus Tracy at the SEC? He's a real bear on this kind of thing. Nail Tillman and Tracy will clap him in irons. Jesus, the head of General Motors doesn't want a problem with Tracy.'

'I've heard he's tough, but fair.'

'Your friend, Damen, is a toughie, too,' Poole said, putting down the car window. 'For him that meeting was just a courtesy call and he had no interest in helping you – until you painted the full King Corp picture. Then he got too interested, I thought. I just hope he's really a White Knight.'

'No problem there,' King replied. 'But I agree, he started out yawning in my face then he sat up and took note.'

'You were giving him inside information, that's why,' Poole said, pointedly. 'The kind of confidential stuff

305

you say Tillman slipped Zanadu. So, get after that bastard before it's too late.'

2

Even throughout Sunday, there was no let-up. They ate sandwiches in the office and, to cut his thirst, King drank iced tea. He was talking briefly with Kate Foy about the shareholders' letter when still another phone rang. He picked it up. 'Yes, this is King.' A moment later, he said, 'Hello, Sir, good to hear from you.' He cupped a hand over the mouthpiece and gestured for silence. 'It's Rickover,' he whispered.

'Mr King,' Rickover boomed, 'tell me what all this is about, this Zanadu thing.'

'We're being raided, Admiral – a tender offer. But we've put together a good team and we're fighting back.'

'Good, good. Glad to hear it.' Rickover had a strong no-nonsense voice, biting off each word precisely as i loath to waste breath. 'Now look here, King, can yo guarantee me you're going to win.'

'No, Sir, I can't go that far, but I'm pretty certain w will.'

'Okay. Now, I cannot and will not get involved in a industrial fight, but I want to tell you something. Yo may not quote me, but you can say what you want. consider you the best manager I've ever worked with i industry.'

'Why, thank you, Admiral.'

'Don't get big-headed, young man. Remember, don't think much of any management. If this Zanad outfit takes you over, I expect their top man to come

306

Washington and see me first. I want his assurance you will be kept on as chief executive. That's all. Goodbye.'

King stood there for a moment, staring at the dead phone, a bemused look on his face. He went back to the table and told the others of the call.

'What does it add up to, Kurt?' asked Ron Poole.

'Hard to figure, but I'd guess it means if Zanadu wins they could be headed for trouble. I won't stay with the company and very few of my top people would stay.'

Kate Foy shook her head to confirm King's statement.

'Rickover has a lot of new business in the pipeline. Knowing him, those orders won't be placed until the smoke clears away. Although he'd prefer us to make his control systems, he could go elsewhere.'

'That could turn out a problem for Zanadu if they win.'

'Damn right it could, Kate. We've got about 200 million invested in plant and equipment for the Rickover programme. If the Admiral decided to get difficult, something he's good at, Zanadu could stand to lose a good few millions in that operation alone. That could happen if this new business isn't placed with us, and soon.'

Ron Poole had been listening intently. 'Could Zanadu sell that division for cash?'

King shook his head. 'Who'd want to buy a monster operation like that unless they had work for the plant? Maybe they could sell the land and buildings, but the equipment is highly specialized to fit that programme. If Rickover placed those orders elsewhere, that division would become a gigantic albatross to Zanadu.'

'And he'll have our bonus scheme round his neck as well,' Kate Foy commented. 'That could cost them 30 million dollars.'

'Whooey,' Poole whistled. 'That's a big bundle. What's it about?'

King explained the company had a legal obligation to about a hundred employees for past services plus pension rights amounting to about 30 million dollars. About half was pensions, the other half bonuses that were earned but not paid out. If the company were taken over the money would have to be paid out immediately.

'Do you mean the company didn't have the money to pay the bonuses when they were earned?' Poole queried.

'Not at all,' King came back, hurriedly. 'It's a special bonus plan. Like other companies we make annual bonuses based on performance, only our people can take it in cash or defer payment until, say, after retirement. Since this reduces the tax bite, most executives have chosen to leave their bonuses with the company and collect interest at prime rate.'

'That's a terrific deal for the company,' Poole said. 'I'll sure tell some of my clients about it if you've no objection.'

'Hell, no. Chip dreamed it up and over the years has grown to a sizeable amount. It lessens our dependence on the banks. Anyway, a year or so ago, protect these people and the money they have left in the directors passed a resolution saying that if an unfriendly takeover resulted in an outside company like Zanadu, getting 25 per cent of our stock and the board opposed the raid, then these moneys were immediately due and payable.'

'And it's around 30 million?'

'In that ballpark.'

'Well, it's a great idea and it slows down a raid, bu

guarantee Zanadu will fight you on it. They'll certainly go to court over it.'

King shook his head and waved his cigarette from side to side. 'Our position is so clear no court in the country would stop those payments.'

'Don't be naïve, Kurt, the courts are generally on the raider's side.'

'We have right on our side, Ron, and that's what matters. These people are owed that money. Take me, for example. I've worked for the company for twelve years which entitles me to a pension which today would be close to a million dollars. Add my bonuses and there's another 600,000 dollars.'

'That's big dough.'

'Sure, but it represents quite a few years – and it could have been more. Look, in 1968, things took a sour turn but even then the directors voted me a bonus. I turned it down. They tried to give me a raise but I nixed that, too. It had been a bad year and I felt I didn't deserve a raise or a bonus.'

'Kurt, you're too much of a Boy Scout.' King felt slightly wounded by that crack but said nothing. Poole went on, 'Anyway, if I know Zanadu, you have about as much chance of getting hold of your million-plus dollars as the proverbial snowball in hell. By the way, does Zanadu know about this bonus scheme?'

'I told them in Schutt's office. I thought Thomas was going into cardiac arrest.'

'No such luck,' commented Kate Foy. Everyone laughed.

King balled up the cellophane from his sandwich and tossed it, adroitly, into the full wastepaper basket. 'Folks, I've some quiet phoning to do in the office down the hall. Put my calls through there, Kate, and you keep

309

cracking on that letter. We should have had that ready by now.'

Kate Foy started to say something but thought better of it. She looked at the draft before her, covered with alterations and suggestions, and shook her dark head.

In the empty office, King slipped off his jacket and lit a cigarette to give him time to think. He stared out at the brilliant sunlit day. On any normal Saturday he would be on the north course of the Los Angeles Country Club finishing eighteen holes about this hour, heading for the card room off the men's grill. If it were raining, he might be sitting playing gin rummy at the California Club, a tall cool one at hand. As he stopped daydreaming and went to pick up the phone, it rang. Ted Thurman's voice came through and knocked King momentarily off his stride. It had slipped his mind completely that he had made a date to meet the head of King Corp's Canadian operation at the Fairmont Hotel in San Francisco for dinner that evening.

'Ted, I'm sorry, I clean forgot about our dinner.'

'Kurt, please don't apologize. I know what you're going through and it must be hell. Anyway, I didn't ca about dinner. I have to tell you something, somethin you should know.' He hesitated.

'What is it, Ted?'

'A month or so ago I had personal problems – a lot back taxes to pay. I needed ready money, so I sold son stock, King stock. I had to tell you in case you thoug my selling the stock had anything to do with the raid my lack of faith in you. I sold before I even heard abo the raid.'

'Look, Ted, you did what you had to do, so do worry about it.'

'Thanks, Kurt, but I feel bad about it on anoth

310

count. I sold at 20 and today 31 doesn't look all that bad, in fact about 160,000 dollars better, and I needed the money.'

King barely heard the last few words. Something was clicking in his mind, and he wanted to let the gears mesh. 'Ted, wait a minute, you said 20. Do you know exactly when you sold it?'

'Not exactly, but I can call Toronto and find out. Is it important?'

'Could be. Try to get the exact dates and come back to me.'

King called Paul Towers on the internal line and told him about his conversation with Thurman then put the question. 'If part of the stock Thurman sold was picked up by Zanadu wouldn't they have a problem, legal or technical? They knew they were going to offer 31 and yet they were buying at 20.'

'Twenty, you say. Sounds like dirty pool to me if he sold to Zanadu. I'll check with Steve.' In a few minutes, Towers called back. 'Steve agrees. If the dates match up we probably have grounds for legal action against Zanadu and, if we find enough other sellers, we might be able to turn it into a class-action suit.'

Thurman confirmed the dates did match. Zanadu had purchased his stock. King asked him to fly to Los Angeles the next morning so that the lawyers could get the legal action started. He put the phone down with growing satisfaction. Taking a memo pad, he began to list the counter moves to balk the takeover. If the toilet-makers, Cross, proved a good buy, they would have an anti-trust suit; if Thurman had been gypped by Zanadu, he could sue them for false pretences; if Baker, their Delaware lawyer, could get the court to rule against Zanadu for their legal error in serving the 13-D, that would delay the takeover process. And finally, if only they could track down the slippery Matthew G. Tillman and force him to confess feeding Zanadu confidential information, they would be home free.

In a few days, Mr Norris Thomas would learn he was in for a real fight.

3

When King left the campaign office it was after nine. At his apartment, he found a note from Frankie. She was out with clients in Newport Beach and was expected to stay the night but could make excuses if he wanted to see her. He stared at the message for some time before crumpling it and dropping it into the waste basket. He couldn't handle two demanding mistresses at once – King Corp and Frankie. Tiredness had cramped his shoulders, his neck and even his head, which seemed to have a tight band round it. A good night to be alone. And not a good night to start drinking.

Tossing his coat on a chair and pulling off his tie, he went into the kitchen, found some tea-bags and put water on to boil. Trancelike, he watched the bubbles form, break away and shoot to the top. His mind was racing with half a hundred problems, bursting like those bubbles, getting no place. When the tea was ready, he carried it into the den. A stack of mail lay unopened and that had never happened to him before. A reflex made him reach for a cigarette, but his pack was empty. Two packs already today, he chided himself, as he went to get a fresh one in the kitchen.

Most of the mail was routine. He segregated the bills, dropped the junk mail in the trash and took the one remaining letter in his hand, staring at it for a long time before slitting it open. Cheap paper and a lopsided letterhead, at least to his eye. Nicholas R. Kravetch, Private Investigator, 2219 Friendship Blvd, Stamford, Conn. 06902.

'Jesus, ' he said to himself, 'Kravetch ought to do something about that address.' He kept staring at the letterhead as if mental concentration could change what he feared would be the contents of the letter. Finally, he steeled himself to read it.

Dear Mr King
This is the report of my investigation which you authorized last April. I am sorry it took so long to complete, but I believe you understand some of the problems my operative and I encountered in conducting surveillance of your wife, Mrs Carolyn Crowley King (who resides at 11 Lower Weed Street, New Canaan, Connecticut).

As you suspected, your wife has been having an affair with a male who also resides in that city. At your direction, I am not including mention of his name in this correspondence.

On seven separate occasions, the suspect couple spent the night together. Four of these nights were spent in a cottage on the grounds of the Parker estate in South Newport, Rhode Island. The cottage is apparently owned by professional acquaintances of the male suspect. The other three nights were spent in the house on Lower Weed Street. On two of those nights, your children were with their maternal grandmother in Darien, Connecticut. On the other night, we were not able to ascertain whether or not the children were in the house.

He put the letter down. He opened his hand and stared at his wet palm for several seconds before running it across his brow. He was perspiring freely. He'd been so sure of his suspicions he did not think the truth would really bother him. But it did, to the point of pain. He had to force his eyes back to the statement he knew would follow.

313

We also ascertained, as is required by law in the state of Connecticut, that the act of sexual intercourse occurred on at least one of these occasions.

If you have further need of my services, please call or write. In accordance with our understanding, I hereby render my bill.

Kravetch's large, elaborate signature squirmed before his eyes. Like a live worm. 'Render my bill' – how unlike a rugged, retired police lieutenant to use that quaint old form of words! 'Render my bill . . . render unto Caesar . . . Caesarian . . . asunder.' The words bounced and ricocheted around in his head like Chinese firecrackers.

'Fuck!' He put the letter down on the table and slammed it with his clenched fist. He was halfway to the living room bar when he about-turned and picked up the cheap sheet which made his hand tingle. Replacing it in its envelope, he opened the closet door to get into the wall safe and leave the letter there. Then he went to make himself a Campari and soda, thinking it safer than gin, which would start a drinking binge.

For a long time he sat on the dark terrace in shirtsleeves. Mood music, laughter and clinking glasses drifted upwards to him from several floors below. What were they playing? 'Indian Summer.' That carried him back on his personal time machine. Back to Bev and Glorious Fenster and all the others. Back to a mental replay of his life with Carolyn, from their first collision that night in California to the early years of promise. When, when, when did they turn sour? When did they both wake up to the fact their love had gone, they had said it all? For the years of separation he had no simple explanation. Neither of them had done anything to end them.

That letter in the safe could. It gave him the chance to hit Carolyn and her psychiatrist friend with a divorce suit which would clear the way for him to marry Frankie. Yet, he knew that letter would lie there, unused. How could he accuse Carolyn when he himself felt so guilty. He could never have lived with himself.

King sat and smoked and stared at the star-bright sky. He thought of his children, his slim dark-haired twins. Eighteen years old! How could they possibly be eighteen years old? He wondered, seriously, if he should ever have become a parent, then discarded that thought, angrily. He had two fine children and it was not too late to get to know them. Only, the image of Carolyn and her psychiatrist clouded and obliterated everything else.

King poured himself a large shot of brandy which he drank as quickly as he dared before he went to bed.

At two in the morning, he woke with a start to find himself tangled in the sheets. He fancied he could still hear laughter from the party, then realized he had heard it in the dream that woke him. Fragments, broken images still stuck to his mind. He was with Carolyn. They were in a strange bedroom, strange in many ways. Everything seemed to have been manufactured in stainless steel or plastic. Wardrobes, Carolyn's dressing-table, the chairs, bedside tables, lamps – they all looked as if turned out by one of his factories. Even the wall-to-wall carpet shone as though made of metal and the wallpaper had a plastic sheen. Carolyn was wearing a sheer pink nightgown, and that, too, glittered as if made of spun steel wool. He was imploring her to take off. Finally, she did so. But when he reached for her, he saw she was also built of plastic like a store-window mannequin. She had hard, high breasts on which his

315

fingers drummed. He felt between her legs. There was nothing. No sex. No cleft. No pubic hair. Just hard plastic.

And the face had changed. It was no longer Carolyn's face. Yet, from somewhere, he heard her laugh (that silvery, scornful laugh that had echoed in his head when he woke up). And her mocking voice. 'Take her, she's all yours. You made her, so you keep her.' Then everything had leaked away out of his head and he had awakened.

King lay in the darkness, shaking his head and laughing to himself. 'Now, how in hell would Freud figure that one out?' he wondered. It had something to do with bringing Maxim and King Corp into their bedroom and choosing the factory-made dummy instead of flesh-and-blood Carolyn. She was accusing him of preferring his work and relegating her to a minor role. Further than that his jaded mind would not take him.

Half an hour later, he got up, rinsed his face with water in the bathroom and did something he had not done in over a year – swallowed a strong sleeping pill.

4

For the next forty-eight hours, King and his senior executives never stopped running. They began the discussions leading to the purchase of the toilet-makers Cross Industries. King spent a couple of hours talking Ted Thurman into suing Zanadu, and on Monday, 2 October 1976, the suit was filed in Los Angeles Superior Court. The complaint alleged Thurman had sold 15,000 shares of King common stock at the time Zanadu was planning to acquire control of King. The suit was for damages – the 160,000 dollars Thurman had lost and one million dollars in punitive damages.

Late Monday afternoon, King suddenly realized the vital letter to the shareholders was still not finished. He called Kate Foy on the carpet. When she walked in, her candid face showed all her frustration. The banking and public relations experts were not so expert; she could never see them all together; and every draft she made came bouncing back with still more suggestions. To crown it all, she had two committees reviewing every line she wrote.

'Kate, I want that letter finished this afternoon.'

Kate threw a bundle of paper on his desk. 'This is draft number twelve and I'm not going to do another. Get all your geniuses in one spot for one hour and maybe we'll all agree for once. Either that, or write it yourself. I'm losing my mind in this madhouse.'

'Take it easy, Kate. Get me six copies of what you've done and I'll get approval right away. You've got the media lined up?'

She nodded. 'The Thursday evening and Friday morning papers.' She left with something like a smile on her face.

An hour later, when the six copies came back with a half-dozen different changes on each, King saw Kate's problem. What was it they said about the Ten Commandments? They were simple and straightforward because God didn't let a committee get in on the act! He called a meeting for the next day and they hammered out a final version. He knew it was flawed, but time was running against them. He avoided Kate's eyes as the meeting broke up, knowing he would only see disapproval there.

Other things were moving: they had filed a suit in

Delaware alleging Zanadu had violated the rules for tender offers; they had set up the acquisition of Cross Industries; they had stepped up the hunt for the elusive Matthew G. Tillman.

Then a blow fell when King heard that federal judge Norman E. Page had been assigned to hear their cases. Several years before, he had found against them on a patent infringement case when the evidence favoured them.

Sam Donaldson, the lawyer who would face Judge Page, smiled at King's tirade against the judge. 'It's the luck of the draw,' he said. 'We drew Page.'

'Okay, so let's get a change of venue and another judge.'

Donaldson shook his head slowly and shrugged. 'I'm sorry, Mr King, but a federal judge cannot be disqualified – no way.'

'Then all we can do is pray.'

XII

On Friday afternoon, Damen of Astroteknik arrived with two executives in the middle of what had become the normal scene in the Schutt offices – something between chaos and outright pandemonium. The 'battle' room overflowed with people and even Steven Schutt's private office, where the meeting had been convened, seemed cramped. Damen had asked for the meeting after spending a whole day going over the report of his people who had been studying King Corp's books. He was pleased King's statements had been based on fact, but had several questions to ask and certain conditions to define.

King had brought Ron Poole, Bud Gorman and Bob McGill with him as well as the three law partners. He began by describing all their moves with the pride of a field commander. He covered the law suits, the Cross acquisition, the call from Admiral Rickover. However, after quarter of an hour, King realized Damen was elsewhere, he was hardly listening.

Suddenly, he raised a hand and interrupted King. 'Kurt, I came here to discuss certain things with you, not to listen to you talk.'

An embarrassed silence followed that remark. Only Damen ignored it. His grating voice went on. He looked round the room as he spoke. 'There are people here I've never met before. Kurt, let's go into some office alone and talk about the question you asked me last Saturday.'

Steve Schutt showed them into an empty office. There, Damen said straight out, 'I want to advise you Astroteknik has an interest in King Corp and would like to proceed. I am ready to recommend to my board they offer King shareholders 33 dollars per share for one hundred per cent of the stock. However, Kurt, I caution you that under no circumstances can this discussion be construed as an offer. I don't have that authority today. There are some loose ends that must be cleared up between us before I can proceed further.'

'Such as?' King was puzzled by this bald statement.

'If Astroteknik should take over King, I would recommend you come on the board of directors and also function as a senior vice-president. However, that would create a problem in compensation in relation to that of my executive vice-president, and therefore some adjustments would be necessary.'

Damen droned on in this vein but King tuned him out for the moment. I've built a company from scratch, he thought, while Astroteknik's vice-president has only worked for the builders. What's more, he's never been a chief executive. Yet, he wants to put me on a lower level. Well, maybe it's not all that important, but it means Damen and I are on slightly different wavelengths.'

'We're a very disciplined group,' Damen was saying as King picked him up again. 'Your outfit seems – how shall I put it? – more free form. For example, my people get along quite well using commercial airlines, but you have your own little Air Force! That will have to be looked at more carefully.' He mentioned other small areas where the company approach was different. Then, he concluded by saying he was bothered and concerned by the steps King was taking against Zanad

320

King had heard enough. Nothing Damen had said struck him as a major problem and was probably idle speculation since a Zanadu victory was unlikely. 'Bill, we can resolve all of these things if we have to call on you for help. I take it you're interested in coming in if we ask you. Right?' Damen nodded.

At King's suggestion, Schutt joined them and Damen repeated what he had just said about price and conditions.

Schutt said his client would consider Damen's comments then added, deliberately, 'It is extremely important to my representation of my client that you define your comments as an offer, if it truly is an offer. Mr Damen, is this an offer of 33 dollars for all the King stock?'

'Goodness, no. Let me clarify. At this point, 33 is simply my current thinking on what would be a proper offer. If and when I bring you an offer, it will be sanctioned by my board. Until then, please consider this conversation to be, as you legal fellows put it, "privileged".' Damen gave a thin smile and King tried vainly to read those curious eyes behind their tinted glasses.

'Clyde Clarke represents you?' Schutt said, and Damen nodded. 'I know him well and will contact him if Mr King wants you to come in. That's the best approach.' Again, Damen nodded. At that, he left with his two executives.

Soon afterwards, Schutt asked King to come to his office. Ron Poole was already there. 'I didn't think you'd mind, Kurt, if Ron joined us. He has most experience in these matters.'

'Of course not. What is it?'

'Well, perhaps I'm being alarmist, but I wanted to tell

you my impressions of the conversation I have just had with Clyde Clarke, Astroteknik's counsel. I got the impression from him that Bill Damen has no real intention of helping King Corp – or Kurt King, personally. I'm beginning to be afraid they have their eye on King for themselves – a sweet acquisition.'

'You've got it all wrong, Steve.' King shook his head vehemently. 'I've known Astroteknik for years and they can be trusted. If and when we need somebody to step in, they'll do it if it's good for them. I'm not asking any favours. They know King's a buy at 50 dollars a share and a steal at 33. They're okay, so don't worry.'

But Ron Poole did look worried. 'Kurt,' he said, 'why not let me take the 33 figure and shop it around? I'll guarantee you a better deal. Hell, I know one outfit, H & V, that will give you more just on my say-so.'

'Thanks, Ron, but I don't want to shop the Astroteknik price and I see no need to run an auction.'

Poole screwed his cigarette butt dead in Schutt's elegant Venetian glass ashtray. He looked at King 'Kurt, my old friend, you are paying me a substantia sum to advise and that's what I'm doing. I don't read this Damen bird the same way you do. You may cal him a friendly, but Caesar thought Brutus was friendly, too, until that stab in the chest. Damen want your company.'

'Ron, you've got it all wrong.'

'That's the Boy Scout in you talking. If you want friendly who'll play by the rules, H & V will go to 3 dollars a share on just my word alone. Let me call the and get you a solid deal.'

'Forget it,' King said, sharply. 'In six months, 35 w be cheap.'

'Kurt, don't get yourself in trouble by turning down a good offer. You could be sued – sued personally.'

King had been reaching into his inside pocket for a cigarette. Suddenly, he stopped and slammed both hands on the table, palms down. He glared at Poole who glared back at him. For the first time in thirty-five years, they had come somewhere near a stand-up row. Schutt was watching them both, quietly, ready to step in if things got out of hand. But King checked his temper before he spoke. 'For Christ's sake, Ron, don't you know that's one of the things that's keeping me awake at night? Whatever I do, the shit falls on me. If I beat Zanadu, some son of a bitch is going to sue me because he didn't get his 31 dollars a share. If we beat them and double our earnings, the son of a bitch who sold on the market at 31 is going to sue me because I didn't tell him about our great prospects.' He got up and walked briskly to the window, still talking. 'No matter what I do, I'm going to be faulted. Twelve years of doing a good job and now some rotten bastard puts me between a rock and a hard place.' He turned to the two others, a thin smile on his face. 'You know, it's almost enough to take the fun out of life.'

'OK, Kurt,' Poole said, giving it one more try. 'But when I look at your company armed with the inside dope, I drool. Now Damen has the same information he's drooling, too.'

'Forget it, Ron. I've known him too long to consider he would double-cross me.'

When King had gone, Poole lingered in Schutt's office, still with that worried look on his face.

'Something bothering you, Ron – I mean other than the obvious?'

'Yeah, Steve, there is. I've known Kurt King since we

weren't old enough to shave. He's a determined man, but I've never seen him this determined. Let me ask you – is he in some kind of financial trouble? I mean, some kind of bind that would be worsened if Zanadu wins?'

'Sit down, Ron.' Schutt reached in his desk drawer and extracted a file, flipped it open to page through a thin document then closed it again. 'Let me meet your question with a question. Could you stop working tomorrow and not have to worry about money, or maintaining your present life style for the rest of your life?'

Poole smiled as he shook his head.

'Kurt King could.' Schutt smiled at Poole's whistle of surprise. 'Exactly my reaction. But let me explain. I mean, he could have before all this started, this raid. He is worth several million dollars. Personally, he has little debt and he owns a good deal of property free and clear. But his real wealth is tied up in his King Corp holdings which amount to quite a few million. Only, he has put himself in a bind by opposing the tender offer.'

Poole had been rolling a cigarette between his fingers while he listened. A reflex made him thrust it back into the pack. 'Yeah,' he said. 'Yeah, he can't very well tell the shareholders not to accept the offer to sell and then do so himself.'

'So, if Zanadu prevails, he'll have to become one of the 49 per cent minority,' Schutt said. 'And if Zanadu can't afford to pay cash for the rest of the stock, they'll merge the remaining 49 per cent into their company and Kurt will wind up with Zanadu stock for his King stock. That could create a very serious problem for him and a few others like Boyd, Hubert and Gorman.'

'Because the Zanadu stock will almost certainly drop

'Right. Without Kurt and other key people to run the company. Zanadu may well get into trouble. And the market will get wind of it and the stock could easily lose up to two-thirds of its present value which would be a tremendous loss of money for Kurt.'

'But Kurt still has well over a million dollars in retirement funds and back bonuses,' Poole said.

'True. But if he walks out, which he will, he'll have to spend years in court trying to get that money. And if he does get it, the legal fees will eat up a big chunk.'

Poole stood up and paced the room before turning to look at Schutt. He was still worried. 'Kurt's right. Whichever way the dice fall, he loses. Yet, for all his personal problems, I don't believe he's thinking about himself for even a minute. His only concern is King Corp.'

Schutt nodded agreement. 'And that's why he could wind up getting badly mauled – financially and emotionally.'

2

'Telephone, Mr King. You can take it in the foreman's office, over there.'

Reluctantly, King broke away from the cluster of men on the plant floor. He and Chip had driven out to make one more personal inspection of the Cross facilities. He had found the products sound, the facilities excellent and the people high-calibre. And it was like a tonic to stand in that factory amid the rumble of heavy machinery blending with the high-pitched whine of fork-lift trucks. The sound of a plant operating at peak effort – a sound he loved.

He picked up the phone.

'Kurt? Steve Schutt. Sorry to bother you, but Judge Page has set a hearing for 3.45 and my people feel you ought to be present.'

'Christ, Steve, I'm sixty miles away! I can start immediately, but it's almost three and with the freeway traffic it'll take at least two hours. Is it really so important?'

'Afraid it is. I wish I'd known sooner but a judge's schedule is a very hard thing to predict. Why don't you see if you can get a chopper? There's a helipad on top of the Occidental Tower. Call me back if you can't get one.'

Within minutes, King was clambering into a four-passenger Hughes 500. Normally, he was a careful passenger when travelling in small aircraft, but his mind was elsewhere – on the court case and the urgency in Schutt's attitude. The helicopter rose smoothly for about thirty feet before the pilot moved the collective and the craft dipped to the right.

Chip Boyd was on the helipad, looking up, his hand shielding his eyes from the sun. Suddenly, he saw the helicopter door slide open and King begin to fall out. His right shoulder and right leg appeared through the open door, the leg flailing for support. Boyd's mouth opened, but he was too petrified to scream. He thought: 'Christ, if Kurt falls, even if he lands on top of the tower he's above breakneck height and he's had it.'

In the helicopter, King, too, thought he was dead. He panicked as he felt himself slide into space. He clutched frantically for the door with his right hand. But the heavy Plexiglas shape was pulling away from him. What could he grab? He thought of the collective but a his father's injunctions and his own instinct kept him from seizing hold of that essential control. Just whe half his body had slipped through the opening, h swung his left arm up and his fingers closed tightly around the tubular door frame.

For several seconds, he hung by that arm until the pilot swung the craft to port and he felt himself sliding back into his seat. He only had time to free his hand before the heavy door banged back into position. Almost frantically, he buckled himself into his seat belt then reached over and locked the door. He was sweating under his collar and through his shirt and his mouth had gone dry. And yet, the pilot had seen nothing!

King put his head back against the rest and closed his eyes. He heard the pilot mutter something but the words did not impinge. He was thinking: 'After this, whatever happens in court will be a piece of cake.'

He walked into court just as the proceedings were starting. Ten of his own people were already there and, at the counsel table, four of Schutt's lawyers sat. Sam Donaldson was addressing the bench along with a short man in a blue, pin-striped suit. Edging himself into a seat, King scrutinized the judge. Norman E. Page had a long, thin face with dyspeptic lines gouged into his cheeks. His bulging forehead was emphasized by the absence of hair. King ran nervous fingers through his own full head of hair and began to worry about bald, ugly-mug judges like Page who might have it in for the younger and better-looking.

'Steve,' King whispered, 'what's going on? I thought we were still in the discovery stage, taking depositions.'

'Normally that's what happens. The idea of discovery proceedings is to speed things up. Some lawyers are notorious for delaying cases so that the other side is beaten by the clock.' Schutt lowered his voice when Judge Page directed a reproving glance their way. 'We went into court this morning to set up the discovery machinery and George Waxman, the dapper little guy in the pinstripe suit, told Page we'd filed another lawsuit without informing the court.'

'The Delaware case?'

'Uhuh. Anyway, Waxman bent the truth considerably and Page got quite exercised about it and really raked Sam Donaldson over the coals, said he was overriding federal jurisdiction.'

'That's the Page I know.'

Schutt leaned closer. 'Now that's a lot of crap because the Delaware action is in the Chancery, the state court system, and Page has no control over that whatsoever. But this Waxman knows how to play Judge Page. The main point is we came into court this morning to deal with the discovery process and we're ending up with something quite different.'

'Meaning what?' King felt a tinge of worry.

'Waxman asked the judge for a temporary restraining order to stop you from acquiring Cross.'

'What!'

'We had no notice of it, no nothing. And we've been working through the lunch hour to prepare our defence. That's why I insisted you get here.'

They went silent as Waxman got to his feet to put the argument against the Cross purchase. Legal arguments always fascinated King. Listening to his opponent's counsel, he invariably felt all was lost, but when his own lawyers said their piece his confidence climbed. Because he expected this ebb and flow, Waxman's remarks did not bother him unduly. No one could surely stop the Cross transaction. It was too good, too beneficial for the company and for the stockholders. He even smiled when Waxman referred to the Cross deal as a tragedy.

Sam Donaldson took the floor. He put forward a careful and solid argument for the Cross acquisition then asked that certain of Waxman's affidavits be stricken from the record. Buoyed up by this presentation, King was startled and deflated when the judge suddenly interrupted.

'Motion denied,' he said in his throaty voice then looked sharply at King who had said 'Ugh' loudly.

Donaldson adroitly switched topics, but it looked to King as if the judge was barely paying attention. However, he cut across Donaldson's argument once again.

'Tell me, counsel, has the acquisition of Cross Industries been completed?'

'No, your Honour, it has not. A letter of intent has been prepared.' Donaldson held up his brief. 'I submit that in the numerous cases cited in my brief, other courts have allowed acquisitions tending to block a tender offer as long as there were valid business reasons involved.'

Judge Page pushed his face forward, over the bench, and clamped his thin lips together. 'In this court, we are not concerned with previous cases, only the one before us now.' His voice had turned chilly in contrast with the friendly tone he had adopted towards Waxman.

'I meant, your Honour, there was valid legal precedent for the King Corp action.'

Judge Page fixed Donaldson with eyes like date-stones. 'We are not here to judge what happened in a dozen other cases which have neither analogy nor bearing on the case before us.'

Then Donaldson tried to develop another argument to counter the judge's objections. But Page held up his hand to stop him. 'Is counsel trying to instruct me in case-law or jurisprudence?'

'No, your Honour,' Donaldson replied, then after a moment's discussion with Paul Towers, he went on, 'Your Honour, if the court pleases, my associate will present the next phase of our argument.' Donaldson sat down, ashen-faced. To King, he appeared to be in mild shock.

Paul Towers made an impressive beginning, dealing with the way in which the Cross Industries transaction had been conducted by King Corp. He then said, 'Your Honour, my learned friend was going to submit that Cross Industries need the help of King Corp to stay in business and save several hundred jobs.'

'Are you sure you have that the right way round, counsel?' Judge Page asked, sarcastically.

'I, ahh, think I have. It was Cross Industries which invited King Corp to study the acquisition of the company.'

'And, of course, it just so happens Cross manufactures merchandise that could create an anti-trust suit against Zanadu, is that your thesis?' Everyone caught the judge's ironic tone.

'But my client considers he has the right to do whatever is necessary to fight off the attempt to take him over,' Towers came back.

'Why exactly does your client want to take over Cross Industries at this point?' the judge persisted. 'Isn't it t learn what they know about Zanadu and help block th tender offer?'

'For Christ's sake,' King murmured to Schutt. 'How far-fetched can you get? We don't have to buy them o to learn all they know – they hate Zanadu so muc they'd tell us everything gladly.'

When Waxman rose once more to speak, the judge listened quietly and with obvious attention but, when Towers ventured even a few words, Page choked him off. King shook his head. It seemed to him Towers had taken on a pleading tone. He sat down and Sam Donaldson got up to reinforce the argument that King Corp had every right to make an acquisition that might block the Zanadu takeover bid.

'Counsel, I do not think businesses have a right to do that.'

'Well, your Honour, the cases we have cited in our memorandum are to the contrary.'

'That's your opinion, counsel, which I don't happen to share,' Judge Page said through thin lips.

'I respectfully insist, your Honour, on the validity of these cases which we have studied very carefully.'

'So have I, counsel,' retorted Judge Page in a tone of finality.

Paul Towers tried another tack. 'Your Honour, can I suggest some form of compromise to enable the acquisition of Cross Industries by my client?'

Page glowered at the lawyer as though he had been insulted. 'Compromise! Compromise! Counsel, let me tell you not to attempt to compromise with me.' He flapped a gowned arm at the group of Zanadu attorneys. 'That is who you have to compromise with. I do not compromise. That is not my job. This court will recess to consider its ruling.'

Following a short break, Judge Page returned to the bench. His face told King they had lost.

'I rule,' said the judge, 'that the application by Zanadu against King Corp to restrain it from acquiring Cross Industries has been granted.

'I further rule that the application by King Corp to acquire Cross Industries is rejected.'

In the nearest bar, they discussed the blow. Kate Foy spoke first. 'He really tore us apart. I thought he was scary.'

'That's the second time we've drawn him and I guess you could say our batting average is perfect – zero for two,' King said.

'Could he be in Zanadu's pocket?' Bud Gorman asked, angrily.

'No, he's not in their pocket.' Paul Towers sipped his drink and looked at their surprised faces. 'There are two things involved,' he went on. 'Page is really close to Waxman, who was his room-mate in law school. Waxman's partner is politically powerful and helped to get the judgeship for Page. But there's nothing crooked in that. The second reason's the important one. Some judges think takeovers are a good thing. They look at the stock price before the raid and the offer, and don't see much else. That's all Page heard and that's the basis for his rulings.' Towers looked at King. 'What's more, he looks at you, Mr King, as some kind of villain who is opposing Zanadu because of selfish motives. That may sound harsh, but it's the way I see it.'

King looked at the young attorney. 'I wish I could disagree with you, Paul,' he said.

3

While everyone else was having a second drink, King called his office from the pay phone to see if there were any urgent messages for him.

'Dozens of calls,' Marianne said, 'but I think I only need to give you two of them, or maybe three.'

'Okay, go ahead.'

'Miss Shore, for one. And then Mr Groves and Mr Martenson want to see you tonight if it is at all possible. They said it was urgent and suggested the California Club at 6.30. Could you do that?'

'Sure. Reserve a private dining room. Did you say there was a third call of some importance?'

'A Miss Rockefeller called. I think it was a local call this time. Do you want the number.'

'Yeah, give it to me, but I won't call her. I'd better call Frankie, though. By the way, I assume Quin and Sam didn't say what they wanted.'

'Nothing, except it's important. How did things go this afternoon, or shouldn't I ask?'

'You shouldn't ask. I'll talk to you tomorrow.'

He looked at the match book cover on which he had written Jessica's phone number. It was the first time he had smiled in hours.

In the cab taking him to the California Club he tried to figure why two of his most influential directors would want to see him.

Quentin 'Quin' Groves was, at seventy, the oldest of ing Corp's directors. In fact, the by-laws had been changed to allow Groves to continue on the board. A wise move, for Groves was extremely able and had excellent connections in the business world, both locally and nationally. A tall, white-maned, handsome man, he had spent years at the Harvard Business School. ing valued his advice, more so now since Groves was a large stockholder in Astroteknik and a close friend of ll Damen.

Sam Martenson was a bit younger and Groves' opposite in many ways. Short, articulate but quiet, he was a tired senior partner in one of Los Angeles' major accounting firms. King would have trusted him with any secret, any confidence, any task.

His cab dropped him at the California Club in its beautiful old building on Flower Street. By far the most prestigious of private clubs for men, it had imposing public rooms with high ceilings, glittering chandeliers and dark mahogany panelling. King took the elevator to the second floor to one of the numerous private dining rooms where Martenson and Groves already waited for him.

Briefly, he outlined what had happened in Judge Page's courtroom and they listened, murmuring sympathetic comments from time to time. As soon as the waiter had brought their drinks and left, he put the question in his mind. 'Why the urgent meeting?'

Quin Groves spoke. 'Kurt, I had lunch with Bill Damen of Astroteknik today, and he was rather frank. As you know, I was one of their founding fathers. Bill seemed upset about what he termed your "legal manoeuvring".'

'"Legal manoeuvring" . . . What did he mean by that?'

'The Cross acquisition, the Delaware suit and the other legal moves designed to block Zanadu. Apparently, Bill feels all this is burning up a lot of energy and money, and it makes King Corp an unstable commodity – from his standpoint, that is.'

King banged his drink on the table. 'Goddamn, it's really none of Damen's business how I fight off Zanadu.'

Groves held up a placatory hand. 'To a degree it is his business, if you expect him to step in and top the offer.'

King shook his head, then snapped, 'First of all

don't think it will ever be necessary. If it is, he can make up his mind at that time. In the meantime, I have two choices – let Zanadu run over us, or fight.' He took another swig of his drink. 'Anyway, I'm just a little pissed off at Damen's attitude. When we last met I told him about our movements against Zanadu. He yawned . . . couldn't have cared less. And now he calls you, Quin, and sets up a luncheon so he can bitch about what I'm doing. Why didn't he call me?'

'He probably thought you were too busy.'

King shook his head. 'You can tell him one of the things he's bitching about is dead – the Cross deal. Judge Page killed that today.'

Groves was relieved that he was cleared to pass on the Cross story. 'The other thing bothering Damen is that you might find a company to buy with preferred stock. He calls it Mickey Mouse stock.'

'Damn him! Have we ever done anything Mickey Mouse? I'm getting tired of hearing myself say we won't acquire any other company unless it's a good business deal. But if we find one and they hold stock that will block Zanadu, so much the better.'

Martenson laid a hand on King's sleeve in a paternal gesture. 'Kurt, don't you see, Damen's concerned the preferred stock in someone else's hands might block him if he decides to be your White Knight?'

'Wait a minute!' King's voice rose again. 'If *he* decides to come in – is that what he said?'

Martenson glanced at Groves, who said, 'Well, more or less. That was certainly his meaning.'

'Those are not the ground rules, gentlemen. From Day one, my position has been that we may ask him to come in and help us. If and when we do, then he has a

335

decision to make.' King lit a cigarette, his hands trembling, to give himself time to control his anger. 'Something else bothers me. Damen seems to be going over my head by approaching you. Yet, up till now I've been looking out for his interests.'

'His interests?' Groves queried.

'Sure, Quin. Since this bid started, I've been literally besieged with calls from brokers and principals, companies that would like to make an offer as a friendly. I've held them all off in favour of Astroteknik. I'm willing to give him first crack if we need help. But if Damen wants to play games then I can sure as hell start an auction.'

Martenson interrupted him as he was going on. 'From what you say, Kurt, Damen really hasn't anything to worry about. Clearly, there's a misunderstanding and I think you should talk to him – the sooner the better.'

King put his drink down. 'I'll call him right now. In fact, why don't we go over to the office and you can both hear what I say?'

Within half an hour, all three were seated in the King Corp office where King reached Damen at home. After exchanging pleasantries, he explained why he was calling. He said that Damen's worries were, for the most part, academic since the Cross deal was ruled out. If King Corp made any purchase with preferred stock, the stockholder would never vote in any way detrimental to Astroteknik.

Damen did not utter until King had finished. Then he said, 'I think I understand what you are trying to tell me. But now I want you to listen to me and listen carefully. If you persist with your legal manoeuvring and are able to stop Zanadu and keep your independence, you will then have another problem. I made yo an offer – 33 dollars per share for all the King stock. If at any time in the future I am asked under oath, in court or in a deposition, whether or not I made you an offer, I'll tell the truth. Should your stockholders then get wind of the offer, and believe me they probably will, then you and your directors will be in serious trouble. Do I make myself clear?'

For a moment, King could not believe what the other man had just said. 'Bill,' he almost shouted, 'what you're saying is simply not the case. When we talked on Friday, you were most careful to say you had no authority to make an offer – and now you're putting pressure on me, which is unfair, completely unfair. You did not make an offer of any kind. What you say now is a damned lie and you know it!'

'You have heard my position,' Damen said, stiffly. 'You'll have to decide what to do. You run your business, I'll run mine. Goodbye.'

Suddenly King felt very alone.

Martenson and Groves were watching him, waiting for him to speak.

'Gentlemen, you heard my side of the conversation, but you're not going to believe what Damen said. He actually threatened me.'

'What!' said the others as one.

King explained what Damen had told him and Groves shook his silver-maned head. 'Well, I'll be damned,' he said. 'He didn't mention anything about a hard offer at lunch.'

'Maybe he'd had a few drinks tonight.'

'Yes, he was half-shot,' Martenson said, hopefully.

King snapped off the desk light, the signal for them to move. 'I'll tell you this, gentlemen – drunk or sober, Mr William Damen is beginning to scare the hell out of

337

me. He has become unpredictable. With friends like him I hardly need enemies.'

As they were leaving the office, the phone rang. King glared at the instrument, focusing all his resentment and frustration on the thing that took up his working day and part of his nights. 'Let it ring,' his mind said even when reflex action had taken him halfway across the room to pick up the handset.

It was high-living Dean Hubert, in town for a rare weekend from his assignment at Tri Corp. 'Kurt, thank God somebody at the California Club overheard where you were going. I've just seen Tillman.'

'Where?' King bellowed the word, then remembered Groves and Martenson were still standing by the door. Cupping a hand over the mouthpiece, he told the directors something urgent had come up and they should go ahead and have dinner without him. 'Okay, Dean, shoot.'

'I was driving downtown and saw Tillman pick up a cab off the stand on Wilshire. I followed him to a club, if that's what it's called, a couple of blocks from the beach at Santa Monica.'

'The club – what's it called?'

'Blithe Spirits, and it looks like a hophead or a junkie joint.'

'Dean, where can I meet you?' Hubert told him the intersection of Olympic and Lincoln boulevards. King said, 'Keep an eye on the club and I'll be with you in a half-hour. We'll nail that bastard this time.'

4

In the cab taking them back to the California Club, Sam Martenson sat kneading the cleft of his upper lip between his thumb and index finger, a mannerism Groves knew. It meant his friend was worried. However, he waited for Martenson to speak.

'Quin, I thought Kurt was going into cardiac arrest when he was talking to Damen. You know, this take-over business could break him up or even kill him before it's all over.'

'That might suit a lot of people,' Groves commented in his dry, throwaway style.

Martenson looked at him, sharply. 'You mean Damen.' When Groves did not reply, the other man persisted. 'Quin, you're closer to Damen than anybody. What sort of game is he playing?'

'Bill's looking out for himself.'

'But he's supposed to be standing by to help Kurt and King Corp, not threatening him. Isn't he?'

'Bill reckons Kurt King is playing a dangerous game and we could all get our fingers burned if he beats Zanadu – and he's putting up a helluva fight.'

For several minutes, Martenson chewed that statement over; he had known Groves for more than thirty years but still found it difficult to unravel the convolutions of the other man's thinking. Finally, he said, 'What you really mean is Damen might be going to steal King Corp from Zanadu under Kurt King's nose and doesn't want complications.'

'Steal!' Groves pretended to be outraged. 'He's our White Knight, isn't he?'

'Our White Knight, if invited. There's something else on your mind?'

A red light pulled them to a halt at the La Brea and Wilshire intersection. Groves sat silent, smoothing his silver mane with a hand until the cab started moving again. Even then, he met Martenson's question with one of his own.

'Sam, have you any idea why Damen hits the bottle?'

'I've never given it a thought. He likes the taste, job stress, personal trouble? You tell me, Quin.'

Groves reflected for another long moment before replying. 'I think it's because Bill Damen's got what I call the Procrustes complex – especially about Kurt King.'

'I'm way out of my depth. Procrustes? You mean that ancient Greek robber who stretched or chopped his victims until they exactly fitted his bed.'

'That's the man. And these days you'll see Procrustes in all those short-assed men who make up for their inadequacy feelings by eliminating everybody a tad above their size. There's a Procrustes in every character who feels inferior.'

'But Damen's as tall as King.'

'Physically, maybe. In everything else he knows he's a pigmy beside Kurt King.'

'Quin, you make it sound as though there was an element of personal vendetta in Damen's behaviour.'

They were entering downtown Los Angeles, the high-rise offices of the business district crowding in on them. Groves stopped the cab several hundred yards from the California Club, saying they would walk the rest of the way for the exercise. When they started walking, he put his arm round Martenson. 'Sam, this for your ear alone. We've been around a longish whi and we both know Kurt King's one of the finest chief executives we've ever met . . .'

'But . . .' Martenson prompted when Groves paused.

'But he may be too nice a guy for this form of infighting – and he's short on psychology.'

'If you mean he hasn't guessed the name of Damen's game, that makes two of us. For God's sake come to the point, Quin.'

But Groves took his time before saying, 'Sam, remember those tremendous golf matches and gin rummy sessions at Palm Springs when Kurt King would make a foursome with Fulton Summers, Astroteknik's president, and a couple of Summers' directors?'

'Sure, I remember. Good buddies, Kurt and Fulton. Good golfers and card-players, too.'

'Well, somebody else who remembers them is Bill Damen.'

'But he was a 30-handicap golfer who never sat in on any of the card games.'

'That's what I mean. Kurt King was at the top table and he was at the bottom one.'

'I'm beginning to get your message.'

'Then, there's Kurt's wife, Carolyn, when she's round, and his girlfriend – they make Cynthia Damen look like the fat lady at the fair. King flies his own plane while Damen prunes his roses. King looks like an ex-Marine and is handsome while Damen looks like a flat-footed, short-sighted bookkeeper. King has been very successful with his company while Damen has to buy success, not build it. See the picture?'

'Yes,' Martenson said. 'So Damen thinks he can get even by grabbing the thing Kurt King treasures most – his company.'

Groves stopped at the club entrance. 'King Corp's the

best buy and the biggest coup Damen will ever make – but he gets a more important prize for him.'

'You mean Kurt King sitting below him at board meetings,' Martenson said. 'Incredible.'

'But true,' Groves said. 'William Procrustes Damen may be about to chop Kurt Sixtus King down to less than his own size.'

'We've got to warn Kurt,' Martenson said.

'No, Sam. There are times when personal considerations outweigh all others. Let King handle it his own way – and we'll keep our own options open.'

5

King had no time to ring and cancel his appointment with Frankie later that evening. He ran to a cab-stand and thrust a ten-dollar bill at the driver to hustle him to his rendezvous with Hubert. At the Blithe Spirits club a doorman looked them over and nodded them downstairs into a basement where a black pianist was strumming a tune beside the long bar, with a white sailor sitting alongside him. The décor was austere. Twenty or thirty tables and chairs, schoolroom type, with unpadded stools at the bar. Beer glasses littered the tables and the bar. Diffuse strip lighting hardly pierced the thick haze of tobacco smoke. A couple of waiters shuffled between the bar and the tables and cubicles along the two sides of the basement, taking orders. But what struck King and Hubert was what they did not see.

There was not a woman in sight.

'Kurt,' Hubert whispered, 'I'm an idiot. They're not hopheads, they're homos. Blithe Spirits . . . the gay boys, get it?'

Hubert did not need to spell it out further. Along the bar and at the tables, male couples were holding hands or pawing each other. From the cubicles, male-soprano giggling came to their ears. With his religious upbringing, Kurt tried hard but vainly not to dislike homosexuals. He felt like throwing up.

'Which one of us is the pansy?' Hubert whispered, grinning, as they sat down at a table. He pitched his voice up a good octave as he ordered gin and tonic for them both.

King was looking around. Tillman was not at the bar or at a table. To his astonishment, he noticed an ageing Hollywood actor, a screen tough-guy, sitting hand-in-hand with a six-foot, two-hundred-pound sailor. In fact, King spotted about a couple of dozen sailors, probably from the naval base a few miles down the coast. Even in the dim light, he recognized two or three faces of young actors from Hollywood's film and TV studios.

They were beginning to imagine Tillman had been and gone when he suddenly appeared from the direction of the toilets. A younger and taller man followed him, and they took a seat in a cubicle against the back wall of the club. King now recognized the man who had looked at several new projects for King Corp. He wondered why he hadn't realized the man was a queer during their several sessions in the King offices. He had that mincing walk and a falsetto lisp when he was proved wrong in argument. King felt rage boiling inside him as he watched the smooth, round face under the thatch of long, blond hair. His companion ordered drinks and King could see his hand caressing Tillman's as they sat opposite each other.

'We haven't got Schutt's subpoena, Kurt.'

'We don't need a fucking subpoena.'

343

Hearing the grim note in King's voice, Hubert looked at him, sharply. 'Take it easy, Kurt!'

King had already risen and was making his way to the cubicle where Tillman and his boyfriend were sitting. When he spotted them, Tillman looked up, scared. His eyes darted from one to the other, and he half-rose as though intending to make a run for it. His boyfriend, a burly, square-faced man in his early thirties, tracked Tillman's gaze and noticed his fear. King and Hubert had, by then, reached their cubicle.

'Who're these guys, Matthew?' the boyfriend asked. 'Do you know them?'

'Yes – but I don't want to meet them,' Tillman replied in his lisping voice.

His boyfriend looked them up and down then thumbed towards the stairs. 'You heard what my friend said – he don't want anything to do with you.' From his attitude, King guessed the man imagined they might be trying to take his lover-man away from him. He spoke quietly to Tillman. 'We only want to talk to you for ten minutes, and then we'll leave you alone,' he said.

'What's all this about?' the boyfriend began, rising King pushed him back into his seat and threw a ten dollar bill on to the table. 'Buy yourself a drink on us and we'll send your friend back in ten minutes.' Without waiting for Tillman to agree, King caught him by the arm and slid him free of the bench seat and pushed him towards the toilet. Hubert followed them.

Once they were inside King put the latch on the door. 'All right, tell us about it,' he said. 'What did you give Norris Thomas of Zanadu that made him so interested in taking over King Corp?'

'I don't know what you're talking about,' Tillman started to say when King grabbed the collar of his

344

leather blouse in both hands and twisted hard enough to cut Tillman's breath.

'You know exactly what I'm talking about – you gave them our phone book with the list of confidential numbers, didn't you?'

'I might have.' Tillman's face was turning red as King applied more pressure on the collar of his blouse. 'All right, maybe I did.'

'What else? What else did you give them?'

'No . . . nothing else.'

King released his hands from the leather jacket to grip Tillman round the neck and squeeze. 'What else, you little bastard? What else? I'll keep on squeezing until you tell me.' As he increased the pressure, Tillman started to struggle then beat at King with his fists. His mouth snapped open as he tried to suck air in. His face had gone purple and he started banging his heels against the toilet wall. Oblivious of all this, King kept on squeezing.

Suddenly, King felt another pair of hands grab his wrists and try to wrest them away from Tillman's neck. A voice bawled in his ear. 'Kurt, for Christ's sake, for Christ's sake, stop it or you'll kill him.'

King dropped his hands. He was shaking with silent rage. Tillman dropped to the floor and they heard him gasping for breath. King turned to observe Hubert staring at him as though he could not believe what he had just witnessed. 'Kurt, you could have murdered that poor bastard,' he muttered. 'Your company isn't worth that. No company's worth that.'

Hubert went and fetched a paper cup and filled it with water. Kneeling, he dribbled the water into Tillman's mouth then helped him to his feet. 'You know

345

our lawyers are hunting for you to serve a subpoena on you,' he said.

'I can't tell them anything about the takeover bid,' Tillman croaked.

'You can tell them what you told Zanadu,' King cut in. 'You told them about our Tri Corp deal, didn't you?'

'Tri Corp? No. What's that, anyway?' Tillman shook his head. He looked and sounded genuine.

'They quizzed you, didn't they? They asked about our profits and prospects,' King insisted.

'All right, they did, but I couldn't tell them anything they didn't know already.' Tillman paused to clear his throat and swallow some more water. 'They were like cops, they asked the questions to which only they knew the answers.' He turned frightened eyes on them. 'So go ahead and serve your subpoena, I had nothing to do with the raid, except the phone list.'

'I believe he's telling the truth,' Hubert whispered.

'Yeah, you're right – damn him.' Without even apologizing to Tillman, King walked out and upstairs and stood for several moments outside, breathing the night air deep into his lungs. Watching him, Hubert wondered about the change that had come over his boss in the short time since the start of the raid. All he heard King repeat on their way downtown was, 'There goes the best chance we had to nail Zanadu.'

6

He was half an hour late for his rendezvous with Frankie and Ron in the Zanzibar lounge of the Beverly Wilshire. As he came in, he spotted them from the door. Frankie had her hand on Ron's shoulder, she had her head down, hair everywhere, laughing at some joke he had made. King was glad somebody could laugh. Glad, too, they got on so well together. It took two double martinis to draw level with them and mellow his temper. He had to unload everything; the helicopter fiasco, the courtroom drama, Damen's threat to expose him, and the incident with Tillman. However, he censored the fact he had nearly throttled the man. 'I don't think I could take another day like that,' he said, gulping his third drink.

'Relax, Kurt, and forget it for a couple of hours,' Ron said, biting back any I-told-you-so remarks about Damen, also a jibe that King might easily grow into a takeover bore. 'We're waiting for Chip who's on his way over from Cross Industries with your Seville.'

'Oh, God, not him.' King's heart-cry turned heads towards them. His own was looking heavenwards. 'In my Seville, my pride and joy. He'll never get it here.'

Frankie and Ron laughed. Of King Corp's top executives, Boyd was the most tranquil – controlled in everything except his garish, outlandish clothing. And anything mechanical. He had only to touch a typewriter, an accounting machine, a car and they developed the 'yips'. Chip was, in fact, accident-prone. Too often for mere probability to explain it, his luggage had gone to one city while he flew to another. His feat of losing his luggage twice on the company plane had become King Corp legend. He put the hex on everything he drove; each of the big, expensive cars the company had bought for him just quit at his touch. Parts dropped off and on one occasion the transmission fell out of his car on the Coast Highway. So, King never allowed him anywhere near his Seville.

Ten minutes later, Chip arrived, provoking a minor

sensation with his maroon-check sports jacket, blue-check shirt, yellow tie and matching trousers. 'I stopped home to change,' he said, 'and give the car time to cool down.'

'Cool down!' King's face had gone white.

'Yeah, your car was making a kinda funny rattle the last few miles.' He burst out laughing, and the others joined him when they saw the stricken look on King's face. 'I'm kidding,' Chip said, holding up both hands in a surrender gesture.

King had to join in the laughter. His three drinks had mellowed his temper. 'Here's one back for yours,' he said, turning to Frankie and Poole. 'You know Chip and I began the day at the Cross factory near Laguna Niguel. Well, Bud Crossman and his key people are Jewish and we're sitting over lunch when Bud says he's glad their being Jewish made no difference. So, Chip pipes up, "Oh, don't worry about that, we're not anti-semantic."'

As Frankie and Poole roared with laughter, Chip looked mystified. 'What's wrong with that. It's a perfectly good word.'

'Of course it is, Chip, but it just isn't the right one,' Frankie said, wiping her eyes. She leaned over and whispered something in Chip's ear. He put his head down in his folded arms, murmuring, 'Oh, no. Oh, no.'

Chip brought his head up and gave his own account of Bud Crossman's reaction to the word, anti-semantic. He was just finishing and everyone was laughing when suddenly King looked across the room and said to himself, 'Oh, oh my God.'

Walking directly towards their table was Jessica Rockefeller. Every man in the room seemed to freeze and rivet his attention on her. Even the bartender, who stopped his hand with a customer's change in it while he had an eyeful.

It looked as though the day was going to end as disastrously as it had begun. However, King was relieved she did not look as blatantly sexy as she could. Yet, there was something so vibrant about her face and figure she made every other woman in the room, including Frankie, look plain. Her hair was dyed a startling light-grey shade, almost white, which went beautifully with the silver pant suit she wore. Several inches of her jacket zipper were open to reveal her cleavage. Her breasts, larger than King remembered them, undulated in such a way it was clear she had nothing on under the jacket. A single piece of Indian jewellery – a turquoise and silver sunbird – hung at her throat.

'Mr King.' She was using her husky Bryn Mawr voice. 'Excuse me for intruding, but when I saw you and your party I simply had to come over and say hello. Do you mind?' Only King perceived the mischief behind the smile she shot the others.

'Of course not.' King made the introductions. 'Frankie, this is Jessica Rockefeller, a business acquaintance from New York . . . Frankie Shore . . .' King realized Ron Poole had Jessica pegged. Chip Boyd, however, stood up and offered his hand as if the First Lady had joined them. Jessica smiled and held on to it somewhat longer than King thought socially necessary.

'Oh, Mr King, I must thank you for the suggestion on Lockheed. It turned out to be a fine investment for me.'

King signalled the waiter and asked Jessica what she wished to drink. Before she replied, she insisted on asking the others if they minded her joining them. Frankie, no doubt wondering what sort of business acquaintance Kurt had with this flamboyant woman, assured her nobody minded.

A few minutes later, when both Frankie and Chip went off to the restrooms and Ron had turned to listen to the piano player, Jessica moved her chair closer to King's. Her hand slid into his lap, her long nails dug into the flesh of his upper thigh. 'Hey, big fellow, how you been? Getting any lately?'

He coughed a little and chose to ignore that question. 'Jessie, you look out of sight as the kids would say.'

'It's my tits.'

'What?'

'My tits. I had them done. Aren't they terrific?'

'They were and are.'

'Want to see them?' Her hand went to the zipper and she turned slightly in the chair.

'No . . . I mean not here and now.' King gave something between a groan and a laugh. 'Look, I got your call but I haven't had the chance to return it. I will, though.'

'Look, honey, I read the papers and I know what those fuckers are trying to do to you. I'm here for at least two weeks, so any time. Hey, how're you with the broad?'

'She's a pretty special friend. We go back a ways.'

Jessica laughed, trailing her fingers lightly against his crotch before removing her hand. 'So do we, sweetie, so do we. But I get the picture.'

King slipped his wallet out of his coat pocket and swiftly palmed two fifties which he pressed into the cleavage below the zipper. Jessica said nothing.

'The guy with his back to you, Poole – he's one of my best pals, a real prince of a guy. Why don't you sta

350

with him after the rest of us leave, and let him think he picked you up? Okay? Give him the full treatment.'

Jessica smiled slowly. 'Well, he's kinda cute – in a dumb-ass way.'

Chip, then Frankie, returned and Jessica said her farewells. King watched, like every other male in the room, the sensuous rhythm of her buttocks as she retreated. At least she had put Judge Page, Damen, Tillman out of his mind for a few moments.

Later that night, after discovering, to his dismay, it was the wrong time of the month for Frankie, he cursed as he tried to sleep. But he admitted his anger was not genuine, for he was so tired he doubted if he would have been much of a bed partner. He thought of Jessica and Ron, and managed some sort of smile.

XIII

As the legal battle with Zanadu began in earnest, lawyers started taking depositions from the major figures on both sides and a mountain of paper built up. Because King and his staff had no reason to tell anything but the truth, the Zanadu attorneys learned very little new. But the King Corp lawyers learned a great deal as they continued to burrow into the pyramid of documents. They knew from Zanadu's original 13-D submission back on Day one that Zanadu was borrowing 100 million dollars to help finance the takeover. The deposition process revealed that at least one Zanadu director had no knowledge of this huge borrowing. Another Zanadu director had no idea what King Corp did. All this strengthened King's resolve to have nothing to do with Norris Thomas or his company.

In the welter of information, King felt they must find some flaw in the Zanadu action. He urged his own people to scan every word rather than rely on the attorneys who might read the legal significance right but miss the business implications.

Kate Foy was the linchpin of this operation. She had moved to a small office of her own to spend all her time filtering information from the lawyers as well as preparing press releases.

One afternoon, she mentioned to one of Schutt's lawyers a certain document the Zanadu attorneys had furnished as part of the discovery process. It was a single piece of paper, part of a memo from Chip Boy to Kurt King about a bond issue for a new glass plant in Salt Lake City. In the margins, King had pencilled notes in his own unique scrawl.

That evening, Kate told King about the paper, saying Tillman had probably slipped it to Zanadu and it might be useful evidence against Tillman.

'Forget Tillman,' King said, explaining he had quizzed the consultant and ruled him out as the informer.

A week later while talking to one of the New York lawyers who had recently been drafted in to help Schutt, Kate heard the name of Edward Foxe, whom she had met and disliked. 'What has that son of a bitch to do with Zanadu?' she asked.

'That's what we're trying to find out. His name keeps cropping up and we want to take his deposition, but we can't run him down.'

Kate was walking away when she suddenly halted, stood still with the colour draining from her face.

'You all right, Kate?'

'Yes, I'm fine. But I think I've found the answer to the whole raid. Foxe, the bond issue, everything fits together. Of course, Tillman had nothing to do with it.'

She rang King and convened an emergency meeting of all the senior executives where she told her story. She and Chip Boyd had met Edward Foxe, vice-president of F. G. Irving's corporate finance division. In fact, King had provided the introduction. Foxe had traded some securities for King's personal account and requested the meeting. He was touting business for his firm of investment bankers.

Kate Foy continued: 'A few days after our meeting, Chip, you gave Mr K a confidential handwritten study about the auto parts group of King Corp, saying it could

353

be spun off for over 300 million dollars. Kurt, you bounced the sheet back saying the figure was optimistic and Chip reworked it to 267 million. Chip's study indicated that half the company could be sold for the book value of the entire company and said the whole group could be liquidated for well over 25 dollars a share.'

King broke in. 'Sure, I remember that, but what's the point?'

'Chip stated he wanted to contact a friend working for Freeman, Constable to discuss the spin-off idea, and you gave him the go-ahead.'

'I'm kind of vague on all this,' King said. 'Wha[t] happened then?'

'Chip couldn't reach his friend, but remembered Fox[e] and called him. I sat in on that meeting as did Bu[d] Gorman and a few others. Foxe was filled in on th[e] details of the spin-off idea and given a copy of Chip'[s] memo. Yet Chip very carefully warned Foxe not onl[y] was the document confidential to outsiders but t[o] company people as well. We didn't want to ups[et] operating heads by spreading news about the remo[te] possibility of a spin-off. Nor did we want an informatio[n] leak that might start a raid.'

Kate paused to look at Chip, who confirmed all th[is] with a glum nod of his head. She took a sip of wat[er] and went on, 'Then the bond issue for the new gla[ss] plant in Salt Lake was discussed. When Foxe said [he] thought his firm could have done a better job than o[ur] own people, Bud Gorman got him a marked-up copy [of] the draft. Foxe asked if he could take this with him [to] review when he had more time. Bud agreed, but w[ith] the caution it was confidential and not pub[lic] information.'

King shook his head, puzzled. 'I don't remember much of this.'

'No reason why you should,' said Kate. 'That was the last we saw of Mr Foxe. He called Chip a few days later to say F. G. Irving had no interest in helping us with the spin-off project. He only surfaced again when he made that call to you, Kurt, the day that the raid was announced.'

'Yeah, he was back to soliciting business. But what about the material we gave him?'

'I think he ran over to Norris Thomas and Zanadu with the whole shmear,' Kate said, determinedly.

'Chip, what do you think?'

'He may well have.'

'Christ's sake!' King snapped. 'Come on, Chip, the age in the Zanadu file from the Salt Lake memo ouldn't have come from anyone else. Kate's dead ght.' He clenched a fist and held it up. 'And to think e spent vital days going after Tillman. Call the law-ers, Kate, and fix a meeting with them first thing morrow.'

eve Schutt had a big smile on his long face when King ished recounting their dealings with Foxe. 'It looks if we've uncovered a 10-b-5 violation,' he said. here's no doubt Foxe gave documents to Zanadu and side information cannot be used by anyone in the rchase or sale of stock. The SEC is tough on this gulation, and so are the courts when you can prove This might even enable us to block Zanadu.'

Schutt said the discovery of one of the Salt Lake pers in the Zanadu file tied Foxe directly with the k. He must also have given them the confidential memo and the spread sheet. But those papers would never appear in the files. They were too hot.

'But Steve, how do we prove Foxe passed on those papers?' King butted in. 'That son of a bitch will lie in his teeth.'

'Maybe not. You know, it's interesting, since Watergate people seem a little more truthful.'

'I sure hope you're right, Steve.'

'For the moment, our biggest problem is to find Foxe and serve him with a subpoena and take his deposition. When his name came up first, our New York people tried to catch him but missed him. And now he's in Hawaii, I hear. He's certainly well named. But don't worry, we'll get him.'

2

During the weeks that followed, Kurt King came neare[r] to throwing in his hand than he ever thought he would[.] Slippery Edward Foxe kept one or two jumps ahead [of] their posse of process-servers, and just when h[e] thought they might be making progress to balk th[e] takeover, another blow would fall. He began to feel th[e] countdown clock was running against him, personall[y] and no way could he stop Zanadu.

There was his court appearance before Judge Pag[e.] He was looking forward to testifying about the pr[o]posed acquisition of Cross Industries to try to persua[de] Page to lift the restraining order.

But Page, looking more dyspeptic and sounding m[ore] acid-tongued than ever, managed to gag him with t[he] help of his friend, George Waxman. Twenty-eight tim[es] Waxman sprang up to object to questions Sam Dona[ld]son put to King. Twenty-seven times King heard t[he] croaking voice from the bench say, 'Objection sustained'. Not once did they pierce the barrier Waxman and Page had erected round them. It was an awesome lesson in the power of a federal judge. King left the court fuming, forced to admit the second round had also gone to Zanadu.

However, a sharp ray of hope appeared one afternoon when King took a call from a shareholder who asked, 'Does King Corp own any planes?'

'Yes, five of them. Why?'

The caller knew a former Civil Aeronautics Board official and suggested King contact him. When he did, the official told King that if his company held an air carrier certificate then any takeover would require CAB approval or otherwise an exemption from the board. King said the company's Falcon Jet – 333KK – did a lot of private charter work when not on King Corp business. Most of those who chartered it were movie stars wishing to travel without being bothered by fans. The CAB official said if the aircraft did turn out to have an air carrier charter, King should call Tom Lowe, a Texas attorney, who had been with the CAB.

When King verified the Falcon was properly certified as an air carrier under Part 135 of CAB regulations, he spoke to Lowe in Austin. He had heard of the raid and would have called King but feared it would look as if he were soliciting business.

'Is your certificate up to date?' he asked. 'Is the plane actually being used for charter work these days?'

'The licence is up to date and the plane is now on charter carrying Colonel Tom Parker, Elvis Presley's manager.'

'Then, Mr King, in my opinion, you have a good

block to Zanadu, and if you can't beat them you can surely delay them.'

Two hours later, King and Paul Towers flew to Texas to meet with Lowe, who explained a certified air carrier could not be purchased by another party without CAB approval, and it made no difference whether it was one aeroplane or a fleet like United Air Lines. And the Board did not act quickly. Lowe cited the landmark case of Ronson in which a raider had bought 10 per cent of Ronson stock disregarding the fact Ronson owned a certified helicopter. The Board stepped in, requiring the stock to be put in a non-voting trust, and this ruling caused the raider such a delay it spoiled his scheme.

King was excited. 'Give it to me straight – what chance does this give us?'

'At this point, I'd rather be in your shoes than Zanadu's.'

'Sounds beautiful, but I feel there's a hitch somewhere.'

Lowe shook his head. 'You have two choices. You can get an advance ruling and maybe have the Justice Department stop Zanadu before they get the stock. Or if you're gutty, you can wait until they get 10 per cent of your stock and the government, in the form of the CAB, will have no choice but to step in. It might take Zanadu anything from ninety days to six months to get CAB permission to go ahead.'

Ninety days! In that time, they could take court action to beat Zanadu. King retained Lowe on the spot and that evening all three flew back to Los Angeles in the company's Lear Jet. They dropped a passenger in Palm Springs, parking at the Combs terminal.

'Mr Lowe, that's what I call a coincidence,' King said as they stretched their legs. He pointed to a plane parked next to them on the apron. It was a Falcon 333KK on the Parker charter.

<h1 style="text-align:center">3</h1>

King's elation was short-lived, swept away by a call from the Securities Exchange Commission officials in Washington who threatened to sue him for false declarations in his letter to King Corp shareholders.

That letter – which had cost them so much sweat, which had been put together by so many highly-paid experts, which had caused Kate Foy to blow her top – had finally appeared in the major newspapers. And, prompted by Zanadu, the SEC had pounced on errors of omission and misleading statements.

King saw at once they were right to complain. How had the lawyers and experts passed the evident falsehood that brokers who bought King Corp stock for Zanadu would get two commissions? That and several other errors angered King and he immediately set Kate Foy to draft a letter correcting the mistakes. Kate herself was devastated by the turn of events.

Schutt acted quickly. His partner, Harry Mandel, who handled SEC matters, flew to Washington to explain King was professionally and personally sorry about the errors and would make a retraction speedily. Mandel assured King the Commission would make no difficulties – but he was dead wrong. The young attorneys assigned to the case were furious with Kurt King and threatened to bring suit. They complained about the King Corp language, specifically objecting to words like 'aid' and 'attack'. King, they contended, had put out false and misleading earnings projections. But their major concern was the payment of the 30 million dollars to the hundred key employees which would be triggered if Zanadu acquired 25 per cent of King stock. No mention of the 30-million-dollar payout had been made in the shareholders' letter. This damaging information had been furnished to the SEC by Zanadu and now King's monologue with Norris Thomas on Day one was coming back to haunt him! The SEC talked about this as if it were a criminal act.

At the end of the week, Harry Mandel called Schutt. 'Jesus, Steve, I feel every time I take one step forward, they make me take two back. Don't tell King this, but these people talk about him like they would about a Mafia godfather. I keep telling them in twelve years of running the company he has never even been looked at by the Commission. An impeccable record. I tell them the letter was written in haste by people Kurt depended on as experts. They don't even listen. I tell you, Steve, they're after his blood.'

'Have you got a plan?'

'Yeah, I guess you better get the retraction letter ready and newspaper space reserved. Telecopy me the final draft and I'll see if I can get it approved in the next day or so.'

Within a day, Kate and the lawyers had drafted the letter and reserved the space. Mandel and the Washington lawyers working with him thought the SEC would accept this. Again he was wrong. Next day, the Commission brought suit against King Corp in Federal Court without giving the company a chance to make amends. However, the lawsuit was settled the day it was brought. King had the option of either fighting in court or consenting to a permanent injunction. Schutt, Mandel and Boyd advised him to fight. He surprised everyone by signing the consent decree. It was a nas-

pill, but he was increasingly concerned about the mounting cost of legal fees; he also felt they should give their energies to fighting Zanadu, not the SEC. However, he admitted later that he had been wrong to give in. He would regret his decision.

The government action and his signing the consent decree were very damaging. Zanadu lost no time in exploiting it, and the press inadvertently co-operated by distorting the significance of the affair. Many shareholders misunderstood, and King insisted on taking the brunt of their abuse. Even friends told him it appeared he'd been caught with his hand in the cookie jar. That bothered him, though not as much as Chip Boyd's report that his thirteen-year-old son had come home from school asking his father why a classmate had said, 'your old man and Kurt King are crooks'.

The anger of certain shareholders was typified by a letter that came to King marked Personal.

Dear Mr King:

I resent very much the way the management of King Corp tried to deceive the owners of the business, the stockholders. Of course, you must realize you have lost credibility by your attempt to corrupt and to betray the people who have invested in it.

Surely you know the difference between what is right and what is wrong. You evaded, you misrepresented, and I gather you even lied about the Zanadu stock tender. You indeed represent all that is bad about the corporate image, and for that I cannot forgive you. I am writing to the Securities and Exchange Commission and to Zanadu to tell them that I hope they will take over and get rid of present management. I'm sure this will not be to my financial interest. But I'm willing to pay the price.

Disgustedly,
C . . . B . . .
Shareholder

Most of the abusive flak stemmed from the 30-million-dollar problem. As the *Wall Street Journal* reported it: 'The Securities Exchange Commission accused King Corp of fighting a tender offer without disclosing that its top management had much to gain financially as a result of the offer.' That paragraph would haunt Kurt King for weeks and weeks.

His anger and concern turned to frustration and Frankie became a target for his pent-up feelings. 'Why am I fighting so hard to defeat Zanadu?' he stormed at her one night. 'Explain that to me, if you can. Why bother to fight when I can make a fortune by just rolling over and playing dead? My critics have got it all completely wrong. Even the great *Wall Street Journal*, quoting the SEC, pointed out that two of our directors who voted to reject the offer stood to receive over 2 million dollars. Chip and myself, that is. But what about the other six directors who voted the same way even though they stood not to make a dime? The *Journal* didn't mention that little fact. Furthermore, that's our money. It's bonuses we could have taken when earned but we chose to defer it. It's our money we loaned to the company. Nobody seems to get the story straight.'

Frankie let him blow off steam; she listened and made sympathetic noises, knowing what pressure he was suffering.

Then, just when King was despairing, the company won a major victory. On 10 November, one day before Zanadu was scheduled to make their official tender offer, King Corp got its first break in the courts. Chancery judge in Delaware found that Zanadu had, in fact, filed improperly and enjoined them from proceeding with the offer.

Zanadu was furious. It had hired the two top attorneys in this special field of corporate law, yet they had bungled their opening move like amateurs.

King was elated. It acted on him like a tonic. He immediately sent a telegram to each of the company's operating heads.

GENTLEMEN:
YOU HAVE PROBABLY READ OF OUR VICTORY IN THE DELAWARE CHANCERY COURT. THOUGH THE WAR GOES ON WE HAVE WON A MAJOR BATTLE. THIS WILL DELAY ZANADU THOUGH FOR HOW LONG IS NOT DETERMINABLE AT THIS TIME. YOUR SUPPORT AND EXPRESSIONS OF CONFIDENCE ARE DEEPLY APPRECIATED. THE OVERALL CONTINUING SUCCESS OF THE COMPANY'S OPERATIONS ARE A TRIBUTE TO YOUR DEVOTION AND HARD WORK. THE SHAREHOLDERS, DIRECTORS AND CORPORATE STAFF SEND THEIR THANKS. DO NOT HESITATE TO CONTACT ME ON ANY MATTER OF IMPORTANCE.

VERY BEST PERSONAL REGARDS
KURT

Steve Schutt explained this victory meant Zanadu would have to file a new and corrected 13-D document on King personally at the King Corp office to restart the tender offer. 'And Kurt,' Schutt continued, 'watch your back and front for they'll tail you round the clock and probably hand you the new file as you walk in the front door one morning.' He thought for a moment. 'Let's see, today's November 10th. They could file again on the 12th, Friday, and start the tender offer on December 1st.'

'But we've put a real crimp on their plans.'

4

The phone woke him with a start and he stared at the instrument as if his look could silence it. Then he shook his head, driving away the last filaments of sleep, and picked up the receiver.

'Mr King, this is Kravetch. I hope I didn't wake you. I remembered your saying you were an early riser.'

'No, no, it's quite all right,' King lied, wondering why in the world a private detective would be calling at this hour.

'I know your case is closed, so to speak, but I ran across something and wondered if you wanted me to follow up on it,' Kravetch went on.

Still bewildered by the call, King stammered, 'I don't know, what is it?'

'You may recall my assistant lives near New Canaan. Quite by accident, though I must say chance plays a larger part in my business than I would want people to know . . .'

'Oh, Jesus,' King groaned inwardly, 'a philosophical private eye at five in the morning.'

'. . . he happened to see your wife, Mrs Carolyn King, twice in the company of the same man. It was not the man whom we reported on earlier. Through discreet enquiry, he found the man was not a local resident. I wondered if you wanted me to find out more about him. There's no charge up to this point, and your account has been paid in full.'

King was in the process of lighting his first cigarette of the day and it triggered a hacking cough. He waited for a moment, hand over the mouthpiece.

'Mr King?'

'Excuse me, I was thinking.' He paused again then spoke slowly. 'No, Mr Kravetch, I think not, but I do appreciate your calling me. Thank you, goodbye.' He put the phone down, quietly, and sat back against the headboard, smoking and staring at nothing.

He needed sleep, but there was so much to do and he could not dispel the unpleasant mood Kravetch's call had created. Finally, he got out of bed, put on an old seersucker robe, lit another cigarette and walked into the living room, where it was almost light.

On top of the bar lay a small pile of photographs, all shots of Frankie taken by a friend whose home-office combination she had recently decorated. A couple of the pictures had turned out unusually well. One almost candid shot showed Frankie staring intently at something out of the camera field. She had a thin pencil laid against one cheek in a quizzical gesture, and her large lower lip was slightly protruding. All the handsome beauty of her face stood out in that snapshot. As King stood gazing at the picture, he tried to remember Frankie's age. He could not. Thirty-two? He wasn't sure. He put the picture down then propped it up against a decanter.

Wandering into his den, he picked up a stack of notes and a small portable dictating machine which he carried into the kitchen. He put the water on for instant coffee and began to page through the notes. Suddenly he stopped, startled by the realization that he had been thinking not about his wife and not about Frankie but about Jessica Rockefeller. Jesus Christ, he said to himself, disgustedly, and snapped on the recorder.

He dictated a note to Chip Boyd cancelling a projected legal action in Canada against Zanadu for breaking the country's foreign exchange regulations; he also quashed the idea of suing Zanadu's directors, the more so because one of them had a heart problem. After making coffee, he dictated a dozen more memos and letters on company business.

When the antique clock in the hallway chimed seven he had a shower, dressed, then started for Schutt's office. On the Santa Monica freeway, he ran into the worst traffic jam he had seen in a year, and that dissipated the good mood his early working session had produced. When he arrived forty-five minutes late, he was loaded for bear.

Steve Schutt triggered his wrath by handing him the day's first problem. Several King directors, worried about his aggressive frontal attack on Zanadu, had begun to talk about hiring attorneys to represent the board. They thought if they did everything King and his lawyers recommended, they would be leaving them selves open to lawsuits.

'They're out of their fucking minds,' King bellowed 'They don't need to worry about being sued. Maybe some idiot will bring a suit later on, particularly on who sold at 30 and then sees the stock shoot up. That' why we have director's insurance. The directors are a covered. Christ, another set of lawyers will really fuc things up.'

Schutt ignored that general slur. 'I don't want to se that happen either, Kurt, but I'm afraid I can unde stand even if I don't share their concern.'

'Oh, for Christ's sake, Steve, they'd want to revie everything and it would be like running a war committee and not by a general and his staff. Damn I've never made a move without considering the dire tors' position. They just can't hire their own lawye and that's it.'

'I'm sorry to say they may go ahead anyway since they don't need your permission.'

King drew a quick, deep breath. Anger surged through him such as he had never felt in his entire adult life. Schutt's trick of twirling that gold pencil between his fingers maddened him. Both his fists had clenched tight. He forced himself to open them. It shocked him to admit he had been on the verge of knocking hell out of Steve Schutt. What was that ancient custom of killing the bearers of bad news? He willed himself calm again.

'Any idea who'd put them up to it, Steve?' he asked.

'I think Martenson and Groves were the mainspring behind the move, if that means anything.'

It did. King said nothing, but he smelled the big, banana-fingered hand of Damen behind the two directors. Hadn't they already acted as Astroteknik's message boys? He filed Schutt's information mentally for future reference. 'All right, let's move to something more positive,' he said, gruffly. 'I'm sick and tired of people telling me they can't find that bastard Foxe to serve him with a subpoena. Thinking of that little bastard who started all this keeps me awake nights. I want him run to earth and I want him now.'

'We're working on it, but Foxe is extremely elusive,' Schutt said.

'Yeah, and he'll stay elusive until Zanadu takes us over unless we do something pretty damn quick.' King looked sharply at Schutt. 'You're not dragging your feet because you represented Foxe's firm in the past, are you?'

Schutt glanced at King, noting the clench of his face and the quick-burning cigarette between his lips. If this case went on too long, Kurt King might well turn paranoid. 'I wish you hadn't said that, Kurt,' he came back. 'You know well, on this matter we're working for you and you alone.'

'Sorry, Steve, I take it back.' He reflected for a moment. 'But what you just said makes me think about an angle we can use. One of our directors has personal friends at the top of F. G. Irving. I'll ask him to let his buddies know I'm furious about Foxe running to cover. I'm preparing a suit against Irving and intend to call a press conference and blow the whole story. So, Irving had better shake the tree and produce Mr Foxe.'

Schutt smiled for the first time that morning. 'I'm not sure you shake a tree to catch a fox, but you have grounds for a suit, so go ahead. Only, soft-pedal it a bit.'

'Jesus, you guys really get me.' King's mood had swung back to angry. 'Why is it the other side never seems to be worried about legal niceties?' He cut Schutt's reply off by scything with his hand. 'Don't bother to answer, I'll talk to you later.' He turned to the papers on his desk and, after a moment's hesitation, Schutt left the room. King knew he had been rude but was in no mind to say sorry.

Irving did promise to co-operate in producing the senior executive, Foxe, but days went by and nothing happened. As the thought of filing yet another law suit appalled him, King did not pursue his threat; but he continued to fume at the idea Foxe was thumbing his nose at all of them.

One afternoon, alone in the conference room, King suddenly slammed a hand on the table. 'Damn, why didn't I think of that before? That might just be it!' He drove to his office, paged through his King Corp phone directory then dialled a number.

'Mr King, this is a pleasant surprise,' said Gardner Barker, a young executive manager in the auto parts division. 'What can I do for you?'

'Gardy, didn't you once tell me you went to UCLA with Ed Foxe from F. G. Irving?'

'That's right.'

'How much of a football fan is Foxe?'

'Fanatic. Goes to all the games. His seats are near mine.'

'Where are your seats?'

'This year we're at tunnel eight about row ten, and Foxe is on the aisle a couple of rows below me.'

'Do you think he'll be at tomorrow's game against USC?'

'You must be kidding, Mr King. It's the biggie every year, and this year it's the one that decides which team of the two goes to the Rose Bowl. If Fast Eddie Foxe is in town he'll be there, you can bet on it.'

'Thanks very much, Gardy, but keep this call to yourself for a day or two.' King hung up and got Steve Schutt on the intercom. 'Can you get a subpoena for Foxe today?'

'Sure. Did your director and Irving smoke him out?'

'No, but I think I know where he's going to be, and I'll nail him myself.'

'You can't do that, Kurt. No company officer or employee can serve him. It has to be somebody else. Does that spoil things?'

'No,' King said, thoughtfully. 'It may better my chances of pulling it off. Just get me the subpoena by the time you close shop tonight.'

Again, he was making calls. He asked Frankie if she would be heartbroken if he didn't take her to the game tomorrow; she reminded him she was a basketball and baseball fan. He promised to call her and see her later that evening. He did not reveal he was taking another girl to the game.

He made one last call and was hanging up when Kate Foy walked in on him. She was astonished to see on his face the biggest smile she had seen in weeks.

5

King knew the meaning of mixed feelings as he watched the game. As a USC fan, he was disappointed they were not winning, but his mood was euphoric when he looked twenty-two rows below his own. There, right on the aisle, was Edward Foxe. He was more like a male model advertising high-fashion casual clothes than vice-president of a top investment banking firm.

'Okay.' King nudged the person seated next to him 'One more dry run.'

'Shit, I'm going to work off so much weight climbing these fucking stairs I'll look like a fucking scarecrow.'

'Yeah, but one of the best-looking, best-paid scare crows I know. Go on.' King gave her right buttock firm slap and with a pretended snarl, Jessica Rockefelle started down the concrete stairs. A real eyeful, she wa wearing white pants, a tailored, lightweight navy blaze and a pale-blue blouse. Her jacket barely covered he bottom and her pants were so tight they appeared have been sprayed on.

Jessica walked two steps past Foxe's seat, havir slowed down – as King had briefed her – to wait un she heard the referee whistle the play dead. Sl stopped and, with strip-teaser's art, removed the jack That raised as much din as the scoreless match h from the men in the vicinity. They saw Jessica w wearing a see-through blouse which gave her breasts their full erotic value. She made no sign that she had heard the hubbub but walked slowly down the stairs.

Only a handful of male fans in that section knew Ricky Bell had just gained twelve yards on a power sweep; all the others knew only that an ash-blonde madonna had descended the stairs showing almost everything from the waist up. They prayed, collectively, that she would be returning by the same route.

As Jessica turned and moved quickly up the stairs, the sight and bounce of her breasts brought a chant from the stands, heralding her coming.

Vince Evans, USC's quarterback, astounded his critics by throwing a thirty-yard strike for a completion, but Edward Foxe missed it. He was eyeing the sexiest girl he had ever seen mounting the stairs towards him.

And then she tripped.

Her small leather purse bounced and slid under his seat. Foxe hated to tear his gaze away from the exquisite pair of breasts that had just come into view, but the opportunity of assisting this girl was too great to miss. He ducked below his seat and found her purse. He handed it to her, smiling. As the striking girl stood in front of him and checked her purse, he murmured, 'Is everything okay, Miss . . . ah?'

Jessica smiled winsomely at him while she slipped on her coat. From it, she palmed a piece of paper, folded over several times, like a thin roadmap. She gave this to Foxe, caressing his hand.

'This is for you, Mr Foxe.'

Foxe stared at the subpoena. All he said was, 'Well, they finally got me.'

Buttoning her jacket, Jessica said, 'Have a nice day.'

In the third quarter, UCLA's Theotis Brown fumbled

and USC safety, Dennis Thurman, grabbed the ball and went forty-seven yards for a score; then Evans faked a pass and ran for another score from the 36. By then, King saw Foxe had already left; he never saw the two UCLA touchdowns that made their losing score a respectable 24 to 14.

Jessica insisted on dining with King. He chose a restaurant favoured by the older USC crowd. After several drinks, he found himself singing along at the bar piano; he remembered a parade of drinks, and eating something, and men and women trying to get Jessica to take off her blazer. He kept trying to remember something he had forgotten to do. Next thing he knew was waking up in Jessica's hotel room. He had a massive hangover but felt strangely proud, and sexually sated. He recalled with a tremendous thrill that Foxe now had the subpoena. Then he remembered he had promised to call Frankie. He cursed himself, shut his eyes and tried to sleep. When everything else failed, he started to count Ancient Greeks jumping out of a Trojan Horse with subpoenas in their hands.

In the first week of December, the Supreme Court of Delaware reversed the decision of the Chancery Court Zanadu was free to begin its raid on King Corp. The original date for the beginning of the tender offer was to have been Armistice Day, 11 November. King's delaying tactics had bought them twenty-seven days. As a result, the new offer date was 7 December anniversary of Pearl Harbor.

XIV

Witnessing the cocky smile on Edward Foxe's face as he sat at the conference table in Schutt's office, King's hopes sagged. Foxe looked nothing like a man who was going to damn himself by admitting he had leaked confidential information. He was chatting quietly with his attorney, as relaxed as if at a restaurant table. He wore an expensive and elegant three-piece suit of tan linen over a white shirt set off by a soft brown tie. A dark-brown Paisley handkerchief flopped from his jacket pocket and a gold chain hung from his waistcoat pockets. King noticed the man's nails were manicured and lacquered. His full head of dark-brown hair was carefully cut and styled. To King, he looked both canny and slippery.

To cross-examine Foxe, Schutt had brought in Barry Learner, an attorney in private practice. King had learned that, even though a lawyer might be a whiz in court, not all of them were good at the cut and thrust of direct questioning. Learner, heavy-set and plain, was an expert at face-to-face interrogations. Like a skilled card-player, he knew what was on the table, what had already been played, and he forgot nothing. His slow, plodding and inoffensive manner was deceptive.

Foxe was accompanied by two attorneys, one of them general counsel for Irving, the other representing Xanadu.

'What's first?' King asked Schutt. 'Do we come right out and ask him if he did what we suspect he did?'

'No,' said Schutt quietly. 'We begin by going through documents to see what our subpoena has wrought. Maybe we'll be lucky, though most often we're not.'

King watched them open the cardboard boxes and check the contents of each file. Within minutes, he could believe neither his eyes nor his ears. Right off the bat, they had stumbled on to the mother lode. The subpoena had asked for all of Foxe's personal files relating to King Corp and Zanadu, plus all the Irving files pertaining to the relationship between the two companies. An amazed King saw every confidential document given to Foxe was there, except for the Salt Lake City paper which had already surfaced. Also, there were memos and letters to Zanadu from both Foxe and his firm. The first exhibit turned out to be the original of the spread sheet with the confidential information Boyd had developed. Another was Boyd's memo to King discussing the auto operations spinoff.

King tried to hide his surprise. But would they be able to get Foxe to admit he had passed the confidential information to Zanadu?

Learner started gently. Yet, within minutes he had clearly established Foxe had been in regular contact with Zanadu while it was planning the raid. Before the serious questioning began, one particularly incriminating bit of evidence emerged. A list of King Corp stock held for investment clients of F. G. Irving had been taken off the computer and passed to Zanadu. Foxe had given two Zanadu officers the list, amounting to almost 11 per cent of outstanding King stock. Foxe claimed this was public information, but his action had unethical overtones.

King sat back and listened to the question-and-answer, totally absorbed like a child finally being allowed to hear something explained that had mystified him for a long time.

This is the picture he saw taking shape: a short time after Foxe's July session with Boyd, he met with the Zanadu people and, armed with confidential information, told one of Zanadu's vice-presidents King Corp would be a good acquisition. That Zanadu executive had said, under oath, his first meeting with Foxe had been in late August, two months before the tender offer.

Yet, Foxe now testified his initial meeting with this man was in early August, and he furnished a copy of a letter to prove this. In fact, the longer Foxe testified, the more his statements conflicted with those of the Zanadu executives. A vice-president of Zanadu swore he had gathered a lot of public information on King all by himself, but Foxe claimed it had come from him.

After a long series of questions and evasive or confusing answers, the moment King had waited for suddenly occurred. Learner was cross-examining Foxe about his meeting with Zanadu people on 25 August in which the King Corp raid had been broached. Foxe kept saying he had given Zanadu only public information but, in his low-key way, Learner kept pressing Foxe to say if he were certain nothing confidential had been handed over.

Suddenly, Learner came back to the paper on the spin-off project for the auto parts division which had been labelled Exhibit One. Had Foxe given Zanadu a copy of this document? Perhaps Foxe was growing tired, perhaps he let his guard down. Whatever the cause, he said, abruptly, 'I read the numbers off Exhibit One to the Zanadu people at the meeting of 25 August, 1976.'

LEARNER: Is it your testimony that you did not give them a copy of the document?

FOXE: That's correct, and the reason is that it wouldn't Xerox.

LEARNER: Do you recall which, if any, numbers you read off to them?

FOXE: I read off most of the numbers on the document.

LEARNER: Do you recall specifically any numbers that you did not refer to in your conversation with them?

FOXE: The second part of Exhibit One consisted of numbers that we did not discuss at the meeting. The first sheet on Exhibit One was what we discussed at the meeting.

LEARNER: Did you indicate, Mr Foxe, to those present at the meeting the source of those numbers?

King held his breath. A hush had fallen over the room, amplifying the quiet hum of the stenographer's machine. For the first time in the deposition, Foxe did not look directly at his questioner.

FOXE: Yes.

LEARNER: And that source was King Corp, was it not?

FOXE: That is correct.

King felt the pulse of his heart. He could have yelled, thrown his hat in the air, jumped up and down Instead, he kept the straightest of faces.

LEARNER: Do you recall, specifically, whether the made notes of that portion of the conversation in whic you referred to the numbers contained in Exhibit One?

FOXE: I believe they did.

LEARNER: Do you know what they did with thos notes at the close of the meeting?

FOXE: I don't know.

LEARNER: Did they at any point ask you to repe anything?

FOXE: Well, not repeat, but several times one of the Zanadu officials asked me to slow down. I think he was writing the numbers down.

LEARNER: You have a clear recollection of his having done so?

FOXE: Yes.

And all this in quiet tones which contrasted with the duplicity of Foxe and the Zanadu executives. Another aspect of Foxe's testimony sickened not only King but Foxe's own counsel. He testified that Gearhart, the raid specialist who represented Zanadu, had offered F. G. Irving the role of dealer-manager in the takeover, a financially rewarding assignment. But when Foxe confessed to one of his superiors he had given Zanadu inside information from King Corp, the senior executive probed further; when he realized Foxe had been given the information in confidence, he knew Irving was on shaky legal and ethical ground and turned down the Gearhart offer. Edward Foxe lost his finder's fee.

Yet, when the raid was announced, he was on the phone that morning trying to persuade King to hire F. G. Irving to help fend off the raid. Having failed to get a fee from the raider, he was trying to get one from the victim. When Foxe blatantly admitted this, his own attorney was so shocked, he said, quite audibly, 'Oh, my God.'

The questioning ended and the participants were leaving the conference room when one of Foxe's attorneys, who knew King socially, took him aside and said, 'Kurt, I'd expected you to say "when F. G. Irving speaks, Zanadu listens".'

King smiled, his pleasure over the Foxe confession amplified by the twisted humour, and responded, 'touché.'

377

When the deposition was finally complete, King modified his opinion of investment bankers. Up to then, he had viewed them as respectable prostitutes; now he looked on them as nothing more than cheap whores.

2

'Jesus, Frankie, you should have seen the look on Foxe's face when it was all over,' King said with a chuckle. 'The bastard was trying to pretend he didn't really spill the beans. He was so shaken that when he left the room he handed me his business card.' He produced it. 'I think I'll have it mounted and put on the mantel.'

They were at the kitchen table in her apartment, finishing the last of many cartons of Chinese food he had sent out for on a sudden, happy impulse. Ron Poole was to meet them later for drinks.

'A real shit. Even his own lawyer expressed disgust with his actions and you know how rare that must be. Still, Foxe tried to make out he wasn't really responsible for the raid by claiming Zanadu didn't understand the insider information he was passing them.'

'What?' she said, laughing at his enthusiasm and his struggle to eat with chopsticks.

'He claimed the figures he read from our internal documents were incomprehensible to the Zanadu people and they told him so at a later meeting.'

'Could that be true?'

'No, it's absolute bullshit. Any idiot with Boyd figures could have got there easily.'

'Ahh!'

'Yeah, and Ron, who knows more than most about these matters, is ready to swear under oath that Foxe's statement is nonsense.'

378

'Speaking of Ron, shouldn't he be here by now?' Frankie had come to welcome Ron's presence on nights like this when King seemed to be able to speak about nothing but the takeover bid. She cursed the raid and the devastating effect it had had on both their lives. She also felt guilty that she couldn't bear some of the load Kurt was carrying, or even understand what was happening in his battle. She looked at him now, saw the circles under his eyes, noted the obvious loss of weight and felt even guiltier. She knew the fact they hadn't slept together in weeks was taking its toll on both of them.

'Kurt,' she said, softly. 'Explain to me the real weight of what happened today. Does Foxe's confession mean you're nearing the end of this nightmare?'

King put down his chopsticks and lit a cigarette while he searched for words that did not depend on business shorthand.

'First, let me explain what he did, then what it means. Foxe went to Zanadu and recommended acquiring King Corp. To help them make up their minds he gave them insider information, confidential to us. That information enabled Zanadu to evaluate our company as no outsider could possibly do.' King stopped to drag on his cigarette, deeply. Frankie could see that even thinking about Foxe and the raid had heightened his tension.

'That information indicated that Zanadu could get control of King for about 300 million dollars, sell off about half of King for about 300 million, and end up with a company twice the size they started with. If things had gone according to the original timetable, by December 2nd they'd have doubled their size and been even moneywise. Not too shabby.'

Frankie shook her head. 'And the only reason Zanadu

could do this was because they had access to information it was illegal for them to have?'

'Exactly right. Now if I could only get Judge Page to step down in favour of you, we'd have it made.'

'Is he still being such a bastard?'

'Bastard's a tame word for him. If I were a lawyer and had to face him I'd find a different job. Up to now we've lost every round in court – but even Page can't ignore that what Foxe has done is a crooked act.'

When Ron arrived, King insisted on visiting a new night spot some friends of his had just invested in and remodelled. Off Wilshire, it turned out a rather loud and flashy place, an instant hit with the so-called beautiful people. Poole could see Frankie did not care for it. She also did not like the fact that King started right off drinking double martinis.

'Wouldn't you rather have a lighter drink, Kurt?'

He stared at her, then said in a sharper tone than he had meant to use, 'If I'd wanted a lighter drink I would have ordered one.' He had never addressed her in that style before.

Ron cut in, 'So, Foxe was the heavy in the piece, eh? He was smiling. He had predicted a leak of some sort.

King smiled back. 'You have my express permission to say, "I told you so". Yeah, he really fingered us. You know it's sickening that an officer with one of the country's major investment houses could be so blatantly dishonest. Well, the important thing is we caught him and we can put an end to this whole rotten business. He reached for his drink.

Poole nearly retorted it might not be all that simple but he bit his tongue. Sensing how desperately his friend needed to hope, he let him hang on to it as long as possible.

King's euphoria lasted no longer than his drink. When he had ordered another, he turned to both of them, 'Maybe I should just say the hell with it, let Zanadu steal the company and play golf every day, cut my handicap from 12 to 6. But I can't do that. It's not what I'm here for. I want to build, create jobs, make good products for people to use. I want to be more than a money-grubber.' His eyes were shining. 'I want to build,' he said. He was a little drunk.

'Kurt.' Frankie took his hand. 'That's really nice and I agree with you, but what do you say we go home now? You look exhausted.'

That sensible idea wasn't what King wanted to hear. Fuelled by the martinis, he wanted to continue feeding the high started by Foxe's admissions. He knew he was tired, but tonight he was determined not to give in to it. 'Damn it all, Frankie, we're just having a good time. If you want to go, then go, Ron and I will stay.'

'Oh, for Christ's sake, Kurt, Ron doesn't want to stay any more than I do.'

Poole was surprised at the way Frankie had spoken for him – even though she happened to be right. Still loyal to King, he disagreed and said he'd be happy to stay. With that, Frankie began to gather her things, cigarettes and lighter, and stuff them into her bag.

'Here,' said King. 'Take the Seville.' He handed her the car park ticket then started to extract a bill from his clip.

'Oh, keep your money,' she snapped, hurt by the sudden unhappy turn of events. 'I can afford the tip. You're not the only one around here in business, you know.'

They stared after her, and Ron stood up. King sat still. 'Jesus,' he said, puzzlement in his voice, 'can you beat that?' He shook his head as if trying to rid himself of the memory of those last few minutes. It seemed to work, for he turned to Poole and said, 'Ron, I've got about a hundred questions to ask you about how we make use of what we learned today. But first I've got to tell you how we finally served the subpoena on Foxe. You remember Jessica, Jessica Rockefeller . . .'

Two hours later they were sitting at the counter of an all-night diner in Santa Monica. Poole had finally persuaded King to leave the lounge and for the last forty-five minutes they had been drinking coffee and talking strategy. When they left in Poole's rented car, King was still asking questions but had sobered up.

Back on Wilshire, a huge Mercedes began to crowd Poole and he slowed to let the car swing across into the right-hand lane. As it cut in, the car clipped the front of Poole's car. Although the sound was horrendous, the rented car had barely a scratch; however, the Mercedes had a broken tail-light assembly and a deep gash on its right rear fender. The Mercedes driver began to berate Poole for driving too slowly, and King watched with amusement as the argument heated up. When he saw Poole's fists clench, he stepped between them.

'Sir,' he said to the red-faced, well-dressed older man who wouldn't have gone a minute in a fight with Poole, 'you must excuse my friend. He was too busy talking to me to pay proper attention to his driving.'

Poole was startled and opened his mouth to object but King waved him away. 'In fact, Sir, I feel rather guilty about the whole thing.' As he spoke, he reached into a pocket and produced something small and white. 'Take this and have the bill sent to me at this address. I'll take care of everything.' He pushed Poole back towards the car. 'The sight of your beautiful car all scratched up makes me feel terrible.'

The man looked at King, then at the card. His face lit up. 'Why, that's very decent of you, sir. Thank you very much, Mr' – he gave another glance at the card – 'Mr Edward Foxe. Very decent indeed.'

'Think nothing of it.'

Back in the car, King told Poole to make a U-turn. When they were safely headed in the opposite direction, he confessed what he had done. For the rest of the ride, they howled like the schoolboys they had been together three decades before.

3

King thought now they had nailed Foxe the battle was all but won. They would merely have to bring a law suit against Zanadu for the illegal use of confidential information to purchase King Corp and start the takeover process. They would also sue Foxe and his company, F. G. Irving, in connection with the same offence.

Of course, he realized Zanadu would claim they had not used Foxe's inside information, but this would be hard to prove in court. King Corp could either elect to go before a State or Federal court, whichever they thought would favour them most. It was while they were debating this point that Steve Schutt put in his word.

'Our big problem is Judge Page,' he said.

'What the hell has he got to do with it?' King came back. 'Surely we can file the suit elsewhere – in Delaware, for instance.'

'Yeah, for God's sake keep away from Page whatever we do,' Ron Poole said. 'I've been in a lot of courts because of takeover bids and I've never seen the kind of treatment he gives you people. And that Waxman guy plays Page like a violin. I think you could lose the best case in that man's court.'

'I agree,' King said. 'I think we should go for a State court. What about right here in California, the Superior Court?'

Paul Towers waved that one down. 'California judges aren't too anxious to handle this kind of case, and with Judge Page in the background, it would be a hot potato for them. Anyway, our main problem is we're running out of time.'

'Paul's right – that's our main problem,' Steve Schutt said. 'Time.'

'Aren't King, Irving and Zanadu, the three companies involved in these suits, all registered in Delaware?' Schutt nodded an affirmative to King's question. 'All right, then why not file in Delaware State Court? We won our only battle there.'

'It's the best choice, Kurt, and it's the right place,' Schutt said. 'Let's get on with it.' He turned to King, a smile creasing his long features. 'You know, Kurt, by the time this is over, you ought to be given an honorary law degree for all you've been forced to learn.'

King did not share the merriment provoked by that remark. All he could think of was that he could probably have put an entire class through law school for the money they were paying in legal fees.

On the opening day of the takeover battle Bob McGill of Newcombe & Styles had delivered a lengthy mono logue on the problems King would face in opposing Zanadu. McGill had predicted the support that would be given to the raider by the banks, the SEC, shareholders and even King employees. The events of the past few weeks had proven McGill's prescience – with one exception, the bankers.

A careful review of the Zanadu documents put another twist to the knife in King and made McGill 100 per cent correct.

A livid Kate Foy burst into King's office. He was on the phone, but turned and looked up, noticing the agitation on her face and the sheaf of papers rattling in her trembling hand. Promising to place the call later, he placed the handset in the cradle and wearily asked, 'What now?'

Her composure far from restored, she exploded, 'Here's the latest! The bastards, I can't believe what we've found now.'

'Easy does it, Kate.' King repeated, 'What now?'

'Now? Now? It's the bank, the loan to Zanadu.'

King, motioning, said, 'Sit down, Kate. We know all about the loan. They got 100 million from Mones Bank, took down the whole loan . . . crazy, but that's what they did. So what?'

Seated and more at ease, she answered, 'Sure, we all know that. But Mr King, who's been your lead bank, whose chestnuts did you pull out of the fire when you straightened out this company and paid off the ton of debt owed them? Which bank, Mr Nice Guy?'

'Kate, don't play games. You know it's Bartletts–American. Hell, you attended the luncheon their chairman threw for us a few months back when we finally cleaned up the short-term borrowings. They're not involved. On Day one Bud Gorman called their senior VP to see if they were participating. We knew that they were the lead bank for Zanadu. Bud got a negative.

385

They made no loan on the raid . . . didn't know anything about it.'

Excitedly, she came back. 'Oh, that too I know, but the Zanadu papers show that Bartletts knew all about the raid. Bartletts gave Zanadu a waiver on their loan agreement so they could borrow the money from Mones.' She tossed the documents on his desk. 'See for yourself, Boy Scout.'

Perplexed, King perused the papers confirming the newest treachery. Staring out of the window he said softly, 'Son of a bitch, well I'm a son of a bitch.' Turning back to Kate, and now louder, 'Kate, it's hard to believe. Zanadu had to get this waiver to borrow the money to attack us, and Bartletts had to know what Zanadu was up to to grant the waiver. Our own bankers sided with Zanadu against us. All they had to do was tell Zanadu that they were not going to grant such a waiver when a valued client was involved. This thing would never have started without Bartletts' help. Get their chairman on the phone for me.'

A few minutes later King was speaking with Derek Newell III. 'Derek, Kurt King here. You know what we've been going through with Zanadu. You do read the *Journal*? As you can well imagine this is a very distressing event in a corporate life, mine too. Now, the latest shock to my system. I find that you granted Zanadu a waiver so they could raid King Corp. Not only that, but at the beginning Bud Gorman called your senior guy, Cooper, I believe, and Bud was told you were not a party to Zanadu's action. A stranger, yes you could help Zanadu to raid a stranger, but King Corp . . . ?'

Newell interrupted, 'Kurt, I'm really sorry. We didn't think this would get out, but evidently it did. They put a lot of pressure on us and after a long debate we decided to give them the waiver . . . really sorry. Now, Cooper told Bud Gorman the truth as he knew it. He really did not know about the waiver. Only one other person in the bank besides myself knew that you were the target. Seriously, I am sorry.'

King's phone slammed down.

He turned to Foy, 'You heard my side, he admits it and says he's sorry and only a couple of people knew about it. Only a little bit pregnant. Kate, I just can't believe what's going on. There's simply no morality, no decency. It's just become an avaricious game these guys play . . . the fast buck . . . no loyalty . . .'

Before the day had ended all of his company's and King's personal banking relationship with Bartletts had been terminated.

The next day's newspaper carried a full-page Bartletts–American ad proclaiming that their new policies were introducing an era of morality into commercial banking. An editorial in the same edition lauded their ethical preachings. King, incredulous, could not believe what he read.

Chip Boyd called them all together to suggest a back-up move in case their law suits failed. In essence, it involved having the King stockholders amend the certificate of incorporation so that no company could take over King Corp unless one of two conditions was met: first, all stockholders are treated equally; and second, the merger is approved by 90 per cent of the stockholders. Zanadu could not fulfil the first condition by tendering for only 51 per cent of the stock, and they could not get a 90 per cent vote if Chip's scheme were adopted.

'It's a great idea,' Ron Poole said. 'Chip, you amaze me.'

'But Chip,' Kate Foy asked, 'won't somebody yell to Judge Page this is just another attempt by entrenched management to keep their jobs?'

'No,' King interjected. He was instantly taken by Boyd's plan. 'Because it would be just the opposite. If Zanadu takes over King, the minority shareholders are going to get a real screwing. When they've canned all of us, they'll merge King Corp into Zanadu and give the 49 per cent minority Zanadu stock for their King stock, which would be worth less than half its present price. And if the shareholders go for Chip's amendment, Thomas and his company will know they can't get a 90 per cent vote on a lousy deal.' He paused to glance round the assembly of King executives and Schutt's lawyers. 'I don't see how even a judge like Page can prevent this. What about the rest of you?'

Everybody saw it King's way. But there was a hitch; the tactic would need the approval of the SEC and all heads turned towards Harry Mandel.

'Right now they don't particularly like us,' Harry said. 'But I'm for the idea and I'll go to Washington and push it past those bastards, though I guarantee I'll come back all bloody. I warn you they'll diddle me around on the language so much that by the time we get the material written to the SEC's satisfaction, the poor shareholder won't know what he's reading or what to vote for. It's so simple that the bureaucrats will fuck up. Or, to make them happy, I'll have to fuck it up. When you're ready, I'll hop on the first plane for Disneyland on the Potomac.'

With a grin, Schutt said, 'Before we proceed, I feel I should comment on Harry's language. Until he joined the firm, it was considered impolite to say "fornicate", but he's managed to teach Paul Towers to say "fuck". And since our association with the King people, the language around here has become even worse, particularly because of them, and partly because of the pressure. And you can stop smiling, Kate Foy, because you're as guilty as the rest of them. Some of your idiomatic references to popular sexual practices came as a revelation to me.'

Kate almost blushed amid the general laughter. Schutt went on, 'Okay, immediately Harry has satisfied the SEC, we print and mail explanatory material to the stockholders. Then we use every means to solicit their vote – phone calls, telegrams and personal meetings. Kurt, we'll call on you to phone and meet some of the larger holders. For all of us, this'll be hard, tough work. And you must also realize that as soon as we get this ball rolling, Zanadu will make an all-out effort to stop us.'

His prediction was accurate. Mandel had a difficult time in Washington getting the SEC to drop a demand that the proxy statement contained the line, 'The sole purpose of this proposed amendment,' was to block Zanadu. He watered this down to read, 'A purpose of the proposed amendment is to dissuade Zanadu from proceeding with its proposed tender offer.'

Ron Poole was frankly outraged by the SEC attitude. 'The way they're treating us it looks to me as if somebody in the SEC is on the side of the raider. Somebody's in somebody's pocket and the whole thing stinks.'

'Surely something's got to work for us,' Kate Foy said. 'We've got the anti-trust suit, the CAB case, the suit against Foxe and this amendment – something's got to work.' She appealed to Poole, who shrugged his doubt.

King called a directors' meeting to approve the final documents. With little debate and in a surprisingly short time, the board approved the idea. When the meeting was officially over, King had a good feeling about the concerted effort everyone was making. He prayed it would last.

4

Within days, George Waxman was on the phone to Schutt, protesting about the action of the King Corp board in calling a stockholders' meeting to approve the amendment which would balk Zanadu.

'Stephen, I have to tell you Karl Gearhart feels the King directors are acting irresponsibly and, to protect his client's interest, he is considering bringing suit against them. Frankly, I'd prefer to avoid another lawsuit, so I'm letting you know the possibility as a courtesy.'

Schutt guessed Waxman was merely acting as a stalking horse for Gearhart, and said, 'I like your sense of humour, George. You know Kurt King has iron-hard grounds for bringing an action against Zanadu directors which I've advised him to do. He has turned me down cold, even though he has been accused of all sorts of pernicious acts against your client.'

'Maybe King's afraid if he brings suit we'll come after his directors and find a lot of dirt beneath the surface.'

'Your humour's running away with you, George. You know they're fine people, dedicated and honest, and you and I know such a suit would be pure harassment. What's the charge – rape? murder?'

'Gearhart's not kidding, Steve. He plans to throw the book at them, ask for damages of 50 million dollars.'

'Why not 100 million?' Schutt came back. 'These people are pillars of the community, all of them above reproach. You wouldn't stand a chance.'

'It might cause them to slow down that crazy King.'

Before Schutt could reply, Waxman suddenly changed his tack without warning. 'Talking about King, how would he feel if we jumped the offer to 33 dollars and let him stay and run the combined companies? I think Norris Thomas might like to take it easy. Please understand, Steve, this is not an offer. I'm simply thinking out loud. My idea and mine alone.'

'Forget it. If you want to make Kurt King a proposition I can get him here in a minute. But to go back to our possible suit against the King directors, you do what Gearhart says you should do. However, I must tell you that if you decide to sue them, I shall have to insist my client authorize me to sue the Zanadu directors.'

'Will he?'

'He has a mind of his own, but I shall make an specially strong recommendation.'

Schutt gave King the gist of his conversation. King said he had no interest either in the combined job or the 3-dollar figure. As for the suit against his directors, he said, angrily, 'It's just harassment, but I just hate to see them subjected to this sort of treatment. It'll take up a lot of their time and the press will screw up the story and make them look bad.'

'What about a counter suit against Zanadu's directors?'

King shook his head. 'It buys us nothing and we need our energy to sell Boyd's proxy idea and nail Foxe.'

King had turned to leave Schutt's office when the phone rang. Schutt signalled him to stay and switched on the speaker phone. It was Waxman, and Schutt told him, 'George, I've put you on the squawk box because Kurt King is here with me. Do you mind?'

'Not at all. You might as well both hear this. Good evening, Mr King.'

'Same to you, Mr Waxman.'

'Gentlemen, I've just spoken with Mr Gearhart in New York. We intend to file suit against your directors before Judge Page in two or three days. However, we will not go ahead if you call off your stockholders' meeting. That's our position. Think about it and call me back by noon tomorrow.'

Before Schutt could answer, King broke in, forcefully: 'Mr Waxman, King speaking. Shove it!' He turned and left the office.

5

During all their meetings, King could see Ron Poole had something other than the legal hassle with Zanadu on his mind. When they broke up one morning, he put a hand on King's shoulder. 'Aah, Kurt, I kinda owe you a bite and swallow and, aah, I booked a table for us at the California Club.' King's eyebrows went up, but he asked nothing. Poole had reserved a window table in the elegant comfort of the main dining room. 'Say, Kurt old buddy, you've lost weight,' he said, running a finger round his own collar to point up his statement.

'No more than I needed to lose,' King said, quickly. 'Come on, Ron, what's up. What's on your mind?'

Poole lit a cigarette. He would have preferred then to have a drink or two before unloading what he had tell King. Already, King had waved the waiter away without even asking Poole if he wanted a drink.

'Well, aah, you recall I had to go back to New York for a few days a week or so ago?' King nodded, so Poole went on, 'I was surprised, no I was startled, to find I had a message to call your wife.' He stared at King.

'Carolyn? What in the world did she call you for? I mean, you hardly know her. Oh, I shouldn't have said that.'

'No, you're basically right. I couldn't figure what she wanted, though I was sure it would have to do with you and the problems you were having. And it did, or does.'

'Did you see her?'

'Yeah, she offered to come in to the city, but as I had two days of business scheduled in Norwich, I said I'd stop by, which is what I did.'

'How did she look?'

That question surprised Poole, who hesitated before answering. 'Well, I'm not sure how to answer that, Kurt. You know I always thought she was one of the two or three most beautiful women I'd ever seen. And she's still beautiful. Looks like a million dollars, the way she carries herself and dresses. She's very fashionably thin, almost bone thin and it gives her a . . . well . . . Jesus, I don't know what to call it.'

'A hardness?' King gazed at Poole, more curiously than unkindly.

'No, a coldness, I think. But that may be too harsh. If you had never known or seen her before, and she walked into a room, you'd be stunned by her beauty.'

King nodded, a thin smile on his lips. 'Still, eh? Well, shouldn't surprise me. Anyway, Ron, what did she want?'

'Kurt, I don't know any way of telling you this other than flat out. Look, I'm dealing strictly with my own impressions here, because she wouldn't come right out and tell me what she wanted other than to ask about you, and the takeover business.' When King said nothing, he continued, 'I got the distinct impression she may be, after all this time, planning some legal action.'

'Divorce.' King uttered the word in a quiet voice.

'I'm afraid that's my impression.'

King said nothing for some moments, then, 'Her sense of timing always did stink.'

'Well, Kurt, I'm not so sure it was accidental.'

'What do you mean?'

'Her message was dated the day after that story about King Corp in the *Wall Street Journal* more or less accusing you of sharp practice.'

'Ron, for Christ's sake, the *Journal* isn't *Harper's* o *Vogue*. Carolyn wouldn't be seen dead reading it.'

'No, but she may well have friends that do. A attorney friend, somebody who has a sentimental inter est in breaking things up between you two.'

King said nothing for several minutes. When the had almost finished eating, he said, 'Did you stop an see her again, on the way back through Connecticut?'

'No, why do you ask?'

'Oh, nothing. Come on, let's finish, we have to g back to work.'

XV

Everyone involved in the takeover battle slogged on through Thanksgiving without a break, most of them putting in several eighteen-hour stints in their seven-day week. As December approached, it seemed the key people would also miss Christmas with their families. Nobody complained. They all knew every chance must be grasped and exploited if the company were to be saved.

Sometimes, it looked as though they had triumphed, only to have their hopes shattered. Like the anti-trust question, for example. King had always felt the proposed takeover would violate the anti-trust laws because of similarities in Zanadu and King Corp product lines. He had his lawyers check this out and they reported they had a reaction from the Justice Department. Yes, the takeover could possibly violate the Clayton Anti-Trust Act. However, before the Justice Department lawyers could make a ruling, they had to study the matter carefully. They sent King and Zanadu a letter requesting a detailed list of both companies' products to enable them to assess the degree of competition that existed. 'This is it at last,' King thought, until he saw the information dateline was 15 January. Too late. By then they would be part of Zanadu. Yet, doubtful as he was, he put his staff to work gathering the information.

A couple of things kept his spirits up. Tom Lowe, the CAB expert, felt he was making progress in Washington with the idea of blocking Zanadu with the air carrier charter. Secondly, he was bucked up by the results of a poll indicating his stockholders favoured the charter amendment on which they were about to vote.

At least he was acting, doing something. He could not stand to lose without putting up the best possible fight. Indeed, he was beginning to feel a renewed surge of hope and fully expected to beat Zanadu. Physically, he seemed to be holding up under all the work and worry, though he was noticeably thinner. He recognized he was spending all his efforts on work and had become obsessed with the takeover battle. He realized it had even begun to alter his concentration. He had driven the busy Santa Monica Freeway so often, his Seville needed no prompting. Yet, twice recently, his mind on the raid, he had gone way beyond the offramp he wanted. Another night, already late for a dinner meeting at the Lakeside Country Club, he was alarmed to find himself pulling up in front of the company hangar at Burbank.

When a business companion told a sex joke at lunch, he was jolted to think he couldn't remember the last time. 'What's sex?' he said to himself, ruefully.

His innate optimism kept him going. He figured several of their defensive moves had merit, in particular the upcoming shareholders' vote, the anti-trust and CAB manoeuvres. His real winner, the stopper, would be the Foxe case and he could hardly wait to get into court with that.

Over and over again, in his mind he played the court scene with Foxe in the accused box. Nowhere could he find a flaw. Even Judge Page must find for them this time. He would have to issue an injunction stopping the raid until Foxe was tried. Then the fun would start

Several nights, when sleep would not come, King imagined the whole scenario. He realized a couple of times he had been smiling in the dark. He warned himself against becoming too obsessed with the whole business.

2

On a Wednesday in early December, King called a special board meeting because the suit against all the directors had been filed by Zanadu. As predicted, Gearhart had thrown the book at them, listing every conceivable count and adding a claim for damages amounting to 50 million dollars. As every director knew the suit was without merit and was mainly harassment, there was little need for detailed discussion of the complaint. But the question of legal costs was raised straight away.

King made no attempt to fudge the question. 'The costs are tremendous, no doubt about that, but I can guarantee that in spite of them, we will exceed the earnings estimates I gave you the day the raid started.'

'Yes, Kurt,' interrupted one of the directors, 'but without this expense you could have shown another 10 cents per share in earnings.'

'Yessir, you're right. But I didn't start the fight, Zanadu did. And if we hadn't spent the money they'd own us today.'

'I guess you're right, but it's certainly a lot of money.'

King sighed. 'As a matter of fact, when this is over, Zanadu and King Corp will have paid lawyers and investment bankers close to 5 million dollars. And some people say takeover bids are good for shareholders. I'll tell you who they're good for – lawyers, bankers and investment bankers.' His voice pitched up, unconsciously, as he continued. 'The banks are netting about 5 per cent of the 100 million Zanadu has borrowed, which comes out to 5 million a year which my pocket calculator makes 13,700 dollars a day.'

'You mean Zanadu actually borrowed the money,' asked an astonished director. 'I thought they only had a commitment.'

'Hell, no, they took the loans down and stashed them in some piggy bank, I guess. I should tell you before we're all through we'll pay investment bankers about 500,000 dollars, and more if they find us a White Knight. Then, if the offer goes through, Zanadu will have to pay 40 cents per share to the brokers who deliver the stock, that is another 4 million. And if you think I'm running up legal bills, just consider what they're paying Gearhart, Moss and Waxman.'

His whole board seemed to be in a state of collective shock as King went on. 'These costs don't reflect time spent on depositions, courts, useless non-business activities, travel, nor the damage to staff morale and the bad effect on our business. All in all, I'd guess there's a waste here of more than 5 million dollars. Takeover bids are good for stockholders?' His voice rose. 'I say "Bullshit!"'

Suddenly, he stood up as though too agitated, too caught up in what he was saying, to keep his seat. He walked round his chair to rest his hands on its back.

'Let me tell you about what I call the social responsibility aspects of a takeover. Let's say Zanadu takes us over. In 1970, Zanadu employed 9,400 people and we had 6,500. Today, we employ over 16,400 and 3,000 of those worked in operations that were essentially bankrupt when we took over. So, we've both created job and saved quite a few. In that same period, Zanadu employment rolls have shrunk by 2,600 jobs, down from 9,400 to 6,800. I don't know what this signifies to the courts, the SEC, the government, bankers or anyone else involved in this whole stinking mess, but to me it means we've been fulfilling an important obligation by creating much-needed jobs while Zanadu has done just the opposite.'

King walked to the window to stare for several minutes at the driving December rain before returning to his chair. No one spoke. He buttoned the jacket of his grey houndstooth Oxxford suit. Everyone was watching him intently, waiting. He had their full attention. One of the directors from the Midwest, who was relatively new to the board, said, 'But hasn't a great deal of our increase in employment come through the companies we bought?'

'No,' King answered firmly. 'At least, damned little of it. Look, our sales have shot up from 250 million dollars to almost a billion dollars in six years. Of that 650-million-plus increase, 80 per cent is internal growth. And you can attribute most of that increase in employment to new products, new processes, better marketing and good management – operating people, that is. Leave me out.'

'So, what do you think will happen if Zanadu wins?' the director persisted.

'If they do, God forbid, they're going to be responsible for over 20,000 jobs. And if they repeat their past performance – and everything about them tells me they will – you can figure in six years they will employ about 20 per cent less, 4,000 jobs down the tubes.'

King sat down again, swivelling his chair round to face down the long table. His voice was lower now.

'I guess it's important that half our shareholders get a premium over market for their stock, but those people like Judge Page, who have such control over our destiny, should consider the social responsibility of management. I've thought a lot about this and played with a lot of numbers.'

For a moment, he referred to the notes in front of him before continuing.

'Those same King Corp shareholders the courts and others have been protecting from the "avarice of entrenched management" – meaning me – are going to realize a premium of about 9½ dollars a share on about 3 million shares, 28.5 million more than they would have received on the market a couple of months ago. A nice piece of change and you might say the banks, courts and government are doing the right thing by taking Zanadu's side. But let's play the numbers game. The jobs I say will disappear means an annual payroll of over 25 million dollars down the tubes, which more or less wipes out the benefit the shareholders will get. And most of them don't need that money as much as the working stiff who has five kids to feed.'

His sigh echoed down the table. He ran the point of his pencil over the figures he had in front of him as though symbolically cancelling them. 'My only problem with that argument is that I can't prove it. Time alone will tell – but gentlemen, I bet I'm right.'

His words hung for a long time in the respectful silence. Papers were shuffled, throats cleared. King lit a cigarette and waited.

Normally Quin Groves was first to speak up directors' meetings, but this time Cass Byrd weighed ahead of him. Though by no means reticent, Byrd nev spoke until he felt he had something useful to contribute, which meant his opinions carried a lot of weight with the others. His twangy, ringing voice filled the conference room.

'You know, gentlemen, that's quite an argument Kurt has just put forth, one that has me thinking about some aspects of this whole tender offer business that I've not thought of before. The idea of social responsibility is quite important and I'd like to get that and a few other points that Kurt made across to some friends back in Washington. When you consider all the facets of a tender offer, there's a lot more to it than just money in the shareholders' pockets. I might also add, as an aside, that tender offers appear to have a wearying effect on management.' He smiled at King.

'You looking at me, Cass? Hell, I'm in great shape. Never felt better, but I've lost twelve pounds. And when I sleep, I sleep just fine, though never for too long at a stretch. Look, when this is all over, I'm off for the desert, La Quinta, for two weeks. And I trust I may do so with your blessing.'

King's impassioned and impromptu speech relieved pent-up feelings, but it still proved an expensive interlude. Six attorneys and one insurance consultant sat in on the meeting. All the meters were running.

3

King had not unloaded everything in front of the board. He had not forgotten the actions or the threats of William V. Damen of Astroteknik, who possibly threw a few handfuls of sand in the works by persuading King directors to hire counsel, and by putting his own interests first. So, he had worked out a long-stop strategy in case all their legal moves fell through.

He drove back to his old office. Funny thing, he had been spending so much time in the Schutt offices, he felt like a stranger in his own. He glanced briefly through mail that Marianne had not considered important before taking a piece of paper from a pocket and picking up the phone. He had three calls to make and would leave the unpleasant one to the end.

He had not seen or spoken to Dean Hubert since the night they had roughed up Tillman. Although a top executive, Hubert had taken little part in the takeover fight, having been working at the Tri Corp plant trying to put the finishing touches to that crucial acquisition.

'Kurt! Great to hear your voice. How are you feeling?'

'Jesus, is everybody worried about my health?' King thought with a slight tinge of paranoia. Aloud, he said, 'Dean, I'm calling because I'd love to announce the Tri Corp acquisition and see the shit hit the fan. How close are you to wrapping it up?'

'It's gonna go, Kurt, but not for a while yet. Jesus, I'd hate to close the deal and see this super outfit turned over to Zanadu. We could run it well, but they wouldn't stand a chance.'

'You're right, but what's your rationale?'

'It's too tough and technical for them. They wouldn't know how to straighten it out let alone where to get the people with the knowhow. They'd really fuck it up.'

King smiled at Hubert's earthy analysis. 'At some point, probably soon, I want you out here to outline the whole Tri Corp deal for the board. Can do?'

'The Lear is here and I can be there in five hours from any time you say.'

'Okay, Dean, you're on stand-by for the next few days.'

'Say, Kurt, I heard your friends at Zanadu just filed suit against the directors. That's got to be horseshit, right?'

'Yeah, but it has aggravation value. There are only eighteen charges covering sixty-nine small-print pages. Two of our directors picked up their copies and filed for Medi-Cal and Workmen's Comp – hernias. Gotta go, Dean. I'll let you know when.'

His next call was to Ron Poole, who was still pressing to be allowed to look for another White Knight. Although keeping faith with Damen, King realized he needed the comfort of a back-up offer.

'Ron, I believe the time has come for you to head back East and talk to those people who might top the Zanadu offer on your say-so. But handle it in absolute confidence. They come in only if we ask them. Just bear in mind I'm confident we have Zanadu beat, so don't approach anyone you can't trust. Tell them everything once you've developed a gentleman's understanding they'll make no offer unless asked.'

'Tell me,' Poole said, 'are you getting worried Damen and Astroteknik will back out?'

'Hell, no, it's too good a deal for them, but you never know. Remember, if we need him he gets first crack. King's association with Astroteknik goes back a long way and I want them to have King Corp if Zanadu can't beat. But he might back out for some crazy reason. When you leave tomorrow? Good. And Ron, try to relax a little if you can. You've been working your tail off since you got here.'

King smoked a cigarette before punching out the

numbers for the third call. Halfway through the ten-digit number, he stopped. He looked at his watch, concluded it was late enough in the day and went over to his hide-away bar. There, he mixed a martini. Back in his chair, he lit another cigarette and stared out of the window at the busy freeway below. Traffic was heavy with shoppers, hurrying in the fading sunshine, trying to make as many purchases as they could before wilting. Christmas in California. Newcomers could never get used to it, always comparing it, unfavourably, with some stereotype of a snowy, candlelit New England scene.

New England. Damn. He shook his head, reached for the phone and punched out the number.

Carolyn answered on the third ring. There was so much expression in her voice he figured she could not be alone. Then he realized that, with the three-hour time difference, he must have found her on her second cocktail.

'Aha,' she said. 'The great man himself. You know this call isn't necessary, Kurt. In fact, I would prefer to have the whole thing handled by the lawyers.'

'Well,' he said too quickly, 'perhaps that would be best since they've been taking care of everything else for years.' Each month, his secretary mailed a cheque for five thousand dollars to his lawyer, Ken Jackson, who paid the mortgage on the New Canaan house and the children's tuition then sent a cheque for the balance to Carolyn.

'If you've called to fight, Kurt, you've caught me at a very bad time. I'm on my second Scotch and feeling, how do you say it in Californiaese? – very mellow.'

'No, no,' he said firmly but without anger. 'I did call to fight. It just seemed to me if we are finally going to divorce we ought at least to talk about it between ourselves.'

'I fail to see any logic whatsoever in that, and besides there's really nothing to talk about. I would think with all the problems you have, a simple thing like a divorce would be far down the list.'

His temper flared, and he began to form an angry response but made himself pause and regain his control. 'As a matter of fact, the two are related in a sense. Carolyn, I have no intention of opposing you on the divorce.' He waited, but she did not come back on that, so he went on, 'I only ask that you hold off a bit, just a few weeks or at the most a couple of months. Let me get this fight over with, and maybe some time to recover. It's been rough. I don't expect to lose, but if I do, I would appreciate some time to . . .'

'To lick your wounds? Sorry, but this divorce is something I should have done years ago, for my own well-being. If the timing happens to be inconvenient, well you'll just have to forgive me.'

King now felt his temper boiling over, despite having warned himself not to get into a slugging match with Carolyn. How he wished he had used that evidence Cravetch had gathered! He should throw some of it in her teeth now – her nights with her lover-man in South Newport, and then inviting him into her own house in New Canaan. But she'd have an answer. She always did. And Jessica was right – he'd always been too soft with women. He told himself to remember Carolyn was the mother of their twins. But even then he could not keep the rage out of his voice as he snapped, 'Your well-being! I suppose your shrink friend agrees with you on that.'

'It happens my psychiatrist is no longer in the area as

I'm sure your friend, Ron Poole, has told you along with all the gory details. He left his wife, married a psychiatric nurse who must be all of twenty-five and moved to New Mexico where they will undoubtedly open a clinic and treat aged neurotics. Perhaps I should reserve a room.'

At a loss for words, King said, 'I'm sorry, Carolyn, I knew nothing about it. I'm sorry because I know you liked him, I mean you valued his help.'

'Don't patronize me, Kurt. You've been doing that ever since we've known each other, or at least ever since your success exceeded that of my father, a gentleman whose name shouldn't be mentioned in the same breath as yours.'

King focused all his attention on her speech, hoping to get some sign that this was alcohol and nothing else talking. He could not and it scared him. She was ranting on. 'Every time you took a step up the ladder it was a slap in the face of my father's memory – a disgrace. Oh I'm so furious I can hardly get my words out.'

She fell quiet and he filled that silence with flashback of their life together. It had all begun to click in his mind. So that's why she never wanted him to get to the top. It would show up her father's failings, which she would never admit. He remembered her saying after his funeral, 'If I couldn't have my father alive, at least wanted money of my own.' She had hated her mother not only because she inherited her husband's money but through jealousy. Then that blazing row they'd had when he'd hinted, merely hinted, her old man had been a failure. His own father had been just a cowboy tinkerer compared with hers, she had said.

Carolyn was talking again, spitting words out like grape pips. 'I'm going to tell you three things, and the

I will hang up on you. One, you've never loved me or anyone else – only your hick father and your nuts-and-bolts business. Two, I'm going ahead with this divorce which will cost you plenty. And three, as for all the trouble you've got yourself into – it couldn't have happened to a more deserving person.'

King was about to shout down the phone, 'And who did you ever love? Not me, just your own snobby self and your bumbling old father.'

Nothing but a dial tone. Mercifully. He had never been too hot at quickfire repartee or arguments with people like Carolyn. He always thought of the right comeback when the street door slammed behind him. Maybe a good thing in this case. He went and built himself another powerful drink.

4

As he took his seat on the bench, Judge Page looked at King as a snake might put an eyelock on a rabbit. It was no longer the distaste of the bald and unprepossessing for the younger, more virile, more handsome, but the scowl of the righteous for the unrighteous. Or so King thought, sitting in the court well behind the phalanx of his own and Zanadu's lawyers. Everybody, it seemed, thought he had played fast and loose with 30 million dollars of company money, giving even him a guilt feeling.

George Waxman's unctuous, ingratiating voice cut across his thoughts. 'I am fully aware we are in court this morning for the specific matter of the proposed cross acquisition which you have already restrained temporarily. However, another matter has arisen that I feel must be brought to the attention of the court in the interests of fairness both to my client and to the share-holders of King Corp.' He gave that hook time to bite.

'Proceed, counsel, this court is willing to hear any matter as long as it is germane.'

'I refer, your Honour, to several actions of the current management of the King Corporation which, in my opinion, are blatant attempts to avoid the jurisdiction of this court.'

That brought Judge Page up in his seat and tightened his thin lips.

Waxman continued, growing more flowery. 'I have just learned that, in an egregious act of management perpetuation, Mr King has sent out a proxy statement to all his shareholders which has no other purpose than to block my client, Zanadu Industries, from acquiring King Corp. I request the court's permission for time to file a complaint asking you to restrain the present management from taking this evasionary step which they purport to be on behalf of the shareholders.'

Sam Donaldson jumped up like a boxer off his stool 'Objection, your Honour.' Page turned his date-stone eyes on him, and Donaldson went on, 'We are here today at our request to hear submissions that th restraint on the Cross Industries transaction should b removed. This matter is irrelevant.'

'Objection overruled.' Page lowered his head to glar at Donaldson through his spiky eyebrows. 'And coun sel, I shall judge what is and what is not relevant in m own court.' He nodded at Waxman. 'You may proceed

'I would also like to bring the court's attention another similar move which also stems from Mr King single-minded desire to retain his position with th company no matter what it costs the shareholders. refer to the fact he has recently filed a suit in t

408

Chancery Court in Delaware against my client and the F. G. Irving company. I would like the court's permission to file a complaint to restrain that action.'

'Objection,' Donaldson called, getting to his feet. 'My learned colleague knows very well this court has no jurisdiction over a state court in another state.'

To King, it seemed Sam Donaldson had blundered into the elephant trap Waxman had dug for him. Page looked as though he would explode. His nostrils flared and he spat his words through clenched teeth. King hoped this hearing would not finish as a duel between Page and Donaldson.

'Objection overruled. Counsel, would you be kind enough to stop trying to teach us all about the law and let us hear what Mr Waxman has to say.'

Waxman turned a broad smile on Donaldson. 'I was about to say, your Honour, that in the interests of consolidating issues and a desire to conserve the court's time, I would at this point also like to ask for relief in regard to the 30-million-dollar remuneration programme devised by Mr King and Mr Boyd. Not only does my client object to the payment of this money in the event of their successful purchase of the King Corp stock, but I have learned that even certain members of Mr King's own board find themselves faced with an improper conflict of interest.'

Another objection by Donaldson was quashed by Page before Waxman went on, 'As a result of these new matters, your Honour, I respectfully submit the Cross case is not the central issue before us today. The crucial issue is the on-going manoeuvring by King Corp management to frustrate the orderly process of a perfectly proper purchase offer. These manoeuvres are jeopardising the position and rights of the shareholders who

409

are, as the court has so accurately put it, the true owners of the company. I ask the court's permission to file these new complaints as soon as my office can prepare them.'

Again Donaldson objected, and again Judge Page overruled him. But the judge still had to deal with the Cross problem first. He swiftly ruled he would take the matter 'under submission'.

As the lawyers whispered to King, this was a clever way of handling it. Had Page refused to set a date or set one too late for King's purposes, an immediate appeal might have been lodged and upheld. By doing virtually nothing, the court was letting the Cross purchase die a slow but certain death.

On Waxman's request, Judge Page moved positively, setting a hearing for the following day on all the matters the Zanadu counsel had raised.

That evening, a meeting was called in the Schutt offices. For the first time, King saw Sam Donaldson lose his cool. 'Never in all my years of trying cases have I felt the treatment was so completely one-sided,' he complained.

'It was rough, Sam, but I see a pot of gold at the end of this rainbow,' Schutt murmured. Donaldson looked at him as though he had gone crazy. Schutt went on 'Look, we'll probably lose tomorrow, but I believe Waxman has gone too far this time and if Page lets him get away with it then we pick up our pot of gold. Do you see, Sam?'

'I'm beginning to, Steve.'

'What the hell are you two talking about?' asked King, exasperated.

'It's like this, Kurt,' Schutt said, 'Waxman is taking into court tomorrow to get a temporary restraining order to stop your shareholders' meeting and payment of the 30 million dollars to key employees. And he'll get it, I'm sure. Page will rule in his favour.'

'He can't do that.' King was steaming at the suggestion.

'Damn it all, a federal judge can do anything! Now listen, Page will give them what they ask for because he's convinced you're a crook – excuse me – who is trying to thwart Zanadu just to keep your job. Page sees himself as the great protector of your shareholders from whom you're stealing 30 million bucks. He'd like to stop the Foxe suit in Delaware, but we've got too much law on our side for him there.'

'Steve, you're losing me,' King said, his mind grappling with the notion that Page might eliminate two of his best defences against Zanadu.

'All right, let's say Page stops us temporarily on the meeting and the 30 million. He has to set an early date to make his injunction permanent, knowing if he doesn't we go to the Appellate Court for them to set the date. He won't risk that.'

King and the others were listening intently as Schutt continued.

'Page will probably say Monday for the hearing on the permanent injunction. And when he does that we go straight to the Court of Appeals in San Francisco and get him overruled. Then, because of the time he has cost us the Appellate Court will stop Zanadu from proceeding with their tender offer until the whole matter has been heard.'

'How?'

'By putting a halt to their purchase of stock for, say, thirty days.'

'That just might be all the time we'd need,' King

murmured, reflectively. 'Hell, I've got Ron Poole in New York right now lining up another White Knight on the off-chance the Astroteknik deal falls through. What kind of timetable are we talking about?'

'I'd expect an Appeals Court decision by Thursday night.'

'What kind of decision?'

Schutt scratched his right temple with his pencil point before replying. 'It's my considered opinion the tribunal will not permit Judge Page to stop a stockholders' meeting, and thus disenfranchise them. As to the 30 million, once we explain things, the court will look at it in a different light. And if Page attempts to stop the Foxe action, we're home free. The Appellate Court will freeze everything until the whole matter can be properly adjudicated.'

Next day, on Schutt's advice, King stayed away from the courtroom, the lawyer fearing that if the judge called on him for any reason, he might not be able to control his temper. It was sound advice, for when Waxman claimed King was spending excessively on legal fees, Judge Page asked if Mr King was in court and could tell them how much was being spent. Cass Byrd, the only other King Corp official there, phoned King and then returned with the information – about 1.7 million dollars.

Page said the shareholders should be protected against such expenditure. He omitted to ask Waxman what Zanadu was spending to press the takeover bid. After hearing the arguments, Judge Page ruled against King Corp on every point: he issued an order restraining them from holding the shareholders' meeting, from making a disbursement of the 30 million dollars in bonus money and from pursuing the Foxe case in

Delaware. In addition, he restrained them from suing Zanadu in any court but his.

Steve Schutt had been right on every point. But he and his lawyers were elated by what seemed a total defeat. It freed them to take the positive step of filing their appeal with the San Francisco Appellate Court.

'Kurt, they've played into our hands,' Schutt said, visibly excited. 'Page's ruling clearly exceeds his authority. He can't block us in Delaware and it's plain crazy to lay down we can't bring an action in any court but his.'

'And the 30 million?'

'On that I can't argue with him too much.'

'Sure, it's not your money. It belongs to one hundred employees.'

'Kurt, I know your position, but it's not our main case. The other rulings are more important in San Francisco, and if we succeed up there you won't even have to worry about the 30 million.'

'I'm touchy about it. Does your timetable still hold good?'

Schutt nodded, then said, 'I'm confident we'll have a hearing in San Francisco by Wednesday and a decision the following day.'

'What's your best guess on the outcome? All right, you hate to be put on the spot, but give it to me anyway. Christ, I'm sure as hell paying for it.'

Schutt gave a slight smile. 'I'll bet six martinis to your one the Court of Appeals will overturn everything and thereby give us the chance to try Foxe in Delaware. They'll stop Zanadu from acquiring the stock until the Foxe case is adjudicated. What follows will take time and you'll have to be patient, but I now believe we'll win. Don't celebrate yet, but the breaks are starting to come our way.'

'It's about time.'

It was a warm night for December and Frankie and King took their after-dinner drinks on to the terrace. Soon, the slight breeze drove them to the *chaise-longue* where they warmed each other. There, a brief kiss led to a longer one, and he began to run his hands up and down Frankie's responsive body. He cupped her breasts, softly, in his hands, impressed with how firm they were – exactly the same as when he had touched them years before.

He brushed his fingers across one nipple which hardened immediately, and he dropped his hand to her legs. Pushing up her skirt, he ran his hand along her smooth thighs then started to caress her sex through her silk panties. Frankie's breath, against his neck, began to come faster. He felt her unzip his fly. She took his penis in her hand and began to fondle and squeeze him, slowly, but each grip slightly more firm than the last.

After another deep kiss, Frankie stood up quickly and pulled off her panties. When she laid down next to him again, King slipped a finger inside her. She was delightfully wet. As he rubbed his finger against her clitoris, she gripped his hand with her warm thighs and groaned. She nipped his neck.

'Oh, come on, honey,' she whispered against his shoulder, 'let's go to bed, it's been too long.'

In bed, they turned to each other with feverish haste. Frankie was breathing even faster now, and she sucked greedily on his tongue while she moved her hand down to his penis. Startled, she found it had gone soft.

'Oh, no. God, I'm sorry, Kurt.'

For a moment, he did not speak. She began to stroke him, alternately fondling his scrotum and his penis, now flaccid and relaxed.

'Frankie,' he said, bitterly, 'it isn't going to work.'

She said nothing but took his hand and put two of his fingers inside her and, at the same time, she bent over and started to take him in her mouth. He pulled away. She drew his head against her breast, and he could feel the animal-like thudding of her heartbeat. He moved his fingers gently at first, then with some force. Frankie moaned and put her arms tightly around him. For a full minute, she thrust against the stiffness of his fingers. Then she gasped as she reached her climax, shuddered for a moment and relaxed her fierce grip.

Moments later, cigarettes lit, she spoke quietly. 'I'm sorry, that was greedy of me,' she said.

He put his free hand gently on the warm flesh of her stomach, caressing it gently. 'I'm the one who should say "sorry". Maybe I should have anticipated this. It's an almost classic case, wouldn't you say?'

There was something in his voice Frankie did not like, so she did not reply. They dressed in silence and went back to the terrace where she made them fresh drinks.

'I'm glad I read *Playboy*,' he said in a dull tone. Still, she did not respond, so he continued. 'That's how it says us big boys have to expect to react during "periods of stress".' He looked at her sitting silent, nursing her drink. 'What's the matter, Frankie, don't you feel like talking?'

She sighed. 'We haven't talked to each other for a long time, honey. Even before this raid business started, we'd been having some pretty long silences.'

'I didn't notice them.' His voice had a contentious touch.

'I know you didn't, and that's part of the trouble.' She got up and walked to the terrace edge. After a moment, she hugged herself against the chill.

'Want a sweater, hon? I'll get it.'

'Yes, please.'

She smiled at him and touched his hand when he snuggled an old cardigan round her shoulders. He stood next to her, his hand lightly on her waist. She was close, but not leaning on him.

He spoke, looking straight ahead at the distant lights. 'My wife wants a divorce. How's that for timing?'

Again, Frankie sighed, though not so deeply. 'Kurt, I think I gave up waiting for that about two years ago. You know, there was a time, about five years ago, when I thought of little else. I wanted to be Mrs Kurt King. I deserved to be, I used to think. But that feeling passed. Now I'm not sure that would be such a good thing.'

She turned towards him and put her hands on each side of his face. 'Kurt, I'm afraid for some time we have been staying with each other out of habit.' He began to object, but she stopped him. 'A warm, wonderful and exciting habit most of the time. But still a habit.' She leaned against him and he caught the smell of her hair a fresh, clean smell so familiar he felt he could track her by it.

'Frankie,' he said, 'you aren't going to do anything right away, are you? I mean, anything abrupt?'

'Of course not, dear.' She hugged him and he could hear the smile in her voice as she said, 'First, we have to get your plumbing working again.'

Later, he watched her as she stood in the foyer, ready to leave, checking her purse for keys and cigarettes. He could not dispel the feeling they were both rather relieved at what had been said. He studied her long silhouette as she bent her head to look in the purse. Then he said something he had been turning over in his mind, debating, for the last fifteen minutes.

'Frankie, you fly to the design show in New York the day after tomorrow, don't you?'

'Yes, why?'

He hesitated, then added, 'I forgot to tell you Ron Poole's in New York and will be for another week. You ought to call him. Marianne can give you his number.'

'Oh, sure, I'll do that, that would be nice.' He was watching her expression intently. Even in that dimly-lit foyer, there was no way to miss the pleasure that flooded her face or the delight in her voice. But as she kissed him she drew back and looked keenly at his face as though searching for a sign. When she failed to find any and he did not say anything, she kissed him quickly and left.

King made a strong drink and carried it to the terrace, but stopped in the doorway to stare at the lights. He did not know why, but suddenly his mind shot back nearly thirty years and brought up the faces of two of the girls he had dated when in college. When he dropped them, Ron had taken them over. Was that the reason? He sat down and took a stiff pull on his drink which made him feel better. He was certain he had done the right thing. Only, it had left him with a sudden and terrible emptiness.

6

On his way out of the Schutt offices, King was stopped by a call from Cassius Byrd which he took on the antique phone that was part of the reception area's period decor. 'You just caught me, Cass. I was going to have lunch with Bill Damen at his request. I guess he wants to make sure he understands the script and he's not to make his offer until I tell him. When? 20 December's the best day for us . . . anything earlier would give Zanadu time to react. Cass, I'm confident we have the bastards stopped and we won't need Astroteknik.'

'Kurt, that's good news. Now, my nickel. I've been doing a lot of thinking about some of the things you said before the meeting the other day. I simply hadn't an idea how unfair and one-sided the whole tender offer situation is, and my experience in Judge Page's court actually scared me. I feel I should have been down in the trenches with you sooner. Look, how about flying to Washington with me next week?'

'Washington? We've got a whole platoon of lawyers there right now, but I'm not sure they're earning their corn.'

'That's because they're not Washington lawyers. Lawyers in the capital know how to get things moving quickly and know how to make sure things don't just rot on the desk of some clerk. I took the liberty of calling Grant Alexander last night.'

'Alexander! Jesus, he's on the other side of the political fence from you, isn't he? I mean, he's been advising Democratic presidents from FDR's day?'

'Grant and I have always gotten along and he owes me a few favours. Look, one of the things he mentioned is that if Judge Page stops us from suing Foxe in Delaware, we should turn the case against him over to the SEC.'

'But we've already given them the story of Foxe.'

'Yes, but to some junior. Grant says we have to speak to Theo Tracy personally. He's in charge of the enforcement division, he's smart, ethical and a real bulldog. Get the Foxe case into his hands and something will happen.'

'Okay, I'm all for the Washington trip. I can stop by and see Admiral Rickover and maybe shake some of his orders loose. Marianne will make us reservations. The Hay-Adams all right with you?'

'Fine. Now, what about this meeting with Damen?'

'I'll fill you in later, Cass. Got to run.'

It was a beautiful Southern California day and King wished they were having lunch within walking distance. As he hurried to his car, he felt good about Byrd's call. He was loyal. About several other directors he wasn't so sure. They were feeling the pressure of the lawsuit Gearhart had brought against them and a few of them were beginning to believe life would be simpler for them if Zanadu won.

Because of these suspicions, he was not releasing additional information to his board. Several directors were too close for comfort to Astroteknik and one thing he wanted to keep 'in-house' was the difference the Tri Corp acquisition would make to the company's earnings structure. Damen might be a friend, but would he stay that way with more than a billion dollars in sales and high profits at stake? To divulge the Tri Corp figures might bring up the dollar signs in his eyes, and King did not want a greedy White Knight at this moment.

In fact, King and Dean Hubert were the only ones

who knew how favourable the impact of Tri Corp would be, having worked it out late one night in a hotel bar. What King referred to as the Hubert–King cocktail napkin analysis indicated the Tri Corp acquisition would double King Corp earnings. That estimate was so highly secret not even Boyd or Kate Foy knew about it, so there was no fear someone would leak it to Damen.

Two thoughts warmed King during his drive to the Bel-Air Hotel meeting. One was Schutt's optimism about the legal outcome of their various cases; the other was the picture of Cass Byrd rubbing shoulders with Democrats. 'Better watch out or somebody's going to ask me to make a campaign contribution to Teddy Kennedy,' he thought. Still grinning, he entered the hotel.

Damen was sitting in a quiet corner. King thought his Bloody Mary looked just right and ordered one, then began to talk with animation. His high spirits seemed catching for even Damen's dour face relaxed into a grin. King was pleased he had removed his trademark dark glasses. Without giving Damen a chance to speak, King launched into his favourite topic – a biting diatribe against Norris Thomas and Zanadu, Foxe and Judge Page, the SEC and lawyers in general, all the dramatis personae of his long nightmare. He outlined the probability of stopping Zanadu and Damen's smile began to slip; the more optimistic King sounded, the more sour Damen's face became. Finally, he interrupted.

'Kurt, I'm listening to you but I'm not sure I'm hearing you. You don't seem to see our viewpoint.'

'Bill, we'll win out, but I have to tell you how much I appreciate your standing in the wings, waiting to help.'

'Kurt.' Damen sounded exasperated. 'Have you

spoken to Steve Schutt? I think there has been some misunderstanding.'

'Yeah, I spoke with Steve before I came here. What do you mean misunderstanding?'

'Didn't Schutt speak with my attorney?'

'Clarke? Yeah, he said basically he'd been told you had an informal discussion with your directors and had the go-ahead to step in and top Zanadu if we need you.'

Damen reached into a pocket and pulled out a sheet of handwritten notes. He glanced at them and was about to speak when their sandwiches arrived. King hungrily took a huge bite of his club sandwich and began to chew while Damen fixed him with a hard look.

'Evidently something's been misunderstood by somebody, you or Schutt or both. So that there's no further misunderstanding, I'll read you from the notes we made at our formal meeting yesterday. Please notice I said formal. How you people got the impression it was informal is a mystery to me, but it no longer makes any difference since you're here and I can give it to you straight.'

King felt his stomach muscles contract. He had a queasy feeling and wondered if he would be able to keep the Bloody Mary and sandwich down.

Damen continued. 'Thursday night, at a dinner meeting, we discussed King Corp at great length. Yesterday, at our formal meeting, I was authorized by a unanimous vote to offer your shareholders 33 dollars per share for any and all of King stock. I am now making that as a formal offer to you.'

'Wait a minute, Bill, slow down. I can hardly believe what I'm hearing. What you're saying doesn't sound very friendly. We asked for your help only if and when we reached the end of the road. We're not there yet, not by at least ten days. I consider this downright unfriendly.'

Damen stared at King with a neutral expression on his round face. 'I don't call it unfriendly, but you call it what you like. Look, it's this simple: you now have an offer. You are obliged to call a meeting of your board and present my offer and then give us a response. So there's no future misunderstanding, I'll read from my notes which were prepared by Clyde Clarke during our board meeting.'

Damen cleared his throat. King stared at his sandwich but did not dare attempt another bite.

'To repeat myself, the offer is for 33 dollars a share, any and all . . . .' Damen stopped. 'Don't you want to take notes?'

King shook his head.

'Okay, maybe you have a good memory, but I don't.'

King had no doubts about his memory. He knew he would never forget any moment of this lunch and every word uttered.

Damen droned on. 'We want the complete agreement of your board that they will eliminate the 30-million dollar payoff to the key people. That we can't swallow, no one could. We want the shareholders' meeting scheduled for the 20th stopped. We understand you have a deal for a huge glass plant in the works – T Corp, I believe it's called. We want that stopped. That about it. Oh, one more thing. We plan to announce our offer on Tuesday, so you'll have to arrange a director meeting for tomorrow or Monday.' He folded his note and put them back in his pocket. He stared at King, his eyes partially shaded. 'Frog eyes,' King thought, his mind grappling with an answer.

You son of a bitch, he thought, gazing at the m

who had just stabbed him in the back. Damen sat, his face a mask. King suppressed the urge to pick up the table, covered with food and drink, and empty its contents on the traitor's lap. Instead, he groped for control, recognizing the need to keep his emotions from blocking his judgement. He must try to reason with Damen.

'Bill,' he said as evenly as he could, 'those points you just raised tell me you don't understand what King Corp is doing. Look, that stockholders' meeting set for the 20th would in no way block you. Your offer for all the stock eliminates the effect of that vote. You're home free. As for the 30 million, if we get into bed with Astroteknik on a friendly basis, it goes away. There is no need for any payout. Anyway, it appears Judge Page has already halted us on that. As for Tri Corp, that's got to be the greatest deal we ever made.'

King stopped in his tracks. He was talking to Damen about Tri Corp, a deal Damen should never have known about. Somebody must have tipped their hand about Tri Corp! Who? Quentin Groves, Sam Martenson or somebody in the Schutt office? Anyway, they couldn't have known the real value of that deal. And here was he almost putting all their Tri Corp cards on the table. He stopped talking about Tri Corp.

'Bill, forget these points. All I need is time – ten days, and maybe even less. Now, say we push this meeting back one week to give me time for the appeal. If we lose, you go ahead and God bless you, but if we win and get the delay I'm counting on then you hold off until everything is adjudicated.'

Damen did not utter and King stared at him, his mind still racing and words tumbling out pell-mell. 'See here, Bill, we're going to overturn Judge Page, hold the stockholders' meeting, block Zanadu and win the Foxe case in Delaware. Frankly, I'm sure Zanadu will fold their tent before the Zanadu case is tried. They're running scared. They'll probably ask us for a bit of money to paper over their wounds. All I'm asking you for is time to stop them. If we don't, you come in with my full support.'

Damen scythed a fleshy hand at him to cut him short. 'We don't have time.'

'You do, Bill, you do. You can come in as late as the 27th, make your announcement and carry the day. But with Christmas on us, you can announce as early as the 21st with no problems.'

'It's no go. Clarke tells me we have to move Tuesday.'

'That's absolute bullshit and you know it. He has to be talking out of both sides of his mouth. Schutt and he agreed to the timetable of the 21st last night.'

To King's anger and astonishment, Damen actually looked bored. He drew his napkin across his mouth then put it on his plate. He signalled the waiter for the bill. 'That's not what Clarke tells me,' he murmured 'And, quite frankly, I'm not interested in what h supposedly said to your lawyer. I go with what m lawyer says to me.'

'For Christ's sake, Bill, we don't need to argue th point. Let's get them together and settle it. You and know the 21st's all right. Goddamn, you told me ho you stepped into the Vaneiron fight on about the la day.'

'Yes, and lost.'

'But not because of time. Someone else topped yo offer and by a good bit. You've plenty of time.'

Again Damen interrupted, this time with a final n in his voice. 'Look, I've had my meeting and my boa

424

doesn't meet again until February. My directors are all over the country – New York, Cincinnati, St Louis – and I don't intend to drag them back just to give you time.'

'Cut the crap,' King snapped. 'You told me yourself the Vaneiron offer was done by a telephonic board meeting you cranked up within hours. All I want is one week.'

Damen ran his accountant's eye carefully over the bill before signing it. King bit his lip, gazing at the square head bent in front of him. Fragments of that sleep-inducing exercise several nights before about the Trojan Horse flitted through his mind. Ron Poole had warned him to beware Greeks bearing gifts and he had gone and invited this Trojan Horse into his stronghold.

Damen raised his head and turned those frog eyes on him. 'Mr King, you have our offer. I suggest you take it to your board.'

Lunch was over.

XVI

King's alarm pulled him out of deep sleep just before six on 16 December. He got up, made himself some strong coffee and drank it with his first cigarette. The night before he had needed a sleeping pill, though he feared it might leave him hung-over. But he felt rested and was looking forward to the board meeting he had called to consider both the Tri Corp purchase and Astroteknik's sudden and treacherous offer. As he dressed, some of his buoyancy returned and his adrenalin had begun to flow.

For forty-eight hours after the Damen bombshell, King could hardly control his fury at the man. Then he began to size up the situation calmly. After all, he had already counted on something like this when he sent Ron Poole east to look for other White Knights. He had, in fact, evolved a rough strategy. By Monday afternoon, he had devised a scheme which was complicated and would demand skill and good timing. But it might just work to save King Corp.

With a small crew he had worked late the previous night to prepare for the meeting. Principally, they had finished an elaborate report on the Tri Corp deal. Dean Hubert had furnished figures proving to Bud Gorman what a marvellous deal it would be. When they were copying down the final figures, a weary Gorman said, 'Kurt, if Zanadu could see these figures, they'd offer 40 dollars a share if they could raise the money.' He looked at King, puzzled. 'But what's our rush now?'

'Directors meet early tomorrow, Bud, and I want them to approve Tri Corp before Cass Byrd and I head off for Washington.'

That left Gorman even more perplexed. 'But what if we get Tri Corp and Zanadu gets us? Why give it to them? Why do them a favour?'

'It wouldn't be a favour, Bud. They'd fuck it up so badly it would be an albatross round their necks.'

On Tuesday morning, the conference room was packed. In addition to the eight directors, there were four people from management, six attorneys from Schutt's office and from Dale Rucker's firm, now representing the directors, McGill and his assistant from Newcombe & Styles plus a court reporter who had come at King's insistence. He did not want any missing testimony or misquotations.

In front of every director was an agenda, reading:

KING CORP
BOARD OF DIRECTORS MEETING – 14 DECEMBER 1976

1 Report on operations
2 Status of Zanadu takeover bid
3 Review of Tri Corp negotiations
4 Discussion of other possible offers for King stock
5 Any other business.

King opened the meeting in a deliberately low key, briefly outlining excellent operating results. When he revealed Judge Page had made his injunctions permanent the day before, Schutt interrupted to say his staff were in San Francisco at that moment, waiting to file the appeal. 'I expect that, after Thursday, you will be able to proceed with your shareholders' meeting and the lawsuit against Mr Foxe,' he said.

Cass Byrd held up a finger. 'Mr Schutt, since you're already out on a limb, why not predict our chances of beating Zanadu?'

Schutt gave a dry cough, then smiled. 'It's my firm belief you will stop them completely, force them to withdraw. Time is now on our side – for once.'

King found the exchange interesting, especially since, at this point, the directors did not officially know about the Astroteknik offer. King had kept it that way to find out if any of his directors or management people might carelessly volunteer information from the other side.

'Gentlemen,' King said, 'let's move on to item three on the agenda. First, please note that each of the Tri Corp folders in front of you carries your name and that all the information is bound into the folder so that it cannot be removed. When we have finished discussing the Tri Corp proposal I want the folders returned to me. As you know, it's not like me to be secretive, but this information is so vital we can't let it out of this room.'

King guessed who would be first to question this procedure and he was not disappointed. Quin Groves interrupted. 'Kurt, don't say you don't trust your own directors.'

'That's not the point, Quin. It is to safeguard you and King Corp. You've been interrogated once by the other side and if they take your depositions again they'll demand you produce any records in your possession. If you don't have them' – here, he tapped the folders – 'then you can't produce them.' He paused to emphasize his next statement. 'If Zanadu or anyone else could see the future offered by the Tri Corp deal, they'd be standing in line to raid us.'

Groves nodded, then put his nose in the Tri Corp papers. King smiled to himself. One person was nibbling at the bait.

With very little discussion, the board agreed on the soundness of the Tri Corp plan. King waited until everyone had his say, then rose to his feet. 'Gentlemen, I now present the *pièce de résistance*, the figures which I consider to be safely conservative. Obviously, at a time like this, I cannot afford to be overly optimistic, but these figures you can put in the bank. In fact, I believe we'll do a lot better.' The room lighting dimmed and the figures flashed on to the screen at the end of the room. King had begun to enjoy himself immensely. 'You'll note in '77 our earnings continue upward on the present curve and the Tri Corp effect is minimal. But in '78, when the deal becomes effective, our earnings more than double and our cash flow jumps to 85 million dollars. Now, you see why I'm so enthusiastic and why I'm keeping this under wraps. This information just can't get out.'

Glancing round the room, he noted the pleased astonishment on every face. He saw, too, that Quin Groves was hastily penning notes on a small pad. He was convinced Groves had taken one hook. He signalled and the projector was shut off. He held up a copy of the resolution in front of every director. 'Gentlemen, management recommends the board approve the resolution authorizing completion as outlined. Any discussion?'

Groves was waving his paper in the air. 'Kurt, it's my guess Damen is, or would be, concerned with the heavy debt we'd be taking on with this deal. How do you intend to handle that? I mean, if we go ahead with this, he may walk away from his offer and we'd be in trouble.'

'For the record,' King replied in a sharper tone, 'at this point in this meeting, Mr Damen has not made an official offer, therefore I'm not sure what he might do. We'll discuss him later. The Tri Corp deal begins as a one-year option to buy the company. A year from now, this board or Zanadu or Astroteknik, or perhaps another company I have in mind' – he paused for a second or two to let that sink in – 'will have to make the decision about the debt problem. But if we don't act today, we'll miss the greatest opportunity ever offered this company. At this very moment, I have no interest in Astroteknik, only in King Corp.'

Cass Byrd moved passage of the resolution, Sam Martenson seconded and the vote was unanimous. All the directors recognized the Tri Corp deal as a great move for the company. King figured Groves also saw it as a great move – for Astroteknik.

Now they moved to item four: Other possible offers for King stock. It was 11.15 and the directors were beginning to relax with the passage of the resolution and the approach of the lunch hour. But King had no intention of letting up. He called in Schutt to report on the Astroteknik offer of 33 dollars per share for all the stock. Schutt listed the conditions: Stop the shareholders' meeting, stop the Tri Corp acquisition, stop the 30-million-dollar bonus payment, and a reply with a unanimous agreement by noon.

That gave them just over half an hour. A heated discussion started. Then the directors requested the legal opinion of McGill. King sat back, relaxed, and watched how the investment banker would play things. McGill had padded his firm's bill, and King also blamed him for the squabble over the shareholders' letter with the SEC, but King expected he would say the right thing.

'Gentlemen, I'm afraid we've had a very limited time to evaluate this new offer. Indeed, Mr King did not bring us into the picture until late yesterday.'

In fact, King had purposely called McGill as late as he could, admitting he was asking the impossible of him. McGill had not had the time to assess the true effect of Tri Corp, and he was forthright about this.

'We don't feel we've been able to do a thorough job,' he said. 'However, based on what we have been able to accomplish, we can say this offer is barely adequate. And that is without taking the Tri Corp proposal into the equation, although Mr King did give us all the information about it. Tri Corp is a future possibility, not a present fact. But even without it, we feel 33 dollars is at the bottom end of what we consider adequate for all King Corp shares.'

Cassius Byrd raised a finger. 'What do you consider an adequate figure?'

'We'd need more time to give you that opinion. Frankly, we didn't have time for what we've given you this morning.'

There were other hands in the air, but King stepped in. He was watching the boardroom clock coming up to noon, and he was now ready to play his trump card. He looked round the table, making eye contact with each director before speaking.

'First of all, I want you to know Bill Damen has turned from a friend to a greedy raider. We furnished him inside information on condition we could call on him if he was interested and needed. He is interested, but at this point he is not needed. At our Saturday meeting, I pleaded with him to wait out this week. He flatly refused. He said time was running out. That, gentlemen, is simple bullshit, excuse the term. Let's go on.

'Astroteknik's offer will expire at noon today unless we meet all their conditions. One of those is the unanimous consent of the board. Therefore, it looks as if the offer will expire. Because I, for one, am going to vote against it.'

'Hey!' came a shout from the table.

'You can't do that,' somebody else called.

'Wait a minute, Kurt.'

Everybody seemed to be shouting at once. Two directors were on their feet waving their papers, and Dale Rucker was semaphoring for attention. The noise level in the crowded room swelled until nobody could hear anybody, and King stepped back several inches as though forced to give way by the reaction to his power play. He was witnessing the first open conflict in all the time he had headed the company. A sudden flash of memory brought back his father's face and words that day in the plane, the day he had sold his shares. Once again, he knew why his father had never wanted to take King Corp public.

Dale Rucker finally got the floor by sheer persistence.

'Mr King, I empathize with you, but you can't unilaterally reject the Astroteknik offer. It puts your other directors in an unfair position and may also put them in legal jeopardy. It could cost all of you shareholder suit for the rest of your lives.'

King paused a moment before answering. 'Dale, appreciate your concern. But Astroteknik started thi new fight and Astroteknik proposed a unanimous vot of the board. So, as a duly elected board member, full convinced I am in good conscience acting in the best interests of the shareholders who elected me, I am voting to reject the Astroteknik offer.'

'Poll the board,' someone shouted.

'What for?' King snapped. 'My single vote against makes it unnecessary and, frankly, I don't care who's for me and who's not. Damen wants this company badly and he'll hang around until a better offer forces him away. And, I might add, I have a few things working to see we get a better offer. But, for the moment, his offer has been rejected.' He looked at his board and said, 'Any other business?' He had a strong urge to declare the meeting adjourned but forced himself to wait, scrutinizing each director's face. He reached inside his jacket for his first cigarette in almost an hour and was relieved he had not quite sweated through his shirt. He lit the cigarette and waited.

Cass Byrd got to his feet. 'Hell, we can't blame Kurt for feeling the way he does about Damen. In my opinion, Damen could certainly have waited a few more days. Look, I propose we let Mr Schutt tell Astroteknik's lawyer we have rejected their initial proposal.' He gave King a wide grin. 'As I see it, they made a mistake by demanding a unanimous vote. But they can modify their offer to require a simple majority and force Kurt's hand that way. So, I'm proposing a recess, not an adjournment, of this board meeting until Thursday.'

Byrd glanced at his fellow-directors and finally Groves spoke. 'Isn't there some way of getting together with Damen's people today so we can settle these problems and meet again tonight?'

King interrupted to prevent Groves from trying to persuade the others to accept his viewpoint. He thanked Byrd and Groves, then said, 'I like the idea of a recess because' – here, he paused slightly to give his next remarks more weight – 'because I'm heading east for meetings with two friendlies who're sure to top Damen's offer without even seeing the Tri Corp numbers. When they see those they'll act fast.'

'Wait a minute, Kurt.' Quin Groves' voice sounded plaintive. 'You told us that information was confidential.'

'Not to friends I can trust.'

'Who are they, your new White Knights?'

'Sorry, Quin, I can't compromise your position by giving you anything but factual information. But I can say I'll be back here by Thursday, two days from now, with a better offer.'

'But what if you don't and we lose Damen?' Groves was now pleading.

'Quin, don't worry, we won't lose Damen. But even if we do, I'm certain we'll beat Zanadu. We'd be crazy to knuckle under at this point.'

King had been watching the clock. He and Byrd were taking Falcon 333KK to Washington, but they had to get there for a midnight dinner at the Jockey Club with Grant Alexander. Pushing the speed limit somewhat, they rolled into Burbank hangar area a few minutes late. Watching for King's Seville, the crew had the engines running, and within minutes they were lifting over Pasadena eastbound.

King had much to ponder on the flight. Schutt, who rode with them as far as the airport, had predicted Gearhart and Waxman would run to Judge Page when they heard of the Damen offer and have him stop it. 'Zanadu has invested well over 2 million in this fight and they won't give up easily,' Schutt said.

To counterbalance Damen's threat, Ron Poole had

reported from New York that one of his companies might go as high as 35 dollars a share for all shares. He felt fairly confident. Tactlessly, Poole mentioned he and Frankie had managed to co-ordinate their schedules for a pleasant dinner together. His voice softened as he spoke of Frankie, and King felt his old friend would have done better to keep that information to himself. He was under enough stress as it was. He had promised himself one drink on the flight and he found himself mixing a third as they were crossing the Arizona–New Mexico line.

Byrd had dropped off to sleep and woke up after half an hour bright-eyed and refreshed. King envied him that ability to catnap.

He turned to King. 'Okay, my friend, I think it's time you enlightened me. I had a feeling I was bailing you out at the meeting. How about it? What's up your sleeve? I know you didn't stage that Tri Corp presentation for nothing.'

King had to laugh. 'Cass, you read my mind. I have to thank you for the speech and the two-day recess. It's exactly what I wanted. As for the Tri Corp ploy, I won't bore you with the details, but you should know some of our directors are very close to Astroteknik and may already have shifted loyalties. The closest is our good friend, Quin Groves. He has a big bunch of their stock and was a founding father of Astroteknik.'

'You must be kidding.'

'No, I'm dead serious.'

'But Kurt, that's hardly ethical . . . I'll be damned. Quin should have disqualified himself from this whole Astroteknik matter.'

'I agree with you, but in fairness we took no vote today and he'll probably disqualify himself if it comes to that. Still, he's been too close to Damen for me to feel comfortable. Anyway, Cass, the reason I gave you all that juicy inside information this morning was to get it to Damen. If he raises his offer it'll be a fair indication that he's got that confidential information.'

'I think I can take it from here,' Byrd said. 'Either he gets scared your new White Knights will outbid him and drops out, which gives you the time you need for your action. Or, he ups his offer, maybe to 35 a share.'

'Exactly, Mr Byrd. He may even go to 38 and I think he will. He needs King because Astroteknik's been flat on its ass for a long time. Their product development is zilch. Remember, Damen's an accountant, not a builder. He has to buy something and King's a steal at 38. At that price, I'd still feel the shareholders were getting the short end of the stick, but nowhere near as short as when this frigging thing began.' King looked away, seeming to study the new snow on the Rockies before going on. 'And that extra two bucks per share would mean a quarter of a million dollars to me, personally. A new house in Palm Springs and a few new toys, as they say.'

'Kurt,' said Byrd in a softer tone, 'that's the first time I've heard you mention your own personal financial situation. You'd come out of it all right then, I mean in case we lost the war?'

Before replying, King lit a cigarette and took a sip of his third martini. 'Come out all right?' he said, repeating Byrd's phrase. 'With the battle that's been going on I've not thought much about it. I don't guess I could even spend the money I'd make. But that kind of life just doesn't interest me.'

'You couldn't really go off to the Springs and pla

golf day after day, could you?' Byrd made it as much a statement as a question.

'No, I couldn't. But if I lose this fight, I'm going to be pretty damn bitter, and I won't feel like building another company for some new son of a bitch to steal. No way!'

They read, chatted and napped. Finally the captain's voice cut in to announce that he was on let-down to Washington National.

'Excuse me,' said Byrd, quietly, 'but I always like to watch this. I like coming into LA, you know, on a clear night it's so damn big, sparkling, but this is something special.'

King smiled. 'I know what you mean, Cass,' he said and leaned over as Byrd pulled the curtain all the way back. Together they stared out of the small window. With the time change from the West Coast it was now dead dark and the lighting around the monuments made them stand out like diamonds on black velvet. There they were, the Washington, the Lincoln and the Jefferson monuments, the last one King's favourite with its handsome rotunda, noble lines and columns. From the air, the federal city was beautiful.

Byrd sighed, 'It's a thrilling sight, but it hides the fact that those who work down there manage to spend a billion dollars a day. It's what someone once called waste camouflaged by grace.'

2

King's physiological clock read three A.M., yet with the early sunlight slanting across the room, he woke early on Wednesday morning. He, Byrd and Grant Alexander had put away such a big meal at the Jockey Club the night before that he skipped breakfast, dressed hurriedly and went for a walk. It was a beautiful morning, already close to 50 degrees. He crossed Lafayette Park, noticed there seemed to be almost as many joggers as pigeons, and stood looking at the grand symmetry of the White House. For good luck he walked once round the Treasury before heading back for the Hay-Adams.

Alexander's office had done its work well. All the meetings they'd asked for were confirmed for that day, except the one with Theo Tracy at the SEC. Byrd explained nobody got to see Tracy at first crack. If they could stay that long, or come back, they could see him on Friday. King was disappointed, having heard so much about the dynamic and even-handed Tracy, but he rationalized his regret by telling himself it gave him more time to visit Admiral Rickover. The admiral's office had asked him to call at eleven o'clock.

With Cass Byrd, he had a fruitful meeting at the Justice Department, now much more disposed to help on the anti-trust aspect of the takeover. King marvelled at the ease with which Byrd cut through Washington bureaucracy and cursed himself for not using the man's political skill and influence earlier. He knew everybody, and at their dinner the evening before had more well wishers than Alexander.

He arrived at Admiral Rickover's office in plenty of time and at eleven precisely was ushered into the presence. After the barest of greetings, Rickover vented his redoubtable temper on takeover bids, and then on King.

'What's happening to you is not free enterprise, it' cannibalism. One company devouring another and without warning. It's a lousy thing. But you' – h

438

stabbed a finger at King's chest – 'you're just as bad. You've been doing it, too!'

It took King five minutes to explain that every time King Corp had acquired a company it was because the other company had wanted to sell for a variety of reasons including lack of money, health, age . . .

Rickover, who carried his 76-plus years with no noticeable strain, nodded his understanding and moved on to his next point. 'What's going to happen to you? Is that outfit, what's the name – Zanadu – going to get you?'

'No, not at this moment. We'll either beat them or some White Knight will step in.'

'White Knight! What the hell are you talking about? Skip the jargon and speak English.'

'It's the name for another company that may step in and bid higher – somebody we could live with.'

'I see. Would you stay on? Would they let you run your own company?'

'Yes, I'm quite sure they would.'

'Okay, good. But I'm goddamn mad at you and some of your people for going around saying I won't give you any business while that raider is in the picture. That's bullshit and you and I both know it. In my position I can't refuse to place orders because ownership changes. How would that look? You can get me in a lot of trouble with those statements. We have a lot of business to place, but I can't take sides in industrial fights. Understand?'

'Yes, Admiral, but I never made such a statement, though I might have implied it. I respect your position, sir, but you must understand that in a fight like this, with your back to the wall, you use any weapon you can. So, I confess I did imply you were holding up certain orders until you could see which way the fight was going. After all, I expected those orders by early November, and it's almost Christmas.'

'Well, I want you to stop implying, too. Another thing bothers me.' Rickover was up, out of his chair now and pacing the room. 'You've been doing work for me for about twelve years, maybe even longer, and you fuck things up once in a while and you overcharge me like everyone else, but overall you do a pretty good job. There's one thing I always thought about you – you were an honest man. Now, I find out you're a goddamn crook who's stealing 30 million dollars from your stockholders.'

'Wait a minute, Admiral, no one's stealing anything. That money belongs to about a hundred key people at King Corp, including myself. The whole damn thing's been twisted, distorted out of proportion. Let me explain.'

'Explain, hell! What about this?' Going to his desk Rickover picked up a clipping from the *Wall Street Journal* and handed it to King. The statements about the 30 million dollars had been underlined in red. As he started to explain, King heard his name called. Captain Clark, the Admiral's right-hand man and an old friend had come into the office and greeted him.

Ignoring their exchange of pleasantries, Rickover snapped, 'You may say taking this money's all right but I can't agree and I think you're a crook. Anyway I'm too busy to hear your cock-and-bull explanation Maybe Clark is a softer touch. Go down to his offi and explain it to him, if you can. It sounds fishy to m Nice to see you. Goodbye.'

Heading for the door, King suddenly noticed all t

'ule decorations in the office. Instinctively, he turned
Jack and said, 'Merry Christmas, Admiral.'

Rickover grunted something in reply, then walked
briskly to the door with King and did something typically unpredictable. 'Girls,' he called into the outer
office, 'Mr King has had a rough go of it lately. I want
you all to stand and sing "Merry Christmas" to him.'

Even though it was only 'Jingle Bells', King felt
himself choking a bit as he listened to them sing. As he
turned to say thanks, Admiral Rickover took his hand
and pulled him back into the office. 'Clark, you wait,
he'll be right with you.' He closed the door. 'Tell me
honestly, King, when do you think you'll have this
mess settled? When will you know for sure if you're
still going to be running your company?'

'In the next few days.'

'Well, get the goddamn thing settled. I have a lot of
business to place, and I can't hold it up much longer.
Get the message?'

King was smiling broadly as he walked down the hall
o Captain Clark's office. Despite his denials, Rickover
vas delaying those orders until he found out where
King stood. Wily old tactician.

Clark listened more receptively to King's account of
he bonus money. 'I think I see your position,' he said.
But you must understand I'm a public servant who
nly knows what he reads in the newspapers, and they
iade you and your cohorts look pretty bad. You know
ie Admiral as well as I do and how hard it is to change
is mind. But I'll see what I can do.'

Tom Lowe, who had flown in just for the afternoon,
ined King and Cass Byrd at CAB headquarters on
onnecticut Avenue. Again, Byrd's presence opened all
ie doors. Although the meeting dragged on, the CAB

officials finally assured them that if Zanadu went ahead without notifying them, they would act to block their takeover. 'You have a probable block and a certain delay,' Lowe told them before flying back to Texas.

Byrd suggested a drink and they walked through the sunshine to the Mayflower where they found a table in the bar. King felt better than he had for weeks. He had Rickover behind him, they could delay the Zanadu takeover to give him time to act, and Byrd was sure Theo Tracy would throw the book at Zanadu and Foxe. 'You know, Cass, for the first time I'm beginning to think we're home and dry in this fight,' he said.

Byrd motioned him to silence and twitched his head towards the table behind him where two well-dressed men were talking loudly.

'Jesus, I just can't take this shit,' one of them was saying. 'Your Congressman friend was very helpful, but the bureaucrats were afraid I might be cutting myself too good a deal, even though it's a good deal for the government. They're in some kind of goddamn stupor, maybe because it's Christmas, and won't make a decision. These people are scared of their own shadows and all they did was push me from office to office. And every office I went into had a half-assed Christmas party going. They're even incompetent drunks. I'm about to go out of my friggin' gourd.'

'That's the system, Kurt, and no one can change it.'

'I know how he feels.' But King thought this time they could beat the system.

Back in his hotel, King was debating whether to take his bag or simply leave it with the desk and pick it up when he returned on Friday to see Tracy when the phone rang.

'Kurt? Steve Schutt. Glad I caught you. I was afraid you might have already left. Look, I know you're coming back for the board meeting tomorrow, but there have been some dramatic developments this end today and I thought you ought to know about them as soon as possible.'

King felt his heart quicken at the note in Schutt's voice. 'Well, give it to me, Steve.'

'It's like this, I've been on the phone with Clyde Clarke for about an hour and a messenger is on his way over here with Astroteknik's revised offer. It's in writing at my insistence, but let me give you the meat of it so you can think about it on the flight tonight.' As King listened intently, Schutt's voice seemed to drop into a lower gear. 'Actually,' he said, 'there's not much to talk about because this looks like the ball game. I just wanted you to know what it's worth.'

'What?' King's knees went weak and he put a hand on the nightstand to steady himself. 'The ball game? We've lost?'

'I'm afraid so, Kurt. But you've put up a helluva fight. Nobody could have done more, believe me. I'm positive you would have won and beaten Zanadu, but Astroteknik just won't wait. You may have lost your company, but you've pulled off a fantastic deal for your shareholders.' Schutt began to speak faster, perhaps relieved at unloading the hard part of his message.

'I have to advise you, Kurt, you can't oppose this any longer. I don't know exactly what happened since your meeting yesterday, but it certainly changed things in double-quick time. Briefly, this is how.'

King felt as though his legs were filling with water. His hand holding the phone to his ear was trembling.

'Astroteknik has changed its position fundamentally. They want you to proceed with the Tri Corp option, drop the 30 million claim and the stockholders' meeting and they'll accept a simple majority supporting their offer. Which means you can't block them the way you did yesterday. They want your answer by noon tomorrow so they can make an immediate announcement and they want this to be followed by your announcement that you support the deal. Or, if you won't support it, they want an announcement from your board.'

'Hold on a minute, Steve. What's the story on the appeal?'

'Bittersweet in the circumstances. Everything is going as planned with a hearing set for tomorrow afternoon and I predict they'll rule in our favour.'

'But it's too late, two fucking days too late. Damn them.'

'That's the way it looks. Kurt, I realize you must b devastated, but listen to the rest of the facts. The fina and most important point and one I can't understand that Damen has jumped his offer.'

'To what? 34, 34.50?'

'Nope, and I'm sure you won't believe it because don't. He's gone to 37.50, and that makes you a her Kurt.'

'Hero, hell. It makes me a rich bum, and they're st stealing it.'

'Now wait a minute, you've pulled off the best de

ever for King Corp shareholders. Paul and Harry, who're sitting right here, have run some quick calculations on those figures and come up with this: Astroteknik ends up by topping their initial offer by more than 12 per cent and in cash they're spending almost two and a half times what Zanadu offered. Your shareholders are getting 80 per cent over market price when the raid started. We can't recall a tender offer that's gone this high in relation to the pre-raid price. Something sure happened since yesterday to make Damen go another 4.50 a share. You and I know he had the deal at 33.'

King felt sick, drained. But, for the moment, he could still think and talk business. 'Steve, we'll never know for sure, but you heard the Tri Corp presentation yesterday, you heard me say I was meeting two friendlies in the East. Well, all that was staged so that somebody could get the information to Damen. Evidently, he got the message.'

'You mean it was all phony? Tri Corp's for real, isn't it?' Schutt sounded apprehensive as though worried about ethics.

'Oh sure, and I was conservative – but the friendlies, they were for the right ear.'

'You mean, they don't exist?'

'Hell no, I threw them in as extra bait for my friend, Damen, and he swallowed it. So, it cost him another 30 million or thereabouts.'

'I doff my hat, and so should your stockholders. Again, Kurt, I'm terribly sorry about the way it has ended. Another couple of days and you'd have done it your way. But from the money standpoint you've done a helluva job. See you tomorrow.'

For a full minute, King stood with the instrument to

his ear as if questioning the reality of that conversation and the import of Schutt's message. Did it always happen like this – a phone ringing in a strange hotel room with news that hit you like a kick in the balls? Just under two months ago, the phone had rung in another hotel and he was told some bandit was going to steal his company. Now another bandit had actually done it.

Suddenly, he banged the handset into its socket and began to curse. 'Fuck every one of those bastards and sons of bitches . . . fuck the Damens and Thomases, the Gearharts and Groves . . . fuck the lot.' A string of even more obscene oaths burst from him as though he were trying to relieve his mental pain.

His legs seemed to go weak, wobbly. He threw himself on the bed to stare at the ceiling, his eyes and mind reflecting its white vacancy. He felt numb, disconnected, voided of all energy. As if someone had plunged a needle into an artery, siphoned the blood out of him and replaced it with iced water. He had a panic urge to flee somewhere, anywhere. Now he knew why stricken animals ran for cover, any cover. He wanted to cut loose from everything – meetings, phones, anything connected with those last two nightmare months. To retreat within himself.

Who would begin to know how he felt with his world ripped apart? Even his family had never understood what his work meant, and especially King Corp. Curious how, at this moment, his thoughts turned to Carolyn and his children. After all, who else had he that he could confide in if not them?

He levered himself off the bed and went into the bathroom where he sluiced his face with cold water then swallowed two aspirins. He dialled Byrd's room and told him the bad news. They both realized 37.

446

was too high for the board to reject when they needed only a simple majority. 'So, I guess there's no point in hanging around here, Cass, and we should head for home.'

Half an hour later, they had checked out and were making for the Page Airways private terminal in a cab. Abruptly, for no reason that he could think of, King turned to Byrd. 'Cass, we're getting out of here a lot earlier than planned. Would you mind if we detoured up to Hartford before heading west. There's somebody I'd like to see. With the time change I'll still have you home by ten.'

'No problem, Kurt. I'll make a call or two. I think I know what you have in mind.'

4

King stood with his hand raised, tentatively, as if afraid to knock on what was still, legally speaking, his own front door. Before he could knock, the door flew open.

'Hey,' said the startled youth, who almost knocked him down. 'Oh, it's you. You really scared me . . . really scared me. I sure didn't expect to see you here. Uh, how are you?'

'Hello, son.'

Randy was dressed casually in jeans, boots, a sweater and a sleeveless, parka-like jacket – even though Connecticut was quite cold. Already taller and thinner than his father, he had hair to his shoulders. Facing each other, they might have been looking into time-warping mirrors. King said the first thing that came into his mind.

'Don't your arms get cold?'

The boy looked surprised, then began to laugh. It

was a good sound, rich, full and not high-pitched. Mannish. King liked it. 'No, they really don't. It has to do with thermal heat retention, I think. Oh, hey, excuse me, come on in.'

'Thank you. Where'll I find your mother?' He looked around the hallway, impressed with its warmth and solidity. Could this be the same house he and Carolyn had first seen so completely empty all those years ago?

'She's not here. She and Sandy are in New Haven for the finals of a one-act play contest. I was just going down to the Heritage to get something to eat and look for some of the guys.'

'The Heritage?'

'It's a new place, downtown. Look, why don't you come along, I mean if you have time?'

'Time?' King smiled, thinking time had dominated his last two months to the exclusion of everything else. 'Oh, I have time.'

Five minutes later they pushed through the doors of a squat, one-storey building that reminded King of a bomb shelter at Quantico. Rock music boomed from a series of speakers hung near the ceiling. Once his eyes adjusted, he could see it was a large, busy place. His ears, he was sure, would never adjust.

'At least there's room to sit down for once,' Randy said, leading them to seats across a table that backed against a wall. Within minutes, perhaps in deference to King's age or the fact he was the only adult in the place wearing a suit, a burly woman came over to take their order. King ordered a martini. 'Sorry.' She laughed. 'Only wine or beer.' He hesitated, looking at his son.

'Let's have a pitcher of beer and two glasses,' Randy said, easily. 'And a large sausage pizza, with extra

448

everything.' He glanced at his father. 'Correction, half everything.' He grinned. 'And half-regular.'

Forty-five minutes later they had finished the pizza and another pitcher of beer. Although he had eaten only a portion of the pizza, King felt bloated. Yet he was happier than he had been for a long time as they pushed through the packed room making for the exit.

A youth in a soft leather sports-coat bumped into King, swung round to look at him. His eyes widened, his mouth dropped open. 'Holy Christ, a Narc,' he muttered and fled.

'He thought you were a drug-squad cop, Dad,' Randy said, laughing out loud.

In the parking lot, the boy looked quizzically at King, who said, 'Look, son, I have to get back to LA tonight, so I can't stay long. People are waiting for me in Hartford, but would you mind if we just drove round for a while?'

'Sure, anything you like. But could I drive? I never drove a rental car before.'

King smiled. 'Go ahead, you'll be amazed how much alike they all are.'

They circled the downtown area which took no time at all, then they were back in the residential section. Soon, the houses seemed quite far from the road, their lights way back.

'Where are we, Randy?'

'Brushy Ridge Road. Over there, through the trees is the estate of Alger Hiss's mother. Or maybe it's his aunt's.'

King smiled in the dark. 'Do you know what Mr Hiss famous for?' His question came out before his mind played back another voice. His own father's. 'And why aggerwing?' he was saying.

There was a quiet chuckle from the driver's seat. 'No, not exactly. Didn't Nixon get him in trouble for playing footsie with the Russians – but a long time ago.'

'Something like that.'

They cruised through Norwalk then left the strip of neon that would never be allowed in New Canaan. Suddenly, along Route 123, King spotted something familiar. 'Hey, isn't this where the ducks are?' He motioned his son to stop, and they got out. King lit a cigarette as they walked over to the frozen pond. 'Want one?' he asked, proffering the packet.

'No thanks.' Randy laughed lightly, then said, 'Ah, you've got me a bit confused.' He looked away from his father then back at him, in the dark. 'I mean, I'm enjoying myself tonight, a lot. But I can't figure it. How come you showed up without calling? It's always been on schedule before.'

The cold made smoking unpleasant for King, and after another drag he flipped the cigarette in a long, glowing arc. It hit the ice and bounced away.

'I lost the King Company today. Another outfit stole it from me. All legal and above board.' He spat out the last words as though they hurt him.

'What? Oh, no Dad. Not grandfather King's company?'

Turning to stare at the boy, startled by his statement he said, 'Yes, your grandfather King's company. Bu I'm surprised. How long have you called it that? . . . mean, considering what your mother thinks.'

'Sandy and I have always called it that. Maybe w should have called it your company, but he actuall started it, right? We always talked about it that way kind of heritage, that sort of thing.'

'Well, I'll be damned.'

XVII

The final board meeting of King Corp under the chairmanship of Kurt S. King, Jr took place on 16 December 1976. It was an anticlimax, with more nervous excitement than actual discussion. Steve Schutt formally presented the new offer, McGill gave it his blessing as an investment banker and the board, in a show of solidarity, voted its unanimous acceptance, even though two of the directors would have stood by King and waited for the Appeal Court decision.

With the release of the pre-arranged announcement, the directors converged on King to congratulate him on his handling of the takeover fight. He excused himself quickly, not wishing to make a public show of his emotion and unable to stand being told what a great job he'd done – in defeat. In the back elevator, going down to the parking garage, he realized tears were streaming down his cheeks. Tears! He couldn't remember when he had last cried.

After driving the Seville around for an hour, like a true Californian, he felt considerably better. He went back to the office, fairly composed, signed a few letters, made a short congratulatory call to Damen as a courtesy then held a quick meeting with Chip Boyd. He instructed Boyd to see that key employees of King knew their rights to exercise their option to exchange their present stock for Astroteknik stock. 'We don't want anyone to lose what they're entitled to,' he told Boyd.

'Frankly, now it's gone this way I'm going to be co-operative to protect our people, but I have a feeling of distrust.'

King had to return to Washington for his scheduled meeting with Theo Tracy, the tough guy of the SEC, merely for the record now the deal had been done. He was on the way out of his office for the airport when Marianne handed him a note:

K.K.

11.00 a.m.

While you were out, Mr Poole called. I spoke with him. He told me to tell you he has a deal pretty well along at 36 dollars. Fine company. They want to meet with you in New York tomorrow morning. I'm to call him back. What do I say?

King stared at the note for a minute, looked up and said quietly to Marianne, 'Honey, you know the story. Just tell him the ball game's over.'

2

Washington's own special brand of one-upmanship was on display when King and Jefferson Harris, an attorney from Grant Alexander's firm, arrived at the SEC to meet with Theo Tracy just before noon on Friday. A fresh-faced young man approached them in the reception area. 'I'm sorry, gentlemen, but Mr Tracy is not available. You're to see Mr David.'

King grabbed Harris by the arm in a gesture of frustration. 'Why travel three thousand miles for this?' he whispered.

'Let's see what we get,' Harris replied.

Joseph David, a staff attorney in his early thirties, listened patiently enough to Harris only to round o

452

King and accuse him of having had designs on Zanadu. It transpired his information came from none other than Edward Foxe.

His temper flashpoint low, King blew up. 'First of all, that's an outright lie. Secondly, Mr David, you seem to have real trouble understanding the difference between public and confidential information.' Incensed that they had turned Foxe's criminal conduct against him, King was near breaking point. He started to speak again when the phone rang. David grabbed the instrument. His eyes grew larger. 'Yes, yes, I'll tell them.' He turned to them. 'Mr Tracy will see you now, gentlemen.'

King stared in astonishment when they entered Tracy's office. Documents lay everywhere along with law journals, newspaper clippings, files and a slew of cardboard boxes. It looked like a lumber room. Tracy, a stocky, balding man in shirtsleeves, was pacing the only clear space, bawling rapidly into the phone, trailing its cord behind him. Suddenly, he slammed the handset into its groove, marched over briskly and shook hands with both men, motioning them to a chair.

'Mr King, I'm busy as hell. What's your story?'

As King talked, Tracy interrupted once or twice but mostly listened, shaking his head in agreement or disagreement from time to time. When King got to the heart of the complaint, Foxe's action in taking inside information to Zanadu, Tracy cut in sharply, 'But we'd have to have that documented.'

King had brought the entire takeover file and quickly found the incriminating documents which he handed to Tracy. His eyes flew across the pages and he mumbled under his breath, 'Lousy, lousy deal.'

Tracy put down the documents and shouted to summon several staff members then lectured them on the mistakes they had made, the signs they had missed. King watched with mixed emotions as the attitudes of these young lawyers changed towards him noticeably. If only Tracy had been involved from the outset!

Tracy asked, 'Outside of this automotive stuff you stupidly gave this fellow Foxe, what else do you people do?' King recited their product lines and mentioned the Rickover relationship. 'He's a tough bastard,' Tracy commented. 'You work for him long?'

'About twelve years.'

Tracy smiled for the first time. 'Then you must do good work, for nobody works for him that long unless they perform.'

He turned the conversation back to the Foxe–Irving–Zanadu relationship and went over the salient points. He walked the two men to the door and shook King's hand. 'No promises, Mr King, but this will be looked into thoroughly. From what I've heard you've taken a real screwing. But I have to hear from the other side. Thanks for coming to see me.'

Looking at his watch, King saw they had been with Tracy for two hours. Those who compared him with Rickover were right. Two of a kind. As Alexander's limousine took him to Dulles Airport, he berated himself and his attorneys for not getting to Tracy sooner 'All Ifs and Buts now,' he thought, wryly.

Back in Los Angeles, he headed for the Bel-Air Hotel deciding too many people would want to contact him a his apartment. He explained to the desk clerk that h needed to sleep through a night and a day. A crisp twenty ensured him that amount of privacy and quiet.

3

When he walked into his apartment building on Sunday afternoon, his box was overflowing with messages and the phone was ringing as he put his key in the lock. Reluctantly back in harness, he hurried to answer it.

'Paul Towers, Kurt. Sorry to be the one to tell you, but there's one last kick in the ass. We've been arguing with the Zanadu and Astroteknik lawyers about the fallout since yesterday morning.'

'What's to argue about? They won, I lost and it's all over.'

'Unfortunately not. Zanadu has been raising holy hell about Astroteknik coming in late and grabbing all the marbles.'

'Paul, skip the sports talk. I'm so tired of this whole fucking thing, tired to the core of my being. Now, what the hell are you talking about and why does it still concern me?'

'Sorry, Kurt, it's like this. Zanadu threatened to go to Judge Page and allege collusion on the part of you and Damen, so to avoid that, the lawyers have agreed to a settlement.'

'What sort of settlement?'

'Zanadu wants two big ones to go away peacefully.'

'Two million dollars!' King gasped.

'Right, and Astroteknik has agreed to cough up.'

'That's crazy. Why would they agree to that?'

'Because Waxman claimed they'd incurred all sorts of costs in unnecessary fights with you, he says you and Damen were in cahoots from the beginning, and he threatened to file suit against Astroteknik, King Corp and the directors of both companies, all of them. He got

455

hold of Clyde Clarke who took it to Damen who bought it against our opinion.'

'The gutless bastard.' King realized he was still holding his overnight bag. He tossed it, angrily, towards the living room. 'Why did he cave in like that?'

'I figure it this way. Damen was authorized to go to 38 dollars per share. With the 37.50 he pays plus the 40 cents to the brokers, he's up to 37.90. The 2 million dollars of hush-money works out at another 16 cents per share. That puts him 6 cents over his limit, not even half a per cent. So, he figures, get it over with.'

While Towers was talking, King had kicked off his shoes and fished a cigarette out of his pack. He took a delicious draw and exhaled. 'Well, it's his money now, but it's still stupid. Christ, doesn't he realize we will still have a suit against Foxe, Irving and Zanadu that could be worth a couple of million dollars itself? We have a strong case now that Theo Tracy himself is interested.'

'Kurt, you don't understand, that's why we've been trying to get you all weekend. That's part of the settlement. All litigation is dropped, including Foxe.'

'What!' King choked himself on the smoke of his cigarette and his fist whitened over the phone handset. 'Jesus Christ! that really is kicking us in the balls after all we've been through to nail that sneaky little bastard.' He ran out of words.

'I know, I agree, but you're not calling the shots any more, Kurt. Damen is. And he's calling some others I haven't told you about. Listen – he wants King Corp to pay the two million not Astroteknik. He settles but you pay. They think it will look better that way. What do you think?'

That question brought the blood rushing to King's head, and set his adrenalin flowing strongly.

'Tell him this from me, Paul. Go fuck yourself. And don't say fornicate! Do you hear me? That's what I think.'

He put the phone down, pulled out the wall plug and took the instrument to the terrace where he plugged it in once more. He began punching the buttons and speaking in a crisp, clear voice with no hint of fatigue. Forty minutes later, he called Paul Towers back.

'Paul, I've reached all my directors but one. The feeling is unanimous – this is blackmail and we, the directors of King Corp, refuse to pay it. As I suggested before, Damen and his crew can go fuck themselves. This may be the last action of the King Corp board, but it's strong and unconditional. No blackmail . . . let Astroteknik pay it. And if I were one of Damen's shareholders I'd bring suit for stupidity.'

Epilogue

Ron Poole had some trouble finding the access road, but once he did it was easy to follow the trail of the construction crew. So cleverly was the house hidden from the eye of the casual motorist that he almost missed it. If the Seville had not been sitting in the half-finished driveway, he might have sailed right by.

He tried the bell, and a series of chimes rang quietly somewhere inside. He waited, impatiently, and was about to try scouting on his own behind the house when the door opened and a short, dark-haired and very dark-eyed girl in a tennis dress stood before him. He would have known her from her mother's face, and from Kurt's. She had something of both.

'Hi, can I help? I'm Sandy King. Are you with the builders, or are you looking for my father, or both?'

Poole shook his head and smiled, momentarily nonplussed. 'Sandy, I'm Ron Poole. Remember me?'

'Oh, what do you know! Sure. Hey, excuse me. I haven't seen you since that time in New Canaan when you came by. Last year, right?

'Right. Where's your Dad?'

'Out back, but I'm not going to tell you what he's doing. You have to see it for yourself. You just won't believe. Want me to give you a tour of this place? It's sort of a drag right now with all the work still going on, but I'd be glad to. It's going to be super.'

'No thanks, Sandy. Ahh, how do you happen to be here . . . I mean, now?'

'Spring break. My brother and I are thinking about transferring out here. He likes Stanford, and I'm going up tomorrow to see Berkeley. Wouldn't that be weird if we ended up out here, with him?' She gave a sort of sideways nod to where her father was working, then looked at Poole, embarrassed. 'They're getting divorced, you know, after all this time.'

She stopped talking and led Poole through the house. It was a beautiful design, long, angular and rambling. Pure California. When they got to the kitchen, Sandy stopped.

'Want a beer?'

'Great. That would be fine.' He took off the jacket of his suit and dropped it on a handsome round oak table that held a light coating of construction dust.

Sandy handed him a can of Coors, then stepped back. 'Aren't you my father's best friend?'

'I like to think so.'

'But aren't you the same person who's going to marry his former girlfriend?'

'Yes, I am.'

'Hmm!' She smiled and glanced at him archly. 'You and Daddy must really be good friends in that case.' A noise from outside caught her attention and she looked out of the window. 'Hey, this is what I mean. Look at this.'

Poole walked over and peered out. There, fifty yards away, across the dichondra which was beginning to turn green, King was shovelling dirt like a madman. He wore cut-off blue jeans, his hair was longer, he was tanned like a beach boy and a coating of sweat added a sheen to his body. As he shovelled, he sang a passable rendition of 'On a Clear Day' so loudly that it could be heard for half a mile in every direction.

'Mr Poole, are you here just to see the new house and everything, or have you come as my father would say "on business"?'

'Well, I did want to see the house, Sandy, but about a month ago your Dad asked me to check into something for him, a company that's developed a new way to make computer chips. He wanted to know how much it would cost to buy and what sort of a deal he could make and all the rest.'

Sandy arched her eyebrows. 'And, let me guess, it looks terrific, right?' Her pretty face broke into a smile.

Poole nodded. He was startled to see in her smile both Kurt King and Carolyn and the senior Kings he had known so long ago.

'Even better than that, Sandy, even better than that.'

He picked up his can of beer and headed across the new lawn.

The world's greatest novelists now available in paperback from Grafton Books

Kurt Vonnegut

Breakfast of Champions	£2.50	☐
Mother Night	£1.95	☐
Slaughterhouse 5	£2.50	☐
Player Piano	£2.95	☐
Welcome to the Monkey House	£1.95	☐
God Bless You, Mr Rosewater	£2.50	☐
Happy Birthday, Wanda June	£1.95	☐
Slapstick	£2.50	☐
Wampeters Foma & Granfalloons (non-fiction)	£2.50	☐
Between Time and Timbuktu (illustrated)	£3.95	☐
Jailbird	£1.95	☐
Palm Sunday	£1.95	☐
Deadeye Dick	£1.95	☐

John Barth

The Sot-Weed Factor	£3.95	☐
Giles Goat-Boy	£2.95	☐
The Floating Opera	£2.50	☐
Letters	£3.95	☐
Sabbatical	£2.50	☐

Tim O'Brien

If I Die in a Combat Zone	£1.95	☐

To order direct from the publisher just tick the titles you want and fill in the order form.

GF

The world's greatest novelists now available in paperback from Grafton Books

To order direct from the publisher just tick the titles you want and fill in the order form. **GF781**

All these books are available at your local bookshop or newsagent, or can be ordered direct from the publisher.

To order direct from the publishers just tick the titles you want and fill in the form below.

Name _____

Address _____

_____

Send to:
Grafton Cash Sales
PO Box 11, Falmouth, Cornwall TR10 9EN.

Please enclose remittance to the value of the cover price plus:

UK 60p for the first book, 25p for the second book plus 15p per copy for each additional book ordered to a maximum charge of £1.90.

BFPO 60p for the first book, 25p for the second book plus 15p per copy for the next 7 books, thereafter 9p per book.

Overseas including Eire £1.25 for the first book, 75p for second book and 28p for each additional book.

Grafton Books reserve the right to show new retail prices on covers which may differ from those previously advertised in the text or elsewhere.